Maid of Honour

Elizabeth Byrd

Maid of Honour

A Novel Set in

The Court of Mary Queen of Scots

1534

St. Martin's Press
New York

Library of Congress Cataloging in Publication Data

Byrd, Elizabeth.
   Maid of honour.

   1. Seton, Hon. Mary, b. ca. 1541—Fiction.
   2. Mary Stuart, Queen of the Scots, 1542-1587—
      Fiction.
I. Title.
PZ4.B995Mai   [PS3552.Y67]   813'.5'4   78-19952
ISBN 0-312-50430-6

For Anna Sendrowski

CHAPTER I

———◆———

I was to remind my Queen to bathe in the May dew this morning but she slept so deeply that I decided to wait until full sunrise. And with no one about I could take my own bath at leisure.

A Scots guard let me through a palace door, bowing, too sleepy for surprise. I pulled my shawl closer, wondering if I were a fool to risk the chill. The sky was beginning to pink as I hurried down terraces of sea-green marble. St Germain-en-Laye was a pride of fountains, of jade and onyx animals peeping through flowers, of posturing marble gods forming a line among the willows. I ran past them into the woods, thoroughly chilled now.

Near a bridle path I found a vast bed of yellow violets, threw off my dress and shift and plunged as I would into a pool. Jesu, it *was* cold, but the fragrance of the crushed violets was exquisite. I rolled about, thinking of how my skin would be improved. It could never achieve the luminous pearl of my Queen's but I could already feel a softness when I sat up and touched the soles of my feet. Then I turned over to press in my face and my hair. No bath can so sparkle the hair as dew, and my blonde locks were darkening a bit with age. I was fifteen.

The horse came so swiftly that I did not hear it until too late. In terror I turned on my side and tried to cover myself. The man would think me wanton, and obviously he was no courtier or he would have ridden on to spare me embarrassment.

A woman's voice drowned the sound of my breathing. 'Who are you? Sit up at once.'

I feared that voice more than any. I rarely feared my own gentle Queen, or Queen Catherine de Medici, who ignored

1

me, but this uncrowned queen – King Henry's mistress – could make me feel smaller than a pebble.

'Lady Seton, is it?' she asked as I sat up to face her, tossing back my hair. There was no pretence of modesty – she had known me since I had arrived from Scotland in my Queen's entourage. She had approved my gowns, warned against corseting, ordered all facets of my elegance as she did the Queen's and the other maids of honour.

I could not curtsy from a bed of violets. I inclined my head and said, 'Your Grace.'

The word suited her. Diane de Poitiers, Duchess of Valentinois, was the most beautiful woman at court; although she was fifty-eight years old, more than twenty years older than King Henry II, she still enchanted him. She wore a loose, white tunic buttoned in pearls to her slender waist, her velvet boots were pearled and so were the pins that held her thick blonde hair. She said that she never tinted her lips or painted her eyelids. Her enemies thought it witchcraft that she had not a wrinkle, but she told us that was because she never smiled or frowned and bade us be chary of our emotions.

'Rise, Lady Seton,' she said.

Trembling, I got to my feet and curtsied.

'I approve that bath,' she said. 'I had one myself – but not in public. Didn't you remark this path?'

I stammered that the violets had been so inviting.

'Suppose some man had seen you wallowing here?'

I begged forgiveness. She lectured me on witlessness and the sin of impulse. Then she said, 'You swear you were not hoping to meet someone here?'

'I swear! The four of us Marys are sworn virgins until our Queen marries.'

'So you've a year to wait,' she said. But her voice had softened. 'I see your body has improved, small-breasted but slim and well-proportioned.' She examined me as if I were a half-finished painting. 'If you stand more erectly it will lend you dignity.'

Then she relented and told me to dress. I said aye (lapsing from French to Scots in my nervousness), I must hurry and

2

arouse the Queen for her bath in the walled garden. Then she said, 'Mind that the sun never reaches her skin, or yours. I have warned you ladies for ten years of the dangers of the sun. . . .'

I was dressing as she talked, for the sun was now up and I was anxious to go to the Queen. Then she nodded, took a small whip to her horse, and was away. This was her early exercise; she rode again at dusk. It perfected the figure, she told us.

Back at the palace I climbed the marble steps to my Queen's suite, pausing to tidy my hair. This was a small adventure I could tell my Queen, for Mary Stuart loved to laugh – wrinkles to her were a distant worry. As I came into her bedchamber she was propped on lacy pillows in her white, brocaded bed, taking a cup of ale from Livingstone, her chestnut hair tangled down her shoulders. It was her despair because it had darkened from blonde like my own.

'Seton,' she said smiling, 'you were meant to rouse me for the May dew. Now it may be too late.'

'Oh no, Madam!' I said. 'I've just been in it and it will surely last the hour.'

'Oh,' she sighed, 'why must you be so truthful? Why may I not have *corrupt* maids? You and Livingstone and Beaton and Fleming fuss like mother hens.'

But that was our duty, our sacred privilege. The four of us, all of her age, had sailed with her from Scotland ten years ago as her maids of honour; we felt a strong sense of responsibility.

'Madam, I met Madame Diane in the woods just now. . . .'

She loved the story, she teased me about summoning the god Pan from the woods, she called for bread and honey – and all this, I suspect, to escape the May dew. But Livingstone was stern and asked, what if Madame Diane came riding by here and found her negligent? At this the Queen pouted and dived out of bed, demanding clothing, and she and I hastened to her private garden, down steps, enclosed by a high, stone wall. Here grew jonquils, and in season roses and flowering trees. A tiny stream ran through it and there were lilies-of-the-valley among the ferns.

3

She flung off her clothes and sprang for the lilies. It seemed to me appropriate; they represented France and she was to marry the Dauphin in April. But I doubt if she made the connection; it was the fragrance of the lilies that she loved most of all perfumes.

She was tall, though so charmingly shaped that she seemed fragile. Her breasts had budded beautifully, high and full, her waist could be circled by one of those ferns, and her legs were slender, approved even by Madame Diane as elegant. So were her hands. Now she rollicked like a puppy in the lilies, turning into the grass and back again.

A maid came to say that my mistress's grandmother, the Duchess Antoinette de Guise, was on the way from her palace of Joinville, and we hurried to the royal dressing-room – panelled in white satin, and full with chests; three brass chests held jewels alone. None of us cared for the stiff farthingales that deformed the figure to a low-waisted V. Still, it was necessary to dress Her Majesty in one, with a velvet gown stamped in gold over it. 'My hair!' she said and I, who was expert in hairdressing if in nothing else, arranged her waves under a heart-shaped cap bordered in sapphires. Then, in her presence chamber where her cloth of state hung above the throne, she said, 'Summon the other Marys. She will want to look you over.'

We made ourselves presentable and then were commanded to sit nearby, I suspected to soothe her nervousness. For the Duchess was as formidable a lady as Madame Diane. In our early years she had shaped the Queen's character and thus our own. The Queen loved her grandmother and we respected her, but a visit from Joinville without formal notice seemed strange.

'At least,' she said, 'we're relieved of our studies this morning.'

She studied politics, statecraft and philosophy with the Cardinal of Lorraine, her magnificent uncle. She also studied with thirty-seven young nobles and noblewomen in whatever palace we chanced to occupy. A great deal of cleaning was required for so large a court as King Henry II's, so we moved from Blois to Fontainebleau to Chambord with its four hun-

4

dred rooms, and on to the castles of Chinon and Amboise. Sometimes there was the elegant Hôtel de Guise in Paris. What we enjoyed most was travelling on the Loire in barges sailed with gold cloth, hunting on the way.

'Is there any news this morning?' she asked Fleming, who, being the most worldly of us and not easily shocked, was kept informed by the tirewomen.

'There's rarely news before breakfast,' Fleming said, for we'd not had time for so much as an apple or a sugar fig. 'But there's always gossip, Madam.'

'We must never listen to it,' the Queen said. She looked down at her little steeple-heeled shoe. Then she said, 'What is it?'

Fleming told us of a brawl between Queen Catherine's stablemen over a buttery maid who, kicking aside the vanquished suitor, had clouted the other over the head with a milk bucket. Then Fleming ruined speculation about a ghost in the woods – it was only a Cistercian monk in his white robes with dispensation to meditate at midnight. Fleming went on, 'If I may be bold, Madam, there's gossip that concerns yourself.'

Her Majesty said, 'It's your duty to tell me.'

'Monsieur Chastelard is madly in love with you.'

Laughter. 'He and his poems! But he is a good poet, and he dances well . . . a pleasant young man despite his religion.'

We thought it odd that despite her own piety she could be tolerant of a Huguenot – a Protestant – but then, he didn't agitate or try to spread the new doctrine, so he was accepted here at court. And he was handsome. I could have wished him her suitor were it not for the vast difference in rank. I hated to think that next year she would mate with the Dauphin – puny, sniffle-nosed, his head too big for his frail body. But that thinking was immature; physical beauty must never count in the matter of true love, and they had loved each other truly for ten years – since almost the moment of meeting. Yet it was strange; she was so beautiful and he so unmanly, despite his hard riding and attempts to be strong and dominating. Poor creature, seemingly still a child at thirteen; by no means an idiot, but dull.

5

And she adored him. Perhaps in gratitude the glum, rather sullen King came to adore her and invited her to his private revels where she must have offered far more amusement than Madame Diane, even if laughter *did* cause wrinkles.

She was laughing now about Pierre de Chastelard. 'He wrote that my eyes are amber jewels; I admired that. There are so few gentlemen about that dare to flatter me because of the Dauphin. So why should I not feed on it a while? At least you girls can flirt, whereas I dare not flutter an eyelid.'

There was a rumpus outside the room and we knew the guard had admitted the Duchess de Guise. Today she was in dark green to compliment a dark red wig. She curtsied deeply to Her Majesty, we curtsied deeply to her. She placed a pearl-handled cane on a couch, sat with Her Majesty's permission and asked that we might be seated.

We were inspected like a regiment. She said that Livingstone's small, tight ruff accentuated her long nose; Beaton's curls were too merry. Fleming, as always, was perfect. I – poor me. She was always kind but I was in truth no beauty except for my figure and dark blue eyes. My mouth was too small and my nose turned up and, despite being the daughter of a lord, my fingers were stubby. It struck me that it was very odd indeed that Her Majesty said I had a very mysterious allure about me that would be fatal to men. I took this as one of her charming efforts to boost my confidence. I felt that the gentlemen who pressed round me did so not for the honour of my presence as an attractive girl, but because I was the Queen's maid of honour.

The Duchess waited for Her Majesty to defend us, which she always did. It was my pallor that she had pounced on this time and the Queen told her that I had been made too busy in the apartments for sun and exercise. Then, said the Duchess, a bit of rose salve on lips and cheeks and a less severe coif to display my hair. Presently she asked for privacy and we were dismissed.

Each of us had our own suite and maids and pages; a large commonroom, too, where we gathered now as sun flared the room; it was the colour of jade. I sat down at a small mosaic table and fretted over my pallor. Wasn't it fashionable? Was

6

not the Queen's so white as to inspire poetry? But Fleming said mine was just a bit sallow and the others agreed it required colouring, so I decided to paint – discreetly. Then we sent for breakfast – we would have to leave it if Her Majesty summoned us – and by now it was so late that we ordered soup and cold capon and spice puffs, as though it were midday. I thought how hungry Her Majesty must be – she loved to eat – yet had deferred taking a proper meal for her grandmother's sake, who, after all, was a mere duchess. Or perhaps they were having cakes and wine.

From childhood we had fretted about her health; she was often sick, and suffered cramps of the stomach at other times. Often she fainted. She had tried to make us keep our promise not to inform the doctors but of course that was futile. Yet she was an expert huntress, fencer, dancer. She chided the Dauphin for riding too long and too hard, yet she often did the same. And how could we command or even advise, though pledged to look after her?

After an hour she summoned us; the Duchess had gone and she was eating meat from a silver tray – too fast, we thought. She was so ardent about everything; but in public so much more regal than poor, fat Queen Catherine, who always seemed clumsy. This was due to the common blood in her, Fleming said. Queen Catherine was the daughter of an Italian banker. All she had brought to France was money and, eventually, seven children who lived. It was rumoured that Madame Diane ordered the times of mating, sending the King to her bed.

Our mistress looked troubled, pushing aside the food. Almost always she confided in us. There never seemed to be a state secret; in truth I doubted she was entrusted with any. She was a cherished and educated ornament to be pushed to power by her marriage, yet even then sure to be dominated by the Cardinal of Lorraine and her other Guise uncles, who in turn dominated the King.

She looked at us sadly. 'I don't know what to do that I haven't done already. Her Grace is concerned with what she calls the Dauphin's "suicidal riding", and so am I. *You* know.'

7

Indeed we knew. The lad, perhaps to show his virility, rode recklessly. Often he turned blue in the face and had to be revived with wine. The stablemen were always prepared with linaments for scratches from tree branches. And his shortness of breath troubled them, though it passed. Once he had ridden a horse nearly to death – speed seemed essential – and neither the King nor the Queen could reason with him. I wondered why they didn't forbid him to ride as he did – after all, he was the future monarch of France.

The Queen spread her hands helplessly. 'What more can I do? I have chased after him and headed him off; I've even begged on my knees. And he smiles and bids me to rise and promises – and then a week later he is off on another mad ride.'

She paused. 'One thing I've not tried. I shall tell him he's not fit to be King if he breaks promises!'

But we all knew that kings broke them as lightly as bread. So did she, of course, for she said, 'No – I shall threaten not to marry him!'

Being so close to her, knowing her love of him and her natural obsession with power, we Marys were certain she would never dare to do this.

'Well?' she asked. 'What do you think, Livvy?'

Livingstone hesitated. 'I think the King should forbid him, Madam. If you suggested to the King—'

'That would seem as if I were saying, "You are negligent of your son."'

'I should beg again,' Fleming said, 'in the name of France.'

It was true that the wedding would be of great political significance to France, strengthening its bonds with Scotland, a rough slap at England who had wanted our Queen for the wife of Prince Edward – and it would put an end to the idea that France was not a major power. Already we had heard of wedding preparations to display – well, France's wealth. Spain would never have achieved this flamboyance because King Philip was cautious, whereas King Henry loved to spread the idea of Catholic magnificence. Or rather, the Cardinal did. We knew who really ruled the royal family.

Her Majesty said, 'I'll have to think on it. Pray on it,' and

8

she rose and dismissed us. She would be going to her oratory and so must we, having missed early Mass.

Each of us had our private oratories, stained-glass set into windows that shaded the light. No palace or castle was ever without these, as familiar as our bedchambers. Now I knelt on the velvet cushion below mine and prayed for the Queen's persuasion of the Dauphin. I forgot all about confessing my sins to God; they seemed so trivial in comparison. Besides, I had my confessor, who would call at dusk. I think that if I had been quite honest with myself I could say that he caused such uneasiness in me that I would rather have turned Protestant for half an hour and spoken to the Almighty directly. Now the very thought of that priest intruded on my prayer for the Dauphin – *damn* him!

Two months passed – it was now July – and it seemed our prayers were answered. The Dauphin curbed his wild riding, though I'll never know how Her Majesty achieved this miracle. We all enjoyed the fêtes that summer, culminating with the Battle of Flowers at Fontainebleau.

It was held at night on the soft green lawns, by torchlight. Our Scots guard and Scottish gentlemen attendants made mock battle of thousands of blooms, and so fiercely that I expected dirks to be drawn. Our Queen was also in native dress, though the plaid was woven of silk because of the heat. Her shoulders were bare, as were ours by her order. French ladies at court imitated this as they did nearly everything she fancied. They even rode in tight green breeks.

From a dais the King raised his hand to end the contest and commanded dancing. We floated from partner to partner, our feet crushing roses. Purple and scarlet rockets sped towards the moon. There was a fountain of wine, and on a long, golden table refreshments of every conceivable cake – quince, apricot, ginger, peach, raspberry – and even the humble raisin cake of Scotland which was one of the few things I remembered from childhood. With cream, it wasn't too bad.

After a dance with plump Monsieur Brantôme, the historian, we sat under the trees and he discussed the poetry of

9

food. 'But it can be practical too,' he said. 'In some cases, it must be. I've no idea what chef of the King's took pity on beggars at the gates and encased in a sheep's stomach fish, complete with its entrails, and meal with onions. I do not recommend it, Lady Seton, but the peasants thrive.'

'Practical?' I asked politely.

'Should you ever return to Scotland you will find it in a different version. Your Queen's mother left here with the recipe for using sheep's entrails.'

I thought of the lovely, elegant Mary de Guise and wondered if she had been brave enough to taste it. She was brave enough to hold the throne as regent against our own conniving lords, against English raiders – against the terrible influx of Protestantism. There was that maniac John Knox, who preached heresy from Edinburgh; Her Majesty said he would surely be placed in some asylum, so mad he was.

Monsieur Guillame claimed me, then another, and I danced until the Queen tired and motioned us to accompany her back to the palace with the Scots who always guarded us. I often wondered against what. There were not even ghosts except the lingering haunt of flowers as we went to our quarters. After my tirewoman had disrobed me and blown out the candles I stood at the window marvelling at the peace of the far woods, the soft clasp of moonlight. We were so safe.

It was in November, at St Germain, that I began to worry about the state of my soul. This was because Father Michael subtly drove in needles. He had been assigned to me after the old priest died but, being young, there was no tolerance in him for me. I was given penances for merely existing.

He was tall, with hair blond as my own but curling inwards. His lips were thick and red. He should have been handsome but his eyes were cold, the colour of pewter. He glided rather than walked, like a woman. He had the soft, insinuating voice of a woman – one who is fully aware of her charm. But I was not charmed – I was afraid of him; and one should not fear one's corridor towards God.

Matters would proceed like this: 'What of the sin of

10

intemperance, my lady? You were not abed until dawn.'

'But my Queen's command—'

'You enjoyed it, did you not? The wine and the kisses.'

'Kisses! I have never in my life kissed a man carnally.'

'Ah, but you think about it, do you not?'

Nearly sixteen, I did think about it as any girl would. After the Queen married we were relieved of our vow to remain virgins, and, indeed, the vow was our own idea. Of course we all looked forward to husbands, children. We Marys talked about that – sometimes teasingly, but often seriously. And we were innocent; we had no idea what love-making was like.

'I think about it, wondering how it would be that a man's lips on mine could sweep me into passion.'

'So you are curious.'

He always put me into the wrong, whereas he considered my true sins to be trivial – such as forgetting to order the right gloves for Her Majesty, such as curling a wig improperly – she loved them in various shades – and my embarrassment about that was intense. But she had forgiven me this great sin whereas Father Michael seemed to invent them for me.

'What about envy?' he asked. 'Do you not envy those born of royal blood?'

I was quick to correct him. 'No! I'm the daughter of George, fourth Earl of Seton. We are related to the finest families of Scotland. . . .'

'Ah,' came the taunting, feminine voice. 'So you bear the sin of pride.'

That I could not help; my father's last letter before he died was to warn me not to encourage suitors who were below me in rank, and now my half-brother, the fifth Earl, was cautioning the same thing. I believe that both of them rather looked down upon the French nobility. Scots of any kind have a ravening pride.

'I suppose I do,' I said, pleased that he was off the pesky subject of carnality.

And so he gave me penances clear to December.

8 December was Her Majesty's sixteenth birthday and gifts had arrived from all over the Catholic world, including a

11

long glass from the Pope so that she could see herself from coif to shoes. It was framed in gold and sapphires and she permitted us all a look before we set about storing the other gifts. A happy day began as she chose her gown for that night's ball – white, with long, mink-lined sleeves. Then the Cardinal arrived and we left them together, thinking what a gift his very presence was to her.

But when she summoned us she was in tears. The Dauphin's attendants had found him crumpled in the snow on a dead horse. He was now unconscious and the Cardinal had given him the last rites. She must go to the bedside.

She didn't care what she wore – cloak quickly put on – nor about her hair, which she tucked under a shawl. The Cardinal waited below to accompany her to the royal wing. And we Marys prayed together just as we were, kneeling on the carpet, *May the Dauphin live.*

I had no political interest beyond hoping that Scotland might hold out against the English and treachery inside the country. I suppose I realised, dimly, that if the Dauphin died there was no French prince for her to marry, Charles being too young. My important concern was their love for one another – that it should end so cruelly after ten years. There were cynics who said that the little boy, aged three, could not have adored her on sight. Why not? She was scarcely older and so they began as playmates, sharing secrets against the grown-up world – a world that none of us understood at the time.

A bell rang below to announce that Her Majesty was in her apartments. Then, the four bells that summoned us. She was sitting on a love-seat, tearless and composed. But her face was strained and the light had gone from her eyes. She motioned us to sit down. Then she said, 'He has regained consciousness but his fever is high and he trembles from chills. Four physicians are with him. I can only wait, out of the way, though Queen Catherine is with him.'

She tried hard to smile. 'Happy birthday to us all. I refuse to mourn a person still alive. Seton, order wine – no, *aqua vitæ.* It's stronger medicine.'

This was a Scottish brew rarely drunk except by Captain

12

Montgomery and others of our guard. It tasted like dank, liquid earth. She tossed hers off in one gulp, so we did the same. She didn't even wince. To her, all things from our native land, or of them, must be honoured, even the screeching pipes that blasted the ear drums.

The drink steadied her voice. 'Unlock my desk, Seton, and bring the little packages.'

While I was away in her study I paused to pick up our gift to her – a golden, lily-shaped brooch with tiny emeralds as stems. The package, wrapped in green velvet, was scented with lily-of-the-valley. When I brought it to her she sniffed, smiled again, opened it and burst into tears.

Perhaps it was the tension of waiting; in any case she soon perked up bravely and fastened it to her gown and thanked us. Our gifts were golden rings marked with our names and *Forever, Marie R.* Forever love, she said, though there had been no room to have love inscribed. In truth, there was no need of it – we knew.

That was a weary day. Messengers would arrive hourly but there was no change in the Dauphin's condition. We tried to play chess. Fleming's lute accompanied Livvy's songs, but they were ill-chosen, being about love, and we sensed that and the music stopped. Beaton asked Her Majesty if she should summon Nichola, the female fool, but she said, 'She could not be amusing today and that would embarrass her.'

As soon as it was dark she retired to her bedchamber, and we sat up by the fire waiting for some more encouraging message. I am certain that she longed for him to call her to his bedside but Queen Catherine was fiercely maternal and, I think, jealous of our Queen. At midnight I picked up my embroidery and said, 'Truly, I'm not sleepy. Why not go to your beds?'

'Why should you be alone?' Beaton asked.

'Call it a birthday gift,' I said as merrily as I could. 'Unless I must waken the Queen, I'll tap on your door at five.'

I did so at five. There had been no change. A page told me that Her Majesty had retired, not to her bed but to her oratory. Yet now she was asleep, her tirewoman said.

At noon the Dauphin asked to see her. She had no idea

13

whether this was to be a parting before his death or a visit to a recovering invalid. She wore a bright green gown -- the colour of life. She wore our brooch. She called for her sable cloak. Under its hood her eyes – those long, 'amber jewelled' eyes – looked out serenely. Some folk might say that she had been trained to bravery but I think it was born in her. She left in the Cardinal's charge, scented with lily-of-the-valley.

The Dauphin recovered, perhaps because by now all of France had prayed for a miracle. But Her Majesty said that he was depressed, possibly from shock of the accident. Nor was he pleased that his parents had forbidden him to ride. His chief amusement now was playing at war with toy soldiers on a vast map of Europe, and in this our Queen joined. She told us that Scotland had conquered England within one hour. The young Earl of Bothwell, who had consistently defended her mother and intercepted English gold intended for our treacherous Scots lords, was made commander.

But now that the Dauphin was safe she longed for air and exercise, and one day late in December, after the celebration of Christmas, she commanded a group of us to hunt. I am maudlin about hurting animals so I carried no falcon on my wrist, no arrows. I think my horse tripped over a rock – under the soft powder of snow. In any case, it stumbled and I was pitched under the giant firs.

My groom and I were well behind the others so he didn't shout for help. Instead he checked his horse and came to me, looking so fearful that I was able to smile. 'It is only my ankle,' I said, 'and I doubt it's broken. But it throbs. . . .'

He had knelt in the snow beside me, still silenced by fright, a new, young groom from Soissons named Raoul, doubtless thinking that he would lose his place for carelessness of me, but how could he have avoided the accident? So as I massaged my ankle I told him that presently I would rise and lean on his arm and try a few steps. My horse was waiting, as if abashed, and I knew I could ride him home.

Raoul lost his fear. 'My lady, you must not try to walk. I shall lift you.'

I had not noticed before the depth of his eyes – grey, with

14

very black pupils. His skin was still dark from summer sun. He had a beautiful mouth, and it was determined. So was his voice. 'I shall carry you now and ride with you.'

I felt the strength of his arms as he picked me up and I forgot the pain of my ankle for a new sensation which I cannot describe. It was a mixture of deep comfort and something else – a stirring in my body. We rode back with his arms about my waist, my horse following. Snow dropped from the tall spruces and I lifted my face to it, wishing the five miles were ten. I dared not turn my head to look at him because in truth, I wanted his mouth on mine. And when we entered the courtyard to a scurry of alarmed servants, and the little adventure was over, I felt almost bereaved.

When I was able to be alone I daydreamed about Raoul, reliving the brief experience with such pleasure that I knew I would have to confess to Father Michael. I even came to dramatise, wondering if Raoul had felt the same way as I; or if I were merely a valuable bundle to pluck from the snow.

My bedchamber was dressed in lilac satin, the ceiling painted in a mosaic of silver. At dusk, without candles, it was vastly romantic. I would stand at the window watching the snow fall on the opposite turrets of the courtyard and feel the most intense joy – and then rip the images away. Imagine, Lady Mary Seton mooning over a groom of the stables! I tried to laugh about it; I failed. I longed to tell someone, and Fleming would surely understand, yet it was so sweetly private until I had to confess to Father Michael – a few days away.

I thought, I must see Raoul before that so that he has no chance to forbid me, and my ankle was quite healed. So I asked Her Majesty's permission to ride – the day was clear and sunny – and she granted it, suggesting that all of us Marys go out together.

I dressed in my most becoming riding costume – scarlet bodice and skirt, scarlet cloak hooded with white marten. With the others I sought the stables where the Master of Horse awaited us. Grooms stood stiffly at attention. Raoul was not among them. Boldly I asked Monsieur de Picon where he was, saying that I wanted to thank him for bringing me safely home.

'Oh,' he said casually, 'he is in service to us at Chinon. The royal children are being moved there, you know.'

This was from some rumour of a Huguenot uprising, but there were many such rumours and we scarce paid attention. They were mainly an unarmed rabble more anxious to focus attention on to their religion than to kill.

But my little romance had been killed. So I buried it in my mind, or tried to, as we set out among the snow-jewelled fields, into the woods.

You may know what Father Michael said to me when I confessed.

'This was lust, my daughter. An attraction of the body that held no spiritual thread.'

He made it seem ugly. I determined not to allow such a thing to happen again and so, when the other Marys chattered of future husbands and babies, I kept silent. It seemed the only righteous way was to marry someone to whom I was not attracted at all and let *him* bear the sin of lust.

My Queen's trousseau occupied us throughout February. We were all skilled needlewomen but the nuns taught us more, and I was astonished by the undergarments and night robes, which they cut so seductively that nakedness seemed innocent. Some of these nuns were Italian, favourites of Queen Catherine, two were Flemish, the rest from Paris, and we worked in a long gallery – measuring, stitching, embroidering. Her Majesty, too, skilfully worked on delicate silks, sewing with gold and silver thread. It was a happy time for her. And it crossed my mind that she would most certainly be free of lust for the poor little Dauphin whom we met oftener now at the various prenuptial parties. But it was sad to see her – tall and so alive – and him forced to look up to her, spindly-legged in his hose and the doublet tight across a pitiful chest. He led her into the dance, bowed her from room to room, brought her wine and food with his own hand. The

16

King looked on with that glumness he usually exhibited in public, but he must have been proud of his son whom we felt was nearing the greatest strain of his life with what grace he could – even our Scots piper, burly Gordon Duncan, had more presence in a ballroom.

Late in the month Scottish commissioners arrived and our Queen bade me receive her half-brother, Lord James Stuart, in my parlour. It may be that she kept him waiting because she was not fully dressed. Or it may have been policy; after all, he and his Protestant lords sought to rule Scotland despite her mother's regency. Furthermore, he was illegitimate and, though she may have been tolerant of that, she could not easily overlook his rebellious activities.

As I showed him to a chair I marvelled how alike their eyes were – long, dark hazel – they had inherited them from King James V of Scotland. And he had a kingly manner, sauvity tinged with arrogance. I believe he was twenty-six, but the dark beard made him seem older. When I moved towards him to pour the requested wine I saw that his eyes were tinged with green. For some reason I thought of a cat, of a cat's slyness, but supposed that was only due to what we had heard of his character. A grave man who did not dally with women, who claimed deep faith in God albeit a Protestant – and who undoubtedly wanted the regency for himself. Her Majesty's mother had enough trouble without his meddling.

He spoke at last. 'You are enjoying France, Lady Seton?'

As though we were visitors. 'I loved it from the time we landed here. The peasants blew us kisses; we were amused by jesters from Brittany to Touraine. Someone garlanded our horses each day and we sat among blossoms – a child's dream.'

He nodded. 'And what do you remember of Scotland?'

'Danger. Until Her Majesty was safe from the English attempts to kidnap her, we little girls were held close on our estates with heavy guard. When we joined her at Dumbarton and set sail we all knew that English warships were out to block our way. Thank God they were tricked.'

He frowned. I had forgotten his personal alliance with the

17

English, who were said to pay him for undermining the kingdom and its religion. Embarrassed, I stopped prattling. Clearly, I was no diplomat.

But he was. 'A child relishes more drama than fact, don't you think? It is all puffed up in one's memory whereas so much was merely rumour. . . .'

Rumour! Was it rumour that King Henry VIII had looted our monasteries, had sent sixteen thousand soldiers to massacre, to mutilate, any Scot in his way, all because Mary of Guise refused our little Queen to be his son's bride? Lord James was so distorting truth that I began to dislike him intensely. I often show very swift judgement and am usually proved right. Here was a man hinting that events that had happened fifteen years ago had not happened at all. He thought me still a child or else a fool.

To my relief a page came to say that Her Majesty would receive him. Slender, erect, he bowed to me and then smiled for the first time. A smile of pitying amusement.

Oh, how I hoped she would not be blinded by sisterly affection but see him as he was – cold, tricky, able to condone murder if not to commit it himself. I supposed he would remain for the wedding.

Presently Beaton joined me, removed her riding hat and let the red-gold curls spill over her shoulders. 'If I didn't love you, my dear, I'd have been jealous that you were chosen to delay Lord James, for we are all curious.'

'I wish,' I said, 'that Lord James had delayed in his mother's womb and been born dead.'

'Jesu! Only a first impression—'

'Was sufficient. He is like the devil. . . .'

But when I told her she said, 'You do so exaggerate, it's from reading romances. And Her Majesty is so clever she'll soon have him as her footstool.'

With all deference to her, I wondered.

Later, at a supper party with Queen Catherine as hostess, Her Majesty entered on her brother's arm. But to my vast relief she did not look proud or happy. She seemed aloof and soon left us to join the Dauphin as though he were protection. Ladies were introduced to Lord James. He was presented

18

to Queen Catherine – not by Her Majesty, but by Duke
Francis de Guise, an uncle.

I was almost certain that she meant to humiliate him; I
was thankful – and uneasy.

CHAPTER II

————◆————

Being a member of the family, I suppose Lord James was present at the handfasting ceremony in the Louvre, but if he expected to parade himself at the wedding in Nôtre Dame I am sure he was not noticed. There was, first, the crimson-gowned clergy, followed by the royal family in such clothes and jewels as I'd never seen or even imagined. As they walked towards the cathedral, rubies and emeralds caught the fire of the April sun. We Marys, in procession behind them, did not see our Queen until she stood at the altar.

It was hot, and my velvet robes encrusted with silver seemed to smother me. The roar of the watching mob was lion-like, if approving. For weeks the humblest folk of Paris had worked to fashion silk roses and sew them on ribbons which were hung on turrets and scaffoldings near the church. Balconies budded royal purple blossoms, tapestries, gold-cloth fleur-de-lis. Wagons of roses had been sent from Provence for the crowd to pelt on us from rooftop or windows.

At last I saw our Queen by taperlight. She looked like a tall, white lily grown in a soil of diamonds. The train of her gown was six yards of massed jewels flowing on crimson. Beside her stood Francis. His narrow shoulders had been widened by an ermine coat but no embellishment could dignify him, a child beside a goddess.

I believe that the weight of her crown troubled her, heavy with diamonds, rubies, emeralds, for twice she touched it as though to tip it back from her face. To her the solemn High Mass must have seemed as endless as it was to me – heat from the tapers and the smell of incense must have been well nigh overpowering. Finally it was over and she said, clearly, 'I salute you, my beloved husband – King of Scotland.'

Of course he was only King-Consort as she was Queen-Dauphine of France but it was like her to be gracious. I wished I could have seen Lord James's reaction to this, but I could catch only a glimpse of his dark red robes over the bowed heads of the high clergy. Then trumpets sounded, the choir boys sang and we invited guests were free to follow the bridal party to the celebrations at the bishop's palace where food and wine were served, and musicians played for dancing. I was not aware at the time that money had been thrown to the mob from the porch of Nôtre Dame, that hundreds of people had perished in a kicking, screaming lust for gold. We danced while others died.

In the late afternoon we moved on, by open litter, to the Palais de Justice where Duke Francis de Guise welcomed us with supper. He had arranged a pageant of ships, cleverly made to sail the floor. King Henry drew our Queen aboard, and though she was smiling it was her false, weary smile. They disembarked at windows facing the Seine and leaned out to look at the fireworks – I am sure she needed air to keep her from fainting, I was in fact ready to run to her faster than any physician, for I knew the symptoms: a little muscle working in her cheek and the trembling of her hands. For a moment her left hand held the huge bridal ring to her cheek; then she turned and walked back to her table. But though she had conquered illness, she could not conquer the evident weight of the crown. She removed it, a fifteen-hour torture. Across the room I saw Lord James smile.

She and the Dauphin spent the night at the Palais de Tournelles and we Marys were given suites there. Janet, her tire-woman, said, 'I never imagined how that gossamer robe would become her, gauze and embroidered lilies. I am not a soft woman, but I wanted to weep.'

'Because she seemed sad?' Livvy asked.

'No, she was serene. But I thought, God forgive me, what waste of a bride.'

21

We were not with her on the honeymoon in a country house in Soissons. But we heard that the Cardinal was there and that her studies were resumed.

My friend Captain Montgomery rode with me one morning and because he was a wise old Scot – well, older than I – I asked him how he felt about Lord James. He checked his horse abruptly so that I did too, and said, 'I think him a ravening wolf. He'd commit any crime to wrest the crown but his nature is cowardly. He will work in the dark.'

'I hope Her Majesty perceives that?'

He shrugged. 'She's so young. But when our Scots commissioners visited Soissons last week, she didn't receive him alone. She gave him no honour. He has sailed home without special favour.'

'What troubles me is her warm heart,' I said, 'and the fact that he looks like the portrait of her father.'

'Aye, but the Cardinal will have taught her shrewdness these past years; no man could be less sentimental. She is in good care.'

Then I burst out, 'But that His Eminence should share their honeymoon!'

'Why not?' he asked wryly. 'Likely there's little enough to occupy her considering that the Dauphin—'

And then he turned red, and stammered an apology.

I liked this blunt soldier, so different from the fawning French courtiers, and I had come to know his heart which was the eager heart of a lad. He longed to distinguish himself, but there were no battles. If he had been permitted to return to Scotland he would surely have joined Lord Bothwell in protecting Her Majesty's mother, and in Border war against the English. But as our Captain of the Guard his life was inactive and wasted.

But the Dauphin had to develop into a man, so the King ended the honeymoon by sending him to a military training camp in Amiens. We expected our Queen at court but she lingered in the château, busy with music and verse-making. We were at Chambord when she returned in July. She seemed more thoughtful than before; obediently she attended functions, but she was often alone in her apartments. Was she meditating on the tangle of Europe? Praying for guidance if decision were required? She had changed from a sparkling young girl to a woman with veiled eyes – more beautiful, less approachable. And when we played pranks, like hiding Livvy's lacy pillow in the stables to comfort new-born kittens, she laughed but without the glee of childhood, whereas a year ago she would have joined in.

Father Michael continued to distress me, for it seemed that I distressed him. He must have seen me ride with Captain Montgomery, for when I paused, with nothing to confess but concern that my hair was darkening, he said, 'What of men? Do you not ride out alone with them?'

'No,' I said, thinking how many courtiers followed us, how rare an occasion it was to be more than half a league from company.

'Do you lie to me or to yourself, daughter?'

'Oh—' I nearly laughed. 'Captain Montgomery is an old friend. There is assuredly no lust.'

'How do you know whether he lusts? That you are not tempting him?'

I found this absurd. I stared at the filigree screen between us, thinking that it separated our natures as well as our bodies. His was so suspicious, and when we met in public my gaiety died – as though it were evil to enjoy the most innocent pleasures. Now I murmured that Captain Montgomery was the very last gentleman to be tempted by me but I knew I had not convinced him because of the penances.

After he had blessed me and left, I wandered out to the balcony and looked down on the dusk-drowsy gardens. This man was insidiously trying to separate me from nature itself, for it came to me that he would find lust at the sight of a bee in a flower. And when I wanted to marry – Jesu, by his standards I would be lower than Mary Magdalene.

Impulsively, I asked audience of our Queen, who had just supped alone. She received me in the small, oval chamber hung with her own pink and silver embroideries. At once she asked me what was wrong, and I told her.

'My poor Seton,' she said, 'confession should make you clean and happy – and close to God.'

23

'I am æons away from God when I'm with him – closer, indeed, to the devil. I think he hates me.'

Calmly, she said, 'It is known that some men who dislike women take refuge in the Church; perhaps he is one of them. But he shall not be allowed to try to twist your mind. I'll speak with the Cardinal about another confessor.'

'Madam, would you?'

'Tomorrow,' she said.

So the next week Father Pierre came to my oratory. His voice was old, deep, patient, truly fatherly. I didn't confess to him my mistrust of Father Michael, though it may have been a sin. I felt like a swimmer who has been tangled in dank reeds and then allowed the freedom of the sea.

The Dauphin returned to court puny as ever, but the sun had made his pox marks less obvious. Wherever we lodged, our suites were close to Her Majesty's. Together we heard that Queen Mary Tudor was dead – a blow to Catholic Europe. In January Sir Nicholas Throckmorton, the English ambassador, came to St Germain with news of the coronation of Elizabeth, who had blatantly proclaimed herself Protestant.

Our Queen spent hours closeted with the Cardinal; often the tapers in her oratory burned until after midnight. We sensed that she was deeply troubled but she confided nothing to us until one rainy afternoon. She looked up from her tapestry frame and said, in a strange little voice, 'Do you realise that I am the rightful Queen of England?'

To our silence she said, 'It's true. The English Parliament declared my cousin Elizabeth unworthy of succession to the crown because she was illegitimate – that was in 1536. In 1544 they restored the right of succession but could not deny that she's a bastard. She has no more legal right to rule England than my brother James has to rule Scotland.'

Fleming said, 'Why, of course – Your Majesty is the great-granddaughter of King Henry VII. How dare she to be so presumptuous?'

Our Queen smiled. 'Perhaps because I haven't stated my rights. His Eminence thinks I should.'

We knew little of the usurper, save that she was now twenty-

five and reputed to be beautiful. But of that we were cynical –
all royal ladies were beautiful, as all warriors were heroes.
Foreign princes, fearful of buying a pig in a poke for wife,
rarely depended on portraits. They sent their most trusted
ambassador to report; but if a fortune were involved or
political prestige, warts and bandy legs or bloat did not matter.
Had not King Henry married Catherine de Medici despite
her blowsiness?

'I must publicly declare my rights,' our Queen said, but
there seemed uncertainty in her voice. 'Soon, the Cardinal
says.'

But I sensed that this wasn't what she wished to do. None
of us Marys, at sixteen, thought boldly, as men do. I remembered tales of English butchery in Scotland and wondered if
Queen Elizabeth might not be as savage as her father, or more
so because of the insult to her pride. She most assuredly had
the military power, if not legal title to cause havoc. My earliest
memory at home at Seton was of a stench so dreadful that I
ran inside the house and was sick on the floor; nor was I
punished, but cuddled by my nurse. It was only later that I
was told that the stench was driven on the wind from huts on
fire at the Border. I had smelled burning flesh.

Of course we asked her what was known of Elizabeth, and
Her Majesty admitted that she was clever. She had appointed
Sir William Cecil Secretary of State and the Cardinal thought
him wily, even loyal – perhaps the best choice of men in
England for a young, inexperienced sovereign. 'As to her
beauty, Sir Nicholas naturally praised golden-red hair and a
divine figure, but our own folk say she's thin as a stalk, plain
of face, with blue eyes cold as a pond. There is no rumour
that she flirts; possibly no prince will want her if – when – I
make claim. I could almost feel pity if she were not arrogantly
ambitious.'

'Spawn of Henry VIII, that is natural to her,' I said, and
again thought of the massacres at home. My father told me
that the English had played football with severed heads, that
babies were used in place of golf balls. This was not so much
intended to frighten me as to create implacable hatred of the
enemy; and though I said nothing to Her Majesty of Sir

25

Nicholas Throckmorton's probable villainy I hoped she was aware of it. At best, he was paid to lie; all diplomats must. Even our young Queen, so truthful, would be forced to do so at times.

She changed the subject as though it no longer interested her; or perhaps the weight of another crown dismayed her. She began to talk of the new clothes we would need for the summer. 'For one appearance, I should like you all in green. Emerald satin for you, Livvy, moss for Fleming, apple colour for Beaton and fern for Seton. In that way you will create a bouquet about me. . . .'

We wore the new dresses in late June to a triple celebration commanded by King Henry to mark the betrothal of his sister Margaret to the Duke of Savoy, his daughter Elizabeth to Philip of Spain – and, most importantly, peace with Spain. Green is said to be the colour of life, and Paris the city of light, but this was the third day of a tournament and I preferred milder sports. Yet the ladies' gallery was merry as we waited for our Queen and the royal family to take their places; iced wines were passed round. Across from us Diane de Poitiers sparkled in white, and her colours never varied –⚜ white in summer, black in winter. She wore her diamond crescent in a fold of her headdress.

Then Queen Catherine was seated in the royal box that was looped with crimson velvet and cloth of gold. I scarcely knew her – yet today I pitied her. The sun beat down on her heavy brown velvets, her excess of fat, and her skin was rough as oats. It was said that she lived on Italian starches which created an unhealthy complexion. Now a servant passed a tray of pink sweets and she stuffed two into her mouth. Her lip paint smeared.

Beaton whispered, 'Where is Queen Mary? She is always on time.'

'And the Dauphin too.' But I was not concerned, only bored; and offended by the unwashed smells of the ladies around us. Had not Madame Diane trained us to bathe every day, we too would have reeked in the sun.

In the gentlemen's gallery I saw Captain Montgomery with the rest of our guard and guessed that he too was bored. To him a tournament was a child's pastime to be watched with polite contempt. It came to my mind then that if ever petition was needed, I might ask my Queen. Any experienced soldier could protect us here but there were few to protect Queen Mary de Guise in Scotland. I decided that tonight at the revel I would ask him if I might make such petition on his behalf. No matter that I would miss him; Father Pierre had said that our missions in life were to be tools for the good of others.

There was a sudden blare of trumpets. Heralds appeared in front of a purple and gold litter, shouting 'Make place for the Queen of England!'

Our Queen, with the Dauphin, was carried to the royal box. But instead of cheers there were gasps of astonishment, for her servants' purple attire was stamped in gold with the arms of England and Ireland as well as Scotland and France. Her guards wore the same crest on their sleeves and breastplates. Never had I seen her look so regal nor so stern. She stared straight at Throckmorton, the English Ambassador, in a sort of cold defiance, and Fleming whispered, 'Jesu! When Queen Elizabeth hears of this . . .' but her words were lost to me through the shouting of the crowd. Her Majesty smiled and kissed her hand to them and trumpets sounded again as King Henry entered the lists.

He too was bold, but in proclamation of his devotion to Madame Diane, for his horse wore her colours – black and white – and he flaunted his love through her symbol of crescent moon, the diamonds set to shine on his saddle-pommel. I paid little attention as he jousted with the Duke of Savoy – and won. Through the long, hot day I was scarcely aware of his triumphs, rather of the mockery of his Queen. Throughout clash of lance and animal roar of crowd I pitied Queen Catherine, so publicly exposed to her husband's infidelity. Her face was a mask; nor did she blink when Diane tossed him a white rose as he galloped toward her 'to receive a favour from my lady'. What thoughts went through that tortuous Italian brain when even her younger children must witness this embarrassment?

Now it was late afternoon. Behind us, the shadows of the Bastille crept like blue fingers. Surely the King was tiring, but he challenged Captain Montgomery to tilting. I saw the captain smile, bow, and shake his shaggy brown head. But apparently it was a command, and he prepared himself to enter the lists. Then Queen Catherine sent her page to the King with a message. He looked up at her impatiently. She sent another page, but the King turned away as if in contempt. Then he and Captain Montgomery levelled their lances and charged, missed one another, circled the field. It was so dusty by now you could scarcely see the hooves of their horses. On the third charge both lances splintered with a raw, shattering noise. The King slumped in his saddle. Grooms hurried to him and eased him on to the ground. I saw his visor raised, but there was no face – only a sea of blood.

Beaton clutched my hand. 'Don't look,' she said. There was a terrible wailing from the crowd. When I dared to look again I saw the King borne away on a litter, Queen Catherine hurrying down supported by the Cardinal. The rest of the royal family followed – we learned later to the Palais des Tournelles, which was nearby. There was nothing for we Marys to do but to return to our Queen's apartments in the palace, though we felt abandoned and useless in the stream of physicians and priests. In all of the confusion I hadn't seen Captain Montgomery since the moment of his victory – or disaster.

We were having wine together in Livvy's parlour when Paul, our Queen's messenger, came to us and told us not to expect her summons tonight, but to retire. He also told us that there were five splinters in the King's eye and temple. They were hoping to probe out the one that had lodged in the brain.

After he had left, Beaton opened the blue mosaic door that led to the balcony and bade us all go out for air. But it was warm. The city of Paris was circled with lights, as always on holidays. And on this, the third day of celebration, of feasting, the air was rank with the smell of decay; of rotting fruit, chicken bones, cheese rinds and vegetable parings. We smelled the dank, slow-flowing Seine. Below us, in torchlight, a crowd murmured. We could see the flash of the gold-trimmed hats of the royal guards.

I thought of Captain Montgomery and wondered where he

28

was this night – and if he prayed. My prayers were for him as strongly as for the King. It had been an honourable joust; in public we had all seen him try to reject it. It was obvious that the King shouldn't have sported for so long. It came to me then that a royal whim can be more unfair than the devil's, because the devil judges the consequences coolly.

Livvy said, 'Save your tears. He is still alive or the mourning-bells would ring.'

No bells rang. There was no sound in all of Paris but the stir of its waiting people, and – catching the mood of dismay – the soft howl of dogs.

Two days later our Queen summoned us to the turret tower she shared with the Dauphin. She was alone, wearing a gown of palest pink, and her hair flowed to her waist. She asked me to arrange it, and as I did so she said, 'I think no man has ever suffered so – he is in constant pain. But he is lucid. He has ordered that the marriage of Margaret and the Duke of Savoy must proceed but doesn't demand our attendance. What a ghastly wedding that will be!'

She tried to smile. 'I sleep, when I can, on a couch in an alcove near his bed. Queen Catherine has a pallet in the same chamber. She insists that she had supernatural warning of disaster – a fearful dream the night before the joust – and she remembers that Luc Gauric had predicted the King's death in single combat. That's why she sent messages into the field begging that the sport be ended.'

Gauric was her astrologer; but in 1555 Nostradamus had also predicted death of 'an old lion, in martial field by a single duel. In a cage of gold he shall put out his eye, two wounds from one, then he shall die a cruel death.' We were all familiar with the prophecies but our Queen was not superstitious so we never discussed such matters. But I could not help but reflect that the King's visor was shiningly gilded, like a cage of gold.

'One of the saddest matters is, he screams for Madame Diane. But she is not admitted.'

The young lion shall overcome the old one, in martial field.

'Madam,' I said, 'Captain Montgomery was my special friend. Where is he now?'

29

'In his own apartments, in prayer – so I hear. The King has pronounced him blameless.'

I wanted to ask if I might go to him – but what comfort could I bring, and it might seem to some in bad taste, so I said nothing.

Beaton, always an optimist, said, 'The King is not dead.'

Her Majesty said, 'No, but send your prayers to St Jude.'

Patron of lost causes. As I gave a final pat to her hair and fastened it with the last golden pin, she said, 'It's ironic that I must look – as usual. If I were to be myself wholly, I'd have no thought of adornment. I love him.'

We knew, and we suspected that he loved her more than he did his slow-witted son. I could remember their first meeting under tall poplars as we were driven towards his hunting spot. Already at thirty he was sad-looking, and even his attire was a melancholy grey with black slashed sleeves. To my childish mind he looked less like a monarch than a stranger at his own court. He stared at our little Queen who sat, draped in fur, in her horse-litter, then rode close and kissed her hand, greeting her as 'my daughter'. She reached out and tickled his moustache and told him how handsome he was, and this made him smile. Then she remembered her prepared speech and thanked him for his protection, for the hospitality of France – for picnics along the way and jesters and windbells. Then she introduced us Marys: 'Lady Livingstone is most graceful at the dance. . . . Lady Beaton plans pranks and wins pillow-fights. . . . Lady Fleming can arrange flowers better than the Mistress of the Household. Lady Seton arranges my hair. . . .'

Gravely, he kissed our hands as though we were the most gifted of adults. Then he ordered a feast of venison in his tent and presented us with gifts – a diamond locket for Her Majesty, sapphire bracelets for us. To Captain Montgomery he gave gold and ruby spurs. Never again did I see the King closely; after that he was a distant figure at formal ceremonies.

Now Her Majesty said, 'This is my first deep grief. If only His Majesty were not so aware – if the agony could be lessened by draughts—'

She returned to her vigil. Eight days later mourning-bells rang from every church in Paris. She summoned her tiring woman to dress her in robes of white. I arranged her hair under a white lace veil and she asked for kohl to spark her exhausted eyes. When she left for the ceremony of allegiance at the Louvre we were afraid that she would collapse.

Normally she would grow dizzy for no apparent reason. Now some inner strength carried her through the King's funeral at Nôtre Dame and the coronation of the Dauphin at Rheims.

Outside the church her husband stumbled with fatigue as he tried to wave to the thousands gathered there in the square; but she stood tall and serene, a white glow beyond the black-clad royal family. Now she was Queen of France, of Scotland and – so we all felt – of England.

As she prepared to enter her carriage with the King a sudden rain scattered the crowd; wind swirled her veil and she caught it aside in a jewel-heavy hand. Then the horses moved off, their hooves pounding wet flowers.

Long live the King. I prayed to God that King Francis would protect Her Majesty as his father had; and surely his love was as deep? But one could not help doubting his wisdom.

There was the Cardinal's wisdom, I thought with relief, as he stood beside the great ladies of France – Dowager Queen Catherine, the Duchess de Guise, Madame Diane. There had been rumour that Queen Catherine would prohibit Diane from attending public ceremonies or find other means to humiliate her old rival, but Catherine, as I watched her move towards her carriage, was listless, a woman with all emotion squeezed out of her, her pop-eyes tearless as they had been at her husband's funeral.

Madame Diane swept her a deep, unnoticed curtsey. Then she came to me and said, 'Please remind Her Majesty that she has granted me audience this evening.'

'I shall, Your Grace.'

Then she said a strange thing, which puzzled me because of the entire court I was least equipped in strength or cleverness. 'I trust you to see that she comes to no harm.'

That evening our Queen received Madame Diane alone, but then sent for us. 'Her Grace wants to bid you farewell.' We sensed that she did not mean a brief farewell; her voice was choked with grief. 'She is retiring to the provinces.'

'I prefer not to call it "banishment",' Diane said, 'but I must obey Queen Catherine's wishes. I have returned to her the crown jewels and given her my château of Chenonceaux – she grants me Chaumont in exchange. I am allowed my other estates. It is very fair.'

Considering there had been speculation that Catherine intended some subtle Italian poison for Diane's wine, it was fair indeed; but I could not imagine Diane 'dethroned' after twenty years of power, or away from court.

'She has interest in her vineyards,' our Queen said bleakly.

Diane nodded. Grief may make a woman ugly; rarely does it beautify. She was flawless of face and body as when we had first met her, and I thought, when she meets the King in heaven she will look just this way, diamonds in her hair.

Fleming, usually self-contained, began to cry and Diane scolded her. 'How many times have I told you that emotion is a waste, and the skin's mortal enemy? Not once have I wept for the King; he would have been appalled.'

Then she asked leave to go, and knelt for our Queen's blessing. She kissed her hand to us and met her attendant in the hallway. The next morning from the balcony of the Queen's apartments we watched her departure in a canopied litter of black velvet stamped with crescent moons of diamonds. Her guard wore her colours of black and white, her ladies and pages were dressed in black and white satin, and behind them rode a number of splendid gentlemen in black doublet and hose, their cloaks trimmed with ermine.

Her Majesty said, in awe, 'Those gentlemen – the old and the young as well – would hope for her hand in marriage. Witchcraft or not, she's uncanny.'

Then Diane looked up at us and waved. We expected no smile.

Before we left for St Germain, Captain Montgomery asked audience of King Francis and, boldly, I contrived to see him as he left the walled garden – in fact I hurried after him lest he reached the street before I had a chance to question him.

32

He turned, surprised, and bowed. He was thinner; he looked older, with creases in his forehead I had not remembered. I said in a burst, 'I've missed you – I worried that you were ill, and no wonder—'

'The wonder is that you should care to speak with me.'

The sundial was a golden bar between us, yet he took a step back. 'How could you help it? All the world knows by now that you tried to refuse King Henry's challenge. You won in honourable combat.'

'And I've won the title "King's Killer". I am forgiven, but so labelled for my lifetime. King Francis understands this, and weeks ago your Queen relieved me from my duties, though she said it was unfair. Today I leave here.'

Now was this the time to urge him to think about Scotland, and all that he could accomplish there as protector of Mary de Guise? But I realised that no killer of a king, however innocent of intent, could defend a queen without marking her, among ill-wishers, as taking advantage of a tragic situation. Aye, she could lean on young Lord Bothwell – cold killer of English traitors – but he had not killed a sovereign.

'Lady Seton,' he said, 'I've cherished you in my mind since you were a lass. If I'd been younger – no matter. This is no time to traffic in sentiment or to indulge dreams. To be blunt, mine is a hired sword and Europe is still a battleground. So, I am leaving—'

I knew he did not want me to ask for where; and perhaps he would travel too far for the knowing, like a dark star. He came to me and kissed my hand, then hurried away.

Summer was nearly over. Beaton expressed all our feelings when she said, 'If only something merry would happen to lift this pall.' There were, of course, no balls, no evenings of music. King Francis, his own master, resumed his desperate rides and once I saw him stagger off his horse in the stables and fall at the feet of a terrified groom. I could not help but resent this heedless, self-centred boy because Her Majesty was so plagued with worry about him that her own health suffered. If she tried to eat, she would vomit; if she did not eat she grew weak. Yet she had marvellous resilience. Livvy said one even-

33

ing, 'I think she gains some strength from God so as to bear a child.'

'What!' Fleming leaned forward from her cushion by the fire. 'She's with child?'

'I didn't mean that – I mean she waits, conserves her strength to that purpose. I'd think it her principal reason for fighting despair.'

'It's the *only* reason for the King's existence,' I said bitterly. 'What else is required of him? Only a body to mate with hers, and he punishes it without a thought of his responsibility. In six months, with another man, there would surely be sign of a baby. I think he is so grossly selfish he cares nothing for her or for France.'

'Perhaps he has no seed,' Livvy said. 'Besides, what is six months? Queen Catherine had to wait eleven years. How can we judge the forces of nature?'

But I maintained my disgust with the King, for Her Majesty was fretted like the wife of a drunkard – only this boy was at more deathly a sport than wine. How much it cost her to appear at ease and unruffled we would never know. She conferred with the Cardinal as always, studied military policy with his brother Duke Francis; then, on advice of physicians who were treating the King for a fever, moved our court to Blois. I think he was too weak to protest the lack of a hunting forest.

We could not publicly celebrate Her Majesty's seventeenth birthday because of mourning for the late King, but we asked her if we might plan a simple revel for her on 8 December. She was pleased, and laughed and said that it must be a state secret, with only her uncles invited, and of course the King, who was much improved.

It was charged by some at court that we Marys, like the lilies of the field, toiled not nor spun. But for days we rehearsed a playlet, spun a poem to our lutes, devised a masked dance and encouraged our female fools to new absurdities. We agreed on a banquet of wine-baked oysters, stuffed breast of veal, plover pies and roasted boar in a sauce of Spanish oranges. We ordered the chef to create a loaf of cheese and walnuts in the long shape of a Scots thistle. Cakes were

34

crowned with golden icing. A long table in our suite was covered with our mutual gift – a silver cloth embroidered with her crests. It would please her to see England, Ireland and Wales there. It would please her to see a plump white kitten tangle itself in a ball of gold thread. True, we would all be seventeen on this birthday but not too removed from childhood, so that Her Majesty would laugh, as she always had, when Livvy danced a fling with a cock-feather fan and bells on her ankles.

It was dusk of that day, the candles lit in our apartment, an hour to spare before guests arrived, when Janet came to us – still in her tiring apron. 'Their Majesties are unable to come. The King has taken to his bed with a racking headache. . . .'

May God damn that boy! I thought. But within hours my anger changed to apprehension, for we heard that Queen Catherine had been summoned from St Germain with a retinue of physicians. A proclamation was made to the people asking for their prayers. Finally, on New Year's Day he was able to attend Mass in the cathedral, leaning on Duke Francis's arm.

Perhaps he knew tranquillity during those two hours, but when he emerged, with the rest of us trailing behind, it was to horror. Instead of blessings the people hurled insults. 'Leper! Child-killer! Monster!'

He scurried into the carriage he shared with Her Majesty and, following in ours, we saw women pluck their children from the road and run for shelter. I felt that we were in some mad dream but the shouts of 'Monster' and the crowd's terror of him were all too real. It seemed inexplicable that those who had offered prayers for his recovery were now cursing him for murder.

Later that day our Queen came to explain. 'It's a plot by the Huguenots; they have managed to convince the credulous that his illness was leprosy, that he bathed in the blood of newborn children killed for his healing. He is ill again, of course – from shock.' She paused and said softly, 'Do any of you remember how he whipped a boy who overturned a turtle in the garden?'

We remembered. He loved all creatures though, unlike

35

myself, he would hunt – a paradox found in many gentle people. It was incredible that even the simplest peasant could imagine King Francis a monster.

'He is shattered,' she said, 'though he understands how the people have been misled, and why. The instigator is one Godfrey de Barry. We've no idea how an adventurer – with the help of another, La Renaudie – gained such swift power over innocent minds. But the Cardinal's spies are at work and he says we will take suitable vengeance.'

'Such swift results cost gold, do they not?' I asked.

She nodded. 'Fomenting rebellion is a costly business – the professional assassin is scarcely for hire in terms of glory – he wants pay.' Then she paused, aware that she had blurted too much, for she added quickly, 'If I said "assassin" I meant "heretic". He wants his grain and his meat, and honey to spread on his loaf, while he smashes the saints. Religious obsession doesn't remove hunger, except in demented persons.'

Fleming asked, 'Madam, tell us truly – is there danger of assassination?'

'There is bitter hatred of the power of the Guise, and thus of us who were educated by the Cardinal. We are not immortal; but neither are we vulnerable, so don't be frightened. If you see a heavier guard, it's merely for precaution.'

At twilight she left us, warning us to keep indoors, to avoid the gardens and the balconies. 'One of you might be mistaken for me.'

We were living now in a red tide of history but heard nothing of what went on outside our painted walls. It was later that we learned that the Cardinal's spies were mingling among the people disguised as beggars, that suspected heretics fattened the rats of the Bastille, that our palace was quietly being surrounded by armed rabble who hid in the deep woods around Blois. De Barry was hunted with every device known to our secret agents, but it seemed he had fled to England. This did not discourage his thousands of followers throughout France or, more immediately, here in Touraine. The Cardinal learned that our palace was to be attacked on the night of 10 March and royal barges sped us up the Loire towards the fortress of Amboise.

Whether Her Majesty assumed bravado for this journey or was actually enjoying the adventure I'm not sure. The nights were warm and starry, and when the gentlemen were at dice or chess we anchored briefly and swam in our shifts. By day we wore peasant dress and learned the art of frying fish. I sat on deck and sketched people curled sleepily on cushions or at work – if one could say that tuning a lute or practising a dance was work. And the poet, Pierre de Chastelard, watched me.

Of course we all knew that this handsome young man was a professed Huguenot but of that sort whose convictions stopped short of mania. Indeed, he was too elegant to allow so much as a frown when our jester perked a friar's hat on his smooth blond head. Ladies adored him, but I still felt that he was in love with our Queen, although now he was watching me – perhaps as a link to her.

'If you will sketch me,' he said, 'I will write you a poem.'

'I'm not as gifted as you; it would be a poor exchange. But I'd be honoured if you'd come over and share these figs with me.'

So, for a while, we sat together on cushions and talked about trivial things, until I said, 'Was a royal party ever threatened with murder for so little reason? Some wealthy person must be giving De Barry money.'

He smiled as though humouring a child. 'That is a clever thought, Lady Seton. It may even have occurred to His Eminence.'

'I'll not be teased,' I said. And then I had a monstrous thought – not a clever one. If it were true that de Barry had fled to England, then perhaps Queen Elizabeth had provided the gold. Hadn't she ample reason to want Mary Stuart dead?

'What ails you, Madam?' he asked.

Could he be a spy? Ah, but when I allow my imagination loose it romps absurdly. I decided that I would be a fool to prattle about my theory – not because he was likely to be dangerous, but because he might laugh.

'Nothing ails me,' I said, 'but I thought how dull we may be shut up in Amboise like prisoners. It's such a murky old place.'

How casually I said that. Amboise proved to be the first of my nightmares.

CHAPTER III

Amboise, high on its rocky cliff, was the strongest castle in France, and the court was well provisioned against siege. But we had only a few Scottish and Swiss halberdiers, so couriers rode to summon help from loyal nobles and to buy sturdy peasants with promise of gold. If we Marys were not frightened by shots in the woods at night it was because our Queen was composed. Her greatest concern was the King's health and he seemed much better, but we all sneezed from the dust of decayed rushes, and the water hauled up for us was stagnant.

Monsieur Chastelard found me in the library one evening; the only books were treatises on warfare and politics of a century past, so, in mutual boredom, we sat down to talk. He told me that our patrols had captured some Huguenots and lodged them below in the dungeons to question them as to the whereabouts of their leaders.

'I have never approved of torture,' he said.

'Do you mean that it is going on now?'

'The thick walls spare us their screaming.'

I felt a little sick. 'The Cardinal is a man of God! Why doesn't he interfere?'

'My dear Lady Seton, he orders it. Like God, he dislikes having his authority tampered with.'

Far below us I heard what sounded like a duel of shots and I hoped that those men who could not escape lay mercifully dead. That night I could not sleep and sat praying by the iron-barred window, my crucifix in my hand. When my maid came to awaken me with bread and ale she remarked on my pallor and said, 'The news is good. A manservant found

Godfrey de Barry last night and shot him. They're stretching his body out like a bat nailed to the bridge, so Gervais said.'

'I don't want to hear such things from you or Gervais,' I said, and dismissed her.

But I could not avoid listening to the talk of the fortress; how Duke Francis had taken six hundred Huguenots prisoner a mile from the town, all now crammed into dungeons and jails. For nearly a month we heard of peasants' dwellings sacked, their occupants dumped into the Loire. Corpses swung from trees and parapets, but this was not sufficient for the Cardinal's vengeance. He commanded public executions in an arena in the square and our Queen came to tell us to attend.

'Would to God I could reason with His Eminence,' she said, and for the first time voiced criticism of the man who had been her idol since childhood. 'He wants to create a great drama written in Huguenot blood; he has ordered our ambassadors to carry the news to every country as an example of Catholic power. I don't think it necessary – they could as well be shot in a private field, with some dignity. But no, he is adamant.'

'Doesn't His Eminence realise that Your Majesty's stomach is frail?' Beaton asked.

'He expects me to steel myself, and so I shall. If I sicken, it will be in my soul – but to weaken would attract suspicion that my sympathies are heretic. Seton, you shall prepare my golden wig for me at dawn. We five shall share some *aqua vitae*. In the arena you shall cluster as close to me as possible, but the Cardinal and the King sit on either side of me.'

'Would it be possible to close your eyes when it becomes too terrible?' Livvy asked, closing her own eyes, shuddering.

'No, foreign ambassadors will be watching for any sign of weakness.' She rose. 'We will wear our white gowns, as usual. Janet is making a new silver-lace ruff for me.'

I said, 'Would it be thought that our mourning white is for the victims as well as for the late King?'

'No,' she said. 'I am told that the traitors to be executed will also wear white – aprons of white. But it's well known that nothing so compliments a flow of blood.'

Not since Roman times, I think, had there been such a carnage for 'entertainment'. A man was roped to four horses and, prodded by flaming lances, they tore his body apart. A boy of no more than thirteen was set on fire so that he ran round in circles. One victim's jaws were nailed together and whips enforced his parade around the arena; another, with his comrades, was dragged over sizzling coals by an iron mechanism. But the worst of all, because it was so cruelly slow, was to see naked bodies gently lowered into vats of boiling oil – raised, then lowered again, before the flesh puffed and shrivelled to scraps of floating fat.

Bishops, priests – none rose from their seats to bless the piles of dead, of dying who screamed out the name of God. The screams and the stench of roasted human meat were such that I gagged and hid my face with my handkerchief. Fleming whispered, 'Look out at the trees,' and added on a sob, 'Think of the springtime.'

Finally, in the afternoon, it was over – for that day. Her Majesty, who was seated far to our left, beyond our view, rose at sound of the trumpets and moved rigidly to the side arch that led to the market square. The Cardinal offered his arm but she shook her head mutely and grasped the King's hand.

The dungeons and jails had been partially emptied and death decorated the town walls. We walked below freshly cut heads; we passed blood-spattered railings that held arms, ears, testicles. A page ahead of us fanned off clouds of flies. And when we reached our tower apartments we saw corpses hanging on the battlements below.

We had expected Her Majesty to rest but, perhaps like ourselves, she required life about her, some assurance that the nightmare was past – for today. She was wearing a pale primrose dressing-gown and said she had bathed; that the King was asleep after a recurrence of his headache. She called for wine and asked us to share it; for a while she did not touch hers but stood by the fireplace where the ashes had grown cold.

'Tomorrow,' she said, 'we are required to witness the be-

41

headings. How many hundreds I am not sure. They may take two days. I think the sight will be less sickening.'

Her voice was curiously toneless. Suddenly rage entered it. ' "Where is the Huguenot God those traitors scream to?" the Cardinal asked me. "Why doesn't He come to their rescue?" I was so near to fainting that I said nothing, but for the first time in all of my life doubted that there is any God at all. This will be a mortal sin to confess to my priest, but one thing I know: if I were truly Queen of France no torture would ever be permitted.'

'But you are truly queen,' I said.

'The Cardinal rules; his is the power. But in Scotland no enemy, however vile, shall be submitted to torture. Execution – yes, if I deem it fair.'

She went to the table and drank from her golden cup. 'I will not abide the hypocrisy of religious leaders in the name of "God". I have advised my mother the Queen to banish John Knox as a rabble-rouser but I grant him his dour conception of God. Is tolerance weak? Then so must be every gentle human emotion. . . .'

Rarely did she talk at such length to us – but then, today she could scarcely confide in the Cardinal, in her ailing husband, or in Queen Catherine to whom she had never been close. Many said that they hated one another – Catherine jealous of Her Majesty's loving conquest of her husband and her son – and Mary contemptuous of competition from a power-greedy woman. But we Marys never heard our Queen utter one word of criticism. It was understood that royalty defended royalty – blocking the door to anarchy, or so we had been taught.

'Seton,' she said, abruptly changing the subject, 'in the early morning you will devise me a new coiffure. Two more days on public display and then I vow my hair can tumble down my back for all I care. And look well to your own appearance, my doves. But then, you never fail me.'

We did not fail her in dignity next day, or the next, but many of the men who stumbled towards the block were so disfigured by previous torture that vomit rose into our mouths before we could swallow it. After more than fifty had perished the headsman grew weary, demanded wine, and began to butcher with a blunted axe.

I turned to look at the Cardinal in his sun-drenched scarlet robes. He was eating an orange.

Chenonceaux was one of the most exquisite châteaux in France. Madame Diane had lavished a fortune on spacious galleries, grottoes, rose gardens. Servants were sent there to make it ready for the court, and after the dark and dusty castle and blood-reeking Amboise we wallowed in the freshness of grassy slopes and forest pools shaded by the arms of willows. Somehow the King was persuaded against riding and hunting. He would lie on a checker-board terrace and manoeuvre his old toy soldiers. The game was always Scotland against England – a game now all too real for our Queen's mother in Edinburgh.

England had not declared war; Queen Elizabeth was more subtle. She took advantage of the power-madness of Scots noblemen and supported them with gold, and I was made to understand that her tactics in undermining the nation were supremely clever; war would have roused the common people who would never forget her father's burning and pillaging. It is one of my faults that I can often see both sides of an issue. Elizabeth had been mortified before the world by our Queen's assumption of her rights. I had to question the Cardinal's wisdom as I now questioned his compassion. I felt that he had placed Scotland in immense danger and, though I scarcely remember it, it had been the land of my birth and thus part of my bones and blood.

Some new tapestries had been hung in the château, for many of the old had depicted Madame Diane as nymph, huntress and Venus. The portrait I had loved as a child – one by Primaticcio – had been removed from the vaulted hall. It had revealed Diane as Diana of the Chase surrounded by cupids playing with dogs at her feet. In its place was a painting of Queen Catherine – pop-eyed, thick-lipped, her headdress of diamonds. We Marys thought the artist as vulgar as his subject.

Seigneur de Brantôme, our young court chronicler, was also

the gossip of the court and so amusing that even our Queen inclined to listen to him. He claimed to record living history, not mere chatter, but we felt that he shaped it to suit his particular audience. Knowing our love of Madame Diane, he praised her as the lost Queen of France, sighed at her banishment to her Château d'Anet in Normandy and stated that she would some day be canonised a saint for her piety and good works. To Queen Catherine he probably called her a harlot.

By King Francis' demand, one room remained as Diane had left it – her bedchamber, which our Queen occupied. White velvet draperies bore crescent moons of silver, as did the great bed curtains. The floor was a mosaic of multicoloured stars, and silver stars with gold shone from the ceiling. Below, the River Cher flowed beside the gardens, now a riot of roses. The pointed towers of the château were reflected in it, and swans glided over the smooth waters.

Our Queen sketched the works of Leonardo and Michelangelo, pouting at her incompetence. She embroidered black velvet cushions sewn with silver tears for Diane's *chaise*. If ever there was a ghost, a living lady haunted Chenonceaux.

The presence of the Cardinal – worldly as he was – did not diminish frivolity. We often breakfasted in a meadow under a spangled tent before the hunt, grateful that the King was subdued, content to train falcons for the sport of others. Perhaps he was frightened for his health. But he danced the stately pavanes his mother revived, chuckled at readings of Rabelais. Our Queen coaxed him to eat, and it is a wonder that none of us perished from the excessively rich food.

At night the King, Queens and the Cardinal dined under a silver-cloth canopy, attended by silver-clothed pages. We shared their long table, set with Cellini's candelabra, salt basins and silver statues. His vases held the fat roses of summer. The pages presented golden trenchers of Médoc oysters, sturgeon, turbot in saffron-cream, heron baked in spice, sugar and rosewater. We ate boiled swan with olives and capers, Genoa artichokes, Barbary cucumbers, Windsor beans in butter, suckling pig stuffed with damsons and raisins, roasted roebuck with mint and fennel sauce. There were the wines – champagne, hypocras, gooseberry and plum, and white grape with

honey. Before the sweets, lemon-water was passed in bowls
afloat with flowers so that we might wash our hands and dry
them on the tablecloth.

One night our Queen was presented with a silver wine-cup
by Queen Catherine. Sitting nearby, I could see that it was
engraved and intricately wrought. A page filled it with the
wine of Burgundy. Our Queen bowed, smiled, sipped. As she
did so, the most lascivious figures of men and women became
apparent on the cup. No one dared to laugh, and in her
innocence our Queen was not aware of it.

'An interesting cup,' Queen Catherine said. 'One of Madame
Diane's doubtless left for Your Majesty. You should examine
it.'

Her Majesty did, and I was tense with embarrassment for
her. We were accustomed to Rabelais and Boccaccio, but this
was crude, revolting, ugly. Diane would never have owned
such cups.

'This must be Italian,' our Queen said finally. 'Florentine.
Some merchant's jest. Vulgar.'

Mindful that Catherine was the daughter of a Florentine
banker, I – perhaps the entire company – caught the insult.
The Cardinal, always silken in diplomacy, pronounced the
cup unique, and King Francis ended the matter by calling for
Rochefort cheese and a brew created by Benedictine monks.

That evening I strolled in the gardens with Monsieur
Gervais, our apothecary. He was a young man of wry humour,
somewhat cynical, and pleasing to women because he seemed
aloof. Though slender and scarcely taller than I, he had
massive shoulders accentuated by the padding of his velvet
doublet, and I admired his curly brown beard. In the torchlight of the grotto it held golden glints. Beaton, who flirted
with him at every opportunity, thought that beard 'pattable',
and praised his smell, which was of fresh herbs.

He seated me on a pink marble bench and said, 'I'm
honoured that you came out with me. To me, you seem
remote. Even Her Majesty is more accessible.'

I disliked admitting to shyness which I think is the most
boring of social afflictions. 'Surely you don't think me
haughty? I have little to be haughty about.'

45

'No? I'm told you come from the proudest family in Scotland. The Setons are second only to the Stuarts in your country.'

'An inherited glory,' I told him.

He looked amused. 'Humility is a royal prerogative. I'd like to know what goes on in that shining head of yours.'

Of course my hair was shining; I had powdered it with gold dust. But in honesty I said, 'I'm inclined to daydream. Sometimes I loathe realities. The other Marys discuss what happened at Amboise but I won't listen – I try to push it from my mind.'

'That's only natural.'

'That Brantôme,' I said, sliding away from the subject of myself, 'does he ever report accurately? I heard him say to the Italian ambassador, "A pity Queen Mary fainted during the executions." '

'Brantôme saw me give her a cloved cloth,' he said. 'I detest the little man – better a ballad peddler than a writer who stoops to fabrication. A poet or a dramatist may soar to imagination, but a historian should be factual.' He paused and smiled down at me. 'I've discovered a facet of you, Lady Seton; a passion for truth.'

'Perhaps that's so—'

A page interrupted us, asking that I go to Her Majesty at once. As we passed the courtyard I saw grooms attending exhausted horses and Gervais surmised that couriers had arrived from Paris. Candles were ablaze throughout the royal suites. With a brief 'Good night' to Gervais, I sped past a guard and up the stairs. In her room of starry velvet Her Majesty lay on a *chaise*, Fleming seated beside her. Monsieur Gurion, her surgeon, was just leaving as I entered. He bowed to me and put his finger to his lips, so I remained silent in the doorway.

Fleming tiptoed over. 'He has given her poppy-brew. God grant her sleep. There is terrible news from Scotland. . . .'

John Knox had persuaded the Lords of Scotland to depose Queen Mary de Guise as Regent. Queen Elizabeth had sent troops to Leith, the port of Edinburgh, and captured the city.

46

It was rumoured that Queen Mary was dying in Edinburgh Castle under siege.

Those were bitter days for our Queen. She made no secret of the fact that the Cardinal had refused her husband's request for French troops. It became clear that Francis was king in name only.

Fresh news brought snippets of comfort. A few loyal Catholic nobles had rallied to the Regent's cause together with the wild young Earl of Bothwell and his Borderers. Our Queen was busy with her secretaries, writing late into the night, encouraging those loyal few, begging her mother to take heart. Strangely, though she knew that her half-brother James was, with Knox, the darkest villain in the drama, she said nothing against him. I marvelled at that; but I was to learn that a bond of blood can be dangerously strong.

Then one afternoon Her Majesty called us to her suite; she was radiant. 'My mother's forces have recaptured Leith! The English have been hurled back! Give thanks for a miracle....'

A few days later, on a hot, calm June afternoon, we were sailing toy boats on the river. Our Queen was paddling barefoot like a child, pushing about a pink-sailed galleon while the King dozed in the shade of willows. A courier came with news that her mother was dead, and all Lord James could write was, 'She was taken of a loathsome swelling of her arms and limbs.' And though Mary de Guise, devoutly Catholic, had asked for a priest, he was denied her. A minister, John Willock, 'counselled her to embrace the True Faith'.

Our Queen was torn between rage at this insult and grief for her mother. She neither ate nor slept, and for two weeks seemed close to death herself. King Francis ordered masses for her, and asked the nation to pray. We Marys felt helpless to provide comfort.

I have mentioned King Francis with some contempt, but it was his adoration that must have supplied her will to live. It could not have been merely the jewels he lavished on her. Perhaps she realised that her death would hasten his own, for during this time he had terrible headaches. In any case, she became strong enough to travel, with the court, to St Germain in August. We all wore black as befitted mourning for a Scot.

In her dark robes our Queen looked frighteningly thin, but she was slowly returning to health.

Somehow she maintained that health despite more shocking news. Sir Nicholas Throckmorton, in fact, asked audience of me before approaching her. Evidently he wished this to be kept secret, for he asked me to meet him near the dovecote.

'Her Majesty's physicians are inclined to lie about the state of her health,' he said. 'I am fond of her. I'd not be the source of a relapse, but I bring a letter from Queen Elizabeth that will assuredly trouble her.'

'Nothing can trouble her more than the King's headaches,' I said. 'Today he has excruciating pain in his right ear. Whatever your mistress has to say will probably be of minor consequence.'

'I could delay a day or two,' he said.

I am sure he meant it kindly, for if there is such a thing as consideration in an ambassador, Sir Nicholas had it. But, rightly or wrongly, I feel that delay solves nothing and that in this case I dared not be a party to concealment. Impulsively I asked, 'Is it war?'

He hesitated. 'I should not discuss it, Lady Seton, but you will know sooner or later. It may be for your Queen worse than a declaration of war. I bear here a copy of the Treaty of Edinburgh. France, England and Scotland are affirmed at peace. All foreign troops shall be dismissed from Scotland; but Queen Mary shall for ever abstain from bearing the title, emblems and arms that rightfully belong to Queen Elizabeth.'

'Jesu!' I said. 'My Queen would never agree.' It seemed like presumption to speak for her but I knew her so well; it would seem like abdication of all justice. 'Go to her, Sir Nicholas. It is likely that anger will distract her from worry about the King. But it won't be anger aganst you – she will know you must act as a tool for your mistress.'

He smiled wanly, kissed my hand, thanked me and left me wondering why I, of all people, should be honoured by his confidence. I felt mature in that moment, and humble. Past the dovecote, in the woods, was a stone shrine lichened green with years. I knelt there for a few moments asking God to protect my Queen and guide her in wisdom. Then I heard

48

distant thunder, glimpsed an arc of sheet lightning, and returned to the palace. Naturally I said nothing to the other Marys about my talk with Sir Nicholas. We dressed for the evening meal and shared it in Livvy's dining-hall – snails with truffles in champagne, the usual roasted meats – but before we had finished a page announced our Queen. We rose, curtsied.

She said, 'I've received a preposterous document from Queen Elizabeth asking me to relinquish my rights. I shall be with my secretaries and will attempt to reply without fury. She is so ill-advised I could feel sorry for her. If there is any change for the worse in the King's condition Gervais will ask you to fetch me. I don't want—' She paused, and I guessed she was about to say 'Queen Catherine'. 'If there must be a vigil, my doves, I want you to be with me.'

The King improved but did not leave his couch. Like the rest of us, he was listless, for the August heat was nearly unbearable. I could not remember a summer when it was necessary for relays of servants to fan us with rounds of woven straw, when damasks were shed in favour of peasant cotton, when to venture outside was to plunge into an oven. Queen Catherine's astrologer warned that the sun intended to broil away the earth – and it seemed credible.

If our Queen received a reply from Elizabeth (I could no longer think of her as 'Queen') she did not mention it. She talked only of the King's health, which now was like a seesaw. And so matters remained until, by the Grace of God, the thunder-storms broke. We were grateful for the violence, though great trees were burned by lightning, and storage sheds caught fire. By the end of September the King was able to dine in the great hall and smile at the jesters.

And in early October we Marys smiled at the antics of Fleming who burst giggling into our library. 'Imagine!' said she. 'The Earl of Bothwell is here! Just arrived from Flanders! And it was I who received him in Her Majesty's presence chamber while she dressed.' She looked down at her simple black gown. 'Had I only known I'd have had my silver ruff – and Seton, look at my hair!'

It was in the smooth chignon she generally wore except that

49

a curl hung down. Usually languid, seemingly bored, she had reverted to a comical childishness, and we teased her about love at first sight.

'Oh, *that*,' she said, 'how absurd can you be? Do you think I'd deign to notice a mere Border Lord with shabby, outmoded clothes and mud on his boots? Of course not. But to think he ventured here through the perils of the sea – the hero of Scotland – the defender of the late Queen – England's worst enemy – and the most magnificent long legs—'

'Of course you didn't notice his legs,' Livvy said. 'What else didn't you notice? His face?'

'I was forced to, it being arrogantly made, with dark eyes that seem to see through one. I felt quite impaled on them. He said to me, "So you are the beautiful Lady Fleming." '

Whenever a woman feels impelled to repeat a compliment she is usually bereft of them, a failure with men; yet here was Fleming, accustomed to admiration, the most beguiling of us four, besotted by this muddy-booted visitor. True, he was Lord High Admiral of Scotland, Lieutenant of the Border, a renowned moor-fighter; but rank could scarcely impress us. So it must be the romance of his defence of Scotland, and that I could understand.

'Are we to meet this paragon?' Beaton asked.

Fleming shrugged. 'I know of no plans for him. I suppose we will.' She turned to me. 'Could you help with my hair? Toinette hasn't your art, and Her Majesty might require me to see him out.'

Her maid brought the silver ruff, and as I brushed and rearranged her hair we learned, amused, the many things that Fleming had not noticed. His hair was a dark, wavy auburn. That his skin was sunbrowned. That he was about twenty-five. After she had left to finish tidying herself in her bedchamber Livvy, who tended to be motherly towards us, said, 'I hope he doesn't stay long at court. Fleming mustn't waste her dreams on a man like that.'

Because of Brantôme's gossip, and letters from our Scots relatives, we knew that from an early age James Hepburn, Earl of Bothwell, had a frightening reputation with women, I mentioned that he was said to dabble in witchcraft.

50

'No,' said Beaton. 'It was my aunt Janet who bewitched him – she over thirty and he a lad of sixteen. She meant no more than friendship at the time, but he abducted her to his castle of Hermitage and there forced her to become his mistress. The affair lasted some years – she was tolerant of his younger conquests – but I believe that her infatuation is over. The point is, not even a Madame Diane could hold such a man. One requires a modicum of fidelity.'

I said, 'I couldn't bear a lover who wasn't wholly mine.' In this way my French education had failed me; it was naïve to expect the impossible. 'When I marry – if I do – what torture to have to share him. When I think of Queen Catherine's long humiliation I could almost pity—'

A page interrupted us. Her Majesty asked that we entertain Lord Bothwell at supper in the oval parlour with no other guests. If we wished to play for him on the virginals or the lute, we might do so. She did not add that in time of mourning there could be no frivolity.

Why I should have tried on two black gowns before choosing a third, I've no idea, or dressed my hair with pearls. Perhaps it was a childish matter of wondering if I could attract a famed adventurer, for after all he had proved to be Scotland's principal patriot.

Bothwell was not muddy-booted now; he wore a dark russet doublet, a short, swirling cape of russet which showed silver-slashed sleeves. Fleming had been right about his legs, but not his eyes. In the candlelight of the table they were a deep gold flecked with brown. And true – they were so bold, so searching, that one felt impaled. His face was lean, hard, full-lipped. When he moved he had the grace of a cat. And, to my surprise, he spoke excellent French.

'Of course,' he said, when Fleming complimented him on this, 'I was educated at the Sorbonne, and one never forgets strict masters. Do you ladies speak Scots?'

We told him that we did, but only for the benefit of our native servants. 'You'd find it a bit of a gabble, my Lord – but then, we'll not be living in Scotland again.'

He did not hide a frown; he had not the mask of a courtier.

51

He said nothing but, 'What do you ladies remember of it?'

We told him the little there was to tell. Lest he be bored, I asked if John Knox was indeed a maniac, rousing the country to Protestantism.

'A fanatic – aye. But with the "lunacy" of Calvin. I abhor the man – I also respect him.'

Livvy asked, 'Yet you are Catholic?'

'I was; now I am a free-thinker. I won't be limited by priests or ministers – only by my own conscience.'

We were shocked, but far too tactful to show it. Fleming said casually, 'You attend no church, my Lord?'

'No. For me, their spires block the stars.'

He spoke crisply of communing with nature at sea, on the moors, in the hills. 'On lonely nights of Border-watch there's little to do but think. You can scarcely see for the mists – there is nothing to do once your men and horses are prepared but to wait for sight of balefire.'

'Balefire?' Beaton asked.

'Balefire', he said impatiently, 'is our method of signal. If the English are sighted at – say – Hawick, huge bales of hay are lighted on the hills. They warn other towns and so stream on to Edinburgh where the castle flares its warning north across the mountains.'

'How vastly romantic!' Beaton said. 'Such warning could have helped us at Amboise.'

'France has poor hills,' he said contemptuously.

'But brave hearts,' I said. 'Her Majesty was unafraid during the siege.'

'Her mother and father were examples of courage, my Lady. It beats in her blood. And I was privileged, for a short time, to meet King Francis. That lad has survived torture without a whimper. His ear was so paining him – yet he contrived to ask me sensible questions about our present defences. He made a little jest about the power of *aqua vitae*. . . .'

Lord Bothwell drank *aqua vitae*, unwatered, after the cheeses. I felt that he was impatient to be gone. Four sheltered young virgins would scarcely appeal to him. When he left us, with his thanks for the evening, I was almost sure that he was bound for wenching in the village.

52

Livvy said, in her mother-hen manner, 'You girls behaved quite well; I was afraid you'd flirt.'

'Useless,' Beaton said morosely, and Fleming nodded. I believe it was the first time that we had felt inadequate in the presence of an attractive man. He returned to Scotland ten days later.

In the early hours of the morning Her Majesty sent a message that the King's ear had abcessed. We were to make ready at once to travel to Orléans' milder climate.

We learned on that journey by curtained litter that the surgeons were disputing about treatment of the ear. Monsieur Gurion advised leeching, Queen Catherine's surgeon wanted to amputate, but a third believed that warmth would effect a cure.

We found no warmth in Orléans; the sky seemed ready for snow. Nor was there warmth of greeting. The townspeople, remembering the old accusation of a monster who bathed in the blood of children, ran screaming at sight of our cavalcade, hurrying to the shelter of shops or houses. The Cardinal and Duke Francis were jeered from balconies and rooftops. Either the King was demented by pain, or stubborn, for he commanded that we pause at the Church of the Jacobins for prayer. Never in all of my life had I felt such cold and draughtiness, nor seen candles flicker like those. As the King knelt at the altar he shivered in his heavy, fur-lined robes and beads of sweat dripped from his forehead. Our Queen, beside him, took his hand and lifted him to his feet. Within half an hour we were in the Hôtel Groslot, closer than the palace, where fires were hastily lit and blankets brought.

It was Monsieur Gervais who told us of what went on in the royal suite: 'I'm a mere apothecary, but this I know – Her Majesty was wise to refuse the treatments offered. Jesu! Queen Catherine says a devil inhabits his ear and would amputate. Lancing is precarious because the ear is rotting. The pus is such a stench that no one now approaches his bed except Her Majesty.'

'Not the Cardinal?' I asked.

'His Eminence sits well away with a handkerchief to his

53

nose. So does Queen Catherine – day after day and night after night. But Her Majesty, she sits beside him and murmurs sweetly, though he cannot reply because he cannot open his mouth.' He paused. 'She – she kisses that mouth.'

Love. So this was love – not the romance I had gleaned from poems and pretty legends, but a force beyond and above the physical. I was devout but, when it came to such a test as hers, I know I would have sickened and failed. They begged her to break her vigil with sleep, food. When they brought her wine she shook her head.

The King died on the night of 5 December.

I doubt that any sovereigns save those murdered have been so unceremoniously buried. On her eighteenth birthday – and ours – we followed the coffin to St Denis, near Paris, and witnessed interment in the basilica. The Cardinal feared that a proper funeral, with the pomp of pallbearers, would incite the Huguenots and offend the people.

We returned to the Hôtel Groslot in Orléans and Her Majesty began her forty-day retirement. It was difficult for us to realise that she was no longer Queen of France, but Dowager Queen. She sent for us to pack the crown jewels to be given to the new King, ten-year-old Charles IX, watching us with as little interest as though we were casing eggs or wrapping potatoes. At the end of that week she showed us the mourning-seal she had devised with her goldsmith – a liquorice tree, whose root is its only value. It was inscribed *Dulce meum terra tegit* – 'My treasure is in the ground.'

Our robes were of mourning white, now – simple, unadorned damasks and velvets. In her apartments, by custom, no daylight was permitted, nor any visitors except Queen Catherine, Charles and the Cardinal – if one excludes her secretaries, for there grew an enormous pile of consoling letters from Europe's rulers, among them Elizabeth of England. These required replies; otherwise she had no duties.

Our presence seemed to help her. She would ask Livvy to read *The Lives of the Saints* but I doubt that she listened because her eyes, once so full of light, were dead. Her voice was toneless.

54

But gradually the world beat in upon her and perhaps as well, because anger returned her to life. On a snowy afternoon she said, 'You've perhaps heard that the Earl of Bedford is here?'

We heard all the gossip from Brantôme, more an ear to a keyhole than a man. 'Yes, Madam,' I said.

'I did him the honour of receiving him, since Queen Elizabeth sent him to "console" me.' She swept aside her lacy white veil with a flick of her hand. 'And just *how* did he console me? He asked me to ratify the Treaty of Edinburgh!'

We had grown to like Throckmorton; to send a stranger to her at such a time was unforgivable, she said, if indelicate; but to intrude on her grief with the resumption of this controversy was appalling. 'Naturally I refused. But I told him that I longed to have a personal interview with the Queen, and I asked for her portrait, saying that this would be true condolence.'

We rarely ventured an opinion when she confided in us, unless she asked. Nor was she asking now, simply emptying herself of resentment.

'*Never* do I relinquish my rights!' she said. 'Not to her, not to treacherous Scots. Lord Bothwell believes my brother James to be at the root of our troubles in Scotland, but in some mad way he defends John Knox. So we did not part as friends.'

Fleming said, as I knew she would, 'You dismissed Lord Bothwell, Madam?'

'He dismissed me as a "French doll" uninterested in my own country. The lout – and yet, I forgive him. He spoke what he thought to be truth. He will continue his military duties.'

'Madam,' I said, astonished, 'do you mean that Bothwell dared to defy you?'

'He'd defy the devil, Christ and all His disciples; but since my mother trusted him beyond all men, so must I. Seton, a great many persons see fit to defy me now that I am a widow.'

Queen Catherine peacocked in her new power, mocked her mourning white with cascades of emeralds and diamonds, and

55

was heard to laugh at some jest of the Cardinal's. She dared to seek out our Queen one evening when she was weary and bring young Charles, the most obnoxious child we ever beheld. He prattled that he would marry our Queen, climbed on to her lap and slobbered kisses. Of course we knew that his mother would never allow him to marry her, that betrothal was the last thing Catherine wanted, but she permitted this disgusting behaviour – for his kisses were not childish.

Pierre de Chastelard entrusted me with a poem to give to Her Majesty. I said, rather sharply, 'If it is a love poem, Pierre, I advise against it. She is beginning to receive offers of marriage that so offend her that she weeps.'

'It is only a poem of consolation,' he said. 'What in the name of God have I to offer her but that?'

So I gave her the poem, tied in white ribbons. She read it and sighed and smiled. 'Thank him for me, Seton. He puts me in mind of a faithful spaniel – not that you should tell him that.'

Then she said, 'You are friends. Does he attract you, dove?'

'No,' I said. 'He strikes me as a play-actor of talent, whereas Ronsard – a great poet – has no need to act.'

It was good to hear her laugh. 'I wasn't asking for comparison of poets. I meant – could you love him?'

'No, Madam.' First, because he so obviously loved her. And he was below me in rank. And he had girlishly pink cheeks under a too-silky beard and his hands were too delicate— Oh, there were a dozen reasons why I could not love him. Then I thought of Raoul, the groom, and the feelings he had roused in me and wondered at Father Michael's insinuation that some day I would shed all my dignity for mere lust. 'I shall be very prudent in love.'

She said, in a sudden rush, 'Love – that I had. I can't aspire to it again. Marriage – I must and I shall repeat it. In a week I'll be receiving foreign ambassadors – all with offers from their sovereigns. The King of Navarre, the Kings of Sweden and Denmark, and the Spanish envoy will probably offer Don Carlos.'

'Oh,' I said, revolted. This son of Philip II was known to be a degenerate, an idiot.

56

'Under the wing of Spain,' she said, 'Scotland would be safe.'

One evening at supper with us Brantôme spoke of the Spanish envoy's superb manners, and I asked if he thought it true that a marriage might be arranged. To my vast relief he said no. Queen Catherine would block the marriage because she wanted Don Carlos for her daughter Marguerite. She had threatened to form an alliance with Elizabeth if our Queen dared to move towards Spanish power.

'Do you really listen at keyholes?' Beaton asked, smiling as he loosened his belt from a plump waist.

'No, I hide behind arrases or climb beneath beds. Seriously, my lady, I've numberless informants, all with some complaint to air, some fear to mention. From scraps I weave information, most of it accurate. What should you like to know?'

Fleming, the transparent fool, asked, 'Is Lord Bothwell handfasted to some lady?'

' "Some lady" is Anna Throndsen, his current mistress. She is Norwegian. He met her when he sailed to plead with King Frederick for a fleet. She followed him to Scotland; but I doubt if he's pledged to her. It's rumoured he wanted her for her jewels, which he sold to pay troops, to hire swords for Scotland. Romantic, is he not?'

'No,' Livvy said, clipping off the word.

'The things men accomplish in the sacred cause of patriotism!' Brantôme plunged greasy hands into a bowl of rosewater. 'Of course the fact that Anna is beautiful makes it just a trifle easier to raise – ah – ardour. He seduced the poor thing with the only weapon that could produce weapons.'

We laughed. I was beginning to like him; and any source of amusement was appreciated in our white desolation. But soon that changed. Her Majesty chose a small house for us in Orléans and we wore violet or grey gowns, admitted sunlight into her apartments and, in the spring, hunted stags in Touraine. There were only a few of us – Scots and French – an intimate little court that excluded Queen Catherine and the Cardinal. In Rheims we paid tribute to the effigy of Her Majesty's mother, journeyed to Joinville to visit her grandmother, and in Paris Her Majesty finally shed her semi-

57

mourning in a gown of cream lace and – joined by the royal family – made a state entry. The crowds were polite but not enthusiastic. I, for one, was apprehensive of some Huguenot mischief and was relieved when we retired to St Germain.

On a warm July night, as moths flirted with death in the taperlight of our card-table, Her Majesty entered unannounced. She wore a pale dressing-gown and her hair coiled to her thighs. We flung down our cards and rose in astonishment.

'Be seated,' she said. 'Perhaps I should have waited until morning to tell you, but I need you close. We sail for Scotland in three weeks.'

Her voice trembled, but she stood proudly erect. And now her voice was bitter. 'No one invites us. No one wants us. But it is all too clear that no one wants us here either, least of all Queen Catherine. And Scotland – torn as it is by treachery – is, after all, my gravest responsibility.'

We nodded, shocked, grieved, silent out of a sense of awe at her bravery, scarcely recovered from the death of her husband, now plunged into what could be called a dangerous prison. I thought of Lord James's green-eyed hostility and shuddered.

'I am advised to request safe conduct of Queen Elizabeth should ill winds blow us to England. I have written to Throckmorton. We shall begin to pack. I have a great deal of furniture, as you know, and it must be gathered together and cased for shipment to Calais. Do you have questions?'

'Do we travel alone?' I asked.

'We may require a surgeon, so Gurion shall go, and Gervais as apothecary, and our chefs; also our servants, French and Scots. I've no doubt but that Brantôme and Chastelard are sincere in their loyalty, and both adventurous young men. Naturally, our priests shall go.'

I thought of the Cardinal who had been teacher, adviser, priest – almost God. 'Seton, your friar is elderly; I suggest he remains here. There are still priests in Edinburgh, and altar boys in protection of my few Catholic nobles. Your families – you will have wonderful reunions.'

'Oh, yes,' Livvy said, but I knew her cheerfulness to be assumed. She was imitating our Queen's attempt at composure.

58

This wrench from France would be like a child's departure from the womb. I could only pray that it was bloodless.

Her voice climbed brightly, falsely. 'Bring wine. We shall drink to an adventure.'

We supervised the packing and crating of seemingly endless treasures – china, crystal, paintings, carpets, tapestries, sculpture, furniture, musical instruments, books, silver. There were casks of wine and honeyed fruits, kitchenware that the chefs required, and what Her Majesty called 'comforts' – toys she had shared with King Francis in childhood, tennis racquets, hunting horns and saddles and bridles. Her jewels, and ours, packed in golden chests, would travel in a wagon under guard, her looking-glasses by horse-litter. Two galleys would be prepared for these things, another would accommodate the royal stud, palfreys, hunting dogs and falcons. A fourth ship would carry passengers.

Her Majesty worried about the brutal cold of Scotland and purchased bolts of woollen cloth to supplement our own elaborate clothing. With favourable winds the voyage would take five days from Calais to Edinburgh's port of Leith. She warned that we might expect storms and asked Gervais to devise a brew against seasickness. 'Though', she added gaily, 'champagne will probably suffice.'

During these last days she was determinedly gay, perhaps in defiance of Queen Catherine and the Cardinal who would have enjoyed an exhibition of grief. They, with France's great nobles, accompanied us to Calais – a splendid procession preceded by our Scots pipers and guard. We had thought to be immediately aboard our ship, but there was delay – in fact, only one ship rode at anchor, the one for the animals. Crates and trunks littered the docks.

There was nothing for our small court to do but take refuge in an inn. The King, the Queen and the Cardinal, after effusive farewells, left us. The only remaining diplomat, Throckmorton took residence with us. English though he was, I felt sorry for him. Daily he seemed to expect a courier from Paris; none came.

He was taking wine with me in the raftered commonroom

59

when Her Majesty joined us. 'I'm told a messenger awaits you, Sir Nicholas.'

He jumped to his feet, requested permission to leave, and she granted it. Smiling, she said, 'At last, the safe conduct.'

But granted only on condition that she ratify the Treaty of Edinburgh. What she said to him in private, I don't know. What she said to us was, 'I should never have asked her a favour. Let the winds blow us where they will.'

On the sixth day we sailed in a galley bearing the banners of France and Scotland. A couch was prepared on deck, at Her Majesty's request, so that she could see the French coast as long as possible. In a white cloak, which flapped in the breeze, she left the couch and stood at the rail. The dawn sky was the colour of a bruised peach.

Suddenly someone shouted, pointing across the harbour. We all hurried to look. A fragile fishing boat had foundered on the rocks, tossing men into the water. In horror, we watched them vanish as the boat split.

'Dear God!' our Queen said. 'What omen is this?'

CHAPTER IV

W e neared Leith on the fourth day but fog immobilised us.
On deck I could see nothing, hear nothing but an occasional
drumbeat from our other ships.

Then it was rumoured that a strange ship blocked our entry
into port. Her Majesty laughed, saying that the English would
not dare harass us so close to home. Yet there was still the
drumbeat of another ship. Finally, in a brief lifting of fog, it
was sighted; it bore the dark blue banner of Scotland. Someone had come to escort us. It proved to be Lord Bothwell,
Lord High Admiral, who had been prowling the area for three
days lest enemy ships tried to molest us. Despite the fog he
sent out a boat, and his messenger came aboard. Her Majesty
said, 'Tidy yourself, dove. Go to your cabin and receive your
brother.'

My half-brother, Lord George Seton, whom I had not seen
since I was five, stood there; he looked younger than his
thirty-two years. My first impression, as he kissed my cheek,
was of a rough, brown beard and fog-damp velvet. He smelled
of sea-salt and musk and brandy-wine. And almost immediately he took on the role of a father.

Had I been ill on the voyage? No, my Lord. Had I slept
properly? Yes, my Lord. I had not been remiss in my duties
to our Queen?

'My Lord,' I said as he seated himself on a bench, 'having
been with Her Majesty all these years I think I know my
duties.'

'Of course,' he said, but as he would to a child. 'And you
are a comfort to her, I'm certain. And comely.'

'Thank you,' I said.

'Perhaps it's the French influence that creates an illusion
of beauty?'

A compliment? I decided to take it so. 'We are adept at illusions, my Lord.'

He smiled. 'I remember you toddling about with a spaniel and half killing him with love.'

'Yes,' I said. 'Cheri was my love.'

'And now, sister?'

'I am not in love.'

'But one plans for the future.'

He was so smug! 'Not I! I am bound to Her Majesty. I doubt if she will care to marry for a long while.'

He nodded. His face was thin, and his lips – even his eyes were narrow, and his body put together with a minimum of flesh.

'You need not fret yourself about a good marriage,' he said. 'When your vow is lifted. . . .'

I do not fret.

'It will all be arranged. Madame Diane de Valentinois was a very wise lady. I subscribe to her advice – "Love if you will, but marry well." '

To bring more lands to the Seton estates? I didn't mean to cross my brother, even in thought, but until now I had been commanded only by the Queen, and he was virtually a stranger. I said, 'I would wish to please my family – and myself. How is my mother?'

'Dispirited. She still grieves for the late Queen Mary and retains her white mourning.'

My mother, Marie Pieris, was French and had been lady-in-waiting to Mary de Guise before she married my father, the fourth Earl Seton. I was her only child. After my father's death she had married the Seigneur de Bryante. In my memory she was merely the fragrance of incense and shadow in a chapel; she was deeply devout, and her few letters to me were full of piety.

I asked, 'Shall I meet her in Edinburgh?'

'No, she wishes to be excused from court for a time, but expects you at Seton when Her Majesty can spare you. For a few weeks you'll be busy settling into the palace of Holyrood House. Alas, the galley bearing your animals is missing. Possibly only fog delays it, but Bothwell remembers Queen Elizabeth's fondness for fine horses and falcons and hounds.'

'Jesu!' I said. 'I think Her Majesty would sooner lose her jewels than the royal stud.'

'Bothwell will search when you are safely landed. I have permission to accompany him.'

I then asked a foolish question. 'Has Lord Bothwell married?'

'No.' He frowned. 'My dear Mary, he couldn't match our lands, he has scant gold and his castles are the bleakest fortresses. You must *not* consider him as a husband.'

I laughed. 'You mistake me, brother; but his amorous history amuses us, like a risqué tale.'

He smiled. 'I forget you are so French. I believe he amuses your mother, too. Well, there was some Norwegian wench he recently packed back to Bergen, but I've no idea who his current prey may be.'

As he rose to leave I asked when we might meet again and he said he would come to Holyrood House after supervising a late harvest, perhaps in mid-September. Then, at Her Majesty's pleasure, he would escort me home for a week or two. Again he kissed my cheek, dutifully, without affection. But affection is earned, not inherited. I judged him to be a very controlled man, sensible and forthright. Her Majesty needed such men in Scotland, rich enough to refuse Elizabeth's bribes and loyal to the Catholic religion.

An hour later, when the Marys came to my cabin to mourn the missing galley and sip a cheering Spanish wine, I told them that my brother was strong and protective, that I looked forward to meeting my mother and my new stepfather.

'You should have a merry visit to Seton with relatives to meet,' Beaton said. 'My family – ah, well, the clergy often frolics too. We can't know what's in store for us, so it's like a romance, the pages of a book unfolding. The captain says it's the most brutal haar he's ever encountered.'

A haar, we had learned, is not an ordinary fog. It is slimy, thick, grey-yellow, borne on east winds, and the Firth of Forth was our prison. We were grateful now for the sound of drum-beats announcing the position of our ships; we were not alone in this waste of water. By God's grace it *must* lift soon.

But not until eight o'clock were we able to scurry to harbour.

63

As a sailor helped me down a rope ladder into a small boat I could see nothing of Leith Landing ahead. I could only smell tar, and sickening fish and plant decay. My elegant velvet cloak was useless against the creeping cold, its hood trickling damp. A triumphal entry! We were groping into Scotland like blinded children.

Lord Arthur Erskine, captain of our guard, identified himself and asked our Queen if she was not expecting an escort of her Scots nobles. 'Indeed,' she said, 'my brother Lord James should be here.'

It seemed to me that his absence was an insult. And then she excused him. 'We were a day early, one cannot reckon a voyage, and doubtless the fog— But find us shelter.'

A few moments later the haar lifted. We had all looked forward to the beauty of our native land but what we saw of Leith was a mutilation – broken warehouses, roofless cottages, weeds. Brantôme reminded us that the English had pillaged the town and when Erskine returned to us he said that there was no building left that could serve as shelter except the home of his friend, Andrew Lamb. 'It is humble, Madam—'

'We shall be humbly grateful,' she said.

Now rain came in sudden torrents and we paused at the arch of the Kirkgate to squeeze against its protective wall. Few people were astir and those who were seemed more concerned with the passage of their sheep through the lanes than with a royal progress. Some children stood in the doorways of huts and stared with mild interest. Our Queen, who had accepted Chastelard's arm, said gaily, 'If the plume in your hat is to survive you'd best give it to Gurion for surgery,' and then plodded on towards Master Lamb's stone house.

He was a gracious host, generous with what he had. But his fireplace was only a hole in the roof, his ale sour, his herrings tough and bony. After we ladies were served he took the gentlemen into another room and his wife entertained our maids and tirewomen in the kitchen. Her Majesty removed her heart-shaped velvet cap, her cloak and shoes, and we set them near the fire to dry on the hearth-mat. I attended to her hair as best I could, drying and braiding it while the other Marys tried to repair themselves.

64

The Queen pretended to think our plight comical, but this was only bravado, for we all knew how she had looked forward to a splendid entrance into the capital. But she said, 'When Lord James comes he will surely have extra horses. He will have received our messenger by now – unless he had left Holyrood House?'

She put the question to herself, but Fleming said, 'I'm sure he'll arrive any moment, Madam.'

Rain battered the windows. I had heard of Scotland's poor roads, impassable in storm, but I could not forgive Lord James's bungling of what should have been a historic occasion. Any loyal subject who lived but two miles away could have, should have, arrived early. Perhaps he disdained such shelter as we had, or to await us at a mean inn; but I felt that this was a deliberate manoeuvre to show her that *he* ruled – not she. It was a way of humiliating her before thousands of Edinburgh folk who expected a legendary beauty, a fairytale princess, and would see an unkempt girl.

She said, 'We have thought of this journey as an adventure. But there may be risks ahead and I've no right to ask you to take them. You'd be safer, perhaps much happier, married. So I absolve you of your vows of chastity. That romantic idea was your own, my doves.'

Livvy asked, shocked, 'You are dismissing us, Madam?'

'No, no. I'm simply stating that I may not marry for years. I'll not deny you that privilege or suitable dowries.' She turned to me and smiled. 'You, Seton, are a wealthy young lady with a prudent brother, but I intend to provide for you all.'

We thanked her but assured her we were prepared for risks and would not dream of leaving her. Then, perhaps because she was secretly miserable, homesick for our France, she spoke with unusual frankness. 'We enter a great web of intrigue. Many of my nobles are in league with Queen Elizabeth. Others are beguiled by John Knox to Protestantism. Scotland is a religious battlefield and I have only contempt for such controversy in the name of God. I will command tolerance for both faiths.'

I asked, 'Madam, shall we have to hide our priests?'

'No! There shall be no priest-baiting.'

Mistress Lamb came in then to announce that Lord James was here. After he had knelt to Her Majesty and kissed her hand he turned and bowed to us. I thought that he looked slyly amused to see us dishevelled. He made some pretence of apology for his delay, then asked if he might present the nobles who waited in the next room. They came in singly, made obeisance, then stepped aside for another.

I judged these to be James's tools in the struggle for power. The old Duke de Châtelherault, who was next in line to the throne, and his son, the Earl of Arran who was said to be mentally unstable; portly Lord Huntly, High Chancellor, Chief of the clan Gordon – he, at least, was a Catholic, but he looked a big-bellied brute, his beard and hair untrimmed. None of these men had the grace to bow to us; they only inclined their heads. And though they wore fine damasks and great golden chains at their throats, they had not a puckle of elegance. It was James who stood regally in wine-red velvet, hands heavy with gold and rubies, saying, as if to peasants, 'You may go now, my lords, and see if horses may be found for the Queen.'

'Do you mean', she asked, 'you brought none from Edinburgh?'

A bland smile. He was so sorry, no message had reached him. Possibly pack-mules might be all Leith had to offer. At least, he said, the rain had stopped and we would not hazard more than mud.

When the lords had left she said, 'It may be that by now Lord Bothwell has found my galley.'

He shrugged and smiled. 'Do you imagine it piracy, Madam? If so, it takes a thief to catch a thief.'

She said, 'If you refer to Bothwell's theft of English gold intended for Scots traitors and intercepted by him for the use of my mother, then I glory in his thievery. So did my husband; the tale amused us both.'

James shrugged. 'It scarcely cemented friendship between cousins.'

'It was a ploy to help my mother,' she said, quietly defiant, 'as I believe he will help me.'

He was wise enough to reply that she, of course, was judge

of all matters. But his condescension was obvious – at least, to me. Then she dismissed him, kindly, saying we must make ready for Edinburgh. I summoned Mistress Lamb for the loan of a sleek-iron for Her Majesty's cloak, but there was none. But by far the worst embarrassment was the choice of animals assembled for us from nearby farms and the town's one stable – mangy nags, mules, and for Her Majesty a bay so hump-backed that it resembled a camel. She protested that she would ride James's glossy stallion but he insisted it was too lively for a woman's control. Lord Arran, toadying, begged that she not risk it – she, the finest rider in France! With a smile, she allowed her brother to help her on to the poor creature. Equally ridiculously mounted, we courtiers, preceded by Erskine and the guard, made our way over the moors towards Edinburgh. I could not help but wonder if the ravens who cawed through the pewter sky and dipped to the grain-fields were birds of ill-omen.

There were bonfires in our honour on the Hill of Calton, just above the city, but the earth was too wet for the piled turf, which sputtered and smoked, sending black swirls into our eyes. A crowd surged forward – some hundred meanly dressed peasants in kirtles and jerkins of brown and grey, so unlike the raffish folk of Paris who would wear crimson or green even to funerals. A few cheered us, but most stared in silence. One grimy woman, barefoot like the rest, was clothed in white linen and to my horror I saw a crucifix embroidered in gold silk and realised it had been an altar cloth.

As we moved past the smoke I could see a wide ravine and beyond lay the walled city, twisting up the jagged back of a hill that was surmounted by a fortress. My first glimpse of Edinburgh Castle reminded me of the ogre's lair in a child's story-book, inhabited by a fearsome giant who threw maidens off the precipice. As I recalled, it was six hundred years old and to me it looked old in evil, hulking against a grim, grey sky. But it was the city's defence, it was magically immune to capture, if ugly, awesome. Below it was a wide lake that doubtless served as a moat – the Nor' Loch I had read of.

It was as though the Castle stretched down an armoured

67

sleeve, and on it rested the turf-roofed town. When we had crossed the ravine above the loch, Brantôme rode close to me and said, 'I think this would be the High Street, my lady – the Royal Mile that runs from the Castle straight to Holyrood House.' Mournfully he added, 'It must have seen more regal processions than ours.'

It was crammed with people who watched our pitiful progress from forestairs, from windows, even from the peaked roofs, and pressed against ox-hide doors. Lord Erskine kept them from the street, his horsemen prodding those who stood in the way with lances. Few cheered but there was, thank God, no disrespect, only immense curiosity. I had been shocked to hear that Her Majesty had been reviled by John Knox as a harlot and had expected his flock to appear and jeer, if not stone, her. But it was an orderly if slow progress through a wide market-place where canvas stalls were set to display a variety of goods. On one corner I saw a gibbet close by a beam which swung butter and salt for weighing. I saw neither nuns nor priests. But beggars were everywhere, and pigs lapping the refuse that was thrown from windows. Those windows, I noticed, were only holes pocking the house-fronts.

We passed St Giles Cathedral – no, Brantôme said, as I pointed to it, it was a 'kirk' now, Knox's church. The saints had been toppled and desecrated, the holy altars burned, the amber oak whitewashed. Across the street a new crowd waited outside a gabled house, and Brantôme said, 'I think it's Knox!'

A man in a black Geneva cloak stood alone at the top of the forestairs, glowering down at us. His beard was a long, yellowish-white, his eyes a savage black, and I thought his face the very essence of cruelty, the mouth shaped to a snarl. Then he raised his hand, and the people near him began to sing some wretched hymn. I caught only a few words: *Daughter of Babylon . . . happy shall he be who dasheth thy little ones against the stones.*

Queen Mary checked her horse. Riding behind her, I could not see her face, only the proud tilt of her head, her unsmiling profile as she looked up at him. It must have been a duel of glances, and I could imagine the contempt of hers matched the anger of his. There was a sudden glint of rubies – she had

68

pulled her cross out from beneath her ermine collar.

Then she turned, motioned to Erskine, and we moved on beyond a murmuring crowd into another. The people did not seem hostile; it was as though they reserved judgement, cautious, perhaps a little anxious. A ripple of terror ran up my spine, for the enemy was at our backs.

But there was no further drama as we rode on to a massive gate called the Netherbow Port – entrances are called ports in Scotland, I remembered – where sentries bowed us through, smiling. Brantôme, whose mind was a map, said this was the Burgh of the Canongate, where the high clergy of our church used to walk in meditation. Now it was a street of stately homes with armorial bearings above the doors. We passed a church – Protestant – hushed in its rose gardens, and a great stone building with a statue of Justice. Little wynds and closes ran off this street, prankish lanes. Then the great stables of Horse Close, and ahead lay the palace of Holyrood House.

To a French-educated lady, it was a poor copy of one of our châteaux, with spires and clown-hatted towers, and it seemed to me small, even for our small court. Next to it was a huge abbey, but roofless – another English atrocity due to the fury of Henry VIII whose 'Butcher Hertford' had pillaged in 1544, laying ruin to three thousand abbeys.

Brantôme said, 'At least the hills are magnificent.'

Stark, high, towering above a forest of oaks, and, in a sense, balanced by the height of the Castle at the other end of the mile. Such a forest should provide good hunting. I hoped that Bothwell would find our missing ship; to train new falcons can be tedious, and several of our dogs were not hounds but pets.

We clattered across a drawbridge and a great gate was unbolted to an outer courtyard which was barren as a barracks – just a square stretch of turf surrounded by high, rock walls. Servants came out and helped us dismount and we followed Lord James through an arch into an inner courtyard. There was an arcaded walk and here at least were flowers – the fat roses of August – but they straggled in untidy beds as though no one had cared for them. Her Majesty turned and said to James, 'Whoever the gardeners may be, I wish to see them in the morning. And I want benches placed here. . . .'

69

Servants came to us then, kneeling to Her Majesty. They wore rough aprons or smocks, according to their sex, and they stared at our velvet-clothed pages and tirewomen and maids with a sort of incredulity. James ordered them to help with the unpacking of the wagons. Belatedly, and obviously embarrassed, an authoritative man in blue damask hurried out – the Master of the Household, I assumed – and after conference with Her Majesty conducted our gentlemen courtiers across the courtyard to what seemed the east wing of the palace. James and the other noblemen led us to the west. At the top of a stone staircase we saw a Great Hall, the walls grimly decorated with rusting boar-spears and stags' heads. There was a tattered banner above one of the fireplaces, a long, deal table and oaken benches.

James turned to us. 'I felt that you four ladies would be comfortable in the suite below Her Majesty's, which was the late King's.' He opened a door which adjoined the Great Hall and led us into the least regal chambers I ever beheld. Indeed, there were five rooms, a bedchamber for each of us and a commonroom. But the furniture was of black oak, heavy and graceless, the gold arras stained and fraying and three shabby tapestries the colour of dung. Rats must have been at the bed-hangings. I would have thought that James lied about the King's habitation here except that a ceiling was carved with the armorial bearings of James V.

Her Majesty said, 'We shall redecorate as soon as possible or my ladies will have nightmares.' She tried to smile. 'What horrors are above for me, my lord?'

The four men jabbered a complaint that they had not had sufficient warning of her arrival, that Holyrood was rarely in use except for hunting parties. We climbed more stone stairs to a large presence chamber hung with rotting grey tapestries of a boar chase. There was a small, stained-glass oratory set in the wall and Her Majesty moved to it and stood for a few moments with her back to us. Then she turned.

'Where is my mother's altar?' she asked.

James stuttered that it was likely in the Castle, where she had spent her last months. For the first time he seemed embarrassed. I guessed that the altar had been burned

70

as 'popish rubbish' along with her other holy comforts.

'Where is her bedchamber?' Her Majesty asked.

He opened the door to a medium-sized room that faced the Royal Mile. An oak-panelled ceiling was carved with the crowned initials of James V and Mary de Guise – the only royal adornment to a dismal boudoir. Beside the fireplace, which was of oak and dirty with ashes, were two small benches. The carpet was of dusty rushes, and the gold velvet bed-hangings were worn and spotted with candlewax. Lord Huntly pulled aside a tapestry near the bed and showed us a spiral staircase that was a private one to our apartments below.

'And this closet?' asked Her Majesty, stepping into a tiny room with one window, part of the tower turret.

'No, Madam, you can see it has a fireplace,' James said.

She laughed wryly. 'I can see it now. I mistook it for a shred of broken tile.' Then she crossed the bedchamber and peered into what James called a 'dressing room'. When Her Majesty wore a full farthingale there would be no room for Janet to dress her.

She said, 'I suppose it must do. I'd not care to lodge in that ghostly old castle. So, gentlemen, thank you.'

But James did not take the dismissal. 'A feast is being prepared in your honour, in the Great Hall – unless Your Majesty is weary?'

'No,' she said, 'we are not weary. We shall be delighted.'

They arranged the hour for nine and when we were alone she said, 'Let us count our blessings. I doubt the roof leaks. The walls are thick. I noted a bath-house just inside the outer court. The glass of my oratory is superb.' She paused. 'Have you any other blessings to count?'

'The two embellished ceilings,' Fleming said.

'Someone has thought of chamber-pots.' Livvy said. 'One pokes from under Your Majesty's bed.'

Beaton had spied satin sheets. 'See, Madam?' she asked, pulling back the velvet spread. 'And clean!'

But I had nothing to add to the 'blessings'. Homesickness was an illness that must not be mentioned, because there was no possible cure for it; there was no possibility of us ever returning to France.

71

'What,' Her Majesty asked, 'no blessing here, Seton?'

I needed to match her gaiety. 'If I embroider the hole in your pillowcase it will make a pretty medallion.'

She smiled and said that we were to bustle for the wine page, find a sleek-iron, arrange for our boxes to be brought up, and guide Janet here. She required a bathing-tub, vats of hot water, and wood for our fireplaces. Our maids must help us dress 'with consequence'. Tonight we must make an impression upon every hostile nobleman who came to gawp at 'French dolls'.

'Scots humour can be crude,' she said, 'and there may be jests that offend us. But I need to win friends and so, within reason, I ask that you exhibit tolerance.'

And then she said, as if she had held in her anger too long, 'That monstrous Master Knox! The way he behaved . . . the effrontery of the old goat! He'll not dare ask audience!'

I said timidly, 'Since he's a subject, and a proven rebel, couldn't you punish him severely? The stocks, or prison?'

'No,' she said. 'That would split my country.' She let down her hair in its limp braids. 'I'll not make a martyr of a madman.'

It was dark before we all had bathed, and we dressed in the dim light from evil-smelling sheep-grease candles. Only our necessities were in our chambers but Janet came down to say that Her Majesty had all she required.

'She has chosen to wear black tonight,' she said, 'as befits Scots mourning. Aye, the violet for your ladyships and she said you must jewel your hair. Lady Seton, she asks for you to arrange hers.'

I followed her up the private spiral staircase, thinking that it was one blessing we had not mentioned, an easy connection between our suites. Her Majesty told me to bind her hair up with jet pins. I thought this too sedate but, at eighteen, facing old men of thirty years or more, dignity was essential. Her necklace of jet and diamonds glittered below the wide, back-sweeping ruff that left her throat bare. Never had I seen her skin so pallidly superb, due, perhaps, to the moisture of the day. Her eyes had a way of taking on the colour of her gown,

72

as opals do; now they were grey-black. She fastened in pear-shaped diamond earrings.

Rings sparkled on her long, thin fingers. King Francis's gifts to her had equalled the crown jewels she had had to return; there were also those inherited from her parents and countless presents from foreign suitors. Even the looking-glasses were bordered with precious stones. I remember Madame Diane, admiring one the Pope had sent, saying: 'Queen Elizabeth has only polished metal. Now, if she had adhered to the true faith she could look herself in the face.'

Her Majesty's face was grave; I think she dreaded this banquet and felt herself to be on trial, rather than honoured. But a blessing arrived – a bouquet of roses from Chastelard. They were white, their hearts centered with ivory and gold. She buried her face in them and scanned a little note and blushed and told Janet to set the roses in water. Then she carried the note to the fireplace and watched it burn.

Two tables were set in the Great Hall. One, raised on a dais, was just large enough to accommodate Her Majesty, James, the old Duke and his son, Arran. There, too, sat a dark-bearded gentleman whose black satin elegance seemed French, though I had never seen him before. Below that table was ours, stretching the full length of the room. We of rank were seated closest to the royal one but a pleasant error had been made, for I sat between Chastelard and Brantôme. Opposite me, next to Fleming, were two men with crudely cut beards and dirty fingernails – Lords Lindsay and Ruthven. Lord Huntly, in a spotted red velvet doublet encrusted with diamonds, ogled poor Livvy, and Beaton, bravely smiling, evaded the drunken pats and squeezes of Lord Morton, a redhead with pig eyes who looked like the portraits of Henry VIII. Below the great salt-cellar sat humbler folk, also according to rank, ending with grooms and stablemen and washer-maids.

The food was prepared by the Scots, and presented grossly. A barrel of oysters was passed, and great lumps of beef and entire chickens which one had to cut oneself with daggers; Huntly pulled his apart with his fingers. There was a pie of

73

blackbirds, unseasoned, ribs of mutton in congealing yellow tallow, and geese boiled with prunes. And, all along our unclothed table, leathern jugs of *aqua vitae*. Her Majesty signalled one of our pages, and soon we had carafes of our red Chinon, the white Vouvray and delicate Anjou. The Scots lords spurned these, though I saw the dark man lift his goblet to Her Majesty.

'Who can that civilised gentleman be?' I asked Brantôme, who was struggling with his mutton.

'That would be Sir William Maitland of Lethington. I know little about him as yet but he is surely in league with Lord James. They all are.'

I studied the dark, saturnine face. 'He is the oldest here. Perhaps forty?'

'An ageless and interesting face,' he said. He relinquished the mutton, looked vainly for something to wipe his hands on and brought out a lacy handkerchief. 'Being but eighteen, my lady, all of these Scots seem old to you. But we are a surprisingly young court compared to most. There's not a greybeard among us.'

Chastelard turned to me and spoke softly. 'Do you know if Her Majesty received my roses?'

'They pleased her,' I told him.

'And did she, by chance, read the sonnet?'

'I believe so,' I said cautiously.

'I was thinking of it throughout the voyage,' he said, 'but I should have polished it – it's unkempt.'

'All of you poets suffer humility,' I said. 'Even our great Ronsard told me he will write one line, or two, and save those for years before adding others.'

He chuckled. 'Ronsard *humble*? He thinks to bestow immortality on each lady he loves, such a conceit – but I accord him genius. Of course he is in love with Her Majesty, but who is not?'

So he had admitted it, nor was I surprised. He had the chance of a snowball in the desert; yet he was a romantic and such folk always create fantasies of success. I hoped I would never create one for myself. I could laugh now at the memory of Raoul.

There was laughter all about us, most of it drunken, because the Lords persisted in *aqua vitae* which in France we used only as medicine against chill or as prevention of shock. In any case, they became rowdy and, when I looked up at the royal table, it seemed that only James and Lething-ton were sober. Now began toasts to Her Majesty, and we all rose in her honour. Some of these toasts offered by Huntly and Ruthven were bawdy but she did not blush. Then she rose to lift her glass to Scotland. It was unfortunate that her little speech ended with a question.

'And so we shall work for the unity of our country, shall we not?'

I had expected a cheer. But Lord Morton, by accident or design, broke wind at that moment and the sound came out precisely as a thunderous question mark. It was appalling; it was also marvellously comic. Her Majesty, perhaps unsure if the insult was contrived or natural, chose to laugh. We all laughed with her except Chastelard, who glowered and put his hand to his dirk-belt. Lord James was not smiling either, and commanded musicians who began to play from a gallery above us.

Mercifully, the most drunken of the lords sprawled over the table and slept – their elbows in plates of fruits and cakes, so that we Marys could ignore them or move from our chairs to less barbaric company. When the musicians paused for wine, a terrible din began outside the windows that faced the inner courtyard. Never have I heard such ill-tuned rebecs and fiddles as came from two hundred serenaders that included a dozen pipers. Her Majesty hurried over to lean out and thank 'my people who are making me so welcome'. We could see that they had lit a bonfire in her honour. A ragged crowd they were, but cheerful, and though James said, 'A pox on them,' she turned to him frowning in the coldest silence, then gave them her full attention. It was a rebuff he deserved, but he seemed to shrug it off. There was no doubt in my mind now that he considered himself King of Scotland and I won-dered if he had sewn seeds of mistrust in her. As I fell asleep that night I thought with sudden gratitude of my own half-brother, a loyal subject, a devout Catholic, and I prayed for

75

his safety at sea. And I prayed that my pet poodle had survived.

Next day, with Her Majesty and the Master of the Household, we explored the palace from cellars to top turrets, he taking note of the repairs she ordered. Much of the panelling had been damaged by woodworm, some walls were green with mildew; she commanded juniper to be burned in braziers in the corridors and the mean little rooms.

'Why', she asked, 'did my grandsire build this place without spacious chambers?'

'Madam,' he said, 'a Scot builds for comfort. We suffer brutal winters, and small chambers hold the heat of the fireplace. In a room the size of the Great Hall there must be two always ablaze else you shiver to cross it.'

'I shiver even to look at it,' she said, and commanded bright new banners, the polishing of boar-spears, and fresh rushes to be laid on the floor, for she wished to conserve her oriental carpets for our suites and for guest quarters. We wandered down jagged stone steps to a kitchen, and this she approved, with its boiling and baking hearths, its sturdy brown beams which supported hams and flitches of bacon hung on rope. She peered into vats of salted beef, winced at barrels of salt herring and then held conference with the chefs. The two Scots were dismissed, our Henri and Gaston were to take their places. The kitchen wenches were lectured on the necessity of garnishing. She told them, 'A dish of meat should look as pretty as yourselves and a dish of pease is embarrassed without a ruff of cream. . . .' She left them adoring her, which was her usual effect on servants, and we went down spiral stairs to the dungeons, now used as wine cellars. Some of our wines were being uncrated but the Scots varlets had placed the bottles standing up on the stone racks. Gently, she explained the correct way of storage. 'They have travelled at sea,' she said, 'flat on their backs, and they must always rest so. Wines love to sleep. If they don't, they are grumpy, and so would you be without beds.'

She laughed with them and accepted a mug of ale, and we moved on to her conquest of other Scots servants. Most of

76

them lived in thatched cottages behind the palace where there was a buttery, brewhouse and pens for fowl. Her Majesty asked for the creation of a herb garden, though the gardener doubted that there would be sufficient sun. We had brought jars of powdered herbs, so she said there was no emergency, but the flower garden must be tidied at once, and the arcade swept of débris.

So the day passed. Our exquisite French and Italian furniture replaced the dreary benches and broken stools. Looking-glasses were hung, carpets laid. At the small dinner she gave in the Great Hall to we exiles from France – though James and Lethington were invited – there was an embroidered cloth on the table and napkins and a pewter basin of roses. There were wax candles in the chandeliers that glowed on crystal, and silver knives instead of dirks.

We had been speaking our laborious Scots most of the day; now we relaxed in French, mindful that both James and Lethington were proficient. Lethington again wore black, which contrasted with his pallid skin and complimented his forked black beard. His long, tapering fingers were not unlike James's, and the two men were similar in manner – suave, silky, reserved if not remote. But Her Majesty was determined that we should be merry. Brantôme helped her. He chattered away about French scandals. 'Queen Catherine's breath was so foul as to sicken a pig. . . . Madame Diane flirts with a nunnery and eleven gentlemen. . . . Ronsard, bereft of a current lady, has written a sonnet to a luscious strawberry. . . .'

Chastelard said, 'His poems to Her Majesty enthrone her for ever. What is your favourite, Madam?'

She said, 'I'm sure you know the one, Pierre. Of course he flatters extravagantly.'

Chastelard leaned towards her, quoting:

> Just as we see, half rosy and half white
> Dawn and the morning star dispel the night,
> In beauty thus beyond compare impearled
> The Queen of Scotland rises on the world.

She chuckled. 'And now the Queen of Scotland must retire

77

from the world, and rise to her apartments. But first, a sleep-ing-cap.'

Wine was poured, and she bade good night to the gentle-men, who escorted us to the guard who waited in the corridor. Her Majesty safely above, and Janet summoned to undress her, we Marys dispersed to our chambers. Mine was so much improved with my pale blue arras and matching bed-curtains that it could have been a nook of Fontainebleau or Chenon-ceaux had it been larger.

I was not sleepy. The candlelight was not half as bright as the moonlight which gilded the window. I looked out and saw the rose garden lying so innocent near the cloistered walk, the arched promenade of long-dead nuns. I felt a need to pray there although my prie-dieu was here with its cushion. To kneel on moist grass was absurd.

Yet I took a shawl, unbolted the door and told the guard where I would be. He bowed and preceded me to the first landing, where another guard unlocked a great, nail-studded door. Then I was in the gardens of the inner courtyard among the roses which were still a riot, a turbulence of bloom which would have displeased Her Majesty. But the benches she had ordered were here and I sat on one, grey stone lichened and furry with green patches of moss. It occurred to me that it might have been moved from the churchyard of the ruined abbey, so old it was. Everything about me was at peace – the pale, moon-drenched roses, the grass covered in silvery dew. Above the wall I could see the high thrust of hills under a spangle of stars.

Facing the east wing, I saw candles blink out, but one remained in a low window and a shadow passed before it. Brantôme lodged in this area and I thought of him recording the events of this day in Holyrood.

In the fragrant silence I was close to prayer, and I knew its shape though I had not formed the words: May God protect Her Majesty against all evil. . . .

But before the thought was complete the shadow at the window became a man, and he sat down so that his face was level with the casement. This was not Brantôme or anyone I knew. His shirt, open at the throat, was primrose in the gold

78

of candlelight. His head was hooded, his face beardless. It was a face I had seen only in classic sculpture – young, strong, stern. The eyes were large, deep-socketed, but I could not see their colour. They did not look down at me but straight across to the opposite side of the palace.

He seemed to be meditating, his hands supporting his chin. There was a ring on his left hand shot with green fire – emeralds? I found myself incomprehensibly jealous that it might be his marriage ring, and that behind him, in the shadows, a wife lay waiting in bed. And what was he meditating on so gravely? And why had I not seen him before?

The pressure of my glance, of my thoughts, must have drawn him, for now he looked down and saw me and, after a moment, smiled. My heart missed a beat. It was preposterous – yet the lines of Ronsard came to haunt the moonlight: 'For love and death are but the self-same thing.'

One does not fall in love with a face, I told myself. It was only the sorcery of moonlight. One cannot fall in love in silence, in mystery, without touch. He is servant to someone, perhaps a valet to one of the Scots lords and will presently snuff out the candle and seek humble quarters behind the palace. He will bed on straw with a washermaid. . . . And yet he wore that ring.

Still, we locked in an embrace of eyes. But I did not smile, for fear of losing dignity. With an effort I broke the magic by rising, picking a rose. Then I turned and entered the palace and dared not look back.

In the morning my maid Isobel withdrew the rose from under my pillow. 'Do you wish to keep this, Madam?'

'Toss it away,' I said, angry that dreams of roses, of him, had troubled my sleep.

It was another busy day. Servants continued to arrange furniture and placed Her Majesty's cloth of state above the throne in her audience chamber. The throne, of carved oak, had seated every monarch since the sainted Margaret. The gold curlicues – thistles and fleur-de-lis – were tarnished, and the velvet cushion shredded by centuries of moths. We placed a new cushion there, of purple stamped with gold, and Her

79

Majesty's altar was fitted into the oratory across the room. I asked, 'Did you not want your mother's holy comforts?'

'I do,' she said. 'I have asked my brother.' And then, deeply sarcastic, 'Of course, Edinburgh Castle is a full mile from here. A terrible journey for altar and prie-dieu, don't you think?'

Beaton said, 'Is it possible that Protestants might attack and demolish such things?'

'That might well be the excuse,' she said, 'though if Lord James cared to disguise the shipment as hay in a wagon I'd not be disturbed.'

She had said 'asked my brother', not commanded. Doubtless this was tact, diplomacy, a fencing for power. But hers was the legal power and I was impatient for her to display it, now, immediately, to demonstrate her authority. When Fleming and I shared flounder and peas in her chamber at noon, she said, 'I marvel at Her Majesty's tolerance of Lord James. Yet, being the King's son, albeit bastard, I suppose he considers himself ruler. Men assume that they are more intelligent than we, whatever their rank.'

'Aye,' I said, for we were speaking Scots for practice. 'But she shouldn't permit it. If ever a man needed a boot in his—'

'Arse,' and she giggled. 'He should have daggered that Morton for the fart; I think it was planned between them.'

'I don't think one can plan a fart,' I said, 'but James should have rebuked him.'

'Lord James,' she corrected.

'I shall call him "my Lord" in public, but to me his rank is the rank of a weed. I wish he'd fester somewhere else.'

'Perhaps she thinks to win him over,' Fleming said, 'to convert him back to the true faith.'

'As simple a problem as Knox,' I said.

She changed the subject to Sir William Maitland of Lethington.

'I welcomed him into the audience chamber this morning and we chatted while Her Majesty kept him waiting. He is much like the diplomats she received in France – shrewd, wily, imperturbable. I felt a sort of cool charm, but I wonder what favour he seeks.'

'Power of some sort,' I said. 'She gropes through a murk of power-mad men.'

'At least he has manners. And he seems finely educated.'

I smiled. 'To charm a maid of honour? I thought you fancied Lord Bothwell.'

'Oh!' she said. 'How susceptible do you think I am?'

'I wouldn't dream of probing an endless history,' I said. 'You were the first of us to fascinate, aged thirteen—'

'Jesu, only a love-sick page, Her Majesty's discard. I haven't the talents of you three. Beaton is so merry, and her red-gold hair . . . Livvy dances so high and handsome as to gain applause . . . and you, my dear Seton, you are unique.'

'Aye,' said I, 'that word covers a multitude of graces which you can't supply, because I haven't them. I'm comely enough, my body is nicely shaped and I wear my clothes well enough, but I have the allure of a dull Mass on a rainy dawn.'

'Oh, you fool!' She tossed a pea at me. 'Always disparaging yourself! Blind to your attributes! In the shadow of the Queen we all assume ourselves to be less lovely than we are. It is not her doing, but ours. She wants us to marry well and happily. . . .'

I was forced to think of the man I had seen last night and I said, 'Do you think we've met all the Scots nobles that are here in residence?'

She nodded. 'And most of them married. But Highlanders and Borderers are sure to make their way here in time. Her Majesty would never allow us to make a *faux pas* in love.'

'I must make a mighty marriage to please my brother,' I said. 'Love is subordinate.'

'But the two *can* be combined,' she said.

Her Majesty came to us then to say that her gold-cloth carpet required mending; it was to be spread in the abbey tomorrow where we would hear Mass. To pray in ruins did not disturb her, she said – here her ancestors had worshipped and, though the roof was broken, we would hear birdsong. She said, 'I shall put aside my mourning and celebrate Christ in a ruby gown. You may wear what colours you wish.'

We spent the afternoon repairing the long, shining carpet, Beaton and Livvy helping. At dusk we were finished, and I

81

went outside to see to the placing of the altar. Strong young pages handled the heavy ivory and oak as though it were dandelion fluff and hung the massive cross in perfect balance. A mist was rising but I loitered after they had gone. The smell of dead honeysuckle was exquisite, and looking up I could see high crags clothed in the royal purple of heather. I could remember that it was harsh to the touch, but from here it seemed a climbing glory of velvet.

A monk emerged from the arcaded walk to the left and stood with his back to me, admiring the altar or perhaps in prayer. Then he turned and saw me and bowed.

'A good evening,' he said.

But I could say nothing.

'I didn't startle you?' he asked.

I shook my head.

'I am Father Black – Adam Black.'

I stammered my name and he came forward in the rising mist. The face was more wonderful than when I glimpsed it at the window, for his eyes were a clear, violet-blue, softening strong, high cheekbones. I felt a pressure below my breast that was acutely painful.

'A good evening,' I said finally.

But the white mists rose about us there in the old, ruined abbey and from somewhere high among the ravaged stones ravens called signal of storm, and beat up in black clouds towards the belfry.

'And a good night to you,' I said, and fled like a frightened child.

CHAPTER V

It was my misfortune that young Lord Arran attached himself to me in the cloistered walk before Mass. Bulbous-eyed,
pox scarred, he smelled of sheep-grease, which he evidently
used to smooth down his spiky hair. He sat down on my bench
and asked me if Her Majesty had chosen a husband.

'*What*?' I asked, then remembered he was mentally un-
balanced, said to be subject to fits. 'Not to my knowledge,' I
said more gently.

'Good. She would suit me very well. When my father dies
I'm next in line to the throne, you know.'

He began to list his qualifications, but I found him so
tedious that I rose and walked round the abbey, while he
chattered beside me. Suddenly we heard an agonised scream.
Through a small crowd of Scots lords who barred the abbey
entrance I saw an altar boy, his head streaming blood, fall to
the grass. Father Black knelt to assist him, and Lord Lindsay
stood above them with a wet, red sword.

I started to run towards Lindsay with some wild thought of
snatching away the sword but our Scots halberdiers inter-
vened just as James and the Queen hurried up. Yet Lindsay
still threatened with his sword, and James drew his. Father
Black lifted the boy and carried him towards the palace, our
surgeon following.

'Sheath that sword!' James shouted.

'So you protect idolaters?'

'I protect the Queen's right to hear Mass.'

Her Majesty moved close to Lindsay and, to my horror, he
shifted his sword so that it was level with her heart. 'I command you to sheath that sword.'

Reluctantly, he did so. Then she said, 'Should that boy die,

God may forgive you – not I. I am sparing you punishment now only because of your rank. But if you attempt murder again, nothing shall save you.'

Arran, still at my side, began to babble that the boy had only a flesh wound; then he began to laugh and to cry. James urged us into the abbey, assuring us that he would guard the gate so that we might worship in peace. Her Majesty put both arms round him and kissed him, and we filed past the Protestant lords into the chill, over the gold-cloth carpet that led to the altar, where someone had placed roses.

Father Joseph celebrated Mass; but I heard scarcely a word. I thought how near to death Father Black had been and thanked God for his safety and prayed for the recovery of the boy. I was also reshaping my opinion of James, though he must have had some wily reason for showing tolerance.

He was waiting with our halberdiers to escort us across to the palace, but the Lords had dispersed and I hoped I had seen the last of Arran, at least for a time. Her Majesty was closeted with James most of the day, taking the noon meal with him in the little room adjoining her bedchamber which had now been fitted out with a table and benches and flowery arras for use for more intimate occasions, since she disliked the Great Hall.

So we Marys idled away the afternoon without duties. Gervais sent me word that the boy's head wound had been successfully treated by Gurion and that he, Gervais, had administered poppy drug and was nursing him.

Beaton, who was embroidering an altar cloth, said, 'On a little walk in the gardens I met a most attractive gentleman – Ogilvie of Boyne. He has come to court for only a few days in hope of greeting Her Majesty and I offered to help him to an audience.'

'Oh, la!' Livvy said, groaning. 'So now we are to have still another love drama? And hopeless as usual. You attract them but you can never hold them. And you know why, I've told you a hundred times: you frighten them off by your eagerness.'

'I? Eager?' Beaton's eyes widened. 'You insult me! I may flirt, of course. . . .'

It was an old argument; I was glad when Her Majesty was announced. She looked radiant. Seated with us, she said, 'Little Jacques is able to take broth and bread. And, because of my brother's firmness, I've nothing more to fear of rebellion among our Lords.'

I said, 'I think they would have murdered Father Black. Arran mumbled something about a burning.'

'Arran!' She dismissed him with a contemptuous smile. Then she said, 'Father Black – I call him Father Adam. He was my mother's confessor during her last two years until she was forbidden a priest. He is now my own confessor and, if you girls wish, he may be yours.'

Beaton and Fleming at once agreed; Livvy preferred to adhere to Father Joseph.

'And you, Seton?' Her Majesty asked. 'You have had priest-problems before, I remember. But Father Adam – being only a few years older than us – understands youth. He does not give penances for over-indulgence in dreams or dancing. Or', she said, with a twinkle, 'for my confessed passion for brandied figs.'

I shook my head. 'Thank you, Madam, but I too would prefer Father Joseph. A somewhat older person would be more – more comforting to me.'

Beaton said, 'I think Father Adam a dreadful waste to woman-kind; the sort of waste there is in some of our pages – those so effeminate that they parody women.'

'Ah,' said Her Majesty, 'but by their very nature they keep my ladies safe. When *real* men are in and out of bedchambers placing candles or wood they can light dangerous emotional fires. The effeminate man is a protector of feminine virtue. His own is not my concern.'

Livvy, who was easily shocked, managed to nod but said nothing. We three agreed with Her Majesty, for we recalled a time when a drunken page attempted to embrace my Isobel; and of mysterious pregnancies among Queen Catherine's women. These pages were usually of good family, often noble-men who went to France for education and found it in service to royalty. Most of ours were far better mannered than the Scots lords.

85

'It will take some weeks before this household is adjusted,' the Queen said. 'Many rooms are deplorable and we must provide against the cold—'

She paused. We could hear deep-throated bells in the distance. She said, 'St Giles. That would be Master Knox summoning another congregation. I'm told he begins at four or five in the morning, even in winter. I am also told that he refers to me as "the Cardinal's whore".' Then she laughed. 'We shall see who wins this contest. My brother insists I should ask him here to dispel his fancies. I intend that he shall be reassured – and an end to this childish hostility.'

But when she left us I thought of James's influence and, later, was mercifully able to forget Adam Black in my prayers for her. Shadows flickered in my sleepy mind – the dark one of Lethington, pawn of James? The churl Morton, the savage Lindsay and the feeble-minded Arran. But when I sank into dreams there seemed to be a golden thread woven by my embroidery needle and it formed the face of Adam Black and awakened me to panic, for the face was drowned in blood.

'I want you present when Master Knox arrives,' Her Majesty said, pressing back the silver lace ruff from the square neck of her gown. 'He'll not be able to say that the Whore of Babylon seduced him to her couch.' I knew her cheerfulness was bravado.

As we waited for him in the audience chamber she said that Master Thomas Randolph, Elizabeth's ambassador, had arrived that morning and, though perhaps thirty-six or thirty-seven, was surprisingly comely and astonishingly kind on hearing of the fracas outside the abbey. 'And he has humour – he laughed with me when he presented Her Majesty's safe conduct permit; and he seemed sincerely sorry about the loss of our animal galley. He says the Queen refers to me not as "cousin" but as cherished "sister". If this is the way she wishes it, why then, I am her most devoted "sister".'

A page announced Lord James Stuart and Master John Knox.

I had no reason to change my first impression of him. He

86

was an old man with a dirty beard and black eyes rimmed with red as though he rarely slept. Those eyes snooped around the chamber as though anxious to detect some sin – and of course they did, for sin to him was Her Majesty's oratory with its holy images.

She began by saying that there were some five hundred thousand persons in Scotland, thirty thousand here in Edinburgh, and these must not be torn apart by religious conviction. 'Together, we may mend the country, Master Knox, in tolerance—'

'The people will not tolerate the Mass, nor will I!' His voice was a snarl, like the set of his mouth. 'To tolerate evil is to deny Jesus Christ!'

'But you do evil by stirring my people to priest-baiting and the wrecking of holy images – and the use of necromancy.'

'So was Christ accused of the black arts,' he said, 'so I must patiently bear such slander.'

'Do you compare yourself to Christ?' she asked. 'Did he ever instigate slaughter and sedition as you have done here, and in England? Did he rip and tear at *any* faith? Foment rebellion, as you have done?'

My God, he then denied the divine right of kings – and said that subjects were not bound to frame their beliefs according to those of their princes. In short, he advocated regicide and we Marys were so appalled that our fingers clutched our crosses. It was as if the very devil spoke, suggesting anarchy and insurrection, and he said that our faith was the Roman harlot.

She said, exhausted of argument, and lamely, 'My conscience does not say so.'

'Conscience requires knowledge, Madam – and you have none.'

I could have struck his sneering mouth; I expected James to rise, at least to rebuke him. But the Bastard sat calmly, one hand in his pocket – a new device set into a doublet – the other, ring-heavy, stroking his beard. His green eyes glittered with enjoyment, that I can swear.

Knox ranted on, stating that Jesus neither said nor commanded Mass at the Last Supper, that Mass was an abomination of God. Her Majesty was shocked to silence. He persisted in the vilest language, which may be comical in a bawdy ballad but not in the mouth of the clergy; for to him our conception of the Virgin was so alien as to make Her out a whore, and it was clear that he thought Her Majesty of that ilk. Finally, and with enormous dignity, she dismissed him and James, and we praised her for fencing so cleverly, but she knew, young as she was, that she had failed as duellist. Yet she was gallant, and never one to whimper or brood. 'Seton,' she said, 'open those shutters. I think we need pure air.'

> Let us drink and sing of love,
> Heedless of
> Felon Care's malignant tooth!
> Age, that pickpurse envious,
> Follow us,
> Crowding on the heels of youth.

The musicians sang Ronsard's lines in the gallery of the Great Hall. But this time the Scots lords were orderly, possibly chided by James for their former drunken behaviour. We drank Anjou and Champagne and sweet wines of the Loire valleys. Beaton flirted with Ogilvie of Boyne, a handsome – if stern-faced lad. The plaid and the cock-plumed bonnet became him, and the burst of sapphire chains at his neck matched his eyes. Lord Huntly frowned at the flirting and Brantôme, beside me, noticed.

'Huntly's daughter, Lady Jean Gordon, is affianced to Ogilvie,' he said. 'Lady Beaton should be warned, if she doesn't know.'

'And how do you know? There's no Lady Jean here.'

'I know everything,' he said, with mock solemnity. 'I am god of the keyhole, remember? Actually, the matter is no secret. The marriage was arranged two years ago and should be celebrated soon.'

Not if Beaton has her way, I thought, watching her clink her wine cup to the lad's, and hearing her call him 'Sweet Alex', and contrive to loose a red-gold curl from her headdress. But now again she was over-eager and thus sure to fail with this rather dour young man who perhaps had never before met a lady from the French court.

To my relief Her Majesty had banished Lord Arran and his father from court because they had protested at the 'Romish sacrilege' of the Mass. Indeed, I think that she was fearful of Arran's madness. Now, it seemed, a quieter madman sat opposite me – Lord Ruthven. He had a coffin-shaped face, deeply scarred. His eyes were very light – strange in contrast to his dark hair – and they were hooded. When a jest was made he did not laugh but sometimes he chuckled to himself, and he had a habit of squeezing any insect that came near him.

That night Her Majesty paid special favour to Lethington, who somehow reminded me of a dark, sheathed sword hilted with gold and jewels; but when the Hall was cleared for dancing, she chose her brother to lead her into the galliard.

When I saw the repulsive Morton smile and come towards me I took Brantôme's hand and said, 'Indeed, I'd love to dance,' though he was not my idea of revel. We danced past a bench where Father Adam sat with Father Joseph and another priest. They must have just arrived, for they had not been at table – and Father Adam smiled at me.

I had been trying to forget him and now his presence spoiled the evening for me. It was absurd, but I wondered if he admired the grace of my gown as it swirled in the dance, my small waist, the plumes that foamed the hem of my skirt. Yet he continued to look at me and I said to Brantôme, 'If you'll dance me out to the corridor I'll take some air.'

'Ill?' he asked solicitously.

'Not yet,' I lied, 'but I'm taking no chances.'

In the corridor I thanked him and said I would be back. I made my way into the garden. Rose petals littered the grass. Only a few shaggy asters survived. I sat on my bench and heard the throb and swirl of a Scottish country dance from above me, the screech of pipers, stomp of feet. Presently I heard the closing of the heavy door and the guard's voice: 'A good night to you, Father.'

I held my breath as Father Adam started across the court-yard. There was no moon, and I was seated far between the

89

cressets that burned at the palace doors so he was not likely to see me. For my own peace of mind I hoped that he would not.

But a night bird called, and he turned, paused by its cry. Then he saw me, hesitated, and came forward.

'Are you weary of the dance, Lady Seton? And so early?'

'Some of those nobles I'd not like as partners so I've escaped for a while.'

He sat down beside me. 'Scotland must seem barbaric after France. But we have our own compensations. The land is so magnificently contrived, as though God were in giant-mood when He made it so high of hills and tumultuous of seas. Brutal, aye. But I prefer it to the daintiness of France and Italy.'

'Even in winter?' I asked, for already I felt the chill of it and always wore a shawl.

'You'll adjust,' he said. 'And if you begin the day with hot buttered porridge by your hearth, the warmth is sealed in. Ask your physician Gurion if this isn't so – besides, your bones are young, Madam.'

I could not mistake the caress in his voice. It was no fantasy of mine that his eyes were soft. I thought of his support of Queen Mary de Guise during her terrible, final months, and now I understood the presence of that superb ring on his finger. What strength she must have summoned from him I could only imagine.

'I'm stupidly young,' I said, as if in confession. 'And one of my sins is suspicion.'

'Of whom?' he asked.

I burst out, 'James. Lord James. I think he permitted the Mass – rather, defended it – to ensure Her Majesty's trust in him. Yet he's a heretic.'

'Perhaps she will convert him,' he said. 'Such fascination as she has may work a miracle. Master Knox has slandered her as "an enchantress" but it seems to me that, like her mother, she enchants sweetly.'

'With ordinary men, yes – because, in their various ways, they fall in love. But not Knox. He sees her as diabolic; he is imprisoned in prejudice.'

90

'Aye.' In the semi-darkness I could not see his face but I thought he was smiling, for he sounded amused. 'He has forbidden the ladies of Edinburgh to wear trains – "Satan's tails", he calls them. Eye and lip paint are abominations before God, says he, but I've never seen him with a clean beard or nails. These are minor matters. His principal fault, to my mind, is that he is not known to go among the poor, the sick, as the humblest friar would do. A shepherd up there on the hills is more tender to his flock.'

'Whom does he tend, then?'

'The wealthy, the ladies who wear tails, who flirt with the new faith as they do their new lovers. As to the poor, he creates a fine exhibition of rhetoric to draw them to kirk. To be frightened with visions of hellfire is more exciting than to sit beside a cold hearth and contemplate their own dreary lives.'

'Do you think him sincere, Father?'

'Utterly. So perhaps was Attila the Hun. But sincerity is not a measure of goodness.'

'Do you think him deranged?'

'Unfortunately – no.'

Father Joseph came out then, followed by his taper-bearer, for now it was entirely dark except for the distant cressets. He paused to greet us, then Father Adam joined him and they left me with their blessings.

I had no heart to rejoin the dancers. For I had come out of my fantasy. No moonlight duped me tonight. I was in love with this man. And worse, instead of fighting the fact, I thought, 'So be it, my vow of chastity shall obtain.' Putting on a smile, I climbed up to the Great Hall to attend Her Majesty.

The next afternoon, on a day of cascading rain, Her Majesty shut herself into a small library on the ground floor. She was writing to Elizabeth in her own hand, and, as she told me, sorely puzzled as how to thank her for safe-conduct deliberately withheld. 'But Lethington advises sweetness and innocent certainty that someone must have bungled. . . . Oh Lord, how I detest this continual intrigue.'

So she was taking Lethington's advice; though I scarcely

knew him, I would trust it more than that of her brother. But my preoccupation was with Father Adam and, in my little oratory, my prayers were that I might be purged of this. The rain beat drearily on the casement. I extinguished the candles and moved restlessly about my chamber. Then a page announced Lord Bothwell.

I tidied my face and received him, explaining that Her Majesty was occupied, rather flattered that he had chosen to come to me. But as he sat down, flinging off his rain-soaked leatherjack and bonnet, he said, 'We have found the missing ship, and most of the animals are safe. But a little dog of yours, collared with your name, is dead.'

'A poodle?'

He nodded. 'I'm sorry, my lady.'

Determined not to cry I said, 'I'll mourn her, my Lord. Where did you find the ship?'

'Anchored off Cumberland, seized by the English on excuse of improper passport. It's being unloaded at Leith Landing. The horses and hunting dogs are lively enough, and the falcons recovering. So the Queen should hunt with pleasure.'

He sounded as if he spoke of a child's amusement, almost with boredom, perhaps because for years he had hunted men. I said, 'You don't care for the chase, my Lord?'

'Oh aye. There's fine sport here in the park, and your brother hopes to welcome Her Majesty for stag-hunting at Seton. He sends you his affectionate regards. . . . Will Her Majesty be long?'

I sent a page to push a note under the door. She must have welcomed interruption, for she summoned Bothwell immediately. I stood at my window wondering if I might ask to go to Seton when the weather cleared. A week or two away from Father Adam might cure me of what could only be infatuation. But when Her Majesty came up in the late afternoon, happy about the ship, she put an end to that hope by saying, 'You Marys are such comfort to me – and who but you can do my hair?'

That night she asked a few of us to sup with her in the tiny room next to her bedchamber. On her right sat Bothwell, on her left Lethington; I was placed next to James who headed

92

the opposite end of the table. It was cramped; and the servants had difficulty placing dishes handed them from the narrow private staircase. It was not a merry party; James glared at Bothwell who appeared to ignore him, and Lethington was virtually silent.

Towards the end of dinner Her Majesty said, 'I've made my decision as to a Privy Council. You, Lord James, shall be my chief adviser.'

Jesu! I thought. So she did trust him. He bowed from his chair almost condescendingly, as though she had offered him an apple. Lethington, said she, was to be Secretary of State, and Bothwell her military expert. 'I shall appoint others later,' she said. 'You three are the nucleus and I expect not only a patching of quarrels but close and kindly co-operation.'

Now they bowed to one another, unsmiling. They pledged her, and their mutual aims, in goblets of malmsey. She rose and said, 'We leave you to talk,' and Chastelard and we Marys trailed after her into the audience chamber where other courtiers joined us for music and ballad peddlars. Ambassador Randolph sat with her in discussion. Fleming, avoiding Lord Morton as most ladies did, drew me on to a window-seat and said, 'He is married!'

'Who?' I asked.

'Lethington.'

'But should you care? A man of his years wouldn't suit you.'

'I've seen him look thirty-five or less, depending on his mood. Ah, but he is so elegant! I think Lethington will make a superb Secretary of State, heretic as he is; perhaps because he is, as cunning as Queen Elizabeth's Cecil.'

Amused, I asked how she knew that. She had, of course, been informed by Brantôme. And then she said, 'Have you met Father Adam Black? Now *there* is a man so handsome and lovable I marvel he has sustained life without some lady's defrocking.'

French priests often had their mistresses and we were accustomed to scandal, winked at by the Cardinal but frowned upon by our Queen. She had no patience with the lasciviousness of the clergy. 'Father Adam – yes, I have met him. I'm

93

sure no woman could tempt him. I think him totally bound by his vows.'

'And Lethington to his wife?'

'How should I know that?' I asked. 'We haven't met her. She's not here at court. Are you being silly?'

She smiled. 'Only wistful. God, here is Morton to pester us.'

But our duty was to be pleasant, and we suffered his foul breath and clumsy compliments. To accelerate our boredom fat-bellied Huntly joined him. He was called 'Cock o' the North', uncouth as his food-stained plaid, but Her Majesty valued him and his Highland clan as loyal Catholics. Even so, I soon became so weary of his attentions that I whispered to Fleming that we should go to our apartments.

'You go,' she said, 'and I'll make your excuses to Her Majesty.'

'And wait for Lethington,' I said, teasing.

'An amusement,' she said, but I thought that she lied. I left the room by the stairs that led to our apartments. I doubted that anyone would miss me. To Morton and Huntly I was only young flesh close to the Queen. Isobel undressed me and pulled the bed-hangings but it was hours before I slept. I could not delay confession, and what could I tell Father Joseph? Only God knew the depth of what I felt.

Her Majesty had had a small chapel restored in the abbey. There were guards at the gate for fear of pillage; but all was serene except my own thoughts.

It was not precisely that I lied to Father Joseph, but I did not tell him the whole truth. I told him that I loved a man who must remain celibate, and that my love was carnal. He told me that if I tried to tempt this man I would be in mortal sin; and as it was he gave me penances. Then I confessed my mistrust of James, which was amounting to hatred, and he asked if it might not be jealousy, which had not occurred to me. He said that the Queen's favour was no small thing to merit, that I must be aware of my ignorance of state matters, and humble, and clean of suspicion. But I left the chapel as depressed as I entered it, whereas usually I had felt relief, even happiness.

94

Brantôme wanted to explore Edinburgh with Gervais, who was curious as to what herbs might be sold in the Grassmarket, and they asked me to ride with them; but I was too depressed. Instead, I put on sturdy leather shoes and walked into the wild thickets of the park, my guard following. Hares scuttered from my path, I glimpsed deer and smelled the beginning of autumn. If I climbed part of the way up the slope towards Arthur's Seat I might tire myself into some peace of mind, but I did not have the energy. I turned back to the palace, walked past the rain-swollen moat, lingered for a few minutes on my bench in the inner courtyard. He might look out and see me.

Jackdaws quarrelled high in the turret towers. Above the thrust of the crags thunder clouds formed. Yet I remained there as the first raindrops fell.

I tried to fix my mind on that night's ball-gown, for Her Majesty was entertaining again – lairds from the Islands, the Highlands, the Borders. I would wear sapphire brocade. I would dance as high and handsomely as Livvy, with peacock feathers in my hair. And if he chanced to be there, watching, I would wave in the whirl of the dance and flirt through the night with anyone who cared to.

'God,' I said, 'I promise. Aye, even Morton.'

Fortunately, Morton did not appear, sending word to Her Majesty that his good friend Ruthven was ill of a mouth-bleed. She bade Gurion attend the invalid, whom she supposed to have the coughing sickness, so thin he was. But the masque was splendid, many in costume, and Livvy, robed as Cleopatra wildly applauded for her dancing. The Great Hall had been decorated with golden branches and gilded wheat. The buffet table had been made attractive with potato-plant vines and I thought that, if Her Majesty was forced to enter some ante-room of hell, she would make it beautiful.

During a lull in the dancing Brantôme gave us the tavern talk of Edinburgh – which was that Her Majesty had turned Holyrood into a brothel and that, according to Knox, no sin was unknown here. 'He says all the priests have their harlots.'

'And do the people believe this nonsense?' I asked.

95

'Yes, most do. He must be a most persuasive preacher. Gervais suggested we join the vast congregation at St Giles to hear him declaim, but I said I'd not want to dirty my mind with such drivel. And he continues to call the Queen an enchantress.'

'She is,' I said, noticing Lindsay's lovesick smirk as he brought her wine. 'She's winning over her rebels, one by one. Charm is an enchantment.'

He said, 'Do you know her marriage intentions?'

I shook my head. 'All I know is that when she received foreign emissaries one morning she said, "If only I could enter a convent and be done with men forever." Yet she feels that it is her duty to marry and have heirs. I suppose Lethington will negotiate as Cupid.'

He laughed. 'And drive a shrewd bargain.'

Her Majesty came up to us and said, 'Seton, my love, I've decided that I shall release you Marys, one by one, for holidays with your families. Fleming shall go first – next week.'

Did she want to get her away from Lethington? If so, that was wise.

'Then Beaton, Livvy – and finally, yourself. I hope you don't mind the delay?'

Her hair, of course. 'No, Madam. I value my brother but I don't find him wildly exciting, and I scarcely remember my mother. She might be a dragon.'

She giggled and kissed my cheek. 'If she is, I'll send Bothwell and all his Borderers to rescue you. Seigneur de Brantôme will write an epic of your escape. . . .'

As she spoke I saw Father Adam at the table with Father Joseph and my heart did that terrible lurch. I was glad – and uneasy – when she took Brantôme as dancing partner so that I was free to go over on the excuse of a wine cup. As the servant poured it Father Adam said, 'Good evening, Lady Seton.'

'Good evening, Father.'

'You are not in costume?'

'I'm not much of an actress,' I said. 'I wouldn't know what role to take.'

'Elaine, the Lily Maid,' he said. 'The court of Camelot was

96

said to be here, you know. Why else is our high hill named Arthur's Seat?'

'His fort was there – supposedly,' Father Joseph said.

I was puzzled by Father Adam's remark. The legends of Elaine are numerous – and she was supposed to have been in love with Sir Lancelot. I imagined he referred to a troubadour's song of the last century in which the lady died spotlessly in a mild passion for the knight, a most confusing allegory. 'Sometimes', I said, 'I find this old place eerie. It's a feeling of being watched by an unseen presence.'

'Ah yes,' said Father Adam. 'I know. I feel it always in the abbey. But the presence is benign, my lady.'

I wanted to say something clever, to hold his attention; but I had no words. Then Father Joseph moved away to talk with Lord Huntly and I thought: Surely he doesn't suspect that this is the celibate gentleman I adore or he'd not leave my side.

'I think it will be an early autumn,' I said. All stupid people depend on the weather for conversation. 'The holly berries have set.'

'And the rowan is reddening.'

I wondered if he, too, was suddenly shy. But surely not because I attracted him? Yet it did seem to me that his eyes held a special tenderness. I said hastily, 'Master Knox will have something to say about this masque; it must be *dreadful* to have to be Protestant!'

He laughed. 'He even saw direful omens when Her Majesty arrived – such a haar, he said, was prescient of doom. He snatches at anything. Yet he calls *us* superstitious.'

We talked then of superstition and I thought that there could be no harm in enjoying his company and I doubted I could tempt him if I tried. I had no such talent at beguilement as Fleming or Beaton.

'Lady Seton.' James was at my side. 'May we dance?'

In a way it was a command. 'Thank you, my Lord.'

I hated him for interrupting. And the pesky man was putting a penance on me because I would have to confess to Father Joseph the resentment I felt.

Next day I discussed with Her Majesty whether half-truths were not akin to lying to one's priest and she thought so.

'Surely our gentle Father Joseph doesn't frighten you?' she asked.

'No, Madam; but my sins do.'

'Shed them, then, by sharing. And I'm sure you don't have any sin on your soul comparable to mine. It's a struggle to control my bitterness and anger at the slanders Master Knox fastens to us. I must meet him again and try to patch matters, but I dread it. I procrastinate. . . .'

So did I, with one excuse or another, neglect the chapel. It took several more days to bring myself to the point of confronting my conscience head on. Finally, one rainy afternoon, I put on a heavy cloak and sent word to Father Joseph that I would meet him about five.

Work had been done on the chapel and the screen between us had been scrolled and gilded. In the deep shadows I said, 'Father, I have sinned in omission of the facts. The celibate gentleman I have mentioned, whom I love, is a holy man, a priest.' I closed my eyes and plunged on. 'He is Father Adam, and though I have not tried to tempt him in a wanton way it's only because I know I'd fail. What I ask of you is, since I take such joy in talking with him, must I avoid him? Is friendship possible?'

There was such a long silence that I wondered if disgust had choked his words. Rain hammered the roof and lightning brightened for a moment an onyx image of the Virgin.

'Yes,' he said. 'Friendship only.'

How strange his voice, like a lute string broken. He said, 'Did you not receive word that Father Joseph is on pilgrimage to Melrose Abbey?'

'*Oh!*'

'I am Father Adam.'

I suppose he could have tricked me to spare me humiliation, for both priests spoke Scots at confession, by the Queen's command. I realised it was as difficult a situation for him as for me, but I doubted whether his embarrassment achieved even a hundredth part of mine.

'Have you more to say?' he asked.

'No.' I had forgotten all about James. I wanted to run from there and hide.

'This man', he said, 'whom you think you love would not merit such devotion; he has nothing to offer but his humble friendship. And you are very young and perhaps prone to loneliness here in a strange country.'

'And suspicious of matters beyond my ken.'

So finally I spoke of James and was glad of penances, but Adam gave me none for the sin of loving him. Perhaps he felt that he had in some way encouraged me. I was relieved to slip out into the wind and the rain, and creep into the palace and weep into my pillow.

I had thought Adam would avoid me but, to my surprise, he seemed to seek me out on the cloistered walk or in the gardens. Very likely he felt sorry for me and in a way responsible. He in no way flirted, the offer of friendship was genuine. We talked of all sorts of things – how the abbey had been founded on a miracle; the dearth of wood in Scotland since the time of James IV, who had felled millions of trees for his great fleet so that most people resorted to turf-fires. He said he was grateful that thus far the autumn was mild so that we, the 'French', could gradually adjust to the climate. We talked of cooking and poetry and the lost art of illuminating holy books.

And I was content, perhaps because I am not truly a sensual person. I did not suffer for lack of his arms, his lips. I thought that perhaps this was the relationship Her Majesty had had with her husband. Perhaps she dreaded the possibility of another kind of marriage.

Yet in November she received Sieur de Moretta, ambassador of the Duke of Ferrara, who was offering marriage. Moretta brought a great retinue so that some of our Scots were lodged, temporarily, in the Canongate. These Italians all spoke French and were good company, and several were talented musicians, which pleased Her Majesty far more than the portrait of the Duke. But she said she would prefer him to Lord Arran.

'Naturally, Madam!' I said as I powdered her hair with gold for the night's ball. 'How could you marry a babbling idiot?'

'Lethington has heard from Queen Elizabeth. She urges my

marriage to Arran. But – this is in confidence, Seton – we are negotiating for Don Carlos.'

Another idiot! I was aghast. But she said, 'Such wealth and power. . . . Catholic protection for Scotland. . . . A block for ever to Queen Elizabeth's and Queen Catherine's ambitions. I think it is my duty if King Philip will agree.'

I nodded, wordless, brushing the gold powder from her golden ruff. I was so immensely sorry for her. Perhaps she knew, for she said, 'This, as yet, is only Lethington's aspiration and Philip is known to take years to make up his mind. Meanwhile, we are free to enjoy what we have. Now, see to your own hair and tonight, if you can, bring some cheer to Chastelard. I've never seen him sulky before.'

So at the ball I coaxed Chastelard into dancing the Canary and prattled about how ugly the Duke's portrait was, so that he seemed rather happier. Towards the end of the entertainment Ambassador Moretta asked to present a special singer from Piedmont and requested silence.

I had never heard a man's voice comparable. It was very deep. I could scarcely credit such a big voice in such a small person. His shoulders were hunched and his short legs seemed like frail sticks. What's more, his chest was not deep. But the huge black eyes blazed as he sang two love songs to his lute. Even Lord Morton was awed.

The Italian bowed to the applause, but humbly. Musicians are not honoured as artists are; ours washed windows and tended fires and sometimes assisted in the kitchen. But now Her Majesty bowed to him from her dais and whispered to me, 'I hope he's a treasure I may wrest from the Duke,' and ordered me to come with her to praise his performance. We crossed the Great Hall to where he stood, the yellow-ribboned lute in his hand.

He was swarthy, thick-lipped, his eyes as magnificent as his voice. He replied to her compliments in French, then in Scots. For a few moments they discussed music and he was witty, cynical, but with a playful grace of expression. She must have been as startled as I that a singer was intelligent, even erudite.

'If only you could remain here,' she said, 'I'd welcome you to court with all my heart. I've a quartet, but no bass, no soloist. Do you think the Duke would release you?'

He said, with mischief, 'Don't you want music in Italy?'

'No!' she said. 'I shan't marry him – but don't tell Moretta.'

He chuckled. 'Ambassador Moretta doesn't welcome my confidences, Madam. I'm only a servant.'

'But you'd be honoured here, I could promise you a happy life, Signor. . . ?'

'Rizzio,' he said. 'David Rizzio.'

CHAPTER VI

We were about to leave the Great Hall when Erskine, the Captain of the Guard, reported that Arran and his father the Duke had left their banishment at Dumbarton and were on the way with ten thousand men to abduct Her Majesty and murder James. Her Majesty, quite calmly, ordered the palace to full defence. Men were summoned from Edinburgh Castle, the town watch aroused and every precaution taken because Holyrood, in its flat meadows, was so vulnerable. The priests came in to comfort frightened ladies while James and Lethington played chess and our Queen passed the small hours in a game of Primero with Brantôme and Chastelard. I wished that I had her poise.

Fleming was with her family but the other Marys displayed the same nonchalance as Her Majesty, and I imitated them; but Father Adam must have sensed my terror, for he said, 'Come, Lady Seton – sit and have wine with me. I think this alarm is a hoax.'

I sat in a far corner with him and I drank and I listened. 'I've been talking with Seigneur de Brantôme who knows every rumour. I myself have heard them, but I believe the fact is that Lords Arran and Bothwell are enemies and that Lord Arran seeks to discredit Bothwell in some insane kidnap plot.'

'But Bothwell isn't here! I think he holds Justice Court on the Borders.'

'No matter,' he said. 'If Arran intended attack, he would have arrived. It's nearly dawn. I suggest you retire.'

'But I can't until Her Majesty does.'

This gave me an excuse to continue our talk. I was no longer frightened; I knew Arran to be demented and I knew

102

Bothwell to be loyal, at least thus far. 'It's all so confusing,' I said. 'Bothwell has turned Protestant but has scant respect for Knox or he'd attend kirk; Lindsay loathes the Mass but now fawns at Her Majesty's heels like a cur. Huntly considers himself King of the Highlands but grovels to her. Morton – now there is the one sound villain – if you wish a consistent one. He can be depended on to annoy and irritate and disgust us ladies.'

'He's in the courtyard with the guard, armed for battle.'

'You see? One can't even depend on *his* black heart. Oh Lord, how they change colour to ambition or mood or brief friendship with one another. Like a rabble of small boys who swear allegiance to a leader one day and boot him out next day in favour of a bigger lad.'

'They lust for power,' he said. 'They try to reach it subtly, in intricate ways. I'm thankful that my nature was never competitive. Nor have I ever cared for riches, else Queen Mary de Guise would have helped me to a bishop's eminence where I'd have felt a great chasm between the people and myself.'

'Do you confess humble folk?' I asked.

'Of course!' He seemed astonished. 'Anyone who cares to come to me. I'm not confined to royalty or nobility – I have also the brewery, the buttery, the kail-wives of the gardens – and midden-cleansers. I should dislike to be apart from any human being in need.'

Her Majesty rose and said, 'I see no reason to keep this tiresome vigil. Go to your beds.'

So we dispersed. There was no attack on the palace, though my brother had heard it rumoured, for he rode in while I was still abed. When I had dressed to receive him he said, 'Arran is a fool, but fools can be dangerous. Thus far his father has been able to control him. . . . Now, I am to report the state of your health to your mother.'

'Tell her I am well.' I made polite inquiries about her lady-ship, and he said she was busy supervising the salting down of meats and fish for the winter; that she fretted about my being cold and catching the New Acquaintance, so she had sent me a coverlid for my bed. I unwrapped an incredibly hideous

103

deerskin spread lined with squirrel; but I managed to praise it, and wrote her a little note and enclosed in it, tied with ribbon, a gold chain of fleurs-de-lis and pearls. Possibly she possessed more jewels than I, but the gesture was important.

'She wishes you to marry well,' he said, 'and she orders you to consult her even before you ask the Queen's permission.'

'I would do that', I said, 'if I'd not taken the vow of chastity.'

'But you are nineteen next month and, as I'd heard, Her Majesty never took the vow seriously; nor can we.'

'The other Marys vowed to her, but I took oath before the Cardinal, so I'm not exempt.'

He smiled. 'Such vows, especially when made in childhood, can be annulled, and His Eminence is sophisticated. At thirteen you didn't know your own mind.'

But I did now. Adam would be my love throughout my life – unconsummated but constant – and it seemed to me that God had foreseen this when He led me to the Cardinal's chapel at St Germain. But I could not argue with my brother because I did not want to distress the family. In time they would accept me as I was.

I sent for refreshment and then he left me, warning me to dress warmly as he hoped the Queen would.

That night I awakened in almost leaden cold. In the light of dying embers I found that coverlid which I had planned to give away and cuddled into it gratefully. From then on it was to be a battle with winter for us all.

The cold was so intense that we were no longer critical of the small rooms because they held the heat of the fireplaces. It was the moisture from the Firth of Forth and the Dutch ocean that was so penetrating, and only on special evenings did we wear our satins and velvets. Beautiful plaids of wool woven by the monks of Newbattle were fashioned into gowns, doublets, cloaks. Our furs were now a necessity.

Her Majesty was still subject to a pain in her side and dizziness. Gervais tended her anxiously with brews of hot milk and honey or Lambswool – hot ale poured over roasted apple pulp. So she escaped colds, and so did we.

104

James courted her with gifts – the most amusing of which was a blackamoor, a young fool named by us 'La Petite Chatte', for she was as full of mischief as a kitten, and as graceful. She could turn cartwheels the length of the Great Hall and back. She could sing in a strange language that made us laugh though we understood not a word of it. She mimicked everything (including a boar-hunt tapestry) and everyone else except the nobility – at least, not to our faces. She had a small, exquisite body like an ebony figurine but when the cold fastened its grip she dressed like a bear in the daytime. For evening she wore the fluffy white rabbit-skins Her Majesty presented. Wherever she ventured in the palace, laughter trailed after her. The only words of our language she cared to learn were, 'please', 'thank you', and 'dance or sing?'

Fleming returned before Christmas and we Marys designed Petite Chatte a warm, holly-red gown with a kirtle beneath that spread like a green fir-tree and a headdress of mistletoe that made her at once absurd and enchanting. I supposed some gentlemen would try to steal kisses from her, but she was rarely still for a moment. And on Christmas Eve she and Rizzio provided our best entertainment in their different ways. He had permission to remain with us, while Ambassador Moretta travelled to Savoy without a bride for his master.

That night, the Great Hall garlanded with greens and holly, our Yule celebration began blithely – all the servants, even the humblest, honoured. Her Majesty danced with her chefs, with her stablemen, with any who asked her, and so did we; and Lord James and other noblemen capered with washer-maids and scullery wenches in great good humour. Our priests sat by, chuckling, and the huge Yule log blazed in one fire-place, while at the opposite end an ox roasted in the other.

Only Chastelard was dour. He would reason that he was, by birth, far in rank above a woodcutter, and yet the Queen seemed to enjoy dancing with that clod. Later she stopped the revel and said, 'I order all men to arms. There is a brawl on the High Street between Lords Arran and Bothwell and it must be stopped. . . .'

So the ball ended. The palace guard, led by James and others, left us. I had assumed it to be a duel, but no –

Brantôme returned an hour later to say that eight hundred men were involved. We women and priests and lower servants ate roasted oxen, but Christmas Eve was spoiled and even Petite Chatte could not make us laugh.

At two in the morning we learned that our forces had prevailed; but Her Majesty was very angry. That day she had her herald proclaim from the Market Cross the banishment of Arran and Bothwell to their estates, not to return to court until after Twelfth Night. She would not have personal enmity destroy her peace, even if the peace of Christ's birthday meant nothing to these two. She was particularly annoyed with Bothwell; Arran was merely a fool.

She raged for hours. I realised that she now considered James to be a sort of saviour. Perhaps she was right. In any case, that evening she told us Marys that she had consented to his marriage to Lady Agnes Keith, a dull, pretty woman. She planned a February wedding.

'He tells me that he has long loved Lady Agnes,' she said.

But my instinct told me that James could love no one but himself.

The snows were heavy; we could not hunt for more than a week, but we built snow forts and threw snowballs at each other – James looking on with amused condescension. On the first mild day there was superb hawking, and later that week Her Majesty rode into Edinburgh. The crowds clustered about her with cheers and blew kisses. Perhaps they suddenly realised that this beautiful young lady was not the wicked sorceress Knox implied – serene on her white palfrey, smiling, gracious, and not averse to a hand patting her boot. On our return, when we all dismounted at the stables of Horse Close, she was radiant. Playfully she took Erskine's sword and touched a wall and said, 'I dub thee White Horse Close to honour my palfreys.' She sang on the way into the palace.

That day she created David Rizzio a *valet de chambre*, and it was he who brought wood and turf while we Marys sat in her audience chamber and discussed how the attitude of her Protestant subjects had come to change so radically. 'What is your opinion, Signor Rizzio?' she asked.

106

He paused, setting down the wood basket. 'I think perhaps, Madam, they have had their hellfire excitement in Master Knox. There is scant glamour in their lives, but they see it in you.' He went on, 'They are warming, gradually, as children to a stranger.'

Chastelard, who had been invited to join us for wine, came in then. Rizzio bowed deeply. Her Majesty asked Chastelard to be seated by the fire, for he persisted in wearing damasks and satins. A page brought champagne as Rizzio lit the tall, golden candelabra. Then they were dismissed.

'Signor Rizzio was telling us. . . .' As Her Majesty talked I could see jealousy plain on Chastelard's face. But she soon had him out of the sulks by the usual practice of praising his poems and saying one should be set to music.

'Why,' she said, 'and who can do that better than Signor Rizzio? For the lute?'

He managed a smile.

'Seek him out then, Pierre, so that he may compose the melody and sing it for us at the next revel.'

Later I thought, how could any man be jealous of the goblin-like valet?

But as the weeks passed it was obvious that other men *were* jealous of Rizzio's sudden rise to favour. The Queen and he were often closeted, talking politics. She said he had read and studied Machiavelli, was as clever as Lethington but with the distinction of being objectively Catholic. Lethington's ambition was an alliance with England, which Rizzio conceded as essential, but he also wanted firmer ties with France and Spain.

Fleming said to me, 'My Lord Lethington is in bad humour these days.'

'Laird,' I corrected, though he was indeed more lordly than Morton or Huntly.

'Well, he's said nothing to me, of course, but I think he mistrusts David Rizzio.'

Very likely. For Her Majesty was now calling him 'Davie' in public. At Lord James's wedding reception Adam remarked, 'Davie is an oddly Scots name for an Italian.' Here was no jealousy, for I knew that he liked Rizzio, and he certainly was not power-mad. 'It sounds – strange.'

Yes – intimate. He was Rizzio's confessor and I could not help but wonder. . . .

'I hope he's not in love with her,' I said.

'I think not – he is too sensible.'

But how sensible was Her Majesty to put him in disfavour with the Lords? Adam bowed and left me; I rejoined the dancers and drank a false toast to the health of the bridegroom.

Master Knox patched a truce between Arran and Bothwell and the Queen laughed at their childishness and allowed them to return to court. But she was restless, anxious to see more of her country, and decided to visit her castle of Falkland with James and his wife and Lethington. She invited Beaton, perhaps to remove her from the affianced Ogilvie of Boyne, and Livvy. Fleming, who now pretended disinterest in Lethington, went also. I remained at Holyrood to attend Her Majesty's jewels, wishing that she had not needed Adam to attend her soul.

Rizzio also remained at Holyrood, and I think this relieved the resident Lords who, if cool, were polite to him. He now served as my *valet de chambre*, but in his free time he composed ballads and conferred with Chastelard – they wanted to please Her Majesty on her return from Falkland. Many of her courtiers, including Brantôme, had now returned to France, so the palace was more comfortable for the Scots. The Master of the Household ordered a vast spring cleaning. Old rushes were burned and new ones gathered with evergreens. Arrases were taken outside and beaten in the sun – the wan sun of March, but with clean, high winds.

I was afraid of the wind. I always had Isobel with me, as if she was an insurance against a collapse of spires. In my own apartment I was grateful for Rizzio's presence, often delaying his tasks to talk. I found him increasingly charming – quietly wise, often amusing. He never gossiped as Brantôme had done, but he knew wonderful stories, and I listened to him like an enthralled child. Because the Queen now asked him to sit down, so did I, and we sometimes played at dice or chess, eating spiced figs, drinking mulled wine; or perhaps he would sing for me.

When he sang love songs I thought of Adam. But I did not fantasise, I was well beyond that. Friendship was deeper, I thought, less transient than romance. In France I had learned of the fragility of marriage, when most men and women took lovers. When one is tied legally, the strings tend to snap. Had Madame Diane married King Henry, I doubt their love would have survived a year.

I mentioned this to Rizzio. 'Am I cynical?'

'I think cynicism healthy, Lady Seton. But as to romance – miracles do happen even in marriage.'

'Would you approve of Her Majesty's marriage to Don Carlos if ever Lethington can effect it?'

My God, I had blurted out a secret and I was appalled. But he said, 'It's a venture close to her heart – or ambition. And union with Spain would solve all of her problems.'

'But heirs? Would they be normal? He is a lunatic.'

He shrugged. 'Who knows? They would rule.'

We had many talks and my admiration for him grew but I was careful that the Lords did not suspect us of being friends. And I hoped they did not know that Her Majesty sent a courier each week with messages for Rizzio. He did not discuss them with me except to say that Falkland provided good hunting – until one night early in April he came to tell me that James had had Arran and Bothwell imprisoned in Edinburgh Castle.

It seemed that Arran had written a letter confessing a plot, implicating Bothwell. They were to have killed Lethington and James and – seizing power – imprisoned Her Majesty in the fortress of Dumbarton. Bothwell had come to Falkland to explain that he had had no part in this and that Arran was clearly insane. Arran was brought to the castle under guard, whimpering and incoherent. But while Her Majesty supped James ordered them both to the dungeons, refusing Bothwell trial.

I asked, 'Do you mean that James defied Her Majesty?'

'Yes, but cleverly. He said that if Bothwell were aquitted, by Scots law Arran must be executed – and that must not

109

happen to one in line to the throne. She was not consulted, for she wants Bothwell free.'

'But that is treason!' I said. 'She can have James's head for treason.'

'Poor lady,' he said gently, 'if she's to save Bothwell she must move cautiously lest he be murdered in his cell. In my small way I advised the courier of this, that she must appear to forgive Lord James or else Bothwell falls to his vengeance.'

Her Majesty returned to Holyrood House looking ill. She showed me a great, pear-shaped diamond ring Elizabeth had sent her with a note: 'Should Your Majesty ever be in any extremity you have only to return this diamond as token and I will come to your assistance.' She had again suggested Arran as husband for 'her dear sister'.

Her Majesty had taken wigs for hunting and so her hair had only needed washing. I tried to cheer her with elaborate arrangements but she was interested only in neatness. I think she was deep into her first disillusion – with James, to whom she was carefully polite – with Lethington, who had stood by to allow outrage – and now with Lord Huntly, who had left court to proclaim himself King of the Highlands in monstrous defiance of her rule. Because he was Catholic, this hurt her the more.

But she remembered the May-dew bath and sank her face into the wild grass at dawn, shivering in her shift as we did. She tried to cheer herself with singing lessons from Rizzio, and she read Latin with Master James Buchanan, a famous scholar. But she seemed to have little heart for frolicking; and one night alone with me she said, 'To think of Bothwell imprisoned – an eagle of a man – my mother's words are etched on my brain: "Trust him beyond any."'

She was so forlorn. I said, 'Madam, eagles are made to soar. He's sure to escape.'

'Scant chance of that, my dove. And now I need him, for Lord Huntly's defiance could lead to a clash and my brother is not' – here she paused – 'not a soldier. I would make a tour of my Highland lands but most evidently Lord Huntly considers them his, and the Gordons are not prone to diplomacy.'

'Then would it be dangerous to go north, Madam?'

Bitterly she said, 'I *am* Queen; I'll travel where I please.'

'And may I go with you?'

'No,' she said. 'I shan't subject my ladies to a rough adventure. Janet will suffice me.'

We began within that week preparations that were for possible war, though nothing was said of it. In the Great Hall armour was polished and guns cleaned and arrows mended. Her Majesty's wardrobe was extended by plumed steel helmets, cutting-scarves to protect her throat, masks to shield her face from dust and wind. Most of her gowns and cloaks were of plaid wool, for the north was said to be cold even in midsummer. We packed only a few royal robes and jewels.

I had thought she might take Adam for her consolation but she did not. Lethington retired to his estates to tend his wife, who was ill. Beaton and Livvy travelled to their families. The Queen left Holyrood, riding with James, and an army of two thousand met them in Edinburgh. That night I followed her with my prayers.

I was nearly certain that Fleming was in love with Lethington because her interest in his wife's illness was intense. We had not met the lady and she was forever speculating as to why. But then, many of the Lords visited court without their families. Holyrood did not have room for non-essential courtiers. Nevertheless, Fleming wondered if he were not ashamed of her for some reason, and I had to smile at her transparency.

Despite my worry that Her Majesty might have to engage in battle, the weeks passed pleasantly for me, for I played golf with Chastelard at Leith Sands, tennis with Rizzio, and we picnicked on the heights of Arthur's Seat and the Salisbury Crags. In the evenings I played chess with Adam who wickedly often allowed me to win; or, with Father Joseph, we played the game of Lamb and Fox. I always thought of James as the fox, and struggled the harder to destroy him. I wondered if he were leading Her Majesty into a Highland trap.

But a courier brought news to Rizzio that she was faring well, gaining men to her army in her progress through Perth

111

and Aberdeenshire; nor did she complain about sleeping in wind-blustered tents, of rain and fog in the mountains, of eternal fog on moors along the coast. 'The people love her,' Rizzio said. 'They are strongly Catholic.'

On 29 August Captain the Lord Erskine galloped in from Edinburgh with astonishing news. 'Lord Bothwell has escaped. This morning, between two and four, guards found his window bars broken in the tower cell.'

'Jesu!' I said. 'But how on earth did he manage it?'

'He climbed down Castle Rock – there was a length of rope found below.' He shook his head, marvelling. 'That terrible height, in the wind – I'd not have risked it for my immortal soul.'

All of us except the Lords were jubilant, and a message was sent to the Queen in Inverness-shire. I laughed to think of James's fury. Rizzio hoped that Bothwell had left the country lest James send secret agents after him.

'As to secret agents,' Rizzio said when we were alone in my chamber, 'Father Adam has done the crown great service.'

'What?' I said.

'He served Queen Mary de Guise in that capacity, under the name of John Noir—'

'But I thought he was her confessor.'

'In secret, Lady Seton.'

So my admiration for Adam became a sort of hero-worship, though of course I never mentioned my knowledge to him. We were often together but I am certain that the innocence of our friendship was obvious. In France, where priests were so often worldly, there might have been gossip, but in Scotland, if they did not respect his religion, they believed in a priest's celibacy.

Yet I felt that, because of his acute intuition, Rizzio knew of my love for Adam. This may have been because I felt compelled to talk of him as women must when they are moonstruck. I would repeat what he had said – mere trifles, interesting perhaps only to me – and Rizzio would listen with those deep black eyes full of what seemed to be sympathy; and again I wondered if, in loving the Queen, he shared my frustration.

112

We had a simple celebration of All Hallows' Eve – bonfires, turnip lanterns grinning in the Great Hall. I acted as hostess to the Lords at supper. They behaved reasonably well, thank heaven. Petite Chatte, dressed as a witch, cackled appropriately and carried a reluctant black cat on her shoulder which at least had the grace to spit. Some young pages flitted about as ghosts, and Rizzio sang a fearsome ballad about the dead rising in churchyards. As the bells of St Giles struck midnight, Chatte screeched like an owl, which terrified poor Fleming. Ambassador Randolph, returned from England, was merrier than usual and I hoped that he brought happier news of Elizabeth. He had come to us while the roads were still passable, before the November storms.

When my taper-bearer saw me to my chamber it seemed to me that tonight the passage was as eerie as the abbey, but I discounted this as my imagination, fed on tales of ghouls and warlocks. As Isobel undressed me and brought another warming-pan to my bed I asked her to pull out the trundle-bed and sleep at the end of mine.

When I was abed she pulled the curtains and I heard her moving about, then the candles died and we were in darkness. A real owl hooted among the trees. A mating call? But I had heard that sometimes it is an announcement of prey – of murder.

Dinna fash yourself, lass, I said to myself in Scots. Superstition is no part of our faith, despite the accusations of Knox. If he had seen our bonfires tonight, assuredly he would have assumed that we worshipped the devil and had held an orgy in his honour.

I heard the click of beads from Isobel's bed. So she was praying. So should I, and I touched my cross, which always lay under my pillow when it was not chained to my belt. There seemed to be a musty smell about me, but that was the ancient, sad perfume of neglect and damp which no burning of juniper could dispel. If ghosts walked in this room, they could only be the kindly ones of the kings James IV and V, the gentle Queen Mary de Guise – and none had died here. Angry at my fancies I willed myself to sleep.

I heard the cock crow. In Edinburgh the town crier would

113

be ringing his bell: 'Five o'clock of a Thursday morning, and all is well.'

But I wondered if all was well with Her Majesty now that she was in Huntly's land; his clan Gordon were said to be savages. At noon I was relieved to have a message from my brother, who had joined her on the way. He spoke of her good health despite the many hardships suffered on the road. 'Were she not a lady I would call her a most gallant gentleman. She has won the hearts of Lord James's army.'

If ever James had thought it his, it seemed now securely hers. He could not hope to rival an enchantress. Nor could Knox. Chastelard reported talk from an Edinburgh tavern: 'A dour old man said there had been a revel of the black mass at Holyrood last night, but he was ridiculed as "daft". They agreed that our Queen, absent or not, would never permit the old, heathen rites. And they drank to her.'

And so I dressed and told myself that Isobel and I had shared childish terror, and thereafter she slept in her own quarters.

Murder is a red word and it did not leave my mind despite the good tidings. Since I had not deliberately sought it or morbidly reflected, it was no sin to confess to Father Joseph. Instead, I spoke of it to Adam. 'The word is a refrain in my mind and I detest it.'

'You took All Hallows too seriously,' he said, smiling. 'You were frightened, and your worry about the Queen combined to upset you. Substitute another word stronger than murder.'

'Safety,' I said.

'Love.'

He looked into my eyes for a moment and then turned away. We were in the garden and he caught a blown leaf in his hand. 'See?' he said, as if that browned leaf was a treasure.

'Yes.'

'An oak leaf.'

'Yes.'

'It is getting dark,' he said. 'I must go to chapel.'

Altar boys went past us with candles ready for lighting.

'Vespers,' he said, as though I did not know.

114

He looked into my eyes again, the leaf in his hand. He opened his mouth as if to speak, then closed it. The wind tossed my veil and tugged at his cowl. Tonight it would whine about the tower turrets. Sometimes it screamed like a madwoman.

I found my voice. 'I'll follow you,' I said, and in silence we took the cobbled path to the abbey.

Gradually news came to us of Her Majesty's victories in the Highlands. Lord Huntly was dead, one of his sons executed, another imprisoned. The Battle of Corrichie had all but destroyed the clan Gordon. Her Majesty wrote on a rain-spattered bit of paper, 'See that apartments are made ready for Lady Jean Gordon who is innocent of any treachery, and now fatherless. She shall serve as lady-in-waiting.'

This more than interested Beaton who, with Livvy, was at Holyrood for Christmas. She told us, in a burst, that she and Ogilvie of Boyne were in love and that he would seek to break his engagement to Lady Jean. 'He says she is immensely wealthy and to him it would have been a most profitable arrangement; but his love was never for her.'

'I doubt Her Majesty will approve a broken bond,' Fleming said. 'Besides, you scarcely know him.'

'As well as you know Lethington.'

They squabbled. I tried to tell them that a married man and one affianced should be considered out of question. Lady Jean, for all we knew, might be coming here to marry Ogilvie with the Queen's blessing. That Lethington's wife was ill did not mean that he would become a widower. Fleming turned on me and said, 'Oh, *you*. You've no idea what love is. You should be a nun!'

'I might well be some day,' I said, for my world was Adam's.

Her Majesty returned looking more beautiful than ever. Victory became her. Her new self-assurance was far from arrogant, but it seemed to us that she had gained even more dignity and I was delighted that her manner towards James was now authoritative. Perhaps he was grateful for Huntly's

115

richest lands – the Earldom of Moray was his reward for his part in the Highland victory. He was humbled, or at least acted so. She spoke to us at once, and freely, of her joy at Bothwell's escape. But a few days later Ambassador Randolph brought word that, in escaping from Scotland, his vessel had been wrecked at Holy Island. The English there had captured him, accusing him of piracy, and he was held in Berwick, pending the justice of Queen Elizabeth.

God knows he had pestered her over the years. Our Queen told us that 'on advice' she had requested Randolph to ask Elizabeth to send Bothwell to her as a fugitive from her own justice. So the letter was written and it was sent by Randolph's courier. Not long afterwards the 'advice' was proved to be Rizzio's.

She now made no secret of the fact that he served as her secretary, and we Marys knew that they were often at work together in her apartments until past midnight. Lethington, now at court again, was nominally Secretary of State but this seemed to us a formality – Rizzio had gained the Queen's confidence. She lavished on him fine clothing, a gold-and-diamond crucifix. He no longer tended her chambers but was given a small house in the Canongate, facing the palace. Here he had servants and all the comforts she could provide.

I said to Adam, 'He deserves his honours, I think. But I am uneasy – the Lords. . . .'

'You must shed your fears,' he said.

Then merriment came with gossip – proved true – that Knox was courting a girl of thirteen, though some put her age at fifteen. In any case, she was nearly fifty years younger than he. Protestants must have been as embarrassed as we were amused by the antics of the old goat; and Lord Ruthven said that Knox only comforted her spiritually, that she was said to be ill. But Chastelard saw her on the High Street in buxom beauty, her kirtle drawn up against the mud, and said that her legs, though plump, were pretty. It was rumoured that Knox wanted to marry her 'for the saving of her soul'. Ha!

Lady Jean Gordon was a relief to Beaton, being a wispy blonde with thin, lank hair and a nose longer than Livvy's. But her figure was admirable, and her hands, so that she had

116

a certain elegance. However, Beaton judged her a bore, and no rival, and she was swiftly assimilated into the household, a quiet young woman whom our Queen seemed sorry for because, of her relatives, only her mother and a brother survived.

On a February night I was preparing for bed when I heard a scream above and hurried up the spiral stairs with Isobel. Janet was holding a robe to Her Majesty's nakedness and a guard was holding Chastelard against the wall at dirk-point. As the other Marys rushed in through the audience chamber the Queen said, 'Quiet! We must not cause alarm.' But Janet had screamed again, and another guard came in with drawn sword.

'Quiet,' she said again, turning her back to us and wriggling into the robe. 'I command silence, or such a scandal—' Her voice trembled. Then she faced Chastelard and the guards. 'There shall be no killing.'

The guards put their weapons aside.

'Pierre,' she said to the cringing poet, 'have you lost all reason? How dare you hide yourself under my bed?'

He mumbled something about love, but he was incoherent.

'Love?' she said with a sort of searing scorn. 'Is it love that seeks to compromise me? I had thought you my friend.'

Again he protested his love, whimpering, one hand to his mouth.

'Leave here,' she said, 'at once. Go to hell, or France, or where you will.' She told the guards to take him to his quarters, to see that he packed his belongings, and to put him out. He might take his horse and they were to escort him to the port of Leith.

The guards removed him, still whimpering. The Queen called for *aqua vitae* and Livvy brought it to her bed. She lay back on the cushions and said, 'He has never been drunk. What madness struck him?'

'Madam,' I said, 'you are right. No loyal lover would attempt this— If Knox knew—'

'Or Queen Elizabeth.' She set down her cup on the little pearled table. 'It almost seems to me – though I may be wrong – that the poor fool was a tool. Someone seeks to dis-

117

credit me. Someone who hopes that whatever marriage plans I have may be blocked.'

I thought of those opposed to the Spanish marriage. Queens Catherine and Elizabeth might suspect negotiations.

We talked for an hour or more and then she dismissed us, reminding us that we must be up early for our progress to the seaside town of St Andrews, to be broken by a visit to Rossend Castle as the guests of Kirkcaldy of Grange, a favoured soldier. I asked if she required us to wear splendid gowns or should we take only woollens. She said, 'Not you, dove. I've just realised you've had no holiday. We'll summon your brother and he'll escort you to Seton.'

'Madam, I don't really care to go. Unless you command it.'

'What? I hear you've the most magnificent palace in Scotland, a splendid golf links and forests— No?' For I had shaken my head. Then she smiled. 'Truly I don't need you, dove; wigs will do for this journey.'

'If I may have a holiday,' I said, 'I would rather spend it here.' Of course I could not say that separation from Adam would make me miserable. 'I could laze about and perhaps Signor Rizzio would teach me to sing. Please, Madam?'

She rose and embraced me. 'Very well, my dove. You're a hug-the-hearth and perhaps when we are all in sea mists we'll envy you. But you really love this place?'

'Yes,' I said, lying for it had such strange, haunted pockets in corridors and abbey. 'It is home to me now.'

So next morning I waved from the drawbridge as Her Majesty left with James, Ambassador Randolph and her retinue of ladies and servants. Her surgeon Gurion was abed of the New Acquaintance but Gervais went with her, and strutted a little as if in charge of the journey. It was a mild and sunny day for February, and when they were out of sight, walking towards White Horse Close, I strolled into the park. It remained a wilderness by Her Majesty's order – coverts for foxes, lairs, hidey-holes and caves for all sorts of game, a fairytale forest where one might expect the wee green folk of the Celts or the bear of the Norse. But I was not here casually; I knew that Adam might come this way as he used to come here for meditation.

118

But I did not see him and returned to my chamber for breakfast. Lady Jean Gordon and I repaired a tapestry – I did not wonder she was left behind; she was so dull. But Her Majesty said this was only because of her bereavement, that in time she would probably blossom to gaiety, shedding her mourning and perhaps marry Alex Ogilvie of Boyne. But she told me that she felt inclined to a convent. 'Men are fortune hunters,' she said bitterly. 'Or triflers.'

Beaton would have been delighted. I suppose I should have felt pity for this wan heiress, but in truth she bored me. So I spent the rest of the afternoon at music with Rizzio and we supped together. Her Majesty had told him of the Chastelard incident and he thought banishment too lenient. If our guards were not trustworthy, if they talked, her reputation would be in shreds. I could only imagine what Philip of Spain would think. But, rather romantically, Rizzio attributed Chastelard's behaviour to simple lust. He thought the man too stupid to be a tool of Catherine or Elizabeth. 'In any case,' he said, 'good riddance. He was a mediocre poet.'

We parted at midnight and Isobel bedded me and left. I had missed seeing Adam but even to know that he was across the courtyard sufficed. I thought, sleepily, perhaps moths are drawn to flame through a desire to perish, but I had no wish to destroy myself, only to live where he was – always where he was. . . .

Isobel awakened me with mulled ale and drew back the window arras. 'Poor Father Black was set upon with cudgels and a dagger last night in the forest – some murderous Protestant, we suppose—'

'Murder!' My ale cup clattered to the carpet. 'Is he dead?'

'Nearly, I think. Monsieur Gurion was roused from his sick-bed and is tending him, but – oh, my lady!'

For in leaving my bed I had fallen, and I am told I fainted.

CHAPTER VII

$\mathbf{Y}$outh and strength and a ravening will to live saved Adam, and of course the skill of Gurion and, I hoped, my prayers. I helped to nurse him and was finally able to coax him to take brose, a thin porridge with strained vegetables, and red wine for his blood. But he was so pallid that I was frightened, cheered only when he was able to take a few steps and felt well enough to complain of the lice.

Meanwhile Rizzio had been in a deep depression which I at first attributed to his worry over Adam and Captain Erskine's inability to hunt down the person responsible for the attack. It had been in darkness and so swift, so sudden, that Adam was sure of nothing but one adversary, seemingly a large man in a black cloak. I suspected Lindsay or Morton, but Erskine dared not question a noble without Her Majesty's authority. But Rizzio said on the second day after the incident, 'Troubles rarely come singly.'

'Do you fear that another priest will be set upon?' I asked.

'No—' He hesitated. Then he said, 'I feel such a weight of responsibility. The Queen's courier awaits a message from me tonight and I've twice destroyed a letter to her.'

'But sooner or later she must know about the attack on Father Black.'

'If it were only that.'

'You may trust me with a secret,' I said, 'if it would help.'

But he shook his head and suggested I send Petite Chatte to amuse Adam, which I did. She returned an hour later mimicking a yawning man who evidently was in no mood for her capers. Rizzio joined me for supper, at my request, though he ate little. Finally he said, 'It's too much to bear alone, my lady, and in time she would tell you herself. Chastelard fol-

120

lowed her to Rossend Castle hoping for pardon and another chance at court. But he entered her apartments secretly at midnight and hid himself in a closet. Her Majesty had just disrobed when he emerged, pushed past Lady Livingstone who was offering her a night robe, and crushed her naked in his arms, kissing her. . . . Lady Beaton ran screaming into the corridor and this roused Lord James and the Laird Kircaldy who with their daggers held Chastelard helpless.'

'Jesu!' I said. 'He must be mad, mad as Arran.'

'I had to consider that, as you'll hear. The screams also roused the rest of the castle, for presently Ambassador Randolph arrived, seeing Her Majesty with only a robe held up to shield her, she'd had no time to put it on. A concourse of people poured in and so the story is certain to spread, a scandal Queen Elizabeth will relish as a cat laps milk.'

'Randolph is sure to tell her?' I asked.

'Of course,' he said, as if I were a naïve child. 'And she in turn will delight in informing the world – so Her Majesty's chances of marriage look bleak indeed. At best she will emerge as a careless flirt, leading on a lover. At worst – Chastelard's mistress. Lord James, says she in her letter to me, was for killing him at once but she said there would be no bloodshed and ordered Chastelard to prison in St Andrews Castle.' He bowed his smooth, dark head and stared at his hands. 'What she requires of me is advice, whether to keep him there or execute him.'

'My poor friend,' I said, touching his shoulder. To ask his advice was a great honour – it superseded her trust in James's counsel – but Rizzio's nature was kind.

'Lord James wants him questioned under torture as to his motive in this matter, for a secret lover does not behave so blatantly. Her Majesty and I reject any form of torture. But, Lady Seton, my letter is finally written, she'll receive it at dawn. I have recommended execution.'

I shuddered. 'Yes.'

'Since the scandal will be carried by Randolph, it's better by far to make it public, even to trumpet her fury so that Knox will not be able to say she was lenient to a lover. I doubt whether he's mad except in passion for her. Yet my head

121

aches with doubts. And my heart aches to be the judge of this matter.'

'I believe you judge rightly,' I said. 'If he remained a prisoner folk would think she favoured him.'

But, as we were silent for a while, I think we both remembered Chastelard as a gentle fop, a man in love beyond hope or wit and, as Rizzio had said of the former incident, too stupid to be a tool or a spy for another Queen.

'What time does the courier leave?' I asked.

'At nine tonight. He is supping.'

'Tell him that I wish to ride with him.'

'But—'

'I am on holiday. Her Majesty might be glad of my presence. If I can comfort her. . . .'

'I'm sure you can.'

'Father Adam is beginning to heal, but I ask that you take him books to cheer him, and see that he doesn't perish of boredom. Chatte hasn't the mind to entertain him, but you do. You'll do this, Signor?'

'Gladly.'

'But if there's any change – should he worsen – you will let me know at once?'

'At once, my lady.'

He kissed my hand and we separated. Before I left I looked in upon Adam. Gurion was just leaving the chamber and whispered, 'He is asleep.' We had a brief conference in the courtyard and he told me that there was now no danger. Certainly my Queen required every assistance during those next days and my principal duty was to her. But if I was right in suspecting that some Mass-infuriated noble had attacked him, Adam was now virtually helpless, so I asked Captain Erskine that he be well guarded, especially when he would be able to walk outside. I called for my groom to make ready to accompany us at nine. The courier, John Aiken, wanted us to leave that night not only for haste but in the hope of out-riding a predicted storm.

It was a tedious, uneventful journey, mainly in mist. At dawn we paused at a mean inn for buttermilk and porridge; then on, following the Firth of Forth until we reached Burntisland where we climbed up to Rossend Castle perched on rocks like a great, wing-spread vulture. Its master, Sir William Kirkcaldy of Grange, was in the courtyard with an armourer and a blacksmith and, though I scarcely knew him, he welcomed me joyfully. John gave me Rizzio's letter and as I followed Sir William up spiral stairs he said that the Queen had for the past two days received no callers but he was sure I would be admitted, and he would have a chamber prepared for me.

Fleming came down a corridor, astonished to see me, and led me to Her Majesty's audience room, where she took my cloak and suggested food, but I told her I had no appetite. I was not bearing happy news and dreaded its effect. Then Fleming left me and I went close to the fire to warm myself.

'My dear one!' Her Majesty came in and embraced me. She was wearing a plaid woollen gown of heather and grey, the sleeves lined with squirrel, but she shivered as we sat by the fire. I gave her Rizzio's letter and she read it and a tear slid down.

'You know about this?' she asked me.

'Yes, Madam.'

'And you think he is right?'

I nodded. 'I see no other course to take. But you know I'm not competent to advise – I only came here to comfort.'

She put her face into her hands and her words were muffled. 'I have never before needed to end the life of a friend. With the Gordons it was war, but Chastelard – kind, winsome, gentle. . . . Still, it is the only means of silencing the gossip, the speculation that we were lovers. Lethington is in England prepared to explain the matter to "my dear sister" – though God knows what Randolph has written her.'

'I wish we had Ambassador Throckmorton back,' I said.

'I believe he liked me too well.'

It was, of course, my duty to tell her of the attack on Adam, and her sorrow about Chastelard changed to anger, and that was good. She praised me for nursing him, for suggesting a heavier guard. If Adam's intended killer were found she would have no compunction about execution.

I asked, 'Does Lord James approve of Chastelard's death?'

123

'Yes, decidedly. But it was Signor Rizzio's advice I planned to abide by.'

I was grateful for this; it seemed to presage the waning of James's influence. She said that she would order Chastelard's execution for 22 February in the town of St Andrews. In her heart she wished to wear mourning white but this would create suspicion; and so we ladies would all wear deep blue or brown, and a simplicity of jewels.

'I must not weep,' she said. 'I *shall* not.'

The market square of St Andrews was a mass of people. They were prodded away by our guards' lances so that the Queen, James, Kirkcaldy and Ambassador Randolph had full view of the black-draped wooden scaffold. We Marys, too, could see – too clearly. All of us were on horseback.

Chastelard, despite the cold wind, had dressed in white satin. The headsman removed a silver ruff from his neck, and his doublet. A black-robed minister stood beside him. A magistrate called for silence and read the death warrant:
. . . 'against the honour, integrity and sacred person of our Sovereign lady Mary, Queen of Scotland and the Isles, Queen Dowager of France, and in payment for said crime to die by the axe. . . .'

His minister said, 'Speak and make peace with God.'

Chastelard recited Ronsard's *Hymn to Death*. Then he was masked and helped to the block. For a moment he stood there, then turned and pointed in Her Majesty's direction. Loudly he said, in French, 'Farewell, most beautiful and cruel mistress.'

She flinched.

I looked away as the executioner raised the axe. When I turned back the golden head bled into a pile of ashes.

When we returned to Edinburgh we learned that Knox was preaching against the 'cruel mistress' who had killed her not-so-secret lover. But Rizzio said that, had she not acted promptly, the scandal would have been far worse. Still, she was morose, and Elizabeth was holding Bothwell in the Tower of London, and Lethington, still at the English court, did not appear to work for release. What he had done, Rizzio told me (for now we were firm friends), was to keep alive marriage negotiations with Spain. King Philip might yet offer Don Carlos.

Adam, quite recovered, went about his duties and we were often together in the gardens where appeared snowdrops, then daffodils and lilac. Her Majesty had corners of the park tidied but enjoyed hunting in the wilderness forest, and was often out for seven or eight hours with falcons or hounds. I preferred to be Mistress of the Picnic, seeing to the linen cloths and cutlery and sturdy trenchers for the broiled game. She always insisted on Rizzio's presence on these outings, with his lute, and Petite Chatte rode a mule and wove garlands for us all, so that our progress was as pretty as it was absurd. Even James sported a daffodil cap and Lord Morton's was a steeple of young ivy. But neither they nor Lord Ruthven were merry persons. Lady Jean Gordon remained her quiet, dull self but Beaton worried that Alex Ogilvie rode to his estates out of cowardice – not quite able to relinquish an affianced heiress. 'If he loved me he would not think twice about breaking the bond.'

'You are thinking in French terms,' I said. 'Here in Scotland a bond is sacred. Father Adam explained that to me. It is far more than a promise to a friend, it is also a promise to God. So your Alex is an honourable man.'

'Pesk take honour!' she said. 'We love one another. Jean is like you – a nun at heart. *She* should break the bond.'

'Perhaps she is not like me,' I said, 'but only modestly waiting and hoping.' Suddenly I felt impelled to defend her. 'True, she is not lively but how would you behave if most of your loved ones were gone? I hear her mother is to come to court, and that may brighten her, but her brother is still imprisoned – the rest of the clan dead – and if Alex is any sort of man he'll not desert her now.'

As she was silent, I said, 'Would you want a man, however lovesome, who would break a bond when you were in the deepest depression of your life?'

She hesitated. 'I can't lie. I want him on any terms. And I'm not the only sinner, Mother Superior Seton. Fleming loves Lethington, wife or not. We—'

125

'How dare you mock me as Mother Superior? I am neither! Never before have I heard you speak crudely—'

'Oh, love, I am sorry, but you are so good—'

'*Good!* What in the name of heaven do you know about my inner thoughts? Good! Do you take timidity and hypocrisy for goodness?'

'Hypocrisy?' she asked. 'Never.'

But I had been assuring myself that I did not want Adam as my lover. I had clothed my lust in altar cloths. And I would continue to because there was no other way.

'Yes,' I said. 'I don't preen myself on any sort of superiority.'

She soothed me by apology and, in forgiveness, I arranged her curls. I felt that Lady Jean had scant chance against her beauty and liveliness but assured myself that it was not my problem. When Alex returned to court it would be his.

Her Majesty was still depressed about Chastelard's death and its reception abroad; she gave no splendid balls. But she perked with amusement when Knox married his 'little lass', Margaret Stewart, and joked that she should send the bride a doll. Then Lethington sent word that Elizabeth had released Lord Bothwell from the Tower on parole and she was jubilant, asking we Marys at a private supper to drink to his good fortune. She was in a mood to confide, and said, 'Rizzio has composed a most clever letter to Her Majesty which I've just signed, saying that I am told Bothwell plagues her for permission to go to France, and that if she cares to grant that permission I'll be relieved of a troublemaker who could well lose his life in the Huguenot brawls.' She laughed. 'But he won't! Now, further, the Virgin Queen is madly in love with Lord Robert Dudley but, thank God, will never marry him – only dally – so I need not worry about her heirs.'

'Can it be true that her vagina is in some way sealed over?' Fleming asked.

Her Majesty shrugged. 'That may be true, or only gossip. But Lethington says that her people adore her. She has no Knox to conspire against her, she is forever visiting almshouses and lavishing gold on the "worthy poor" – gold stolen from our abbeys by her father, and she wears jewels wrenched from

126

the eyes of our madonnas. And yet, if only she and I could talk close in privacy we might realise that ambassadors may have misrepresented. Secondhand-talk is apt to be prejudiced. Cousins we surely are – sisters we might be in spirit.'

So it seemed her dream was to meet Elizabeth; her ambition to marry Don Carlos. I admired her political objectivity but marvelled because she was so emotional and feminine a creature, weeping over a dead puppy and attending its burial in the woods.

But if she was prone to regard Elizabeth as a potential sister, Ambassador Randolph returned from England and destroyed that fantasy with the grossest of messages: Elizabeth suggested that our Queen marry Lord Robert Dudley, whom she planned to create Earl of Leicester on Michaelmas Day. Her cast-off lover, her Master of Horse, whose ancestors bore a taint of treason, who was so churlish of behaviour that, when playing tennis with the Duke of Norfolk in Elizabeth's presence, he had snatched a napkin from her hand to wipe his sweaty face. An oaf in plumes and ermine – this reject to become the King of Scotland?

Since Her Majesty had told us about this in fury, I asked Rizzio what would be the diplomatic reply. 'It's intended as an insult, of course,' he said, 'but Her Majesty is prepared to write an affectionate letter saying that she will consider him as husband, since her "dear sister" is offering the most precious jewel of her court. . . . In that manner we are able to prevent suspicion of negotiations with Spain. Queen Elizabeth is not the only royal lady who may make use of eternal vacillation.'

He chuckled. 'In a manner, Lady Seton, this is a comedy.'

It was not comical for Her Majesty to grant Elizabeth a favour that seemed excessive – to pardon Lord Matthew Lennox who had been exiled by her mother for treason twenty years before. But our new envoy to England, Sir James Melville, strongly advised this. Lennox headed the Catholic party in England and his son, Lord Henry Darnley was – after our Queen – heir to Elizabeth's throne. So Lennox was invited to Scotland in September.

Meanwhile, Her Majesty pretended to consider Dudley in

127

marriage and a sweet correspondence ensued between the two 'sisters'. There was still no word from King Philip and we Marys waited in suspense, for none of us wanted our Queen married to an imbecile who was said to torture children and small animals. Nor for all the grandeur of Spain did we want to leave Scotland. Fleming remained in love with Lethington, who would not desert his ailing wife. Beaton could not be sure Ogilvie would follow her, nor I that Adam would be asked to accompany us. Livvy was beginning to fall in love with William Sempill, younger son of Lord Sempill, whose superb dancing excelled her own – though doubtless she had a less frivolous reason. Yet we realised that to Her Majesty power was security and she had been trained to place it before personal happiness.

Lord Lennox arrived at court and was graciously received. In return, Elizabeth allowed Bothwell to go to France. But when Melville returned from England in October he was closeted with Her Majesty for so long that we worried. Had he borne good news she would not have rejected both the noon and evening meals, but entertained him in the Great Hall.

Late at night she summoned me and I found Rizzio with them by the library fire. She said abruptly, 'Lady Seton, do you remember Lennox's son, Lord Darnley?'

Vaguely I did. He had come to France on a visit of condolence after King Francis's death and she had received him briefly. 'A pale, blond boy of great height, was he not? Gangling.'

'He failed to impress me at all,' she said, 'but that was perhaps due to my grief.'

'He would not be forgotten now, Madam,' Melville said. 'He's an astonishingly handsome lad – man.'

'Three years younger than I,' she said.

'Your Majesty need not consider that. And he has been raised to please you by his ambitious mother, Lady Lennox. When Ronsard was engaged as your verse-master, so one was chosen for Lord Henry. Your interest in music created his. He excels in sports. Every facet of his education parallels your own. And with the major consideration of his heritage to

128

Queen Elizabeth's throne, such a marriage should prove provident.'

'He *is* Catholic,' Her Majesty said, but wearily. 'But from what you tell me, Elizabeth wouldn't approve.'

Melville said, 'She'll approve no suitable marriage for you, Madam. And, as I told you, she knows of the negotiations with Spain and threatens war if you marry Don Carlos. Dudley – I should say Leicester now he is an earl – is a red herring tossed in the trail. She knows you won't take her lover, and I'd vow he still is, for during the ceremony of his elevation in rank she tickled his neck inside his ruff. And she made a coarse jest, that if you'd marry him she'd come to Scotland and share the same – household.'

'Bed,' said Her Majesty contemptuously. 'Is she Queen or fishwife to speak to an ambassador so? Well, I am in no mood to consider a lesser husband than Don Carlos.'

She dismissed us and Rizzio followed me into the corridor with our taper-bearers. After Sir James had left with his, he spoke French so that our Scots servants could not understand. 'Perhaps I am a romantic at heart, but I think Lord Darnley would bring her the love she's never known. And should Queen Elizabeth die without heirs, there's no question that they'd inherit England.'

'Shall you pray for that?' I asked.

'Perhaps hopelessly,' he said, and bowed and left me at my door.

Lethington received King Philip's letter. Negotiations for the marriage were firmly ended. Perhaps the scandal of Chastelard had been the cause, but the excuse was that the Cardinal of Lorraine, through Queen Catherine, had offered Her Majesty to Archduke Charles of Austria – and without her permission.

You can imagine her fury, being pushed about like an ivory Queen on a political chessboard. In her distress she spoke to us freely. True, the Archduke was Catholic, but no great match. She was angry with her brother James who inconsistently advocated the Archduke and rejected Lord Darnley because he, and Knox, would not accept a Catholic husband into Scotland. So! She would send for Darnley and judge for herself. If not a splendid marriage, it would please the Pope and the rest of Catholic Europe. 'Who knows?' she asked cynically. 'It might even please me. . . .'

In February we Marys accompanied her to James's country castle, a cliff-side retreat facing the Firth of Forth. Wemyss Castle was elegantly furnished but I was appalled, for it seemed a museum of holy images and furniture stolen from our monasteries and used casually on floors, stairs and walls. In my bedchamber I avoided treading on the beaded face of the Virgin which dominated a blue carpet. Adam, who was with us, told me that the wine-cup on his night-table was the sort to serve at Communion.

Here was grave insult to Her Majesty's faith but she made no complaint. I felt that perhaps she was afraid of her brother; or else had good reason to employ diplomacy. This was soon apparent because, after she had granted Livvy's petition to marry Sempill, and James had given a ball in their honour, she told him that she expected Lord Darnley to arrive on 17 February. 'We shall expect entertainment,' she said, as we sat down to dinner, 'as befits an honoured visitor who might think Scotland primitive.'

'Of course, Madam.'

'We know that he is high in Queen Elizabeth's favour, despite his religion,' she said, and there was mischief in her eyes. 'We shall be pleasing her, shall we not?'

His voice was as stiff as the pleats of his ruff. 'Indeed, Madam.'

I felt certain that he did not want her to marry. A Scots king, whether Catholic or Protestant, would put an end to his power. For as Earl of Moray he did have power over the rich Highlands, and thus the ability to raise an army.

'What sort of entertainment?' she asked, including Lady Jean in the question.

'Chatte is most amusing,' Lady Jean said timidly, 'and blackamoors are rare even to the English, I'd think.'

James said, 'But Chatte has an unfortunate tendency to mimicry. Somehow she must be made to understand that it's offensive.'

130

'My dear brother,' our Queen said, 'has the wench offended *you?*'

His dignity was impaired. 'Certainly not, Madam. She'd not dare ridicule us – but I've seen her pretending to be Father Adam, bible in hand and eyes raised to heaven—'

'He has a sense of humour,' I said, and received the stab of those cold, green eyes. Our Queen said merrily that someone must try to teach Chatte English, and why not Father Adam who had the patience of a saint?

So the lessons began. I was present at the first and it was clear from the start that, though she was willing, she expected a reward for each word learned, as our poodles expected tidbits for a successful somersault. So there was a tray of apples, dates and Spanish oranges. When she had learned to say 'Welcome, my Lord Darnley', in subsequent lessons she achieved a golden locket from the Queen. Within two weeks she made amazing progress, though how much she understood was a puzzle to Adam. He thought she parroted.

During this time Alex Ogilvie walked a tightrope between Lady Jean and Beaton, and I disliked him intensely. If he truly loved Beaton, he had not the courage to relinquish the heiress, so both ladies were made miserable. Still, my own love was more than questionable.

For though we scarcely touched hands, except when Adam helped me down a slope to the beach, there was lightning between us. More often than not, I did not trust my voice and he, too, was silent as we gathered sea-shells which were fashioned into absurd necklaces for Chatte. We fished with Her Majesty, joined in building sand castles. But even in company I felt that we were alone.

Being so alone in my thoughts of him, I desperately needed a confidante. Certainly I could not shock the Marys, and our Queen might have dismissed him in order to heal my heart. Who would understand? Who always did offer the great gift of sympathy? Rizzio, of course.

I found him in the music chamber studying manuscripts at his desk and he seated me beside him. He said that Her Majesty had commanded some English songs to be presented to Lord Darnley at the banquet. Did I have some request?

131

'Not for advice,' I said, 'for the problem is not to be solved.' And I blurted out my love for Adam. 'Forgive me, Signor, but I *had* to tell someone. . . .'

'I'm not surprised,' he said gently. 'Nor am I distressed for you, because you've been so radiant of late. I see no reason why you shouldn't love one another for the rest of your lives. Marriage can be happy rarely but romance endures.'

As I smiled at him in gratitude he said, 'Not that I speak from experience, my lady. No woman has ever desired me – they admire broad shoulders and strong legs. I've learned to stifle passion.'

'Except in your singing,' I said. 'There it comes in a great tide, like a sea-surge. And it suffices?'

He hesitated. 'It substitutes.'

'You're fortunate in not being a woman,' I said. 'I'm expected to marry, to bear children – one reason I delay visiting my family. My mother is sure to pry and probe and perhaps match-make. What shall I say to excuse myself?'

'Half-truths are convenient. You are deeply religious. Dangle a future convent and they can't but respect you.'

I laughed. 'How far in the future? The length of Adam's life, and he might live till ninety! So might we both.'

'God grant it, my lady.'

Impulsively, I reached for his hand. He clasped mine.

From that time on I thought of Rizzio as my dearest friend. Adam, though we had never kissed, was my lover.

On the afternoon that we expected Lord Darnley Her Majesty asked that I take special care with the arrangement of her hair. Nothing seemed to please her. Finally she said, laughing, 'Just make me look demure if I can't look seventeen,' and this I achieved with a circlet of white velvet bows. Because we knew Darnley was tall, she was able to wear her steeple-heeled shoes with the pearl and emerald embroidery.

We Marys were not introduced to His Lordship until just before that night's banquet in a chamber off the Great Hall. Tall! He was a giant, but no longer awkward. His shoulders were magnificent, as were his legs in their puffed breeches. Slender, elegant in primrose velvet and topaz jewels, he bowed to us with the graciousness of a king. I had never seen before a man whom I would have called 'exquisite' – large, limpid, hazel eyes, skin like pale gold satin, wavy golden hair. His chin was strong, rather stubborn, else he would have been flawed by a look of excessive gentleness.

Her Majesty had spent several hours with him and was calling him 'Harry' with what seemed to be genuine affection. And no wonder – his mother, Lady Lennox, had trained him from childhood to please her. A less ambitious woman might have been dissuaded when Her Majesty married the Dauphin, but she had obviously not given up hope. In any case, Lord Harry was a most amusing guest, both at supper and later. Chatte, in guise of a poodle, nuzzled his foot and tried to climb into his lap but he only laughed and tossed her a beef bone. After Rizzio sang for us, he discussed music with Her Majesty – not as an amateur, but with wisdom. If he had not been Catholic I think even James and Lethington would have warmed to him. As it was, they were politely attentive.

Next day I said to Adam. 'You weren't near enough at table to notice how charming Lord Harry was to everyone, and how Her Majesty's eyes were soft with a sort of pride in him. You must meet him.'

'I did,' he said, 'when he came in to admire Lord James's library with Her Majesty. They talked of books and then she said what a sacrilege it was that so many holy volumes had been burned with the abbeys. You have never heard sympathy so sincerely spoken. He said that *The Lives of the Saints* was his most beloved reading.'

'So you approve him?' I asked.

'I've rarely seen a more accomplished courtier.'

Usually Adam was forthright but now he did not return my glance but went to the window where the sea mists had risen to cloud the glass. Gulls screamed out in the Forth as fishing boats came in.

'Do you mean you don't trust him?' I asked.

He turned in a whirl of his white robes. 'Who am I to judge? Who am I to trust even myself? For all my learning, I haven't the wisdom of a vole. Else I would ask favour to leave here while I can.'

133

Because of his love for me, as yet unstated but urgent as the air we breathed. I realised then how I had tricked myself into thinking that we could endure celibacy – perhaps apart, but not together. My conscience tried to reply but my heart refused the words 'Yes, you must go.'

I tried to hide my tears with my sleeve. He said, 'Mary, what in the name of heaven or hell are we to do?'

That question was answered by the sound of laughter in the corridor and then knocks on the door. Chatte stood outside surrounded by some men of the household who had placed her on stilts. She tottered down the hall with a yellow wig on her hair and the facsimile of a man's doublet and hose. 'King,' she said. 'King Harry.'

'You imp!' I said. 'How dare you mimic a guest? Who put you up to this insolence?'

Of course she did not understand but the tone of my voice frightened her, for she jumped off the stilts and disappeared. I scolded the grooms and taper-bearers and told them that only their servitude to Lord James saved them from immediate dismissal. 'If your lord knew,' I said, 'it could be a flogging.'

One of them spoke boldly. 'My lord provided the stilts,' he said. 'He thought it amusing that she should practise and perform tonight.'

There was nothing else to say, and I felt ridiculous. With what dignity I could muster I waved them off, closed the door and asked Adam what to do. He thought for a moment and then suggested that we both seek audience with James rather than tell Her Majesty. 'Leave it to me,' he said.

When James admitted us into his apartments he was wearing a dressing-gown of dark mink and his hair was damp from a bath. He motioned to a valet, who scuttled off, then smiled. 'I hear there has been some misunderstanding, Lady Seton. The blackamoor wench is in truth a fool. She understands nothing. How appalling that she used the stilts, which were intended for a dwarf in a future masque.'

Never had I heard a weaker fabrication. 'I keep costumes for various entertainments. Being a natural mimic she chose to emulate a giant, whereas I had in mind the dress of a frog.'

134

He spread his long, slender hands. 'You know, Father, how hopeless she is in learning our language?'

Adam said, 'The language barrier is immense, my Lord,' and he spoke the truth. 'What we came to prevent was insult to Lord Darnley – intended or not.'

'Her Majesty would have been more than appalled,' I said.

James nodded, patting his moist hair. 'I shall punish the wench—'

'No!' I said, forgetting his rank. 'It's enough that I frightened her. Besides, she is Her Majesty's property, subject only to her.'

My anger, my years of mistrusting him, had culminated in this defiance. I would have stupidly said more but Adam interrupted smoothly, assuring James that he could make Chatte understand that the stilts and the yellow wig were forbidden. 'I am sure that she knows already, for Lady Seton was vehement.'

James pretended gratitude for our visit; he was not so facile an actor as to bring warmth to his eyes or his voice. As we left him, separating in the corridor, we both knew that his power-lust was so strong that he would use any tool to drive Lord Harry from Scotland.

But after the dancing that night, alone in my chamber, near to sleep, I thought only of Adam: 'Mary, what in the name of heaven or hell are we to do?'

The court returned to Edinburgh. There was a false spring which sometimes comes in late February and Her Majesty commanded hawking each day, leading the chase with Lord Harry. He excelled in sport as, apparently, in every other skill. There was music and there were costume balls and in March a banquet to celebrate Livvy's wedding. When the cake was cut Her Majesty's slice contained the bride bean and she blushed like a girl.

In fact she behaved like a girl, racing with Lord Harry up the windy height of Arthur's Seat, romping with the dogs and, of course, dancing. It was obvious that she adored dancing with a man taller than she – they looked splendid and his grace matched hers. He pleased her in more subtle ways by taking a fancy to Rizzio and having lute lessons, which Her Majesty thought unnecessary. He was attentive to her ladies without being flirtatious and, as I told Adam, why should he not be an accomplished courtier? Why mistrust a gallant young man who even seemed to charm the Protestant lords with his humour and gaiety?

Adam was morose. One evening on our bench during a revel he said that he must make a decision about us. 'I can't expect you to live my life – to give you nothing but sterile love. I mustn't thieve you of marriage and children. And yet – God help me, when I watch you dance in another man's arms I could murder.'

'Truly,' I said, 'I want no other man, ever.'

'I've decided to go to Newbattle Abbey – aye, a retreat. In a month or two you may have forgotten me—'

'Is my nature so changeable?' I asked.

'Youth is adaptable. And Her Majesty agrees to what she believes to be a holiday from the gaiety here, bless her innocence. So, my lady, I leave in the morning.'

He raised my hand and kissed it and left me. I supposed that God had guided his thoughts but at that moment I mortally hated God for interfering. And on Friday I pretended illness so as to avoid confession.

Her Majesty commanded Fleming and me to her bed-chamber one evening and said, 'I've had a message from Lord Bothwell. He's in hiding at his Castle of Crichton and begs that I come there for vital news. It must be secret. I shall want a disguise. Seton, take a blonde wig and I'll conceal myself in Fleming's yellow cloak, with the hood, and ride Fleming's horse.'

'Crichton!' I said. 'Do you ride twelve miles alone?'

'I can trust my groom,' she said, 'but no one must know of my absence or they will raise the town watch. I've told my brother and Lord Harry that I've a headache. On no account let them enter this room. Harry is' – she smiled – 'deep in affection. He might want to bring violets or primroses or inquire of me. I leave this to your wits.'

So when she had left us we placed pillows in her bed to simulate a sleeping body, leaving one curtain open since an

136

invalid requires air. We placed a vial of medicine on the table and a spoon. Except for firelight the chamber was dim. And, indeed, we had the odd fancy that the bed was occupied.

'What news could Bothwell bring that would require her to take such a dangerous ride?' Fleming asked from her chair.

'He's been in France,' I said. 'Perhaps he has news from there.'

She said, 'I hope it's not some intrigue that will upset her. She's become so happy.'

'Yes. Lord Harry seems so perfect for her.'

Fleming said, 'William [meaning Lethington] says little to me of politics but he believes that Knox would never accept a Catholic king.'

'Knox is not Scotland. He pounds his pulpit to no avail.'

There was a timid knock at the door and I ran to it. But it was only Lady Jean asking after the Queen. 'Lord Darnley told me to bring her this.'

I took the small, linen-wrapped package and whispered that the Queen was asleep – a mere headache. When she had gone I placed the gift on the bed. 'He is perhaps ambitious of kingship,' I said, 'but so addled with love! So was King Francis. So was Chastelard. So are all men – even, in his way, King Henry.'

'And Bothwell,' Fleming said.

'What?'

'Why else should he try to return here, a fugitive from justice? What does he stand to gain with enemies like Lord James, Morton, Lindsay? You may call it loyalty but he is no fool to endanger his life for a mere concept.'

We argued a while but more to shed our uneasiness than to score points. Four hours crept by. Fleming dozed and my thoughts went to Adam. He was certain to return spiritually cleansed of the sin of carnal love, whereas I had no means to fight it. Even if he did decide to forsake his vows and marry me, we would disgrace Her Majesty and provide Knox with evidence of 'the infamy of Catholic friars, who secretly cohabit with all women'. No, we could not marry. Perhaps I would find courage to write to him and ask if the Queen would grant him permanent leave at Newbattle.

137

It was after four when Her Majesty returned. We heard her at the door speaking to the guard: 'The Queen has summoned me,' and his, 'Aye, Lady Fleming.' We removed her cloak and she tossed off the wig. 'No one missed me?'

'Lord Harry sent you a gift, Madam.'

She unwrapped it at once – a heart-shaped ruby brooch edged in diamonds – and read a little note. 'He is so dear – and Bothwell is so abominably wrong about him! He had the effrontery to hint that Harry's reputation in England is obscene, that Queen Elizabeth is well aware of this and pretends to block a possible marriage between us so as to trick me into it. Bothwell says that she manoeuvred Lennox into Scotland as preface to the son's arrival. He tells me to expect threats of war from her if I marry, whereas nothing would please her more.'

'Madam,' I said, 'such intrigues are beyond my wits. And why is Lord Harry so disreputable?'

'Bothwell says he mingles with boys, not women. That he might be incapable of normal love, of fathering heirs. That he drinks secretly, and to excess. Isn't that preposterous? In these many weeks has he been anything but impeccably behaved?'

Fleming and I agreed that he had seemed wondrously sober, considerate of the potent *aqua vitae* as we were ourselves. 'As to consorting with abnormal creatures,' the Queen said, 'only a true man could kiss a woman as he has kissed me. There was further slander – that Lord Harry abuses servants – dirked a page's finger because he had presented a wilted salad, whipped his valet for a loose button. Bothwell said that if such things have not occurred here it's because Lord Harry knows he is on trial; but that, given power, he would revert to whatever gross habits may please him.'

I asked timidly, 'Is it possible, Madam, that Bothwell is jealous and wants you for himself?'

She laughed, but wanly. 'If that were so, I'd not have returned here in safety, in honour. He has a long history of taking any woman he wants. No, I believe he spoke the truth but as he saw it, and finally he insulted me by saying that my wits were befogged by lust. This, of course, enraged me. He said he no longer had patience to warn, to reason with me, and

138

would be off to France this week. I so lost my temper that I told him I'd have his head if he returned. So we parted enemies.'

We were silent in sympathy. She held Harry's jewel in her hand, then cuddled it against her cheek. 'Call Janet to bed me. Perhaps, by dawn, I shall sleep.'

I heard nothing from Adam, nor did I write to him for fear of disturbing what peace he might have attained. Rizzio was my principal comfort and when the court went hunting we read verse or sang together, for my voice was improving. Since Her Majesty had told him what Bothwell had said, he and I both observed Lord Harry more closely but could only imagine that Bothwell had been the victim of vicious gossip. Elizabeth and Secretary Cecil were a wily pair, doubtless in league with James, Morton and other hostile Protestants.

In May we moved to the fortress of Stirling, which guards the Highlands. The view from my high, barred casement was of moors pleated with flowering trees, of sunlit mountain peaks, of a grey-roofed town that nestled at the base of rocks. Lord Harry was stricken with measles, attended by Gurion and Gervais, and Her Majesty persisted in nursing him, often until midnight. Her love for him was so evident to us all as to be indiscreet. We heard that Knox, in Edinburgh, was proclaiming her a harlot. She laughed. James was sulky – she laughed. She filled the sickroom with flowers and one evening at supper proclaimed with delight that Lord Harry's skin was healed without a blemish. We applauded as though a war had been won.

Lady Lethington died and Fleming was overjoyed – but tried to conceal it, certain that she would become his next wife. Beaton confided to me that Alex Ogilvie of Boyne had finally promised her marriage, and would ask our Queen's sanction later. Why later? Because he was sure that the Queen would marry Lord Harry and had no wish to carry off a maid of honour before the royal wedding.

I had thought it one of his eternal vacillations but one sunset I was strolling on the battlements when Lady Jean joined me. She favoured grey gowns as extension of mourning

139

and always reminded me of a nun, with her fair hair tucked into veils. She said, 'A good evening to you, Lady Seton,' and, as if weary, leaned against the side of a wall.

'That is dusty,' I said. 'You'll spoil your gown.'

'I will change,' she said listlessly. And then, to my astonishment, she turned and began to sob. Impulsively I put my arms round her and she, who had always seemed coldly reticent, spilled out the story of Alex, of long love since childhood, and now he had told her that he wanted Mary Beaton for wife. '. . . having lost most of my family, too, I see nothing to live for. I walk here on these heights and long for the courage to throw myself down. . . .'

I took her to her chamber and offered such comfort as I could. When her love-blindness lifted she would see Alex as a very ordinary young man easily beguiled by Beaton's flattery, probably susceptible to any pretty woman of high position. 'You are well rid of him,' I said, 'and it's time you shed your mourning and asserted your own beauty.'

'I have none,' she said.

But within an hour I had taught her the art of subtle painting, defined the mouth – her best feature – plucked the eyebrows to delicate arcs and fluffed her golden hair. Her long nose was, I told her, aristocratic (she was able to laugh at that). I called for her maid to pad out the bosom of a wine-red gown and it moved fluidly as she went to her looking-glass. She was as graceful as any of us.

Then I wove garnets and pearls into her hair and, when the supper gong sounded, felt immensely proud of my creation. In my own chamber Isobel dressed me hurriedly and I was nearly last at table. But, to my perplexity, the royal table on the dais was empty except for the silver service, goblets and flowers.

Rizzio rose to seat me. 'Her Majesty has commanded that supper proceed without her.'

So Lord Harry was not recovering? He said, very softly, 'Queen Elizabeth has sent word by Randolph from Edinburgh that she will acknowledge Her Majesty as successor to the English throne—'

'Thank God!'

'– *if* she will relinquish Lord Harry and marry Leicester.'

Dudley – Leicester – whatever he was now called. 'Surely her answer is no?'

'It is no. At the moment she is in furious argument with Lord James and Lethington. But she is determined to marry Lord Harry at any cost.'

A servant interrupted by sliding trenchers of duckling between us.

'The cost', Rizzio said, 'may be too high.'

CHAPTER VIII

The price exacted by James for acceptance of Lord Harry was that Her Majesty legitimise him. She said that he was born a bastard and would die one. He gave her three months to revoke her decision. If she did not, he had six thousand armed men, Knox to rally others and, due to her gift of Highland lands, countless more. Lethington implored her to marry Dudley and thus ensure the succession. She could never win a war against James, said he, with her personal guard of halberdiers and archers. But he would remain neutral whatever the outcome. She suggested he visit his estates, and ordered James from court.

It was rumoured that Her Majesty and Lord Harry were secretly betrothed in Rizzio's apartments at Stirling, but we ladies doubted that – she was waiting for dispensation from the Pope for first cousins to marry. But she did create him Earl of Ross and, in July, Duke of Albany. They were as entranced a couple as one could imagine. She wore pink gowns with roses in her hair, gathered and placed roses in every vase and ordered them scattered on the dining-tables. Only Rizzio seemed grave. When I visited him one evening in his study to talk of Adam he said, 'At least you are ruled by common sense, my lady. You give absence a chance to heal you. But Her Majesty is intent on marriage whether the Pope sends permission or not. If His Holiness refuses, then the marriage is illegal, her heirs illegitimate and the crown of England remote as those stars.'

We were sitting on a bench by the casement window and the fragrance of the rose gardens was heavy. 'I've done all I can to ensure that Lord James cannot harm her. She has forgiven Lord Bothwell and summoned him from France. We've released Lord George Gordon from prison to rouse what is left of his clan – but if James is passionate for war, as I think, our chances are slim. Have no doubt that Queen Elizabeth will help him.'

'But Bothwell,' I said. 'If any man can control the Borders, he can.'

'If he can get through to us. Likely James has a network of spies watching the coasts.'

The court moved to Edinburgh. On 29 July at the Market Cross trumpeters proclaimed Henry Darnley, Earl of Ross and Duke of Albany, 'King of this our Kingdom'. Marriage banns were posted on the Canongate kirk. Thousands of bewildered townspeople heard Knox snarl from his forestairs about the carnal union of beasts fed on the filth of Rome. But if he had hoped to unleash armed men on Holyrood, he failed. At four o'clock on that Sunday morning we Marys – with only the married Livvy absent – prepared the bridal attire with Lady Jean and the tirewoman. Her Majesty explained that this wedding must in no respect seem frivolous. 'I want no gauds, no frippery. I'm in truth a widow and shall go to the altar attired as one.'

I gasped when Janet brought out the mourning robe Her Majesty had worn at King Francis's interment. It seemed sinister, ill-omened.

Only her face was radiant, and her voice. 'Be happy for me, my doves. I marry in the true faith and nothing nags my conscience.'

Although the Pope had not yet sent dispensation. . . .

'Your King loves you as I do. See to it that he is always addressed as "Sire".' She smiled. 'What a hopping about you have had with his titles from "My Lord" to "Your Grace".' She paused. 'I trust that you Marys will be comfortable in the new quarters prepared for you.'

Of course he must have the apartments below, with the private staircase. Our chambers were to be decorated in our favourite colours and our furniture was pleasantly arranged. 'Seton,' she said on a sudden thought, 'see to it that Father Adam's bedchamber is properly neat, and his study – I'd quite forgot.'

Stuttering, I asked, 'He is expected?'

'He is here,' she said.

I concealed my delight. 'And my brother, Lord George?'

'Sent his regrets. I think he feels you neglect your family, though naturally he'd not say so.'

Certainly I intended no rift in the family but my loves were here.

'You had better go to Seton soon,' she said, and then with mischief, 'I shan't lose your brother's allegiance because you choose to avoid your family.'

'He's your staunchest friend,' I told her; and I could not imagine his reason for not attending this wedding. Her Majesty went to her oratory for private prayer and we ladies sat in silence. I am sure we all prayed for her happiness but her sombre attire had deadened our gaiety.

When the abbey bells rang out they sounded funereal. We followed Her Majesty down the staircase, Beaton bearing her train. Below us stood Rizzio, Ambassador Melville, her half-sister the Countess of Argyll and a few Catholic lords. None smiled. The path to the chapel was massed with soldiers, servants and townspeople, solemnly silent. Lords Lennox and Atholl met Her Majesty and she walked to the altar between them. Tall white candles glowed on a bank of roses and broom. The Dean of Restalrig came forward with Adam and Father Joseph and the lords stepped back as the King came to her side.

I swept Bothwell's gossip from my mind. Here was so perfect a portrait of what I can only call innocence – the wavy gold hair still with its boyish whorl at the parting, the guileless eyes, the expression of tenderness mingled with awe. He wore jewelled white satin but of simple design. This was no swaggering peacock, but a humble bridegroom.

Our Queen extended her hand for three rings symbolising the Trinity. After prayers, after Mass, after the nuptial kiss, the King left the chapel first, and we ladies scattered roses from a basket near the altar and Her Majesty walked the flowery path into the sunrise – a strange grey-gold. In her bedchamber we removed the hideous robes and dressed her in pale ivory damask and emeralds. I placed an emerald tiara

144

on her hair. 'I want no crown to weight me,' she said. 'I shall dance lightly!'

We danced after the banquet at noon – we were beginning a four-day revel made happier for her by news that Philip of Spain sanctioned the match and sent a pair of turquoise goblets, though they preferred to share a loving-cup at the evening feast. At the priests' table, which was removed from the others by a rose-twined gate, I saw Adam lift his glass to me, and in the midst of talk and toasts no one noticed that I, in turn, drank to him. At midnight the bride and groom were still dancing – and I with a succession of lords. Lady Jean did not lack for partners either and Beaton whispered, 'She is somehow more attractive,' and I giggled.

No one noticed that I slipped out into the garden shortly after Adam left. He was waiting on our bench.

'You have been well? Content?' he asked.

'Content. And you?'

He shook his head. 'No. But I feel stronger in spirit. I believe I can offer friendship now in truth, and that is to advise you to find – to accept – a love I can't offer.'

What I had dreaded became reality. 'I know you're right for us both but I – am I to mate just because I'm young? Without the slightest maternal feeling? To transfer wealth to a husband who will please my family? Oh, doubtless I can endure the farce – many women do.'

'My darling,' he said, but he did not touch me. 'I can't imagine any other course. You're not a nun at heart, you've felt too much of the world to relinquish it. If I were a prioress I would not even allow you as novice because the beat of this life throbs in you as I think it should. You are devout, yes, but your nature is to be free as a falcon. The jess – the restraint of a convent would sicken you.'

He looked into my eyes. 'In convents I have talked with wise superiors. They often shelter ladies who wish to flee the world. But the Church understands that these would be better at peace in the solitude of seaside cottages, aye, a hired home or any refuge not ruled by religion or relatives. Peace of mind doesn't come by enforcement.'

'No,' I said. 'But if you offer me only crumbs of friendship,

145

'I'll be content because I can't enforce love for any other man.'

Wind rose, sweeping pink petals across the grass. Then Father Joseph came to us and told Adam that it was time to bless the bridal bed, and I followed them upstairs. They turned to the King's apartments, I continued up to Her Majesty's bedchamber where Janet had laid out a pale pink nightdress girdled with silver, and a silver tissue robe. 'I've been waiting for her since midnight,' Janet said. 'If he was your husband, would you prefer to *dance*?'

I laughed. 'That's an indiscreet question.'

Beaton and Fleming came in and I thought they both looked troubled. They admired the night attire and sprinkled it with lily-of-the-valley. Fleming sent Janet to close the windows of the audience chamber and blow out the tapers there. Then she said, 'Seton – he is drunk.'

'Staggering,' Beaton said. 'His servants are helping him to bed.'

Shocked, I asked, 'How could he, on such a night?'

And then Her Majesty came in, smiling the set smile she adopted as a façade. 'Ah,' she said gaily, 'I hope you've enjoyed the revel as much as I.' She hummed a tune as Janet undressed her, then slipped into the pink and silver and sat down for me to remove her hairpins and brush out the long waves that fell to her waist. Then she went to the private staircase, holding a candle. She cast a tall, slender shadow on the wall.

'Good night, my doves,' she said.

'May God bless Your Majesty,' I said, and she left us.

That façade of a smile was evident during the following days and I prayed that it was merely the strain of entertaining the many Catholic nobles who came to pay their respects to the new King. Lady Jean's brother, Lord George Gordon, had been released from prison and arrived with their mother, and after I wrote to my brother he came to stay a few days before taking me to Seton. I left Edinburgh reluctantly and uneasily because I felt that Her Majesty was unprotected. From what I had observed of the King, he was sober only in the saddle, which was eight hours of the day. Her brother James was in

146

Stirling and said to be raising an army against her. Rizzio had no time to talk with me, involved as he was with foreign correspondence. Above all, it was a wrench to leave Adam. He had called me 'My darling' – he loved me in his way, and that must suffice.

George and I travelled with his guard through rain from Edinburgh to Musselburgh, seven miles of flat land; stopped at Blinkbonny for bannocks and ale at an inn and, after monotonous farmlands, turned through Seton village up to Seton Palace. Rebuilt after the English had burned it in 1544 it stood, magnificent, in splendid gardens. We arrived at dusk, weary and wet, in the torchlight of the courtyard. George said that my stepfather was in Glasgow, my mother was indisposed but would meet us for supper in the Great Hall. He gave me into the care of a young maid, Elspeth, who preceded me up a splendidly carved oak staircase into my suite.

There were wax candelabra reflecting a painted ceiling in my bedchamber, and cherubs of oak formed the four posts of the bed. I shed my damp clothing and bathed in a wooden tub by the fire. Elspeth, though a Scot, chattered in French as she unpacked my chest of clothing and approved a silky plaid gown buttoned in gold. 'It is cold this summer, I suggest the furred shawl.' She was kindly and yet vastly respectful, the perfect tirewoman, and I felt at home – until I went down to meet my mother.

She was taller than I, dark and beautiful but showing the pain her back caused her. I knelt and kissed the hem of her black damask skirt and she bade me rise and kissed both my cheeks in the French manner. But she was formal as wine was served in her withdrawing room, asking if I preferred French or Spanish, did I approve of my suite, was I comfortable. True, I had had no daughterly feeling during our years of separation but I had been prepared for a giving and sharing of affection. There was only courtesy. I judged her to be honest in that there was no burst of sentimentality. Madame Marie de Bryante was a firmly practical Frenchwoman whose emotions, if any, were as strictly laced as her V-shaped waist. She had all our Queen's dignity but none of her impulsive warmth or gaiety. She inquired of our Queen's health, and

147

hoped that the honeymoon frolics had been pleasant. Finally came the question anyone might ask : 'What is your opinion of King Henry?'

Did one lie to those sharp black eyes? 'Most charming, Madame, but – thus far – frivolous. Of course, on honeymoon. . . .'

'I've heard that the boy is not continent – that he indulged in excesses at the English court. Why had Her Majesty no warning?'

Bothwell had warned her but I would not betray a confidence. 'I think she's in love,' I said, 'and doubtless he'll grow to responsibility as he matures.'

Her smile was wry. 'Spawned of a traitor, he comes of rotten seed, my dear. But what's done is done – and at least he is Catholic.' A gong sounded below and she rose. 'Supper.'

The Great Hall was roofed with the arms of France and Scotland, the Seton crest, and inlaid gold and silver. Of my relatives only George and his wife Isobel were in residence, she a prim young lady of about my own age, one of those dutiful girls who addressed her husband as 'My Lord' and seemed in awe of my mother. We all spoke in French and the food was worthy of Her Majesty's own French chefs. Beyond our small table about forty servants dined below the salt; during the meal musicians played behind a screen of blue mosaic.

Madame my mother explained her malaise as an inflammation of the back and retired early. So did Lady Isobel. George and I sat by the fire in his charter room and I asked him why he had not attended the Queen's wedding.

'In my heart I couldn't have celebrated it,' he said. 'I've heard of that dissolute lad since he was fourteen and I marvel that she fell into what can only be Elizabeth's trap.'

'Yes.' But for some reason I tried to defend this. 'He's not crude or gross as Morton and Lindsay – he doesn't swear or belch – he is just stupidly tipsy when he isn't at sport in the forest.'

He sighed. 'The barrel fevers are said to be caused by nerves, yet I'm told he controlled himself throughout the courtship. Now he is King he imagines he can revert to his

148

former vices. And Her Majesty – do you think she can reform him?'

'We don't discuss such matters,' I said. 'Whatever misery she may feel she bears alone. Unless she confides in Rizzio. And after all, brother, he doesn't yet act as sovereign. She hasn't granted him the crown matrimonial.'

'Oh, but she will. Her nature is to be generous and you may be sure the lad will pout for power.'

I was afraid so but I felt sure that Rizzio would advise her wisely. In a sense, Rizzio was to her what Adam was to me – the quintessence of friendship and, in its way, holy.

My mother awakened me next morning – I suspect to see how I looked without paint or hairdress. As we ate our breakfast, she inquired of my duties to the Queen and reminded me that she had held the same position at the court of the late Queen Mary. 'Never was there so gallant a lady . . . I remember when we were holed up like rats in the Castle how she commanded the cannons and, warning us of a bombardment, said, "Ladies, take neither ale nor wine lest it spill on your gowns." Until Lord Bothwell came to relieve her she was our only general.'

I told her that our Queen had sent for Bothwell and she said, 'I think he and George and the young Earl Huntly are all she can depend upon at the moment. Lord James has bought Kirkcaldy of Grange, or so we hear.'

'Madame,' I said, 'both Queens employed Father Black as confessor – was he yours?'

She nodded. 'He was young then, remarkably handsome and as remarkably daring in carrying messages to our friends. Priests, of course, were shot on sight in the streets of Edinburgh. We ladies of his height lent him gowns and veils as disguise, and once a brave little page carried his train . . . it all sounds so highly melodramatic, doesn't it? Is he your confessor, my dear?'

'No, Father Joseph. But Father Black is my friend.'

As I knew she would, she asked about other friends. Was there no man I fancied? 'A pity. You are twenty-three. We must find someone suitable.'

'Madame,' I said, 'please don't trouble yourself. I intend to

149

devote my life to my Queen, as I swore to the Cardinal years ago. A husband's embraces would not please me, nor do I long for children. So, I beg you, keep my dowry for whoever in the family most needs it.'

I had expected argument. She merely shrugged and said, 'If you are certain, then you relieve me of the tedious business of match-making. As to your dowry, however, you will accept it whenever or however you like, as your due. Now, let us dress and I will walk with you before my back begins to tire.'

That morning we visited the restored chapel – still incomplete but with the beautiful tombs of my ancestors – then walked along the wooded paths that bordered great hunting forests. Before noon we paused at the stables where George was conferring with an Irish dealer and shaking his head. When the man had gone my mother said, 'Mary is to choose a horse for this afternoon.'

'I'd like a ride,' I said, 'but not for hawking.'

'Show her the grey palfrey,' my mother said, and George led out the most magnificent horse I had ever seen. Then she said, 'No need to saddle – ride her,' and George lifted me up and we were away – I say 'we' for correctness but we were one force, one element. As I dismounted George said, 'She is yours. To keep.'

My mother said, 'Part of your dowry. I've explained your situation.'

As I thanked them for the gift, I thanked them silently for their understanding. At dinner we enjoyed trying to name her, for, though part English, her name was an unpronounceable Arabian. Lady Isobel, less shy now, suggested several but they seemed to me too coy. I would not be riding a lovable pet but an animal capable of great courage and endurance and to call her 'Chérie' or 'Bijou' would denigrate her. So for a few days we dispensed with a name as I rode her, saddled in Spanish leather and with silver-embellished reins, around the vast estate.

George, Isobel and I played golf on the links, and I won an archery match, though George triumphed at tennis. A few neighbours came to dine, and there was music. Then one dusk a courier arrived from Holyrood to tell my brother that James,

150

commanded to appear in Edinburgh by Her Majesty within six days, had not arrived. At the Market Cross he was proclaimed an outlaw.

George said, 'I've written to Her Majesty that I'll gather the loyal men of this area when she sends the word.'

'If only I could fight!' I said. 'I've loathed that man most of my life.'

'Not more than I,' George said. My mother quite calmly hoped that someone would assassinate him before he bathed Scotland in blood.

Next day my stepfather returned from Glasgow where he had been to the sheep and cattle markets. Tall, brown-bearded, I assumed he had once been handsome but age had crumpled his face and I suspected that beard was dyed. I found him merry, with a Frenchman's gallantry, and it pleased me that he was so attentive to my mother, bringing her shawls, admonishing her to use her stick when her back troubled her. He seemed delighted when I told him of the gift of the palfrey and we rode together the following day so that he might show me the herds of Highland cattle he had purchased, and the sheep.

I was enjoying my visit when Her Majesty's courier arrived on 24 August. George was to summon his men to arms at once and meet her in Stirling on the 26th. I was to remain at Seton until further notice.

Our messengers sped throughout the countryside and nearly a thousand men accompanied George from Seton village. The weather was perfect, pipers pranced in advance of the army and, despite my fear of James's ability to raise massive forces with Elizabeth's help, I felt a sort of exultation. That evening my mother and stepfather and I held special prayers in the chapel, which all of the remaining servants attended. And the yellow and crimson banner of Scotland was raised below the cross of Christ.

We learned, through couriers, that our Queen had headed her small army (and that the King had worn a gold corselet and red plumed hat) and reached Glasgow only to find that James had fled, for on the way five thousand men had joined her.

151

He had circled back to Edinburgh, with thirteen hundred horsemen – certain of gaining recruits through Knox. But though Knox, on the steps of St Giles, shouted for volunteers, the guns of Edinburgh Castle were safely in the hands of loyal Lord Erskine.

James fled to Dumfries on the Border while our army subdued rebels in St Andrews and Dundee. Our Queen returned, triumphant, to Edinburgh but spies reported that Elizabeth was sending James gold and ammunition and arming men to join his depleted forces. A courier brought me a personal note from Rizzio: 'May I suggest you return now? Her Majesty is not well. You would be a welcome stimulant.'

And so, with the blessings of my mother and stepfather, I rode under guard of their servants to Edinburgh. We entered a storm near Musselburgh. Most horses are timid of thunder and lightning; not so my palfrey. She shied just once on the old Roman bridge, then plunged on, leading the other horses, and in that moment I named her Fearless.

The grooms in White Horse Close gathered to admire her, to tend and feed her while I hurried into the palace. I went at once to Rizzio's study where he drew me to the fire and dried my cloak and boots. Then he sent for *aqua vitae* and I sipped it while he told me of Her Majesty's condition.

'Her nerves are frayed. She can't eat properly, or sleep. Gervais and Gurion attend her, but wisely, I think, she refuses poppy-drug because she wants her mind alert to James's next move. But' – he spread his stubby hands – 'there is no one we can trust on strategy, on military matters. Lethington is here, but remains neutral, nor do I think we could trust his advice if he gave it. Erskine understands only cannon, not the subtleties of war. In short, she needs, most desperately, a general.'

'But what can *I* do?' I asked.

'Keep her abed as much as you can. She roams this palace like a sleepwalker after our midnight talks. And she will not awaken Lady Fleming or Lady Beaton, whereas I believe she would rely on you for comfort because she feels such strength in your very presence.'

'Why?' I asked.

152

'Your serenity,' he said.

I found Her Majesty in the library with the King – and she looked as nearly a ruin as a beautiful woman can; her face was pallid, her hair down, her eyes puffed from lack of sleep. Even her ruff was unpleated as though she had not changed her gown for days. But the King, attired in gold cloth, stretched long legs to the fire and drank from Philip's jewelled goblet. As she sprang up from her desk to embrace me he yawned, ignoring my curtsey.

She asked about my holiday, praised my brother's enterprise in raising men so quickly, then seated me and said, 'We've been in luck thus far but there are rumours that Queen Elizabeth is mobilising an army in Carlisle to support James's. And my agents tell me that three English warships prowl our east coast, four on the west – so Bothwell could not possibly reach us by sea. He may already be caught at a time when I need him to command our forces—'

'*I* command our forces,' the King said.

'Oh, of course, love,' she said carelessly, as if to a small child. 'Seton, you'd best go and change for supper, I'll come up with you,' and we left the room together, my curtsey ignored again.

We separated to dress but later she came to my chamber, dismissed Isobel and sat on the bed, continuing to worry that Bothwell was trapped. 'And time passes dangerously. The almanac predicts storms beginning in early October – if we're to move on the Border, we must start soon – but why fret you with matters beyond your control?'

'God knows I've no military wisdom,' I said, 'but God also knows how essential Bothwell is to us. If we pray for his safe return—'

'We shall,' she said. 'Never before shall I have prayed so earnestly and yet so hopelessly. St Jude and St Andrew. . . . See that Father Black attends the chapel at six.'

She left me and I sought Adam in his quarters. He was reading and, when his page announced me, dropped his book and came forward to take both hands. 'I've missed you so,' he said.

'You were in my thoughts, too.'

153

He released my hands, seated me, and after I had told him the Queen commanded chapel, he said, 'With pleasure. And I've my personal prayers for her peace of mind. The King is an impediment to everything she tries to do, an almost constant embarrassment in public and God knows what hell in private. Two of his servants were "set upon" last week – Her Majesty tried to hush the truth and they complied by lying and saying they'd fought one another. So you'll see Jacques with a bandaged nose and Hubert with front teeth missing.'

'He was drunk, of course?'

Adam nodded. 'The young pages are afraid of him. One asked to be transferred to the suite of Lord Huntly, saying he lacked experience, which Her Majesty took to be shyness of serving royalty. She was sympathetic, and promised that if he served Huntly well he could look forward to resuming his place with the King.'

'She is not usually obtuse,' I said.

'I think she finds every possible excuse for him, as a woman in love will.'

As her confessor he knew far more than he would tell me, of course. And he had said she was in love. I hoped so, for it is said love may create miracles.

Reluctantly I left Adam. As reluctantly I left the candlelit chapel, but with some amusement that both Her Majesty and I were praying for the return of a pirate Protestant, a renegade, some said a brute. Bothwell was Scotland's only hope.

Lady Jean was overjoyed that her mother and brother had been summoned to court and shed her grey gowns for violet and azure. She would never be a beauty, but she had a certain quiet charm and enormous tact. For example, when the King knocked over a plate of meat at dinner, she apologised, saying her sleeve had been caught in the trencher. 'These long-flowing sleeves should be abolished,' she said. And she was also discreet:

'If I were you, Lady Mary, I'd remove your superb palfrey from the Close to the stables in the woods. There could be -- temptation.'

'But the grooms would never—'

154

'Perhaps not. But it seems so valuable an animal, more beautiful than the Queen's own. She has given two Spanish jennets to the King,' she added casually. 'He has such a passion for animals of all sorts. Imagine, he's requested a pair of lions!'

I had my groom stable Fearless with the humbler horses. If the King had demanded her, there could only have been contention with the Queen who would have refused him. Thereafter I was careful to ride in the mornings, when he was asleep; he rarely awakened until after ten when Taylor, his valet, brought him breakfast and prinked him for a day of hawking.

And the days lengthened slowly towards the predicted storms. On the night of 20 September Her Majesty was closeted with Rizzio and, kissing me good night, asked that I remain in the next room with the door open. 'Ours shall also be open,' she said, 'to prevent gossip.'

To me this was one more indication of the King's immaturity, and I sat down to read but was too nervous to do so. If he came and made a scene I did not know if she could control him. But two hours passed and I was dozing when a guard came to my door and said that a man in the courtyard begged to see Her Majesty on a matter of life and death.

This seemed suspicious to me, for our couriers stated their names. 'He looks like a minister,' the guard said.

That seemed stranger still. I went down with the guard to the great, nail-studded door where another guard and a halberdier stood watch on the stranger. He was taller than both, in a shabby, black Geneva cloak, a big-brimmed hat pulled over his eyes and a face-concealing muffler. He turned towards me as I came forward and bowed. 'I believe we have met, Lady Seton. Of course you fail to remember my name – being a poor relation to the Hepburns—'

Bothwell! James Hepburn, Earl of Bothwell. Quickly I said, 'If it's a matter of life and death, reverend sir, you may come in, and I'll summon the Queen.'

A guard escorted us up the stairs. Then, alone with Bothwell in my room, I all but embraced him in my thankfulness. He threw off the disguise and revealed a doublet crusted with

155

mud, torn hose and a shirt grey with dust. The wavy, dark-red hair was snarled with burrs and he said, 'Can you find me some sort of robe or will the Queen receive me as I am?'

'Just as you are, my Lord. You're an answer to prayer.'

'How is she?'

I told him.

'And the King?' he asked.

I hesitated and he said, 'Ill?' with such hopefulness that I smiled as I shook my head. Then I went to the next room where she and Rizzio were studying maps.

'Lord Bothwell is here, Madam.'

She jumped up and he met her in the doorway, bowing. She said softly, 'Thank God. I'd almost despaired.' Whether from shock or, more likely, exhaustion, she swayed and he caught her in his arms as she fainted. He carried her to a bench, Rizzio brought brandy-wine and she revived quickly. She began to ask how he had managed to get there but he said, 'You are going to bed at once – and alone.'

She rose obediently, tottered a few steps, and he picked her up. I ran ahead into the corridor and led the way, past the astonished guard, to her bedchamber, taking the private stairs, fairly certain that the King had retired below. Janet was summoned and the Queen said, 'Don't worry – I am all right.'

We closed the door and Bothwell spoke to the guard. 'It's Her Majesty's command that no one disturbs her. *No one.*'

While Bothwell rejoined Rizzio I had a room made ready for him and gave Isobel instructions to borrow doublet and hose from a sixfoot halberdier, a shirt and jerkin. Though she was trained to obedience without question, she asked, 'Is it a secret matter, Madam?'

'For the moment. In the room next to Signor Rizzio's study you'll find a cloak to clean, a hat and muffler to brush. See that they're placed in the gentleman's quarters. And a bathing tub.'

It was nearly three o'clock when I stopped to bid Bothwell and Rizzio good night; they were deep in talk but I needed to tell Bothwell where his room was. He thanked me briefly, tersely courteous.

In my bedchamber Isobel was waiting by the fire. As she

undressed me she said, 'I've mended a hole in his cloak, my lady, and placed a bible near his candle.'

Doubtless a bullet hole, I thought. 'The guards say he's a minister, Madam.'

'Our Queen is tolerant of all faiths,' I said, wanting to laugh. 'In fact, I think she is rather happy that he's here.'

She looked puzzled and I said, 'Any faith is said to move mountains.'

Bothwell would move armies across brutal hills, against the summits of James's treachery and Elizabeth's golden guile. From boyhood he had learned the skills of guerrilla warfare, and had mastered them. He knew the whims of weather and nosed it like a hound. If he were polite to Her Majesty's almanacs I'd be surprised.

'Good day, Isobel,' I said, for dawn was near. 'Sleep well.'

Fleming awakened me at noon. 'Her Majesty is still asleep and I don't know what to do – the King demands to see her but the guard prevented him, and he's in a rage. Janet came out and he struck her. . . .'

I hurriedly dressed and followed Fleming to the Queen's audience chamber. Beaton was there alone with the sobbing maid.

I examined her face, badly reddened by slaps. 'Janet,' I said, 'you will say nothing of this to Her Majesty. Be a brave lass and forget the matter. Lady Beaton will take you to Monsieur Gervais for a draught to quiet you, then go to your own chamber.'

Our maids were gentlewomen. She looked at me through tears and said, 'Monsieur Gervais might be curious. If I may just rest a while?'

Beaton accompanied her to her room. I summoned the guard from the corridor and said, 'Angus, I thank you in Her Majesty's name for your protection of her. You will, of course, forget the matter.'

He nodded, made a clumsy bow.

'The King was not aware that Her Majesty was exhausted to the point of illness. In protecting her sleep you did her great service.'

157

'My privilege,' he said, and was dismissed to his post.

Fleming said, 'Dear heaven, what a morning! Rizzio didn't appear for breakfast and his valet says he mustn't be disturbed. Not even for Mass! Some stranger occupies the chamber next to his and a page looking in saw pistols and a bible by his bed. Gaston flung a haddock at Henri in dispute over a sauce and Lethington is in a pout about something. . . .'

I told her that Bothwell was the stranger and that it would be best not to tell Lethington until Her Majesty did so. 'He's probably pouting now because she consults with Rizzio but it's his own fault for announcing his neutrality. Perhaps you should consider a less cautious suitor.'

'But he's not a traitor,' she said angrily.

'Not yet,' I said, and left her.

Her Majesty and the King were at dinner – she looking marvellously rested, and apparently she had coaxed him into good humour. He was affable to Bothwell, who wore the guard's clothes with nonchalance, but from my part of the table I heard none of their conversation, only occasional laughter in which Lethington joined. Rizzio said to me, 'I've urged her to spend the day hawking. There may not be another for a long while.'

I had thought Bothwell would join them but as I left the hall he said, 'I'm riding into Edinburgh to see my tailor and my bootmaker. Would you care to come with me?'

I went with him and after we had ordered him new clothes we descended into a wine cellar and he asked the landlord for claret, and in privacy he sped through his adventures as though they might bore a lady. He had received the Queen's message in France, hurried to Belgium to collect arms and ammunition for her, thence to the Low Countries for more. 'They should reach us this week. My agents warned me of Queen Elizabeth's traps, so I hired a pinnace and sailed up the east coast of Scotland. Her Majesty's warship *The Aid* scarcely aided me but I managed to outrun her. At the mouth of the Tweed she fired on me but all she caught was my cloak.'

'So nearly killed!' I said.

'I rowed out of range,' he said casually. 'But when I landed

158

off a Border bay I knew that Lord James's men would be alerted. I could never enter Edinburgh without disguise. So my page Paris and I stopped at a moor kirk to pray.'

'I know you've turned Protestant, my Lord,' I said, 'but I marvel that your faith sustained you.'

'Faith?' he asked, refilling our mugs. 'Urgency. We propped the minister against his pulpit, removed his clothes, gave him mine and so I proceeded as an innocent cleric. Oh, and we relieved him of two old horses which I'll presently put to pasture.'

Impudence so understated that it seemed to him merely logic. 'But I'd not meant to bore you with my little tale. Rizzio has been my friend, but he dissembles. He will discuss Lord James, the mood of your changeable nobles and the possible mood of the weather. God knows, the mood of the weather is in my very guts, and the almanacs be damned. We'll march to meet James when I sense the time – no sooner. Lady Seton, have you the courage to tell me the truth?'

'That depends on your question.'

'It concerns the King. I talked with Huntly this morning. He told me that during the campaign the King was a posturing ass, halting the army outside Stirling to take out a mirror and plump the plumes of his hat. Wherever a crowd gathered, he peacocked, blowing kisses, throwing largesse from his saddle bag – when Her Majesty is pawning her jewels to pay her soldiers.'

'I'm not surprised,' I said.

'My question is this: is there any way of suggesting to her that, when the army moves, he's best left at home with the women and the poodles?'

'I'm afraid not,' I said. 'You would only offend her.'

'She's that deep in love, then?' he asked grimly.

'She's made her choice, my Lord.'

He swore. 'Then there's nothing for it but to carry our national embarrassment with us. I expect he'll demand pink armour with rosebuds on his spurs. Well, let's be off to find a tailor for Paris and leatherjacks for both of us.'

As we rose from the table I asked, 'That stained dirk – you didn't kill the minister?'

'Oh, no,' he said. 'Someone on the moor – one of James's spies, I think.' He sounded bored. As we climbed the steps to the street he said, 'I appreciate your discretion, my lady. If ever I may do you a service, you've only to command me.'

'Very well,' I said. 'Rid us of James – for ever.'

CHAPTER IX

———◆———

Bothwell roused his Borderers and on 9 October, with twelve thousand men, Her Majesty headed her army towards Dumfries. She wore a helmet, a breast-plate, pistols at her saddle bows. The King, of course, glittered as one might expect, but was undeniably handsome in a scarlet, sable-trimmed cloak. In contrast, Bothwell, Huntly and the other loyal Lords in leatherjacks and cutting-scarves looked like ruffians.

During their absence Adam and I had leisure to be together. I felt no passage of time, for in a dream time is limitless. The only realities were marked, for me, by the need to be present at meals, to help Lady Jean and her mother embroider a Christmas gift for Her Majesty. Fleming and Beaton had made a silken gown of apple green and we were sewing on the silver signs of the zodiac around the hem.

When Beaton had left the room Lady Huntly – a plump, stately lady – said, 'I had hoped by now to be stitching bridal attire for my daughter.'

'Mother!' Jean said.

'There are no secrets among us that don't become rumours,' Lady Huntly said placidly. She was one of those forthright Highland women who speaks her mind however tactlessly. 'Lady Fleming, is Lady Beaton actually engaged to Alex?'

Fleming stammered that she was not sure. When Alex returned from the war it might soon be clear.

'It is clear,' Jean said. 'Let's not discuss it.'

Then Lady Huntly turned to talk about fate and destiny and said that she had the second sight. 'I have told Jean not to fret about spinsterhood – she will, in fact, have three husbands.'

We wanted to laugh at this prophecy. Jean, looking

161

miserable, said, 'If you must predict the future, perhaps Lady Seton would care to hear hers.'

I had no faith in such superstition but to please Jean I said I would.

Lady Huntly studied me, narrowing shrewd, blue eyes. Then she said, 'There is great love. There is—' Then she paused. 'When a veil descends, I can't see through it.'

Chatte came in, a merciful interruption. Her animal tricks reminded me of the lions and I said, 'I shan't be at ease if lions are brought here for the King. I can't imagine what pleasure they'd give him.'

'Lions are royal beasts,' Lady Huntly said.

'So are ermines,' Jean said. 'Why can't he keep *them*?'

None of us spoke direct criticism of the King, for that would be treason, but we seemed to condemn him silently. And I wished I could have told Bothwell to kill the King. To kill James was his duty. To kill the King would be pleasure. And had he not always indulged his pleasures?

Her Majesty, the King and our army returned with glorious news. Ten thousand troops had chased James and his army over the Border into England. The traitors were in exile at Newcastle, Elizabeth, expected to assist and harbour them, was cool. She detested failure, especially as she had poured gold into it. So the Queen of England and Cecil were the joke of Catholic Europe.

Furthermore, the Pope's dispensation of marriage had finally arrived, so Her Majesty rode on a tide of triumph. From my brother I heard that she had led her army like a man, uncomplaining of the long, difficult march, of all the hazards involved. Bothwell, who had been wry of women in combat conditions, could not praise her more than in telling Rizzio, 'She was a match for her mother.'

We held a victory ball on All Hallows Eve. Rizzio did not dance, though even with humped shoulders he played at tennis and at the butts. Perhaps he thought himself ungraceful. In any case, I joined him at the great bowl of punch and as the dancers frisked by we clinked goblets, silently happy.

Then we turned as Bothwell came up with Lady Jean. She

162

was wearing a deep blue gown, the points of the sleeves tied with gold. Her hair shimmered under its golden headdress, and she smelled of rose-attar. At the same time Beaton and Alex joined us.

Lady Jean extended her hand to Alex. 'I hear that you are to be congratulated.'

He took her hand for a moment, red-faced, and stammered his thanks.

'And may you be happy, Lady Beaton,' Lady Jean said.

So the Queen had granted them permission to marry. Possibly she would grant any request on this triumphant night but I was sorry beyond words for Lady Jean, whose eyes were like dead candles. Rizzio, with his born tact, asked Lady Jean to come behind the musicians' screen and admire his new lute. As Beaton and Alex joined the dancers Bothwell said, 'I thought Lady Jean was affianced to Alex.'

'For years,' I said. 'But Beaton entranced him.'

'So,' he said. 'I suppose I must rid myself of the concept that bonds are sacred.'

'But love—'

'Oh, love,' he said contemptuously. 'A pledge is a pledge.'

'Would you honour such a pledge if you fell out of love?' I asked, not in defence of Alex but because I was curious.

'I honour all pledges,' he said. 'So, I think, does Huntly. If it weren't for Her Majesty's approval – which I marvel at – he'd avenge his sister.'

I thought of what Adam would think and say. 'This isn't war, my Lord, and what does vengeance achieve?'

He looked down at me, tawny head tilted in mockery. 'It often achieves death, Lady Seton. I regret I was unable to fulfil your request regarding James Stuart. But I didn't pledge myself, now did I? I knew he'd bolt like a hare.'

'But suppose you'd cornered him?'

He implied with his gestures that James would have been gutted. I had sensed the violence of Morton, Lindsay and the skeletal Ruthven, but they would act in passion. Bothwell had no such confusion of mind. His killings would be cold, deliberate extermination.

He laughed. 'In time he'll pay for his treachery. Meanwhile,

163

we may be amused by Elizabeth's embarrassment. . . . Will you dance?'

We joined the dancers in The Skip; after my brother claimed me, Bothwell danced with the Queen. Both were dressed in gold, and in the golden light from the high, oak chandeliers they moved together in dazzling grace. The King, one hand on his goblet, was slumped in his chair.

George told me that he would return to Seton next day and, as he danced me to the door, said, 'Why doesn't she summon his servants to take him to bed?'

The King was vomiting on the table.

Bothwell returned to his castle of Hermitage as Lieutenant General of the Marches, guardian of the Borders. At supper one night the King, drunk as usual, protested to Her Majesty that his father deserved the post. Rarely did she lose her temper publicly, but we all heard her say, 'It's not a suitable post for an ageing man. And it requires courage and experience.'

He glared down the table at Rizzio. 'Is this the advice of your boolie-backed friend?'

'It's my command,' she said. 'Lord Lennox remains in Glasgow.'

The flash of her eyes, the tone of her voice, silenced him. Chatte was ordered to perform, perhaps to distract him. During her song Rizzio left the hall, bowing to Their Majesties, and I followed him into the corridor.

'How obnoxious!' I said.

'I gather that he is demanding the crown matrimonial that would give him full power with her. I suppose he suspects I've advised against it.'

A taper-bearer approached us and Rizzio said, 'Will you have a sleep-cup with me, Lady Seton?' and we went to his apartments where his valet brought wine and stirred the fire. We shared a couch newly covered with beaded damask. 'Her gift,' he said. 'I can't stem her generosity.'

'Why should you try?' I asked.

He went to his desk and brought a letter to show me. It was from our ambassador, Melville, stating that Elizabeth was complaining of James's presumption. 'It is all owing to an

Italian named David whom the Queen of Scotland loves and favours and grants more credit and authority than are authorised by her affairs and honour. It is said by the Earl of Moray [James] that this David is her lover.'

'But how could Melville think that?'

'No, no, he quotes Queen Elizabeth. Lord James must find some scapegoat for his current distress, and I am convenient. Our Queen refuses to take this letter seriously, in fact laughs. She flatters me that I am akin to Queen Elizabeth's Cecil, that she is hotly jealous that Scotland should have a secretary of like calibre – that in resigning my position I'd play into English hands.'

'Surely you'd not resign?'

He said, 'I'd prefer to work in the shadows. But Her Majesty flaunts me despite the gossip. I've warned her but she won't listen. When she finds love, loyalty, she can't reward it sufficiently.'

'Because it's rare in Scotland,' I said bitterly.

'Because it's her nature, as well. So impulsive, yet I can't enjoy the gifts she heaps on me. I have my quarters here, my house in the Canongate, clothing and jewels – and every honour she confers points to scandal. The Protestant lords here at court think me a Papal spy if not a lover. And the King, who seemed my friend – well, you heard him tonight.

'I'm not a coward, neither am I a hero, Lady Seton. I feel so strongly that I should leave her service for our mutual salvation. I'm a wealthy man now. I could return to Piedmont with only a quarter of my riches and still live comfortably to old age. That's what my mind orders me to do.'

'But your heart?' I asked.

The great, dark eyes were luminous. 'How can she struggle alone through mazes of intrigue? Lethington is a weathercock, blowing to the winds of success – I hear he is with us tomorrow. Huntly, Bothwell and your good brother are soldiers, not schemers. As to the rest, you know the pack, and all in league with Knox.' He lowered his voice. 'Perhaps the King is, too. He was seen a few days ago leaving Knox's house on the High Street.'

'But that's impossible! Who saw him?'

165

'One of my servants, on an errand to the goldsmith next door. He said that, though he wore drab clothes, he couldn't disguise his great height. And he came out furtively.'

'But the King is so staunch a Catholic.'

'I can only think it some conspiracy that takes precedence over religious conviction. My duty is to inform Her Majesty but I've no proof, for his face was hidden.'

Such information would only trouble Her Majesty and yet, if the King was conniving with Knox, she should be the first to know. 'She—'

A page tapped at the door and announced Her Majesty. She smiled as we rose and said, 'I can't sleep. So I dressed again and wandered about and saw the light in your window, David.'

'You're so welcome, Madam,' he said. She refused the wine he offered and I asked permission to retire.

'Not unless you are weary, Seton.' She took a chair. 'I can trust you in any matter. The King, maudlin in drink, took a fit of guilt. Knox sent for him on Monday and suggested that he was being duped – by you, David. He said that so long as you were my lover, I would deny the King the crown matrimonial.'

'And the King *believed* this?' Rizzio asked.

'Not entirely. He asked me to deny the accusation. Of course I did – and then he said, "Prove it, and give me the crown." '

'You dare not,' Rizzio said. 'We've talked of his irresponsibility before. But what you can do is to dismiss me. That should end his dealings with Knox.'

She turned to me. 'Seton, you know little of politics. But if you were in my position, with only a handful of loyal men, would you let your principal and cleverest adviser go?'

Despite his love for her, I was sure, in time, he would be happier in his own country. Unlike Bothwell, who could laugh at his enemies, he was emotionally vulnerable. And yet my duty was to her.

'No,' I said finally. 'I couldn't let him go, Madam. No matter what evil gossip, I couldn't.'

She nodded, eyes soft for us both. 'And I can't.'

She gave me permission to retire then, and pressed my hand

as I passed her. At the door I turned to curtsey. The tall tapers were guttering, wind moved the arras near the window in eerie semblance of a hunt. I shivered as I wished them a good night.

In early December the Queen ordered the cleansing of Holyrood, and we moved to Linlithgow Palace where she had been born. It faced a beautiful loch which we hoped would freeze over for skating and the hunting was renowned. Ambassador Randolph was with us. Bothwell came for the hawking. Adam and I walked in the snowy fields and played chess with Rizzio while the others danced. The Great Hall was magnificent, rock-walled but made warm by painted cloths and tapestries, and fires of enormous logs. What depressed me, however, was a chapel which adjoined it. In a loft above lepers were confined, peering out of a little window during our Mass.

At supper on our mutual birthday Her Majesty wore white velvet and diamonds, a white fox shawl covering her bare shoulders. She rose as the feast ended and said, 'I am so happy to tell you that, if God wills, the King and I present an heir to Scotland in June.'

We cheered and shouted congratulations. This would be bitter news for the Virgin Queen, but Ambassador Randolph went up to kiss our Queen's hand and to join in the toasts. The King, who was drunk, pounded the table for silence and slurred some sort of speech, ending with, 'As God's my witness, the child is mine.'

There was a shocked silence.

'It's true,' he said. 'Who dares to question it?'

I do not know what the Queen whispered to him. It must have been agony to smile serenely, then to face us and command the musicians in the gallery to prepare for dancing. The tables were cleared and set against the walls. She led the King from the hall, and they did not return.

Joining Adam in the card-room I said, 'If only Randolph hadn't been here – Elizabeth will gloat over this.'

He nodded. 'I almost wonder if the King isn't in her pay.'

'She'd never trust such a man.'

'But we can't doubt that she manoeuvred Lennox into

Scotland, preparing the way for his son.' Then he said, 'A sorry birthday for you, too, ending as it has.'

'I've had many gifts. Your friendship is the greatest.'

'Love,' he said. 'You know that.'

Chatte interrupted us by bounding up in a whirl of peacock feathers and turning a somersault at our feet. I patted her and she mischiefed off into another room, shrieking like a peacock, but I had no heart for laughter, nor had he. Then Bothwell strode through the room without a word to us, glaring.

'What's amiss with him?' Adam asked.

'Some insult, I suppose. He has a hot temper.'

We played at cards, but only as an excuse to be close. We separated before midnight. I looked into the Great Hall and was joined by Bothwell.

'Have you just killed someone?' I asked, hoping to tease him into good humour.

'I was tempted,' he said. 'But even I resist regicide.'

Then he said, bluntly, 'The King's servants couldn't handle him to bed. I went up to his chamber, summoned by his valet. Taylor was frightened and asked me to go in alone. But the King was in bed – with one of Her Majesty's young pages.'

'Jesu!' I said. 'And where was she?'

'Near the bed, and near to fainting. I think she had just come in. . . . The page fled, poor devil, stumbling over his breeches. I urged her to her own chamber. And I urged her to divorce.'

'But you're Protestant,' I said. 'You can't know what you're asking of her. She'd lose every shred of Catholic respect.'

'So she told me,' he said. 'Sot, pervert, she will never divorce him. He lies on Scotland like a fog, like a haar. Or, if you like, whore.'

'Whores are paid.'

'So is he paid – from her innocence. Horses, jewels, attire – lions. His fancy for lions is interesting. Perhaps he thinks to mate with one?'

I shuddered. 'Do you think he's mad, my Lord?'

'Only for power. For drink.'

'God help her,' I said. 'She's tied to him for the rest of her life.'

168

'It's trite but true that life is full of surprises,' and he wished me a good night as I left him.

Their Majesties did not appear at breakfast or dinner but in the afternoon she closed the chapel to the court and remained there with Adam for more than two hours. I hoped he could bring her some comfort. At supper the King drank only a cup of ale and his subdued behaviour seemed to plead for her forgiveness. She paid him little attention, wearing her fixed smile as she talked with Lethington and Randolph. There was no dancing, no music. Bothwell and Lady Jean played chess in the card-room afterwards, others played Primero. The King retired but Her Majesty lingered, moving restlessly from one group to another, watching the games. I had never felt so sorry for her; to join the King was obviously repugnant to her. Adam sat talking with Father Joseph and examined some book. In the candlelight his face – even when, occasionally, he smiled – was sad. But it was Her Majesty who required such comfort as I could give, so I went to her and said, 'Have you any task for me, Madam – I've accomplished nothing for you since we've been here.'

'There is nothing to do but to amuse yourself,' she said, 'unless you care to embroider some clothes for the baby?'

'I'd delight in that!'

She said that one of our seamstresses was making shirts and bibs; that the christening robe would be made by nuns in Edinburgh at the convent of St Catherine. 'Didn't you suspect my pregnancy, Seton? You are always observant.'

I shook my head. 'Your Majesty is still slender. But I noticed that you travelled here by horse litter.'

'So I shall if there's distance. But I can still ride out a mile or two for hawking.'

Lady Huntly joined us, silent until Her Majesty said, 'I hear you've the sight. Do you predict for me, or are you shy?'

'I have studied your horoscope, Madam, and your stars are in the ascendant. But my own vision tells me that you will bear a son. However, you must guard your health from now until July . . . be prudent. And guard against a fair-haired man.'

The fool! No one at court was so fair as the King.

'That', said the Queen, her voice sharp as a dirk, 'I shall do. Is there any other warning?'

Lady Huntly hesitated. Not through tact, for she had none. She blinked, shook her head, and her skin, which was normally ruddy, had paled. Each freckle stood out. 'You'll excuse me, Madam. A veil obscures the future.'

'As well, perhaps,' Her Majesty said, managing to laugh.

Lady Huntly asked permission to retire; it was granted. I said, 'I think her anxious to be truthful, but she is also sufficiently shrewd not to guess at the future as a gypsy might. And yet, can you believe it, she predicts three husbands for her daughter?'

Her Majesty's laugh was almost genuine. 'If ever there was wishful prophecy! But poor Lady Jean is likely never to marry. Alex was her first love and, I'm certain, the last. I granted my consent to his union with Beaton because no one should marry out of duty unless it's a matter of political expediency. He could have made Lady Jean far more miserable than she is.'

Perhaps by infidelity; certainly by lack of passion. I was suddenly thankful that I was beyond the need to marry. And it occurred to me that the bible states that there is no marriage in heaven. A condemnation of that institution on earth?

The next few days were filled with Christmas preparations. The King drank sparingly and on the surface the days passed pleasantly for the Queen. I tried not to think of her nights alone with him.

At supper on Twelfth Night I was astonished when Her Majesty, wearing her apple-green gown, rose from the dais to announce the engagement of Lady Jean and Bothwell. They had been much together, but they both enjoyed sport so I had assumed a mutual devotion to boar- and stag-hunting. As we toasted them they seemed gravely calm, quite unlike a couple in love, with no excitement about them. Only Lady Huntly dimpled and blushed as though she were the bride-to-be. When I saw Adam I said, 'It's extraordinary to me. Unless he is marrying her for money. He's always admitted he has none. It must be a matter of convenience.'

170

'But that Lady Jean would agree if he were merely a fortune-hunter? I think not. After all, he is a great Lord, high in the Queen's esteem. The Gordons are ambitious to hold that esteem, I'd think. And any lady, rejected in love as she's been, might find her pride regained.'

'Then why doesn't she strut a bit in triumph?'

'It's not her nature,' he said.

But as a man he was not interested as I was. It was Fleming who gave me her views. 'He is nearly thirty-one, and mindful that he must have a legitimate heir. God knows how many seeds he's sown among wenches, now he seeks respectability.' There was a flutter of her old attraction to him. 'If you weren't so spiritual, my dear, you'd be aware of his sensuality.'

'I'm not that obtuse,' I said. 'But it's the sensuality that should repel Lady Jean. She's said she would always love Alex. And I believe her.'

'She might change,' Fleming said. 'But I grant you they're an odd pair.'

But next morning I met Lady Jean alone and when I kissed her cool, pale cheek and again wished her happiness she said, 'Thank you. I ask only a measure of contentment and homes of my own away from court.' Sun from the arched window touched her eyes – still lightless and dead. 'I cannot bear to see Alex again; now I need not. And I have – Seton – I shall have dignity.'

Tears fell but she turned her head and I pretended not to notice. We separated. I had a compulsion to call out to her 'Wait! End this farce!' But I do not trust intuition and so I let the moment pass and climbed the spiral stairs to the tower called 'The Hawk's' where I went to work with the seamstress, embroidering silver and gold on white – Her Majesty's crest.

'Her Majesty is wise to choose white,' Dame Menzies said. 'One hopes it is a son, but it's a known fact that wine-bibbers father daughters.'

'You refer to the King,' I said coldly.

'Och, well, who doesn't know it, Madam? Taylor tells me he drinks through the night – alone. No one cares to go near him. And do you know, a page fled the palace before Christmas? His Majesty must have set upon him cruelly.'

171

'You will not listen to such gossip,' I said. 'It only brews mischief. And you don't discuss your masters.'

'Indeed not,' she said. Like Lady Huntly, she was a Highland woman, tart of tongue and truthful. 'But the King is not my master. That English oaf—'

'Quiet!' I said.

She subsided with an apology. But the firm set of her mouth, her chin, belied her humility. What she said accounted for Her Majesty's reluctance to be alone with the King. And whatever she had confessed to Adam had tarnished his glossy handsomeness. I loved him the more for what he obviously suffered for her sake. I understood his silences when we were together and accepted them.

When I left her I chanced to meet Lord Ruthven at the foot of the stairs. Tall, cadaverous, he tried to step aside to let me pass, but was taken with a fit of coughing so violent that he stumbled. I disliked him but had to help him.

'I'll summon your servant,' I said. 'He'll take you to Gurion.'

But the servant came running. His name I remembered – Henry Yair – because, among others, he annoyed Chatte with his attentions and the Queen had reprimanded him. He was as tall and gaunt as his master, sly-eyed. I said, 'Take Lord Ruthven to the surgeon.'

'Yes, my lady.'

But Ruthven protested that he needed only to lie down, so I proceeded on my way. Passing the King's bedchamber I heard a drunken laugh which soared into a high giggle.

We returned to Edinburgh by way of Melville Castle, one of Her Majesty's hunting seats on the banks of the river North Esk. There was good sport, which kept the King sober, but she joined it for only one day and spent most of her time with Rizzio. And on the morning of our departure, as we gathered near the stables to await our horses, she said, 'Signor, I've a favour to ask.'

'Anything, Madam,' he said.

'We need trees at this spot. You will plant a few to commemorate our visit.'

172

All of us heard her, and it was as if she had said plainly, 'You are the most honoured person in court.' Ruthven and Morton glared, the King turned red with fury and Bothwell moved towards Rizzio as though to protect him. I could not fathom why she should order this – with Randolph to carry the gossip – except in extreme anger, a need to humiliate her husband.

Poor Rizzio looked all but honoured, but he attempted a smile and carried out her command. As he planted two ash trees, an oak and a Spanish chestnut, Bothwell stood beside him. Then the Queen thanked Rizzio and in virtual silence we set off on the Dalkeith road to ride the six miles to Holyrood, she and the King in a horse litter.

That night I said to Adam, 'I think she's in vengeful mood. Surely with good reason, but can't you warn her?'

'I shall,' he said, 'a warning clothed in piety and embroidered with all the counsel of forgiveness. But devout as she is, I doubt that she'll take it to heart.'

As to forgiveness, it implies forgetting. I knew she could never forget what she had seen in the King's bed. Nor, of course, could she forgive or forget James's treason. Within a few days she forfeited his lands and those of the other exiled rebels and summoned them to appear in Edinburgh in March before Parliament, to stand trial.

There seemed a sort of elation when she spoke of it, and this was shared by Bothwell. Since the Borders were under control he was more at court, and they were often together, alone or with Rizzio. If I had been engaged to him I would have been forlorn, but Jean was not in love with Bothwell. And even if she had been, what chance would any woman have against Her Majesty? I had never seen a more beautiful woman, for even Madame Diane could not match her. And her charm was of the sort that made each person she talked to feel a glow of well-being. She simply implied, without words, that one had value. She would listen intently, her glance never strayed from one's face, her attention never wandered.

But Bothwell's attention certainly wandered from Lady Jean. He was polite in her company but abstracted. Once she asked him a question at breakfast but he was watching Her

Majesty make a fan from a napkin and did not hear her. When Her Majesty was absent he watched the door from which she might enter. His face expressed nothing, but his eyes seemed almost wistful. Still, he was no fool and I told myself that protective fathers looked at daughters that way.

The lions arrived, with seemingly half of Edinburgh following. Our hunt-master and men with whips placed them in a pit which had been dug for them behind the palace, walled for safety. The King, in violet velvet, observed a ceremony of welcome from a chamber in the south wing, and threw them meat. They roared for more and he laughed and withheld it, hoping they would fight. But Her Majesty said pointedly that she could not afford a dead animal, and left as more meat was brought.

I followed her with other ladies and she said, 'I wish I could return the brutes, for he'll soon lose interest.'

Then she said, 'May we see the bridal gown?' and turned to Lady Jean, who led us to her chamber. From a chest her maid took a silver-cloth dress with a long train and sleeves lined in white taffeta embroidered in pearls. Lady Jean thanked Her Majesty for providing the materials and the pearl coif for her hair. Lady Huntly added her thanks and said, 'If my daughter could be beautiful, these things would make her more so.'

Her Majesty, whose figure was thickening, said, 'If only I had her waist!' Then she praised Lady Jean's hair and asked that I arrange it before the wedding, which was to be on 22 February. No Catholics would attend the ceremony in the Canongate Protestant Church.

Her Majesty's face suddenly shadowed. She said, 'I feel weary,' and left us abruptly. Perhaps her pregnancy? Why, then, should tears stand in her eyes? I followed her into the corridor and asked if she needed the surgeon or apothecary.

'No,' she said, 'I'm not ill.'

As we separated on the main staircase she spoke over a sob. 'I am really quite all right.'

The wedding reception was given by Master Kinloch, a prosperous Edinburgh merchant. As we rode to his house on the

174

High Street the King took the cheers of the crowd as intended solely for himself; I had never seen him preen so, blowing kisses, bestowing blessings with drunken graciousness. Her Majesty deliberately sped her horse past him. As we passed the Canongate the wedding bells rang out and we caught a glimpse of guests emerging and their servants bringing them sacks of barley to toss.

At Kinloch House the ballroom was festooned with gilded wheat tied in white ribbons, there was a screen of evergreen boughs and waxed white roses for the musicians. The King went at once to a bowl of brandy-wine punch. Beaton arrived with Alex, her husband of two months. At first I marvelled that Lady Jean had invited them, then realised it was a matter of pride. Beaton was merely the wife of a laird; Lady Jean was the Countess of Bothwell.

When trumpets announced the wedding party we all stood aside except the King who stood in their way as though intent on focusing attention on himself. He did not succeed; Her Majesty contrived to sweep past him and kiss Jean and extend her hand to Bothwell. Then they moved among the guests until they came to Beaton and Alex. Jean curtsied to him and kissed Beaton. There seemed to be no strain. But Jean did not approach Alex for the rest of that revel.

I had never thought of Bothwell as a formal person; he had too much independence to conform to the minutiae of court etiquette. Yet he was almost stiffly correct, greeting the nobles in order of precedence, standing at last beside Rizzio. It was only later that I realised he had not even spoken to the King.

But by now the King was sodden, slumped into a chair. When Rizzio sang he looked up sulkily. Nor did he join the dancers. Perhaps he retained enough sense to know that he would stumble. And stumble he did when dinner was announced and Taylor led him to the table.

There were two spangled canopies at either end. The King sat alone under one, the Queen at the other with Jean and Bothwell on either side of her. My misfortune was to be near the King, under a maypole of ribbons, so that I was all too aware of his blank eyes and dribbling mouth. Also, I was seated between the odious Morton and the equally odious

175

George Douglas, who was Morton's illegitimate brother and, I was certain, suspicious of Rizzio as the Queen's lover. He was always making little jests at Rizzio's expense, such as, 'He is so hideous he must possess a vial of aphrodisiacs for the ladies.' To compound my boredom, Lindsay sat opposite me and ogled, making me sorry that I had chosen a low-cut gown with back-flared ruff.

The King ate nothing, though his favourite cock's kidneys and artichoke hearts were served; he was interested only in the contents of his golden goblet. I hoped he would be too drunk to attend that night's banquet at Holyrood. The Queen had commanded four days of celebration for Jean and Bothwell – a tournament, Highland games, masques and playlets.

'. . . look like a ripe peach,' Lindsay said, leaning towards me.

Then Sir James Balfour mercifully rose to propose a toast to the Queen's unborn child, as future ruler of Scotland and England. All of us rose except the King. Randolph drank as though he meant it, as a diplomat must. During the silence the King said loudly, 'I've a suitable name for the child.'

'James,' said Her Majesty from the other end of the table, 'after my father.'

'No,' said the King. He pointed to Rizzio. 'Solomon, son of David.'

I saw Bothwell's hand move to his dirk but the Queen clutched him and whispered, so he remained rigidly beside her. There was no sound in the room but the chirp of caged birds in their place by the casement, and the tinkle of a music-box in the chamber beyond.

Then Her Majesty moved to the door, and Master Kinloch followed her. She gave him her hand to kiss. 'I thank you for your hospitality,' she said. 'I hope you will join us tonight.'

Then she was gone. We remained, stunned, standing, except for the King. No one approached him. Then Master Kinloch returned and bade the feast to proceed. The King slept, a pink-faced corpse. There was eating and drinking and music. But there was no laughter. And until the King awakened none of us could leave.

Rizzio sat as erectly as his humped shoulders would allow.

176

Those close to him evidently dared not speak to him, until Bothwell leaned across Jean and said, 'Signor, have you time for tennis in the morning?'

The great dark eyes turned gratefully. 'If my Lord wishes.'

Bless Bothwell, I thought. Then Lady Huntly said, 'What, tennis in the *morning*, my Lord?'

But it was an excuse for bawdy chuckles, and the tension was eased.

Jean and Bothwell left for Crichton for a two-week honeymoon. Shortly afterwards Lethington accused Randolph of smuggling three thousand pounds to James and the exiled rebels. In council meeting the Queen asked Randolph if he could disprove this; he asked her to prove it. But Lethington did provide sufficient evidence to convince her, and she dismissed the ambassador, writing Elizabeth a note of explanation. Elizabeth replied tersely that she was forgiving James and intended to take him into favour.

One thing we marvelled at – the King had taken Rizzio into favour. If Her Majesty contrived this, or if his scant good sense prevailed, I do not know. But it was a relief to Rizzio even though he told me, 'He hopes to win the crown matrimonial through me – which he won't.'

March surprisingly came in like a lamb. One sunny afternoon Adam and I sat in a thicket of white birches, a private castle, and I told him that I had dreamed of him the night before. 'It was so sweet that it was nearly unbearable.'

'Can you describe it?' he asked.

'I can't. It would be as if I tried to describe a colour you had never seen or music you'd never heard.'

'Ah,' he said, 'that is the essence of religious experience. Dreams, I think, are a preparation for heaven. We voyage strangely in dreams, yet we're never surprised. And the voyage to an after-life must be strange, but we shan't be frightened or surprised by what we see.'

'In my dream', I said, 'I think we had wings and were flying among stars. If that follows death, then I long for death.'

Suddenly his arms were round me and I was lying on the grass with his lips on mine. I smelled the sandalwood of his

177

robes, the fragrance of crushed violets. Faint and far off I heard hunting horns and the high, silver sound of hounds.

Oh, my love, I said silently, for I could not move my lips from his, my love, my love. . . .

CHAPTER X

By 9 March wind buffeted Holyrood. It excited the lions in the pit and made them roar, which pleased the King. But high winds make me uneasy, and the Queen shared this feeling. She had summoned me to bring a case of her documents to the library, where she sat at her desk near the fire. She said, 'Even the walls seem to shudder, as though we were attacked by battering-rams.'

'Rather the wind than the English,' I said.

'Or my brother.'

She said she was working on her speech to Parliament, to be delivered in three days when James and the rebels would appear in Edinburgh on charges of treason. We had heard that the town was filling with people anxious to witness the trial, and that Morton's kinsmen, the 'Black Douglases', crammed the hostels not occupied by Bothwell's Borderers. Bothwell had left Jean at Crichton and was with us for the Parliamentary session.

'Balfour will help me with the legal terminology,' she said. 'Summon him here.'

I found Sir James at a late breakfast with Bothwell in the Great Hall, and he left us. Bothwell was eating frumenty. I had never cared for that sodden mass of wheat boiled with milk and eggs but I asked a servant for the honey that accompanies it, and bread. While we sat at the nearly empty table another servant tipped the remnants of ale mugs and wine glasses into a basin to be given to the poor at the gates, with left-over oatcakes.

'Have you seen the King today?' I asked.

'Briefly, on the way to the tennis court with Rizzio.'

'But how can they play against this wind?'

He shrugged. 'You know the King's whims. And Rizzio is

179

wise to humour them. And of course it prevents the King's interruption of the Queen's work.'

I was thinking of kings, of the history they make, but thus far his would be inept. And as he grew older he would become even weaker in judgement if he continued drinking. I said, 'I wonder what Buchanan is writing of the King, or if he dares to be truthful?'

'Buchanan suits history to his own prejudices. But I doubt he gives the King more than a page.'

It was an acid jest, but I laughed. And I laughed again as Chatte, in a monkey-suit, came in and climbed the screen that shielded musicians at dinner. Evidently she was practising, quite unaware of us.

'I wonder what that mysterious mind contains,' I said. 'Father Black taught her a little but he thought her a true primitive, learning as a parrot does.'

Bothwell said, 'She is a beautiful lass – and, like so many, an unmitigated bore.'

'I think her adorable.'

'But she demands laughter as professional humorists do. I've told Jean to reject minstrels, mummers, ballad peddlers from our doors. Fling them food or money, but for the love of God spare me their insistence that they are amusing.'

'But you've a sense of humour, my Lord.'

'Aye, in my way. But it is the natural human comedy that makes me laugh, not the designed, the artful, the rehearsed. "Look at me," Chatte implies, "am I not hilarious?" It's a challenge – and I refuse it because no jester can command amusement.'

I nearly said, 'No one can command *you*.'

Henry Yair came in bearing his master's silver tray and set it on a sideboard. Ruthven had not been at a meal for several weeks. The King visited him in his bedchamber with Morton and Lindsay and George Douglas and I think they played at cards. I said to Bothwell, 'That Yair probably expects more gold than Ruthven will leave him. He's arrogant with other servants and even bold with Taylor.'

'Ruthven isn't ungenerous,' Bothwell said. 'Mark the fine new livery Yair is wearing and the gold chains at his neck. My

180

page Paris, who knows everything, says that Ruthven gave him a garnet-hilted dirk yesterday.'

We left the hall and I went to my chamber to primp. Adam had made me feel beautiful, and so there was an impetus to achieve it. Isobel mixed a mask of white lead for my face, plucked and darkened my eyebrows. She brought me a hot brew of wine and honeyed vinegar and I cleaned my teeth with a little roll of linen, grateful that they were still intact. After all, I was twenty-four. But, dressed in sea-blue with a perky silver-lace ruff, I did not look so old, perhaps because I was happy. My only concern was the weather. Privacy with Adam could only be achieved out of doors, and I prayed that the wind would leave us.

But it did not. When Her Majesty summoned me to her bedchamber at dusk, it screamed in the tower turrets and blew soot and twigs down into the fireplace. But she was in merry mood, her speech completed. She wanted to celebrate and the tiny supper-room was being prepared. 'You will seek out and invite these people for seven o'clock: Lord Robert [an illegitimate brother, as loyal as James was treacherous], the Countess of Argyll, Rizzio and Captain Erskine. The chamber is too small for more. Remind Gaston that I shall require beef.'

It was Lent but she was in the sixth month of her pregnancy and Gurion had insisted that she must have red meat to build the baby's strength. The Pope had sent her dispensation. I was sure he wanted a Catholic heir to the English throne as much as she did.

'Oh,' she said, as I started towards the door, 'Tell David to bring his lute. He will sing against the wind.'

As I went on my errands I wondered if she had forgotten to invite the King or deliberately ignored him. I decided that she wanted to relax without him.

Only Rizzio seemed depressed about the invitation. He said, 'If I must, but – it is a command, Lady Seton?'

I nodded. 'She wants music.'

He said, 'Please tell Her Majesty that I am too much honoured.' Then he smiled. 'The King honours me with tennis, now the Queen—'

181

'The King is not invited,' I said.

I expected relief. Instead his smile vanished; but after a few moments he said, 'Seven o'clock, then.'

There seemed no hope of being with Adam that night. We could only glance at one another during supper in the Great Hall. Many of the Lords usually there were absent; so was the King. So there was a predominance of women. Lady Huntly said that her son and Bothwell were supping in private in his chamber; 'I think to gamble later. And I'm torn – I want them both to win, so the best I can hope for is a stalemate.'

Above the wind, that seemingly eternal wind, we heard the lions roar.

'Damn the creatures,' Fleming said.

Then we heard screams. They seemed to emanate from inside the palace, from above. Had the lions somehow got inside and savaged someone – a drunken action of the King? But as I wondered the screams became agonised and I knew they came from the Queen's audience chamber. Fleming and I jumped up from the table and ran through the hall towards the main staircase, and men followed us. Looking up I saw a red-soaked thing, like the carcass of an animal, booted down. But it was not a carcass; it was clothed in scraps of velvet, and heron feathers scattered like snow from the sleeves. It was Rizzio, and it lay at our feet with eyes open and aware, until it choked, gurgling, on the blood that spewed from the throat.

Morton came down and spat on the broken face. 'So perish vermin.'

But I saw a dagger in the corpse and recognised it as the King's. Then Bothwell, Huntly and other loyal lords pushed us aside and climbed the stairs and I remembered nothing else but someone – I think a guard – carrying me.

Apparently I revived quickly, in Fleming's chamber. She was being sick. I calmed her and sent her frightened page for *aqua vitae*, for her maid cowered in her dressing-closet and would not come out. The drink soothed us and lent me courage. Fleming begged me not to leave the room but I went out –

no guard was in the corridor – and, stepping over Rizzio, climbed the slippery, red staircase to the audience chamber.

The door was locked. I listened and then, mercifully, I heard Her Majesty's voice raised in anger, and knew she was alive. Again I stepped over what was left of Rizzio, over a widening pool of blood, and hurried towards my apartments. Then I thought, I must see Adam, no one will notice indiscretion on this night, nor question the need for a priest. I turned and ran along the corridor to his wing.

From the end of it – and no guard in sight – I saw someone leaning against the stone walls, retching. It seemed as though a naked black statue had come down from its onyx niche to weep and vomit. But I was in a state of nightmare and so anything seemed possible. Then the statue raised its head and saw me and wobbled towards me and said, 'He. He.'

I thought, Chatte has been raped. Her black hair spilled down her back, there was blood on her body but there seemed to be no wound when I examined her. She was shiny with blood but it was not hers.

'He,' she said again, tears pouring down her face, her breasts. *'He.'*

She stumbled to Adam's door and opened it.

He lay with his blood soaking into a white night-shirt over white blankets. Through his heart was a garnet-hilted dagger. I remember every detail of that bed. Above it was a stark iron crucifix; a small table with a bible and a candle in an iron holder were the only other furniture. On the white pillow were scattered black hairpins.

It was Adam who lay there but his face was so distorted that it seemed inhuman. The open eyes glared. Behind me Chatte was moaning and I saw her struggling into a dressing-gown. Then I moved towards the door but paused and went back and forced myself to pull out the dagger. It took all of my strength. As I turned Chatte screamed, thinking I intended it for her, and ran out. But I wanted it as evidence against Henry Yair; he might return to dispose of it.

There was no one in the corridor but a great clamour outside from the courtyard, and cries of 'A-Douglas! A-Douglas!' This was the battle-shout of Morton's kinsmen. I hurried to my room and was about to open the door when I saw the Countess of Argyll coming towards me, leaning on the arm of her page. Her face was grey, she could scarcely walk, and I said to the page, 'Bring her in here.'

I concealed the dagger under my long-flowing sleeve, and they followed me into my chamber, where Isobel jumped up to assist the Countess to my bed. Then I placed the dagger behind the arras. As I went to a chair Isobel said, 'Oh, God! You are hurt!'

There was blood on my gown. 'No. Now, I have scant strength, and you must help me use it. We must revive Lady Argyll, too. Run after the page and send him for *aqua vitae* – quickly!'

She obeyed. Then I drew my chair to the bed. Lady Argyll said in a whisper, 'I will be all right, I think.'

Her voice was so weak I should not have made her talk but I had to ask if Her Majesty was safe.

She nodded. 'But imprisoned in her room . . . Morton's men surround the palace.'

When the drink came she sat up on the bolster, sipped, shuddered, sipped again. I, too, took a little. Isobel stirred up the fire. The wind had died.

'Father Black is dead,' I said.

'He too? They killed Rizzio . . . I saw it all. . . .'

She said that the celebration had been a merry one until the King had come in by the private stairs and, being drunk, had thrown a pall on the party. 'Her Majesty, of course, was constrained to be polite but she was clearly exasperated, and that table is so small that he crowded her, sliding his arm round her waist. Then, suddenly, Lord Ruthven came in through the arch of the bedchamber. . . . Over his nightclothes he wore black armour, an iron cap. I swear to you he looked like the devil – forked beard, white face, wild eyes. And he held a sword.

'We all jumped up. Her Majesty asked him how he dared to intrude. He said, "I come for the poltroon, Rizzio. He has been here too long."

'She demanded explanation, and Ruthven said, "Ask the King."

184

'But the King denied any knowledge. Ruthven said that Rizzio had offended against Her Majesty's honour and that of the King and the country. He came across the threshold and unsheathed his sword, pointing it at Rizzio. Her Majesty sprang between them, shielding Rizzio, and threatening Ruthven with death if he didn't leave us. Erskine and Lord Robert drew their daggers but then – oh God!'

She shut her eyes as though to shut out memory, then opened them. 'I don't know how many men crashed in behind Ruthven. There was Morton, Kerr, Lindsay, George Douglas and his servants, Patrick Bellenden, Henry Yair . . . they were all armed, and as they rushed towards Rizzio the table overturned. I managed to snatch a candle from the candelabra and held it, for the fire in the hearth was so small. The Queen continued to shield Rizzio, but it was useless, for Ruthven pushed her into the King's arms and she was held there, while Bellenden pointed a dagger to her back and Kerr pressed a pistol to her stomach. All this while she begged for Rizzio's life, promising the men anything they asked if they'd spare him. But George Douglas drove a dagger into Rizzio's back and dragged him on his knees through the bedchamber. I don't know how I managed to follow with that candle, for what I saw no human should ever see.'

Nor I what I had seen in Adam's chamber.

'You mind the fringe on her Majesty's bed? Rizzio caught hold of it, the dagger in his back, screaming. Lindsay wore an iron glove and hammered Rizzio's fingers so that he lost his grasp, and I saw fingers fall to the floor like white sausages. And that pack of wolves finished him off in the audience chamber, all plunging in daggers, howling and slashing, and someone hurled him down the staircase. He was nearly naked but for his sleeves. . . . I heard Her Majesty vomit in the fireplace and went to her and led her back to her bedchamber and helped her to her bed, for she was close to fainting. But she regained strength and when we heard the Douglas war-cry outside she sprang up and ran to the supper-room where Ruthven and the King were drinking from a bottle which had somehow survived. She bent and picked up Rizzio's smashed lute, cradled it, with its torn yellow ribbons, against her

185

and said, pointing at Ruthven, "You'll die for this!"

'But he blamed the matter on the King, and the King's guilt was so plain – his face confessed to the plot, and though I did not see him stab Rizzio, I saw the golden hilt of his dagger in the body. There was then a hammering at the door of the audience chamber; the Queen and I ran there but Ruthven was ahead of us and opened the door. We had only a glimpse of Bothwell and Huntly and Atholl. The Queen shouted to them for help but Ruthven ordered her to be quiet, took a paper from his belt and said, "Look well. It's a bond signed by His Majesty, he has commanded this and your imprisonment here."

'There were thumping boots on the staircase, like an army, and Ruthven said to the Lords, "Morton's men. Go to your quarters if you value your lives." '

Her voice was a croak now. 'They had to go. They were so outnumbered. Ruthven bolted the door and told Her Majesty that she was confined to these chambers, that if she tried to escape she would be shot. I said, "Do you realise she carries a child, the heir to two thrones? Murder is one thing, but regicide. . . . Can you bear to burn in hell?" But he shrugged and said that death was upon him anyway, that he intended no crime against Her Majesty. But she must not, he repeated, try to escape. Eighty of Morton's halberdiers were to guard against that.

'The King came whimpering up. He said he would protect her if she would accept him kindly, for this was none of his doing. She knew, as I did, that he lied, and spat at him like a cat.

'You didn't see her at the start of supper, so beautiful, so serene, prattling of the speech she had finished for Parliament. Eyes so bright, but now they were like gleaming daggers, and the King took a step back, as though impaled on them. You never could imagine a giant of a man so fearful of a fragile woman, but he was, although she was his prisoner. When Ruthven ordered Lord Robert, Erskine and me to leave I think he was afraid that Ruthven would leave too, for he pawed at his armoured shoulder and said "You will stay."

'Ruthven shook him off and said, yes, for only a moment.

186

I begged that the Queen, with child as she was, required some of her ladies but he said no, and I was shoved out . . . and here I am, unable to help her.'

'I, too. Is it useless to try?'

'Utterly. You'd have to meet Morton's wolves on the stairs – I am not so pretty as you, Lady Seton, but on my way out they leered and jested.'

'If only she could have a priest, then,' I said. 'Or was it a massacre of them?'

'I don't know,' she said. 'Are you sure Father Black is dead?'

'Yes. I am very sure of that. His blood is on my gown.' I told her what had happened, but I omitted the presence of Chatte. Perhaps it was because of loyalty to Adam – I did not want his memory smirched and I was almost certain that Chatte had entered his chamber in innocence. But then she had decided to tease him and had climbed into the bed naked when Henry Yair had come in to kill.

'If only I could see the Queen,' I said. 'I want to show her Yair's dagger—'

'She has seen enough,' Lady Argyll said. 'I'll marvel if the baby lives another day. Pray for her, Lady Seton.'

And pray for the dead. When she left me I dismissed Isobel and lit candles in my oratory and knelt and prayed for Adam and for Rizzio, for souls in purgatory.

For love and death are but the selfsame thing.

My sleep was so troubled that I rose before dawn and went to the window. In the light of cressets I could see Morton's men covering the courtyard like a dark quilt. The benches were piled with metal – weapons, I suppose, breast plates. I dressed myself in a black gown. I felt hollow, weak from weeping. If I were to try to help Her Majesty I must not fall ill, so at dawn I ventured to the Great Hall, for food was served early to the servants. A few of them sat at a little table, and rose to bow or curtsey when they saw me. I asked for an egg stirred into milk and took my usual place at the banquet table.

Gaston himself came to serve me; he wanted news of the

Queen and I told him what I knew, and asked him to sit beside me. He said that rumours flew about like evil birds, even the truth was preferable to mystery. For a fact he knew that Father Joseph and Father Roche were alive; they had passed through on their way to the chapel, followed by grave diggers. He supposed that Father Black and Signor Rizzio were given decent burial somewhere in the gardens. 'Do you know', he said, 'that Signor Rizzio was said to be a spy of the Pope? And Father Black, too.'

'Only rumour,' I said. 'A convenient excuse for murder.... Tell me, is Her Majesty denied food? Have you sent food to her?'

He shook his head. 'Taylor was here for wine for the King.'

'I wish I could take her bread and milk and a paste of liver—'

'No, my lady. You can't go past the Douglases. I hear the staircase is thick with them. And they're drinking.'

Then what should I do? I dared not linger here, for any of them, or the ones in the courtyard, might appear, demanding breakfast. Then I saw Lady Huntly come in, grey hair straggling, a robe over her nightclothes.

She asked Gaston for a dish of eggs, and ale, and sat down with me. 'My appearance must be pardoned,' she said, 'but I was roused but two hours ago by one of Her Majesty's guards and sent to her, and the King told me she was in severe pain of her belly and was like to lose the child.'

As I exclaimed she said, 'But wait. Even though the King stood at the bed, listening and watching, she contrived by a wink to let me know that this was a ruse. She begged me to stay with her until a midwife could be sent from town. I could see that the King was thoroughly frightened, and that this was what she wanted, so I said it might be well to summon a priest to administer the last rites. She moaned some weak reply and the King's teeth chattered with terror. Then I asked if she could possibly walk to the privy – the only place for privacy – for elimination might ease her. The King believed this, but trotted beside us with the guard and would have entered but I warned him it could be a bloody business.' She laughed. 'I had him in such nerves that he remained outside. And then

188

Her Majesty blessed me and said she wished me to take a message to Bothwell, to tell him that she had convinced the King that he was in danger here. In short, that they hoped to meet Bothwell tomorrow night and take refuge at Dunbar.'

She paused as Gaston served her, then when he was gone she resumed. 'I promised to get him the message but told her that he and my son had escaped last night and were riding towards your palace at Seton to raise a rescuing army for her.'

'They escaped from *here*?' I was incredulous. 'Do you know how?'

'Yes, I was there, imprisoned with them in the south-wing chamber. Bothwell looked down on the lions' pit and said that the wall was unguarded. They lowered a rope and bed sheets. When they descended the lions roared and I thought they were done for but they ran and cleared the wall and in the dawn light I could see they were safe. Her Majesty marvelled.'

'But how can you get a message to Seton?' I asked.

'At that time I didn't know . . . but when you assure her you'll do something, you do. A few minutes ago I told Paris that his master commanded him to follow on to Seton and take the same escape route over the wall. Bothwell is his god, and so he obeyed, and his courage was such that it revived mine, and I pulled up the sheets, re-knotted them, and saw him safely over that wall.

'But to resume. Now the King was rapping on the wall of the privy and asking if she were alive, and I told him yes, but not to enter. She whispered to me that Lord James was expected here today with a strong force of men—'

'He dares to come here? Not to trial, but *here*?'

'Aye. But mark my words, Lady Seton, she will contrive to hoodwink him. Her play-acting is superb. I rose to it and when I opened the privy door, I bade the King carry her back to the bed else a great flux lose her the child . . . and he believed me, as I pretended both terror and tears. He said that he would demand the midwife if he had to fight all the Douglases himself. This was wine-talk, of course, but he knows himself guilty of Rizzio's death and, she said, of his name on a bond with the traitors, and if the child *should* die she would have him exiled.'

189

'If the midwife comes, can she be trusted?'

'I'll see to that,' Lady Huntly said, 'if I have to bribe her. But the people are with Her Majesty. The provost and the town guard heard the ringing of the alarm bell last night from the Canongate and swarmed to Her Majesty's help, but the King called down that all was well, only a brawl, and Rizzio killed by jealous Scots servants. She tried to lean out and shout the truth but she told me the King pushed her aside and threatened to cut her to collops if she moved again to the casement. She dared not and so he assured the crowd that she was safe, and it dispersed. But, she said, they must have some suspicion. So, I think, will the midwife. Her Majesty can wile anyone.'

'The King, perhaps,' I said, 'because he's afraid of her.'

'No, no, she is all sweetness to him, calling him her saviour, the only man she trusts . . . blaming Morton and Ruthven. Ah, she is clever!'

But could she wile James? I doubted it, and I dreaded his coming here. Then I said, 'Does she know that Father Black was murdered in his bed last night?'

'No!' She clattered down her ale cup.

Omitting Chatte, I told her what I had seen and of the dagger I held as evidence against Yair. Then Lady Huntly and I separated, she promising to come to me when she had further news.

I went to the chapel. It was guarded by Morton's men but they allowed me in. Father Joseph was there. I told him that I had heard of Adam's death. Where was he buried?

'Come,' he said, 'I will show you.'

We walked through the churchyard and he paused by the abbey wall. There were two new graves, both unmarked. 'That on the left is Father Black's.'

I had not a flower to lay there, only my heart. I knelt and kissed the moist earth. It was rumpled, cold. I longed to stay there but was lifted to my feet. 'We will hold Requiem Mass', he said, 'when Her Majesty is free.'

Back in the chapel we lit candles. Father Roche joined us. In silence we prayed, but for the first time in my life I felt that no one listened. Or if He did, He was the wind, for the

190

candles flickered, and when Father Joseph opened the door for me they died.

Later that morning, alone in my chamber, I thought that if Her Majesty were able to escape it might be weeks before she knew of Henry Yair's treachery, and he might dodge her justice. If she was as strong-hearted as Lady Huntly said, then she would accept Adam's death and want to act – perhaps through Bothwell. I was full of the need for vengeance, and knew that it must be swift.

So I disguised myself in one of Isobel's gowns, padding it, for she was larger than I. I hid my hair under a black shawl and, with great care, painted a few pox-marks on my face. Then I took up a little basket belonging to Isobel and put in bottles to look like medicines. Under these I slid the dagger, wrapped in a handkerchief.

Six of Morton's men confronted me at the top of the main staircase. I said timidly, 'Is the midwife here? She told me to come to assist her.'

'She is not here,' one of them said.

'Oh God,' I said, 'late? I'm told the babe may be dying—'

'Go in,' the men said, all of them speaking together in a rush. They unbolted the door and almost pushed me in.

The audience chamber was a splinter of broken chairs. Rizzio's progress to the staircase was marked by a trail of rusted blood on the carpet. There was also a trail of heron feathers, scraps of velvet, a slashed slipper. In the doorway of Her Majesty's bedchamber I paused to force down vomit. I prayed that the King was too drunk to recognise me.

'Your Majesty,' I called out. 'The midwife is late, but I am her helper.'

'Come in,' she called.

To my relief, she was alone. I went to the bed and said, in a whisper, 'I'm Seton. I came to—'

'Dove, it is dangerous,' she said, springing up from her pillows. 'The King has retired below but I'm told to expect my brother at any time and you shan't be caught here.'

'I could use the private stairs.'

'So may he. Quickly, then – what brings you?'

191

Her face was calm but very pale. Her hair was crusted with blood at the ends. She must have bent over Rizzio in an attempt to help him.

I told her about Adam's murder; but I would always omit the presence of Chatte for his own protection and because of my own theory of his innocence. I pulled out the dagger. 'It's Henry Yair's.'

'Keep it for me,' she said, ice in her voice. 'Keep it safely in your chamber. Such evidence could be stolen from me.'

As I replaced it in my basket I said, 'I saw Rizzio's grave, and Father Adam's . . . near the abbey.'

'I marvel their bodies weren't thrown to the lions. What priests survive?'

I told her. Then she said, 'We will hold a proper service as soon as possible. In deference to my mother's memory, I must honour Adam Black.'

I stared at her.

'She trusted him,' she said. 'So did I, and he was your friend. But – last night before supper I went to the chapel on impulse. He was with Chatte, embracing her. They didn't hear me, and I crept away. It was difficult to be merry with my guests. Today I'd have dismissed him, and her.'

Chilled, I could only nod.

'But he didn't deserve death. And Henry Yair shall hang with the rest of the curs.'

I did not want to reveal Lady Huntly's story of the escape plan lest I plunge that lady into trouble, but I said, 'When you manage to escape, may I go with you?' After all, Seton was my home.

'No,' she said. 'I shan't involve you in danger.'

We heard a mighty shouting in the courtyard and she said, 'Go, quickly, that is likely my brother. Go the way you came.'

I called through the bolted door and the guards opened it. They asked fearfully if the child was born – or dead. I said that I believed it lived, stammered a need for poppy-drug, and ran down the stairs to my chamber. Isobel screamed as she saw me, thinking me a stranger. I told her merely that Her Majesty was alive and reasonably well. Then I bathed. She asked timidly about the blood on my blue gown, and because

192

it so troubled her I said, 'I must have brushed against Signor Rizzio's body. Toss out the gown – I'll never want it again.'

I started to dismiss her but she had the habit of a mother hen with a chick, ordered my page to bring me food and wine. I marvelled that the servants behaved by rote, as though matters were normal. But my guard had been supplanted by one of Morton's men, Isobel said, within the last few minutes. He stood in the corridor smoking coltsfoot and his body stank.

When I tried to sleep my mind circled and spun coloured pictures. I strained to will away the ones of Adam – white-robed against a flowering tree, white-robed against an autumn-spilling oak, moving in white among the white tapers of the chapel – and then the pictures changed to a scarlet bed and I would open my eyes, blink, and sink towards sleep only to be shuddered awake by the Queen's picture of Chatte in his arms, black clutched to white, red lips pressed.

I sat up in tears. No longer could I cling to excuses for him. A man, perhaps, a worldly man might have argued that his love for me had so troubled his passion that he had vented it on an animal. Lust and love are said to be as separate, yet close, as yolk and white of egg. This may be true but few women can believe it.

If he had truly loved me, remembered the depth of our kisses, could he have allowed Chatte into his bed? But I found that I was not jealous of her. One does not strike a bitch, a lapdog that demands affection of the master. And that she loved him I had no doubt.

Unwittingly, perhaps, but unmercifully, he had used us.

But it takes time for the soft heart to harden, for illusion to die. If Her Majesty had only permitted me to go to Seton, I felt that I could convalesce there in the peace of the country and heal my heart and regain my independence of him where there were no memories of him. But memories of Rizzio? There would always be music to probe and taunt in every Great Hall of my life. It is said that life is short. They lie. It can seem an endless corridor when the candles are dim and you do not know where you are going.

For the rest of that day I worried that Her Majesty might be rash to try to escape. For one thing, she was burdened with the King. Then there was James, his men and Morton's surrounding the palace. Isobel reported that a horde of them had taken over the Great Hall for eating, drinking, dicing.

Fleming came to me and I told her most of what had happened, but was careful to say not a word about the escape plot for fear she might be in touch with Lethington, on his estates – she, of course, trusted him through love but he changed colour too often for my taste. She had heard a rumour that the King had struck Taylor for daring to order him wine. 'I require no wine, no spirits, they are offensive to me.' I wondered how it was possible for Her Majesty to win him to total sobriety – unless she had managed to penetrate that addled brain with the fact that, unless he kept his wits, no escape was possible.

'Some of James's men called for a jester, and Lindsay called for Chatte, but she could not be found. Her chamber is deserted but if she has indeed managed to leave here she took nothing. All of her costumes are in the robing-closet, trinkets still on her dressing-chest, and on a bench a robe stiff with blood, but that is the mystery, for she was not at Rizzio's stabbing . . . poor lass, what has happened to her?'

I shook my head. 'Fright of the situation, I suppose, and not able to fathom our language she's fled somehow – somewhere.'

'A black wench won't travel far,' she said. 'God, this place is so evil I can't blame her for needing clean air. Signor Rizzio – Gurion and Gervais laid out the corpse. They said there were fifty-six stab-wounds in that little shred that was left. They marked this down in a book, as they do herbs and medicines given, and when I asked why they told me it was evidence that the Queen might need.'

Fleming and I supped in my chamber, but without appetite. When she left me at half past ten I hoped to have news from Lady Huntly, but she did not appear. Never have I seen a sand glass shift so slowly, nor the hands of a clock. I began to wonder if Her Majesty had relinquished the idea of escape, and I hoped that she had, for I could not bear the thought of her shot down on staircase or in courtyard.

At two in the morning I retired. Again dreams of Adam plagued me. Awake, the thought of suicide came to me and so I rose and went to my oratory and fought this devilish corruption through prayer. It was a battle which left me weak but triumphant. I had my Queen to live for – if she survived.

I did not leave my chamber that day. The palace seemed ominously quiet, as if the soldiers had been commanded to silence by James. Isobel begged to send for food but I was weary of forcing it and told her to seek her own. She did so, and returned to say that the troops were withdrawing and we marvelled at such a miracle.

Lady Huntly came to me after supper. After I had dismissed Isobel she said, 'I have seen the Queen . . . she is well. The midwife came and helped me to frighten the King again, and Lord James, too. In short, a bargain was made. The Queen agreed to sign a bond of pardon for Lord James, Morton and all the rest in return for her freedom.'

'I suppose she could do nothing else,' I said, bitter at the thought that murder should go unpunished. 'But will they honour that bond? Is she truly free?'

She chuckled and lowered her voice. 'What a lass! She has so convinced the lords of her illness that the troops have been withdrawn and she says she is too weak to sign the bond until morning. And by morning she and the King will be at Seton.'

I was thrilled. 'But can she trust the King?'

'He is convinced that if he remains here the Lords will murder *him*. She's worked him into such a pitch of panic that he has actually stopped drinking lest he blunder. So, with God's help, they should be on the road by midnight.'

'If only I could join them!'

'She plans to take only a tirewoman, the King's equerry, Captain Erskine and one of his soldiers. They'll escape through the cellar and the burial vaults that lead to the church-yard.'

She left me then, and I prayed for their safety. Next day those of us who sought breakfast in the Great Hall learned that Their Majesties were missing, and I pretended astonishment.

195

Gaston asked to speak to me in private and talked softly by the fireplace. 'I was checking the bolt of the wine cellars at half past twelve. I saw them coming silently, and as silently left the door open and stood aside so as not to startle them. But, God forgive me, I was curious, and so I followed on tiptoe, through the burial vaults. When they reached the churchyard the King stumbled over a mound. It was Signor Rizzio's grave, though how she knew it I'm not certain since Father Black's is nearby. Anyway, she knelt and made the sign of the cross in the earth with her gloved hand. And she said the strangest thing. "I swear another shall lie as low before a year has passed." '

'Lord James,' I said.

'Perhaps. But the King was trembling. She looked at him with loathing for just an instant and then she said, "Come, my dear love," and they hurried to their horses. Where do you suppose they've gone, my lady?'

'I've no idea,' I said.

CHAPTER XI

Six days later Her Majesty returned to Edinburgh heading four thousand spearmen, but she did not come back to Holyrood. Instead, she took residence in the Clamshell Turnpike House in Bell's Wynd. Bothwell came to escort Fleming and me there at her request. While we waited for Fleming he and I took wine in the Great Hall.

'Did you go to Seton?' I asked.

No, Her Majesty had felt sufficiently strong to ride on seventeen miles to his fortress of Dunbar on the Dutch Ocean. 'She was magnificent, always at her best in time of crisis. But the King – another matter. True, my men and I surprised them on the road as they neared Seton and he thought us highwaymen. But caring nothing for the Queen's safety, that a nine-mile ride with child had tired her, he took fright, lashed her horse and shouted for her to follow. She protested her condition and he said, "If this babe dies we can have another." So the King fled with his equerry and I had to send men after him to escort him to Dunbar. When he joined us he sulked that the castle was poorly furnished – good God, a fortress is no sweet bower – and began drinking again. She had wheedled him into trust of her love but then she showed her contempt, as she does now. And she told me that she no longer can love the child in her belly because it is his.'

I said, 'Poor lady.'

'But not one complaint, not one whine, and I had to order her to bed that first night at Dunbar.'

I had to smile at the thought of the Queen being ordered, and he said, 'But I'm master there and she was exhausted. I carried her up to a chamber and placed her on a horsehide pallet.'

One does not expect a soldier to recount such details of

197

peace when an army is gathering at sunrise, summoned by his couriers. But he spoke of the peat fire in Her Majesty's room, how she cuddled into blankets rough as pebbles and asked him to remain until she slept.

He was in love; I knew that now. Perhaps she, too. That would account for her depression on his wedding night. I could imagine them perfectly matched – adventuresome, courageous, steeped in the same tradition of honour. To them a bond was sacred, and so she had fled rather than sign the one offered by the traitors.

'Where are the traitors?' I asked.

'James Stuart has fled to St Andrews. We think it expedient to pardon him and so split his alliance with Morton and the other conspirators, else he'll follow them to England and seek Elizabeth's help. But she won't allow him or Lethington to court until she is calm enough to pretend forgiveness. Besides, I want James at court.'

'Are you mad, sir?' I asked.

'I want him where he can be watched. And Lethington, whose crime may seem indifference, bears watching as well. The King, of course, is terrified of James's return to favour. He thinks he'll be murdered.'

'If only James would kill the King he could be executed for regicide!'

Bothwell laughed. 'James is too clever for that.' He drained his wine-goblet. 'Do you know that Knox, too, has fled? He calls it a "call" to Ayrshire – but at a most convenient time, as our army advanced on the town. Seventy-three involved in Rizzio's death were declared outlaws today at the Market Cross.'

'Henry Yair?' I asked.

'Aye. Small fry—'

'No! Didn't you know he murdered Adam – Father Black?'

He knew but did not seem greatly shocked and naturally he did not know that I was bereaved.

When Fleming was ready we rode into the city, nearly deafened by the Castle cannon. This was both warning to rebels and celebration of Her Majesty's return. I was glad to leave Holyrood and its memories.

198

The Turnpike House was embellished with clam-shells on its staircase tower, partly as decoration, partly because some superstitious builder had used them as protection against witches, for witches are supposedly unable to cross water, and the shells symbolised the sea. Bothwell had fortified the house with field-guns in the garden and hundreds of his Borderers protected it from the Wynd to the High Street.

My brother George welcomed us and led Isobel and me to our suite, which was small but adequate, furnished with things brought from the Castle. George said that Her Majesty had decided to move us all to the Castle, where she would feel safest, before her confinement.

We talked privately before supper. He said that at one time he had had reservations about Bothwell, some moral because of his abandonment of various mistresses; and of his impulsiveness. But now he had none. 'He's not the soul of tact, but I'd trust him with my life. So must Her Majesty. She has no one else.'

Greatly daring, because he *was* so moral, I asked, 'Do you think that she and Bothwell are in love?'

He hesitated. Then he said, 'I don't know, but they are together every spare moment, and he never mentions Jean, nor has the Queen sent to Crichton for her. The King is conspicuously ignored.' Swiftly he changed the subject. 'You've such a pallor, so thin – you must try to forget Signor Rizzio's death, and the priest's. Perhaps you'll be allowed to visit Seton. Your mother wants you.'

My tears came. 'I would love to come. But I shan't ask her. She sent for me. Fleming and I have always been of some comfort, like old pillows.'

He put his arms round me, and I cried the harder, remembering Adam's embrace. But gradually I regained composure and we separated to dress. I had just arranged jet in my hair when my page announced the Queen, and she came in wearing a full, black gown that concealed her figure. She embraced me and said, 'Sit down.'

I did so but she stood with her back to the fire.

'Do you still have Yair's dagger?' she asked.

'Yes, Madam.'

'You can dispose of the wretched thing. You need give no evidence and, if I could command your forgetfulness, I would.'

I could not question her decision. I said, 'I will try to forget.'

'In time, perhaps, we both will. And the tragedy of Chatte.'

'What!'

'I'm told she was found dead on a slope of Arthur's Seat. She must have run out witless in the night. In any case, an animal got her. . . .

'Ah, Seton,' she said, coming to stand by me. 'All we can do is attend Mass for them tomorrow at the abbey. There shall be flowers for their graves—'

I had never before interrupted her but I did now. 'No. Forgive me, I can't. I'm not as brave as you. I would lose control.'

'Very well.' She patted my hand. 'I understand.'

Of course she did not; Mass had always been my comfort. But I had said farewell to Adam in my own way, and one need not be crucified twice.

The Queen asked Fleming and me to attend a meeting of the Privy Council at Parliament House, and we sat in the oak-panelled gallery with other ladies of the court. It proved to be a private trial of the King. Red-faced, stammering, he protested innocence of Rizzio's murder. 'I only consented to the recall of the rebels without Her Majesty's knowledge and I admit this was wrong.'

My brother pointed to a copy of the murder bond. 'And your name on this is forged, Sire?'

'I was forced to sign it, a Douglas dagger at my side. How could I help it?'

The Queen said, 'We are forced to mock justice, Sire. You will nail proclamation of your innocence at the Market Cross in an attempt to fool our good people. This will be done for the sake of the child, to establish your honour.'

The King turned arrogant. 'Who questions the honour of a King? Only my peers may judge me, and none ranks above me.'

200

For a long moment she studied him. Then she said, 'I rank above you. And I'll strip you of honour as you sought to strip me.' She turned to her nobles who sat at a long writing-table. 'Mark well this traitor. He betrayed me as Queen and wife, betrayed the Church he was sworn to defend and then betrayed his bond of conspiracy. Except by my command he attends no public functions, shares in no councils, signs no documents.' She paused and looked at Lady Jean's brother. 'Lord Chancellor Huntly, all coins bearing his image shall be withdrawn from circulation.'

The King's face had turned from red to white. The full mouth became a seam.

'You dare to humiliate me, Madam?' he said, but she ignored him and ordered a list made.

'As an example to the exiled murderers we shall hang, draw and quarter their henchmen who held Holyrood in power. With them shall perish Henry Yair, servant to Lord Ruthven, murderer of Father Adam Black.'

I thought that Adam, in his compassion, would not have wanted such grisly punishment – but *I* did. It was justice.

We dispersed. Back at our house I removed the dagger from its hiding place – despite the Queen's command I had kept it lest, after all, it was required as evidence. It was rusty with blood and I shuddered as I buried it in a bucket of dead ashes from the fireplace. Some poor fellow would find it and sell it for the value of the garnets.

A week later Lady Huntly, Lady Argyll and I rode to a goldsmith's shop to take Her Majesty's watch for repair. It was a mild day – the false spring that preceded April – and, our mission accomplished, we decided to exercise our horses in the royal park. As we approached the Netherbow Port I looked up. There on the turrets of the gate was a row of heads, still fresh. Henry Yair grinned at me in the sunlight.

Since Bothwell remained with us I expected Jean to join us, and when she did not I asked her brother if she ailed.

'No,' he said, 'she is laying out gardens at Crichton.'

And each night her husband and our Queen were alone in

201

her apartments. I did not wonder that there was discussion of what attitude Elizabeth was taking to Morton and the rebels, of when to summon Lethington and James back to court. But if she were in thrall I could not blame her, for the King neglected her when he might have made amends and vindicated himself. Had he genuinely asked for forgiveness she might have granted him at least kind regard and restored his honours. But his drinking was more offensive than ever. He was like a child given spirits – rather, a young boy who became first merry, then pettish, argumentative, hostile, sloppy and stumbling. Isobel told me that all of the servants avoided him (as indeed his peers did) and that even his valet Taylor had spoken of leaving his service. Her Majesty had had to bribe Taylor to stay. Standen, his equerry, was similarly rewarded. It was his duty to accompany the King on his nightly rounds of the taverns and brothels of Edinburgh and see him safely home.

So I could understand if the Queen had turned her love to Bothwell. She was still young and it must have been terrible to contemplate a lifetime with the King.

We moved into Edinburgh Castle by degrees – much of our furniture moved there from Holyrood – and were settled by 3 June. Margaret Asteane, the midwife, became the most important member of the household, presented with an elegant black velvet gown and embroidered apron. Lady Margaret Reres, expecting a child at a similar time to Her Majesty, would serve as wet-nurse. There was general cheerfulness but, Jesu! I had never been so depressed.

It was not only my loneliness for Adam; it was the very look of that grim old fortress. Redecoration had not helped it. Braziers of musk and juniper could not dispel the smell of age, of centuries of rats and mice and mould and middens. For her confinement the Queen had chosen a tiny, oak-panelled bedchamber eight feet square that scarcely accommodated her bed, which was dressed with blue taffeta and velvet with gold-cloth curtains. There was just space for the cradle. But she said that such a room would hold the heat of the fireplace and keep her warm, and she enjoyed the view from the mullioned window and made a little jest: 'I look down on St Giles.' It so pleased her that Knox had fled.

Adjoining the tiny room was a large antechamber which overlooked the town wall and the High Street. It contained her favourite chairs and tables, tapestries and painted cloths, books and writing-cabinets. There were tapers in topaz holders, a screen of gold. It was royal in contrast to the humble, rock-walled quarters we courtiers shared and she spent most of her time there until the birth began.

James arrived with his wife, Lady Agnes, both effusively sweet to Her Majesty. She had pardoned him for complicity in murder and they played their innocent parts. His attempt at acting the good brother was that sort of spurious sincerity that looks his victim in the eye and flatters with the voice. But I was present with Bothwell in the antechamber when, Her Majesty resting on the couch, he said, 'God grant that the child is not of dark complexion.'

'The King is fair,' she said, 'and I was blonde as a child.'

'But Rizzio – and our father – was dark.'

His hatred of her compelled this, I think, to create worry, to compound her fear of birth. But Bothwell said, swiftly and with laughter, 'I'm redheaded and only one of my bastard children has my colouring. Your father and his mistress were both dark, were they not?'

For the first time I saw James lose poise. He stuttered, 'My mother, the Lady Margaret Douglas, has gone grey . . . one ages on a remote island . . . Lochleven is swept by winds. . . .'

Her Majesty was most obviously amused. I wondered if Bothwell's tactlessness was not often deliberate. In any case, when she and I were left alone she was almost gay, though we ladies knew that she dreaded the birth. Jean, who arrived from Crichton next day with a cartload of garden flowers, which she placed in Her Majesty's apartments, told me that she was happily surprised that no gossip had reached us. 'Knox has spread word throughout Scotland that the baby is Rizzio's . . . he expects a misshapen darkling. His sermons in Ayr are tantamount to curses on her – stillbirth.'

Bothwell left for the Border next day, saying he would be of more use there than at women's business, and, though James did not know it, Paris and Bothwell's other agents had him under surveillance. Now the Castle began to crowd with visitors – Du Croc, the French ambassador, Sir William Stanley, Elizabeth's envoy; bishops, priests, physicians. Beaton and Livingstone rode in from their estates, and we had a happy reunion.

The Queen, when not in conference, engaged in her vast correspondence, and her new secretary was Rizzio's brother Joseph. He had been a very minor member of the court, first a window-washer, then a page when David was elevated. Now eighteen, he was a slender, well-shaped lad who spoke excellent French and wrote a fine hand. Her Majesty entrusted him with her correspondence to the Cardinal, Queen Catherine and King Charles but she was careful not to honour him with lavish gifts or rouse the jealousy that had killed his brother. At that time she was surrounded by loyal Lords (except for James) but most were Protestant and she was taking no chances.

Her Majesty, accompanied by we Marys, ventured out one morning to the tiny, wind-swept chapel of St Margaret, built at the order of Saint Margaret, perched like a white eagle on a summit overlooking the town. We had insisted she rest against the cannon before we climbed down. When we entered her apartments the first pain struck. I ran for Gurion and Arnault, another surgeon. The midwife hurried in.

Her labour seemed endless and I feared we would lose her. My only comfort was in talking with Lady Reres, who had made swift recovery from her own confinement. She was a fat, vulgar woman but reassuring. 'Her Majesty has cared for herself despite the many recent shocks. Gervais tells me she has eaten wisely – as I never do – and taken milk and red meat and fresh salads. She is not so frail as she looks, my lady. And the pains are but natural and a first child is the most difficult. . . .'

I say she was vulgar because she prattled about a past affair with Bothwell, and in too much detail. 'When he was a lad he enjoyed older women. First my sister Janet, then myself when I was thirty. Will you believe it, he taught *us* the arts of love? He is naturally sensual, and with so much imagination—'

204

'I'm sure of it,' I said. 'Now, as to Her Majesty's condition—'

But she would not be interrupted. '. . . that I wonder he married that prim Gordon woman except to enrich himself. And it hasn't proved necessary. I'm told she – the Queen – has given him the Abbey of Haddington, all the lands around Dunbar—'

The interruption this time was a page announcing Jean. She said, 'I looked in but I couldn't bear it. How in the name of God can she? Lady Seton, I came to warn you not to go there until it's over. We can do nothing.'

I thanked her; coward as I was, I could not go to see her unless she asked for me. When she left Lady Reres chuckled. 'I wonder if she suspects he is bedding her serving maid, Bessie Crawford. They meet in a ruined tower at Haddington. . . .'

But I made an excuse and left her and sought my own chamber. It was not until dawn that Fleming came to me and told me that Her Majesty had given birth to a fine son. She was well.

As I dressed, the Castle cannon thundered, awakening Isobel who came to help me into an azure gown. This was no time for woe-weeds. Far below we heard a triumph of bells from every church in Edinburgh. I was torn between exultance and awe. My page brought ale and honeyed bread and I ate with appetite for the first time in weeks. Then I went towards Her Majesty's apartments where a crowd waited in the corridor.

James, dour in black and silver, came towards me. The green eyes were lightless, his head was bent. Then he looked up and attempted a smile and said, 'Good morning, Lady Seton. A *very* good morning, isn't it?'

I curtsied. 'Have you seen the baby, my Lord?'

He nodded. 'A lusty prince.'

I could not resist, 'And a fair colouring, my Lord?'

'Yes. Pale hair.' Those words were spoken as a dirge. Again he attempted a smile and moved on past me.

The antechamber was a mass of people when I pushed through. As maids of honour we Marys took precedence over most of the nobles and I was able to reach the tiny bedroom.

It was packed full and I had to stand on tiptoe to see over the shoulders of the King, the Bishop of Ross and the two ambassadors. Her Majesty lay propped on pillows, the baby beside her. To my surprise there was a slight blush on her cheeks, her eyes were bright, alert. She removed a lacy cloth from the infant and said, looking up at the King, 'Sire, God has given us a son, begotten by none but you.'

The King went crimson.

'I protest to God, as I shall answer to Him on the day of judgement, that this is your son. I wish all here to bear witness. For he is so much your son that I fear it will be the worse for him hereafter.'

Awkwardly, he bent and kissed the fluff of golden hair.

She continued relentlessly: 'Stand aside, Sire. I require clean air.'

I suppose he reeked of *aqua vitae*. Then she turned to Sir William Stanley, Elizabeth's envoy. 'This is the son I hope will be first to unite the kingdoms of Scotland and England.'

'Shall he succeed before Your Majesty and his father?' Sir William asked.

'His father has betrayed me. We are broken.'

The King spoke in a sort of bleat. 'Is this your promise to forgive and forget?'

'I made no such promise. If Kerr's pistol had fired, there would be no prince, no queen. You may go, Sire.'

The King left the room, lowering his head to avoid the low arch of the door. We who were left came forward to curtsey or bow or kneel in respect to the prince. Courtiers crowded in and we made place for them but as I left Her Majesty halted me.

'Seton, send a courier to Lord Bothwell and tell him that all is well.'

Jean had come up beside me. 'He's at Hermitage, Lady Seton.'

'No,' the Queen said, 'that would be yesterday. Today he is in Jedburgh.'

Our ambassador to England, Sir James Melville, arrived a few days later. I received him in the audience chamber and he looked a muddy mess from the roads. He apologised but said he had ridden hard from Greenwich. He would bathe and dress before he asked audience of Her Majesty.

But when she heard his voice from her bedchamber she came in, leaning on Lady Reres's arm. Eased on to the couch and dismissing the wet-nurse she said, 'And how does my "dear sister" fare?'

'Ill of her kidneys, Madam, and her teeth rage her, but the barber can't induce her to pull them. At thirty-three one expects these ailments. And when I told her of your happy delivery I think you'd have pitied her the more. She broke off dancing – aye, she dances even in illness – and said, summoning her ladies, "The Queen of Scots is mother of a fair son, and I am but barren stock." Then she retired. But a few hours later she sent for me and I am to convey to Your Majesty her good wishes as your child's godmother. If she is able, she will come to the christening with the gift of a golden font.'

Her Majesty's eyes were soft. 'May God bless her! At last we *are* sisters. Barring your diplomacy, sir, and that of other kind envoys, we have been awash on a sea of misunderstanding. Women must talk with one another, personally, to shape a peace.' She turned to me. 'You remember when my tire-women were jealous of Janet, though I play no favourites? Months of tedious, ineffectual peace-making on your part until you told me and I was able to assure them, each one, that I required their special attention and valued their different arts? No man could have achieved that. And with due respect, Sir James, no man can contend with two queens, two mistresses.'

'We can only try,' he said.

'You try superbly. But she and I will succeed.' She laughed. 'I intended no jest of succession to her throne. We will hold the christening at Stirling Castle, I think, and offer her good Highland sport after a royal welcome here.'

Sir James was young but his brow was furrowed. He was frowning now. 'I'm certain she meant what she said, Madam, but you know how she vacillates. Even if her health permits the journey, Cecil may advise her against it. Time may pass—'

'But I require time for overseas visitors to attend the

christening,' the Queen said. 'It can't be until the late autumn.'

That frown was now a deep rut. 'Madam, don't depend on it. On her arrival. I've reported her fair words, and precisely. But—' He glanced at me. 'Forgive me, Lady Seton, some matters must be private.'

Her Majesty dismissed me in her gentle way. And I was pleased to escape from talk of what I was sure were Cecil's stubborn machinations. Her Majesty might or might not meet Elizabeth but she had triumphed with an heir to both thrones. James was powerless, Bothwell and his men guarded Scotland. My nightmares were subsiding.

But at dusk Her Majesty summoned me to her bedchamber and said, after her page had brought us clary, 'You may as well hear the rest. Sir James had private conversation with Dudley, Earl of Leicester. He said, "Queen Elizabeth had no intention of my wedding the Queen of Scots. Lord Henry Darnley was her choice." '

'Does Your Majesty mean that she actually instigated your marriage?'

She nodded, and her face was bleak. 'I was duped. It was fiendishly clever. She knew what he was and would become. She offered the knot and I strengthened it, tied it, and bound myself.'

I did not know what to say, but she did. 'We are finally aware of the truth, and truth is freedom. I'm free of a maze.'

But she could never be free of the King, I thought as I left her. Unless James – but, as Bothwell had said, he was too clever. Yet the cleverest are capable of blundering.

Slender again, Her Majesty was ardent to look her best and from sketches sent her from France we devised new arrangements for her hair. But she did not order new gowns; the King had previously demanded more attire and more adornment than she could afford. And our army cost a great deal to maintain, here and on the Border.

One evening she said to me, 'Seton, I have wondered whether to give you this ring, whether it would bring you joy or sorrow. Gervais found it on Father Black's finger – my mother's gift to him.'

The emerald ring I had noticed on that first night when I had seen him at his window. She extended it in a little case of velvet.

'Thank you,' I said, 'but I'd rather not be reminded of him.' It was the one thing I had not seen when I approached the bed.

'Very well,' she said, mistaking my reluctance, 'but you must try to forgive him, as I have. That he was tempted by Chatte in the chapel doesn't mean that he seduced her. I was wrong – a hasty conclusion. I realise that now; to doubt a man of God is to doubt God himself.'

'Yes, Madam.' I would never disillusion her. 'It's kind of you to offer the ring, but I could never wear it happily – as you don't wear the diamond you gave to Signor Rizzio.'

'It has been sold,' she said. 'The King coveted it.' Then she said, 'Please be here at seven to arrange my hair – we will try the new swirl, and a dust of diamonds. You Marys will wear your amber taffetas, with topaz, and I the silver brocade. Bothwell is returning,' she said, and there was a lilt in her voice. 'I'm giving a banquet in the Great Hall.'

That enormous hall was ablaze with a thousand candles as we entered, and the table, which seated sixty, festooned with roses. At her table on the dais the honoured guests were Bothwell, Jean and, of necessity, James and his wife. There was no chair for the King.

If the fragrance of the roses had not reminded me of Adam and the gardens of Holyrood I could have been happy. The suave Melville talked about English fashions – ruffs from Spain had been introduced for ladies, nineteen yards of linen, forcing them to dine with great discomfort. 'Imagine a soup spoon two feet long,' said he. 'Queen Elizabeth has put an end to the silly style—'

He paused. The King had entered. He stood behind the Queen's chair. The room was silenced.

She turned. 'You wished something, Sire?' Obviously bored, impatient, she waited.

'Just to bid you a good evening.'

He was seemingly sober, and the blue eyes begged mercy. He kissed her hand.

She pulled it away abruptly. 'Henri,' she called to a servant, 'bring me a basin – my hand is dirtied.'

As the basin was brought the King said, 'Oh, Madam, do I deserve this?'

'You do. You babble your troubles to the scum of the town, you dare to boast of your virility – fathering my child though the King of France failed. I have agents; I know what's said in the taverns. Now, get you to some whore – no decent woman will have you.'

The King crept away. I knew she was justified but I could not help pity him. Adam had said that there is no man on earth bereft of God's gift of goodness. The King had misused the gift and lost it, but he so wanted to restore it.

The Queen said, 'I apologise for this intrusion on your gaiety.' She lifted her wine-glass. 'Drink and eat and continue your talk.'

James clinked his glass with hers. She said, smiling, 'Do you know, my dear brother, there can be no compromise with traitors?' and bade the musicians play. She granted Bothwell the first dance.

At two months the little prince – who would be christened James – was left in the care and protection of the Earl of Mar while our Queen visited Lady Mar in Alloa. Her health had declined and she required sea breezes and, I suspect, a separation from the King. She was accompanied by James, his wife and her tirewomen. I was free to visit my family at Seton.

The holiday was precisely what I needed. Madame my mother feared it was dull for me in the country but I assured her that I would prefer no guests other than family friends and, knowing what I had endured at Holyrood, she understood. We spent hours in the garden, she instructing her gardeners in the arts of French topiary. We rode together through miles of golden gorse. She possessed the gift of silence but when I exclaimed over the beauty of the dovecote, which was built like a blue toy castle, or admired her tapestry work, she chattered like a girl of my own age, and she charmed and pampered me. The coldness of our first meeting was forgotten.

George returned after some weeks with Bothwell on the

Border. I suppose one could have labelled him a stolid man but I treasured his lack of imagination. I was weary of exciting personalities, of rumour and intrigue, and I clung to him as a barnacle to a rock. We talked of nothing more vital than the harvest. With my stepfather I rode the barley fields and drank the rough ale and ate the rough bread of the workers at noon. We visited the cottage tenants and he took note of their needs – a thatching of roof, a new door, whatever was required. To the ailing or elderly we took clothing and peats against the coming autumn. Busy as I was, my heart began to heal; the disillusion ebbed. Madame my mother gave me a silken mask to protect my complexion from the sun but it soaked through my body, the fresh air stimulated my appetite and I no longer saw the wraith of myself in the looking-glass.

Her Majesty honoured me with two letters, one from Edinburgh in August stating that she had recovered her health at Alloa and was transacting state business. There was no need for me to return as she planned to hunt at country castles during the early autumn. The other, from Glenarton, reported excellent sport in the forests, and a surprise visit from Bothwell. I gathered that neither the King nor Jean had joined her party, though she did mention that James had brought in six fine stags. 'The christening shall be at Stirling in December. The prince thrives.'

I also received a letter from Fleming who had accompanied Lord and Lady Mar to Stirling with the prince. '. . . so odd, the baby does not resemble either Her Majesty or the King. His hair is no longer golden, but brown. A dear infant, but not likely to become handsome as his parents. . . . My beloved Lethington returns to court in September, to be neutral is not to be disloyal, and may God be praised that Her Majesty has forgiven him. Here is a secret, we have her permission to marry, his mourning is over . . . and you shall dance at my wedding when we return to Holyrood. . . .'

Madame my mother and I ordered a glittering night-robe for Fleming – white satin sewed with pearls at throat and hem and tiny velvet violets. Soon after the seamstresses had completed it Her Majesty summoned me to Edinburgh and George escorted me. The cart that followed was weighty with gifts from my family – a prie-dieu of mosaic cushioned in crimson, a silver altar with a most beautiful painting of Christ to hang above it; a turkey carpet, vases from the Orient, embellished firewood buckets and a bathing-tub of mahogany lined with marble. Madame my mother surprised me with a new ruby velvet gown and a mink-lined cloak to match. George gave me a ruby necklace and earrings. 'Anything you require for the christening shall be granted,' he said. 'We must think of a suitable gift for the prince.'

At Holyrood I was given my former apartments and for the first few nights, the wind mourning about the turrets, I was plunged back into depression. But I climbed out of it gradually and resumed my duties. There were wigs to cleanse and new ones to curl, seamstresses to instruct as bolts of cloth arrived from Paris. Clearly Her Majesty intended to dazzle her guests when we joined them at Stirling in December. The King was there now visiting the baby. Bothwell was in residence with us.

After their wedding ceremony we celebrated with a reception in the Great Hall for Fleming and Lethington, the usual dancing and fireworks and bonfires on the hills. On the second day a mock tournament was held in the outer courtyard, Her Majesty insisting on blunt lances, remembering too well the death of King Henry. After Bothwell had jousted with my brother – and won – Lethington triumphed over Huntly. Then the winners fought and I am certain out of gallantry that Bothwell allowed the older man to vanquish him. After supper that night I told him so and he laughed but admitted nothing.

I said, 'Since I saw Her Majesty she seems to have shed years – she looks eighteen.'

He nodded. 'Separation from the King was excellent medicine. But late in the summer we found proof that he was conspiring against her, writing to the Pope and the Kings of France and Spain that she was heretic and immoral and that he should be recognised as leader of Catholic Britain. We took care to reveal all this to James. Oh, so piously he said such scum should not be allowed to meddle in foreign affairs, that Lethington should handle them.'

'But aren't they a dangerous pair?'

'Not if carefully watched. And both are allied against the King. That's why he dares not come here.'

But shortly after, on 29 September, the King did come to Holyrood, unannounced, at ten in the evening. Her Majesty had asked me to be present for a conference on christening arrangements with ambassador Du Croc, James, Lord Glencairn and Bothwell and we were in her audience chamber when a page summoned her, at the King's request, to talk with him in the courtyard. Alone.

She was terrified that the baby might be ill, and I brought her cloak and Bothwell escorted us downstairs and outside. The King, on horseback with his servants, refused to dismount. Obviously he was afraid to enter the palace, especially when he saw Bothwell. He bleated out that all was well at Stirling but that he had suffered intense humiliation in Scotland and intended to go abroad and live in France.

'Oh no, Sire!' Her Majesty was aghast. If he did not appear for the christening, it was tantamount to refusing to acknowledge the child.

'Sire, we cannot discuss this in the cold. . . .'

It was ten minutes before she was able to persuade him to come inside, promising that he would not be harmed, and suggesting that he needed *aqua vitae* to warm him after the long ride. In short, he agreed if they could confer in private.

Of course it was not private. And in the audience chamber the Lords were merciless when he stammered out his intention to leave the country. Du Croc said that the rulers of France would not receive him, nor would any other Catholic country. James stated that it would be a most dangerous error of judgement. 'In fact, Sire, it would be a fatal error.'

Bothwell said, 'You are safe in Scotland, Sire. But once away we couldn't control your enemies. You'd leave yourself at the mercy of Morton and the exiles.'

The King had thus far maintained a shred of dignity. Now it collapsed. 'You have all misunderstood. I thought only of a holiday abroad. But I can't stay here—'

'Stirling has such pleasant hunting,' Her Majesty said. 'You would be happier there, Sire.'

He left us, saying that he would not see us until December.

Bothwell escorted him down and when returned said, 'I promised him protection at Stirling and I keep my word. Because, for once, Your Majesty needs him.'

There was an outbreak of cattle and sheep stealing on the south-western Border and Bothwell left to subdue it and bring offenders to trial. Our Queen, who had never travelled to that area, decided to meet him in Jedburgh and hold Justice Court. She sent me ahead to rent a suitable house for her, accompanied by our tirewomen, her physician Arnault and a guard of gentlemen.

It was a pleasant journey in early October. We reached the village of Jedburgh well after dark but were made welcome at a spacious inn where the service was so splendid that I decided it could lodge the servants and soldiers who could not be accommodated in her house. I discovered a suitable house at once. It was scarcely twenty years old and fortified, with a park that bordered a river. It was built of fieldstone and the small rooms would hold the heat of the fireplaces. Back at the inn I sent a courier to Edinburgh listing the furnishings that would be required.

Her Majesty arrived with James, Huntly, Lethington and the Bishop of Ross, priests, pages and armed guard. Before she even removed her cloak she told me that Bothwell had been gravely wounded in pursuit of a highwayman on the moors of Liddesdale.

'Oh God, Seton – he has head injuries, a smashed thigh and left hand. His servants carted him to Hermitage Castle. Paris will bring us news.'

She was too distraught to tour the house and ordered me to assign rooms to the courtiers and household servants and put her chefs to work. She would rest, but if Paris arrived I was to admit him at once, no matter what the hour.

He arrived at midnight, dusty but grinning. His master was out of danger but required rest. Her Majesty said that she would ride to Hermitage in the morning but Paris told her that Bothwell's physician advised that there be no visitors for a week.

Her Majesty's relief was marked by instant vitality. In the

214

dining-room she herself served Paris wine, ordered cold meats and salad, laughed at tiny things and behaved, generally, as if she herself had been rescued from death. Never in my life with her had I seen her so joyous. When Paris retired, to return to Hermitage at daybreak, she scribbled a letter to Bothwell that Paris would carry in his pouch and sent for a sleepy servant to unpack his favourite Spanish wine.

Next day she supervised the placing of furniture from Holyrood and the finest went, not to her own quarters, but to a chamber prepared for Bothwell's convalescence. At dusk she commanded Mass in the abbey and Bishop Ross officiated. For her it was a Mass of thanksgiving and afterwards, still in a state of elation, she herself went to the gate of the house where beggars had gathered and gave them basins of food and a bag of gold and ordered a hogshead of ale lifted across to them. In the torchlight they knelt in gratitude and blessed her and she said, 'I am most truly blessed of all women alive.'

James was not in such a happy state. It must have seemed to him that his old enemy had been resurrected from near death only to be deified, for all she could talk of was Bothwell and how we must make his convalescence here restful but amusing. Lethington, however, was so anxious to win her full forgiveness and trust that he sent for certain of his books that Bothwell might enjoy. With Her Majesty's permission he would send for Fleming who was training their musicians to more than adequate skill. And so, within two days, Fleming was with us and Her Majesty was recalling Bothwell's favourite Border ballads.

One might have thought that these were preparations for a king's visit; in her heart I think Bothwell *was* king. But she was mindful of her duties in Jedburgh, and during that first week went to the assizes and judged criminal cases, fining prisoners but executing none, fixing prices, settling disputes between quarrelling Elliotts, Johnstones and Armstrongs who were akin to the clans of the Highlands and must be brought to harmony. Fleming and I attended one such session and Her Majesty judged a coffined corpse, as was Scottish custom. The testimony against him was, she said, based on long prejudice. True, he was a sheep-thief but so were his accusers. 'May his soul rest in peace and may you mend your ways to achieve such peace. . . .'

The people loved her, as they always did when Knox's voice was silenced. Knox was in Ayrshire and possibly in self-imposed exile. He knew that she was not vengeful but I think the old goat feared his own embarrassment more than any punishment. A rabble-rouser who cannot rouse becomes a fool.

Precisely one week after news of Bothwell's accident, the Queen commanded James to escort her to Hermitage. I was present, in the parlour, but he spoke as if they were alone: 'That is mad, Madam. To ride over thirty miles of rugged hills, and the mists upon us on pathless roads—'

'We will leave at sunrise,' she said, 'before the mists come down.'

'But on returning? I'm told the castle is only a peel tower for defence, with no accommodation for women. Your Majesty could not rest there overnight.'

'Jean was there—'

'But is now at Crichton. Another reason why I implore Your Majesty not to go. Gossip, particularly now before the christening, can only harm you and folk will assume that you – that is, that you have transferred your love from Rizzio to Bothwell – untrue as that is,' he said hastily.

But just as hastily she said, 'What do I care for gossip? I can't stem indecency or vile speculation, and your presence would check it if I did care. If Jean and the King are absent, they are about their own concerns. My concern is to visit a loyal Lord wounded in my service. If you're not prepared to accompany me, my guard will suffice.'

So of course he agreed. I prayed for her safety on the dark, sodden moors, over treacherous peat-hags. The most expert horsewoman could fall into a bog, nor did I trust James to save her. Such an 'accident' would be convenient to him. He had only then to arrange the King's murder and he would rule Scotland, acting as regent for the prince.

With Elizabeth's blessing?

I passed the time at darts with Fleming and Joseph Rizzio.

216

Lethington and Huntly and the Bishop occupied the long day in the little library. I wandered restlessly from room to room, listening for hoofbeats through the beat of rain.

Finally, at seven o'clock, Her Majesty arrived with James, wet, muddy, radiant. But she said she was weary and wanted only soup and I had it taken to her chamber. She told me that Bothwell was unable as yet to walk, but had promised to come by horse-litter the next week.

At dawn Isobel awakened me to say that Arnault had been summoned to her – she had a cruel pain in her side, and high fever. I hurried to her in my dressing-robe but the physician barred my way. The fever climbed higher in the afternoon; she vomited blood. With James and Fleming I waited in the adjoining parlour. Then Arnault came to us and said that she had fainted after returning from the privy and had been unconscious for two hours. 'I've lanced her veins and bled her . . . I think we should send for the King.'

James nodded, and a courier was summoned. I said, 'On your way out, send up another courier.'

'For what?' James asked as the man bowed out.

'Bothwell should know,' I said, for Her Majesty would wish that.

'Perhaps you take too much upon yourself, my lady?'

I controlled my fury. 'Then it's a risk I'll take, my lord.'

He shrugged. 'Very well. But what can an invalid do?'

Fleming said, 'What can any of us do? But he should be informed.'

So another courier sped to Hermitage.

The next day Her Majesty's vision blurred. We were admitted to her bedchamber and she could not see us, though she recognised our voices. Two days later she asked Bishop Ross to take her confession and when he joined us in the parlour there were tears in his eyes. 'Lord James, you and the ladies may go in to pay your last respects but she won't know you.'

Huntly and Lethington joined us at her bedside. She was mumbling, her eyes closed, and I think she spoke of her child, to commend him to the care of his godmother – Elizabeth. Then she said, 'David, it is so windy, so windy,' and indeed

217

there was a wind, for Fleming had opened the casement to release her soul.

We kept vigil until six that morning. Several times she murmured 'Bothwell' in a desperate whimper. Then convulsions racked her body and she could no longer speak. There was a commotion outside, a tramping of feet on the stairs and the door flew open. Bothwell's servants carried him in on a litter.

I have never heard such a roar of anger. 'Close that casement! Arnault – give her brandy-wine!'

'My Lord, how can I? Her jaws are rigid—'

'Pry them open!'

Arnault did so. At Bothwell's order the Queen's arms and legs were bandaged and jerked by his servants to restore circulation, a merciless tossing, and I could not but agree when James shouted, 'Stop! Let her die in peace.'

But these men were Bothwell's and they obeyed their master. Fleming and I retreated to a far corner but we both saw James go to the chest by the casement and open Her Majesty's jewel case for a careful examination. Perhaps I was delirious for in my anger at this I ran to him. 'The most valuable', I said, 'are locked away from thieves.'

'Indeed,' he said calmly. 'How wise.'

Three hours later the men, streaming sweat, pulled back from the bed, and Her Majesty moaned but turned of her own volition on to her side. Daring now to come close, I saw colour in her face, her eyes opened and she said, 'Bothwell is here? Seton, is he here?'

'I'm on a damned litter,' Bothwell said, 'but I'm here and here I'll stay.'

CHAPTER XII

Nearly a week later the King arrived, excusing his tardiness by saying that the courier could not find him; he had been hunting. Her Majesty was now able to sit up in bed and take food, and she received him kindly – at first. But whatever he said or did so offended her that she soon ordered him away and I heard him run down the stairs, shouting for his groom. He was off to Stirling.

Her Majesty was able to walk before Bothwell could, and she was often in his chamber. I was chaperon. This made me uncomfortable, for they so obviously longed to be alone and listen and look only at each other.

We made plans for the christening and agreed that her gown would be of white satin embroidered with emeralds, emeralds to clasp the points of her sleeves. He disputed her idea of a white wig but we argued that it would be unique and beautiful with a coif of emeralds. She pleased him by ordering him to wear blue, symbol of loyalty, and his Borderers should dress in the same colour. 'Sapphire blue for you, my Lord – satin, I think. After all, you shall be host.'

'Host!' He sat up straight. 'Are you mad, love – Madam?'

'I'll not have the King welcome my guests. Even sober he'd mistake one ambassador for another, create a muddle. All I demand from him is his presence at the Chapel Royal for the ceremony.'

She turned to me, asking me to invite my parents, but Madame my mother had wished to be excused. 'I'll ask, Madam, but though she is able to ride around the estate, the journey to Stirling, even by litter, would damage her back.'

She sent for Joseph Rizzio and made a list of expected guests. Then Gaston was summoned to arrange the menu for the various occasions.

When it was time for me to eat Fleming relieved me and I was often forced to share the company of James and Lethington. I came to admire Lethington, if not to trust him implicitly. I could now understand why he so charmed Fleming, and why he had proved valuable in our dealings with Elizabeth. It was not his dark, urbane good looks, though they helped. It was his subtle flattery. Women, even royal women, were so often treated with condescension, as pretty children, their most serious ideas tossed off as whims. But Lethington listened attentively to whatever I had to say, expanded my thought – be it ever so slender – and polished it to wisdom. And so one was made to glow in his presence and achieve importance. The Queen had the same rare gift but hers, given in love, was emotional, his intellectual. James, for all his cleverness, could not fence in conversation without turning dour or bitter. Lethington enjoyed a duel of wits but, modestly, sheathed his sword at the point of winning.

When the invalids had fully recovered we left Jedburgh for Edinburgh, making slow progress, resting at Kelso and Home Castle. Elizabeth had granted permission for us to ride through English territory so we followed the River Tweed to Berwick and at Coldingham – well named, because the weather became frigid at the east coast – we paused to visit Bothwell's sister Janet, widow of James's brother. Her little son Francis Stuart looked so like Bothwell, and Her Majesty was entranced by his red curls.

It was decided that sea air would benefit Her Majesty, so instead of returning to Holyrood we took residence at Craigmillar Castle, two miles from the city. She sent for warmer clothing, and also a red velvet gown and exotic perfumes.

These mid-November evenings she played chess with Bothwell alone, though the door was open to her presence chamber where the rest of us sat by the fire, Fleming and I at embroidery, the gentleman dicing or working at a puzzle. The puzzle to me was that Her Majesty, who had always received Rizzio in private, now made a point of that open door, and it seemed almost a coy way of stating, 'We have nothing to hide.'

One night she wore the red gown, which bared her shoulders in the Italian style and framed them in white fox. She and

Bothwell chatted with us briefly, then went in to chess. A page announced the King, and James sprang up, as we all did.

The tall figure muffled to the chin in furs swaggered in with the insolence of brandy-courage, demanding to see the Queen. I hurried in to her and whispered, 'The King, Madam – I think he is drunk.'

When she entered, Bothwell behind her, the King sidled up to her and bent to kiss her shoulder. She retreated in disgust. 'Sit down and state your business, Sire.'

But he followed her amorously, daring to touch her bosom. I was fearful that Bothwell might draw his dagger, there was such rage in his face, but Lethington moved swiftly to take the King's cloak and this small diversion distracted the King from Her Majesty. 'What do you want?' she asked as he tossed the cloak on the floor.

'You. My rights.' He turned to us. 'I'll be alone with my wife.'

'I refuse to be alone with you, Sire,' she said.

'Then I refuse to acknowledge your bastard child.'

Bothwell moved towards him. He said something but so softly that I did not hear it. The King backed away until he stood at the rock wall.

Lethington's mind was the sort that skips past the drama of the moment and thinks ahead. To him the christening was all-important – the King's presence must be achieved at any cost – so he said calmly, 'Do sit down, Sire. You're weary from your journey. Lady Seton, order wine.'

I was glad to escape for a moment and call a page, and when bottle and goblets arrived I busied myself serving. But this time the King was not distracted, though he drank. He said sullenly that the baby's hair had darkened and his skin sallowed so that he could be taken for Italian. 'Either I remain here with you with the rights of a husband, or I go to my father's house in Glasgow. Is that clear, Mary?'

She blinked, then quite perceptibly shuddered. 'Yes, Sire. Remain if you wish, though I – yes, remain.'

James, damn him, looked pleased; so did Lethington. They did not care what she suffered during the next nineteen nights before we went to Stirling.

221

Then Bothwell said, 'Your Majesty, is this fair to him? Is it honourable for you all to keep the truth from him?'

'What do you mean?' Her Majesty asked.

'With all respect, Madam,' he said, 'the King should be warned that guests are expected here within the week.'

'What *do* you mean?' James asked impatiently.

'You know, my Lord. It would be a pity for the King to meet Morton, his Douglas kin, Kerr—'

'No!' the King said. All of his bravado had shrivelled. In a croak he asked Her Majesty, 'Is this true? You have pardoned them?'

She hesitated. Then she took the escape Bothwell had offered her. 'I have pardoned them.' So rarely did she lie but now she embroidered the lie. 'If you stayed here, Sire, I couldn't control such a pack. We could not protect you against murder.'

The King bent, unsteadily, and whirled on his cloak. Bothwell said, 'Let it be known that you'll attend the christening and no one will dare to molest you. You have my pledge of protection at Stirling.'

'Your guard will be doubled, Sire,' the Queen said.

He nodded mutely. And he left us.

Lethington placed another log on the fire and James said, 'Of course you must pardon the exiles now, Madam, since Lord Bothwell has forced it.'

'The choice is hers,' Bothwell said curtly. 'I said what I thought to be expedient.'

James, of course, would want Morton returned to favour to unite the Douglases against both the King and Bothwell – for Bothwell had become the most powerful noble in Scotland and doubtless James suspected he was her lover as well. Cleverly, he said, 'Madam, you have always honoured your word, and the King has your word that the exiles are pardoned. Your conscience wouldn't permit a turnabout, would it?'

In that moment I prayed that she would relinquish conscience but the Bastard had struck her Achilles' heel – rather, her pride in a pledge. 'I will pardon them,' she said. 'I loathe every one, but I'll pardon them.'

If souls can protest across the barriers of death, Adam and Rizzio must have screamed in that room. Alone in my chamber I thought of the fifteen dagger slashes that had killed my lover. Her Majesty had lost only friends.

Since Fleming and I had been present during that crisis the men now talked freely when we were about, and so did the Queen during our stay at Craigmillar. After the christening, she contemplated annulment of her marriage but Lethington said that, even if His Holiness granted it on the grounds of consanguinity, the prince would be declared illegitimate and lose his claim to both thrones. But if she would agree to divorce. . . .

Protestants cannot possibly realise what they ask when they suggest divorce to a Roman Catholic, and the Queen was lay leader of Catholic Scotland. But her desperation to be rid of the King was such that she agreed that Lethington could negotiate with the Pope on her behalf. He, James and Lord Argyll, who was skilled in legal matters, had her permission to petition.

But she said to me, 'Seton, it's sin on my soul. And yet, a greater sin is that, if I am burdened by the King for life, I would contemplate ending my life. It's a choice between divorce and suicide.'

I comforted her as best I could by saying that divorce was the only means of her survival, both as woman and as sovereign. Bothwell had stated that it would not prevent her son from his inheritance; his Catholic parents had divorced and he had succeeded to title and estates. Fleming was more shocked than I by Her Majesty's decision. 'It's quite incredible – and that you, Mother Superior, take it so calmly!'

I checked my temper and merely reminded her that she had married a Protestant and had no right to practise hypocrisy. Nor should either of us expect the Queen to behave like a saint. She had not and would not break her vow of defending her faith in Scotland. If the Pope granted petition of divorce, and for so many good reasons, he would in fact also grant her the freedom to rule without impediment.

223

'You're still Catholic at heart, despite your marriage. So will Her Majesty be.'

We made a pact not to discuss the matter again; old friends should keep peace and our differences were niggling. Her hair was thick and smooth as honey, and I complimented her on it. She said that my figure was exquisite. In such silly ways do women maintain friendship when thoughts are diverse.

Bothwell left us abruptly – I noticed his absence at breakfast and asked Her Majesty if it was a recurrence of his illness.

'No,' she said. She looked miserable. 'It's a recurrence of Jean.'

She realised she had blurted this out, and assumed her forced smile. 'Poor dear, she's had really no chance of a honeymoon but two weeks of these nine months. He's returned to Haddington.'

'She's with child?' I asked.

'Oh, no,' she said, as if such a thing was beyond belief. 'He brings her here tomorrow. By my command.'

I wondered why, and she answered my unspoken question.

'Because I've honoured him beyond my other nobles there is sure to be gossip,' she said, 'as there was about Chastelard and Rizzio. The presence of a wife should stem it.'

I thought, if it were not for the coming christening she would never bow to the idea of gossip. Then she said, 'Instruct the housekeeper that he shall have his usual chamber, and she the one with the flowered arras.'

They could not have been further apart.

Always Stirling Castle would remind me of Edinburgh Castle, so lofty it was on its rocks, seemingly disdainful of the grey-roofed town that nestled far below. Our progress through the town was slow because of so many foreign visitors lodged in inns or private homes commanded by Her Majesty. Shops were crammed, and stables; in tavern yards, despite the cold, tables were set with food for those who watched cock fights or wrestling. Most of these spectators were servants who could not be accommodated in the castle. An ambassador might bring a train of fifty besides the ladies of his family, sons and priests. Guests in the castle had come from Venice, Rome,

Spain, Savoy, Flanders, France and England. Elizabeth sent the Earl of Bedford as her envoy and his retinue was vast and elegant.

Bothwell, in sapphire satin, welcomed each guest into the Great Hall, then Her Majesty led them to ermine-covered tables that displayed gifts for the prince. My favourite among the treasures was a diamond chain and pendant from King Charles of France, who would be the baby's godfather, and a great golden and jewelled font from his godmother Elizabeth. Presently Her Majesty went to her dais and sat down to receive a new contingent of guests. She looked superb in her white and emerald gown, and the white wig became her, but already she seemed weary.

Bothwell, coming to stand beside me, whispered, 'She's apprehensive about the King. He's sulking in his apartments. I've means of getting him down but she says that, as long as it's known he's in the castle, he's not required for the ceremony.'

He, Jean and other Protestants remained outside while we journeyed from nursery to the Chapel Royal in a path of light from the high-held tapers of our noblemen. My brother George smiled at me as I passed by in my velvet gown and rubies. I blew him so tiny a kiss that no one but he noticed.

In the chapel, where white candles blazed against the dusk, the Comte de Brienne, King Charles's representative, walked to the altar and set down the prince on an embroidered cushion. I was astonished to see that the child, now six months of age, did look foreign. His hair was dark and his skin sand-coloured. He lay tranquilly in ten yards of silver cloth, then looked up to stare at the glitter of the jewelled font. The priests gathered with ewer, salt vat and basin and de Brienne lifted him, unprotesting, across the font to the Countess of Argyll who served as proxy for Elizabeth.

The holy water was sprinkled. I prayed, as I knew Her Majesty did, that this child would some day rule a united Scotland and England. The Archbishop of St Andrews, in a haze of incense, said, 'I christen thee Charles James Stuart. . . .'

From the rear of the chapel trumpets sounded and a herald repeated the name and titles three times. Again in a path of

225

light, and with musicians playing, we returned the prince to his nursery.

Supper was served in the Great Hall, the Queen at one end of the principal table and de Brienne and Bedford on her right and left, James and the Pope's envoy, Lethington and the Savoyard ambassador in between. Bothwell, at the end of the table, had been given the King's place.

From the gallery above I looked down, with the other Marys, on the sixty guests below. It was good to be reunited as we always were by state occasions, but because gentlemen sat between us our conversation was constrained. I had noticed several things – Bothwell's obvious eminence, the relegation of Jean to a table here on the gallery and the unfortunate error of her being placed next to Alex of Boyne. Watching them from the distance of four other tables I saw him speak, saw her reply so formally. Then, as if with enormous effort, she leaned forward to talk with my brother, who must have seemed a lifeline from her embarrassment. I decided to inform Her Majesty so that tomorrow Jean might be placed elsewhere.

But there was no chance to approach her that night. She danced late, as we all did, when the tables were removed and the musicians arrived. It was, of course, a king's privilege to accompany a queen in the Royal Galliard, but she danced it with Bothwell. It seemed to me that she was increasingly reckless – and this in sight of watchful ambassadors. I could not but wonder what His Holiness the Pope would think when his emissary related the King's absence and Her Majesty's capering with another man, a subject of lesser degree, and Bothwell's reputation with women was ugly. What possible chance was there of his granting her petition of divorce?

Naturally, the King's absence was commented on next day, but subtly. I was asked, 'Is he ill? Is he truly here?' and I replied, 'Certainly he is here, and he is ill of a slight fever.'

But we of the household knew that the barrel-fever plagued him. Taylor, his valet, told Bothwell that he could scarcely supply the bottles demanded and was frightened by the King's rampaging. When sober for a few hours he was prey to hallucination and imagined that Morton and his kin stood outside the door to stab him so that he dared not leave his

226

apartments. Bothwell said to me, 'Such fears are convenient to us. His presence would only embarrass the Queen.'

The King sent Taylor to the various ambassadors, asking that they come to him in conference. None agreed. Apparently his letters to their rulers denigrating Her Majesty had created disgust; and this was a relief to us all. But if she continued to favour Bothwell so publicly, she negated Catholic respect.

A mock battle ended the revels on the evening of 19 December. Bothwell had contrived a fearsome attack on a miniature fortress but to we ladies it was all too real as fire tongued the wooden parapets, as men ran from it through a rain of fireballs, as the entire edifice exploded in the snow in a hellish roar and spew. It shattered my ears, it frightened Her Majesty and she ran to Bothwell for protection. He, at least, realised that some explanation should be made to the sharp-eyed guests, and he said, 'Madam, my apologies, I should have asked your permission for gunpowder.'

She emerged from his cloak and spoke severely. 'Indeed you should have. Horrible, deafening . . . go and comfort your good lady, she has run away.'

He bowed and followed Jean into the castle.

James, who stood beside me with Lethington, said, 'Gunpowder is tricky. I'd not risk it as entertainment. The fool!'

Lethington said, 'Perhaps Lord Bothwell is practising?'

By Christmas Eve all of our foreign guests had left and James took the Earl of Bedford to St Andrews for the holidays. George returned to Seton with gifts for my family. The married Marys rode to their country estates. Only Bothwell and Jean, Lord and Lady Mar and Lord Robert Stuart remained – and the King.

He sent for Her Majesty; he had begged to join us for the night's Yule festivities but she had refused. 'He'll not make a spectacle of himself dancing with the young maids and the pages. He'll not spoil our serenity.'

I could not help but feel pity for him.

She said, 'I told him that some English guests were stopping at Newcastle with documents of pardon for his fellow murderers.'

So we were not surprised that the King and his servants and

his guard fled that night despite a snowstorm. Nor was I surprised by Jean's increasing melancholy. Her husband and the Queen seemed almost oblivious of anyone else. When she danced, as was customary, with the male attendants, he could scarcely wait to break in. And that, on Christmas Eve, is *not* customary.

Two days later we moved to Drummond Castle, twenty miles away in Perthshire, to hunt. As we entered the stone hall I noticed a motto carved on the gallery: *Gang Warily.* If only she would.

I was thankful for the sport that took them out into the frosty moors in pursuit of bucks and small game. Lady Mar sat with me by the largest fire in the smallest chamber and chattered about the prince, whom she adored, about the wisdom of his remaining at Stirling under guard and with physicians. 'I've suggested to Her Majesty that the clear air is so preferable to Edinburgh's – I still remember the stink of the Castle moat and the dank, evil mists of Holyrood. The boy should thrive at Stirling and I think Her Majesty plans to keep him there.'

Perhaps I misjudged Her Majesty, but I had not noticed a normal maternal concern for the boy except to protect him. She had not cooed over him at birth, was not effusive about 'the wee treasure' as her ladies were, was content for Lady Reres to croon over the cradle. I attributed this to her overwhelming hatred of the father, for always before she had displayed love for little creatures.

Close to dawn I went to the privy. In old castles which are merely used for hunting lodges these are not built into one's suite, but usually at the end of a corridor over a moat. With a candle, I found the nearest. As I came out I heard voices from the Queen's bedchamber. They were low, but I recognised Bothwell's. I heard her say, 'love'.

In my bed, the candle still alight, I tried to find innocent reasons for this; something might have alarmed her and she had summoned him – then why not to the adjoining presence chamber? Was it possible that there had been a third voice – Jean's? I wanted so desperately to clutch at innocent reasons but they eluded me entirely.

228

I was not shocked – I had loved a priest. But I was overwhelmed by fear and the terrible red word came back into my mind, for traitors had been pardoned and, for all his courage and enterprise, Bothwell was target for dozens of proven murderers. All lusted for power, and Morton's kinsmen even followed a tradition: 'The Stuarts were born to the throne; and the Douglases born to thieve it.' Every Scottish child learns that adage and every Scottish ruler must remember it.

Neither the Queen nor Bothwell appeared for breakfast. Jean's eyes seemed red from weeping, not for love of him – I doubt she felt it – but from shattered pride. She said, 'When my husband and I are fully packed, and the horses ready, we go to Crichton.'

'And miss the sport?' asked Lady Mar, quite unaware of a double meaning.

'It is cold here,' Jean said, 'and I'm not well.'

Still Her Majesty did not appear. At eleven Bothwell summoned Jean for departure and from an arrow-slit I watched their progress down the rocky slope through the snow.

At dusk Her Majesty joined us, more beautiful in a simple blue woollen gown than ever I had seen her attired in splendour. She wore no wig but her own hair sparkled. So did her eyes. They were dreamy, full of light, and she smiled without reason as though she could not help it. She even smiled when the King's courier asked audience, and when she returned to us before supper she said serenely, 'The King is taken with smallpox at his father's house in Glasgow. It will probably not be fatal. In any case, I'm sending Gervais and Gurion from Edinburgh to attend him.'

There was no doubt of her happiness. And as I had been compelled to talk of Adam, so she talked of Bothwell. Within three days he would meet us at Callander Castle where Livvy and her husband planned New Year's revels for us. She hoped he would not forget to bring her a new cross-bow. He had trained a falcon for her but thus far refused to name it. What name did we suggest?

It was not my place to suggest that it was more than unwise to prattle so of Bothwell but she continued until he joined us

229

at Callander – without Jean. There they were almost constantly together in the forest, in the castle at cards or chess, building a portly snowman in the garden. After dancing she would retire about midnight. Soon after he would call for his taper-bearer and bid us a good night.

We returned to Holyrood by Twelfth Night and the merry-making continued, with James, Lethington, my brother and other nobles and their ladies. The King's suite was given to Bothwell, but Jean did not come to share it. When I thought of the private stairs that linked his suite with hers I marvelled that she could be so indiscreet. James must have suspected a love affair by now but their recklessness probably pleased him. However she could be discredited was to his ultimate advantage.

Couriers arrived each day, by Her Majesty's command, to bring reports of the King. His fever was still severe, his skin badly marked. 'Smallpox!' Bothwell said to me. 'Nonsense. It's likely the yaws caught from some slut or he-bawd.'

On a morning in mid-January Her Majesty sent word to my maid and to Fleming's that we must dress in black. So the King had died! But no, we were to receive Lord Morton and the rebels in the audience chamber, our attire to remind them of the mourning they had created here. She would deliberately keep them waiting. We were not to offer them refreshment or our hands to kiss.

Morton, their spokesman, fawned forward, Lindsay behind him. I stared into his pig-eyes and the odious creature smoothed his heavy red beard, preening. He inquired of my health, of my brother, then wished Fleming happiness in her marriage. Were we aware that Lord Ruthven had died of the coughing sickness?

We replied distantly, and I was relieved when James and Lethington came in, wryly amused by James's hauteur towards his former friends. Presently the Queen entered, with Bothwell, and took her place in the chair of state on the dais.

She said, 'My Lords, none of you is welcome at court. But you have received my pardon – all but George Douglas, who struck the first blow, and Kerr, who threatened me with a pistol.'

230

Morton said, 'Madam, we humbly implore—'

'So did Signor Rizzio implore,' she said, 'so doubtless did Father Black implore of Yair.'

'But Madam,' Morton said, 'the King instigated those deaths.'

'Of a Catholic priest?' she asked scornfully. 'But if that were true, your loyalty was to me, not to him. Those of you who are pardoned are not forgiven. And next time you set upon one of my friends you'll die at the Market Cross as common criminals. This I swear.'

She dismissed them.

That afternoon Bothwell's agents reported that the King's servants were outfitting an English ship at anchor in the Clyde. Obviously he was planning to sail when he had recovered but Her Majesty's delight changed to terror when Paris told her that he planned to kidnap the prince.

That rumour was sufficient to send Bothwell's Borderers to Stirling immediately. Bothwell and Her Majesty changed into riding clothes and they followed within the hour accompanied by spearmen and halberdiers. As she left she said to me, 'See that a nursery is arranged and accommodation for Lady Reres next to it. We'll return in two days.'

At supper Lethington said that he doubted the King had courage or wit for such an enterprise, and merely wanted to frighten Her Majesty; it was a bid for attention. But James disagreed – the fool was desperate, he said. She was wise to remove the child.

It was true that Holyrood's climate would be less salubrious for the Prince. I ordered sweet herbs to be burned in the nursery after it had been aired; and when Her Majesty returned with Bothwell, Gurion and Gervais, the last named brought braziers of clove. After Father Joseph had sprinkled holy water on the tiny pillow and the baby was asleep, I asked Gervais if the King truly had smallpox.

'His skin is pitted,' he said, 'but, as Gurion says, it's difficult to judge between smallpox, leprosy and – forgive me, my lady – the French disease. We think it likely the latter, for he's been near no lepers.'

'Is he able to eat, drink?'

231

'Yes, my lady. He's out of danger but niggled by fear that his skin will be for ever marked, so he wears silken gloves to prevent his scratching in sleep, and received us – his physicians – in a silken mask. A lady's vanity is nothing compared to his.'

A year ago no one would have talked so frankly of the King for fear of treason. Now, himself a proven traitor, we had no such qualms. As the days passed Her Majesty's post-bags were swollen with letters from France, Savoy, Spain, Flanders and every friend bade her beware of the King. In the library, when I went in for a book one evening, Joseph Rizzio said, 'Lady Seton, if you have influence with Her Majesty – and I know you do – ask that she takes her correspondence more seriously. She's inclined to toss off warnings about the King as though they were dandelion fluff.'

Because her world was bounded by Bothwell now?

'She heeded my brother's advice, but I'm so young. I feel powerless . . . frustrated by her very gaiety. Now that the prince is here, safe, guarded, she seems to live for the moment, but I assure you the moment is late.' He indicated a pile of parchments on the writing table. 'Almost all of them are warnings. The King wants her dead.'

I confided in Lethington what Rizzio had said. As Secretary of State the problem was his, and he told me that he was more than aware of it. He knew that Lord Lennox's house in Glasgow was a nest of conspirators in league with the King and was in agreement with Bothwell that the plots must be ripped apart.

It was Isobel who informed me that a flurry of packing was taking place in Her Majesty's apartments and presently the Queen herself came to me looking as if she had not slept, and she had not even bothered to change from last night's gown. Seated by the hearth she stared bleakly into the fire. Then she said, 'Tomorrow I go to Glasgow to visit the King and to try to bring him back to Edinburgh.'

'But is it safe, Madam?'

'I'll be well guarded. And I suppose I'm well advised to go. Bothwell says I must. They all agree that he must be

232

placed away from conspiracy or he may do us a mischief.'

Timidly I asked, 'What of the possibility of divorce?'

'Hopeless,' she said. There was something strange in her manner that I could not fathom. I did not think she was *afraid*. No, it was as though she bore a cruel weight, for her shoulders slumped and, when a log tumbled, she jumped.

'Does Your Majesty want me with you?' I asked.

'Oh no!' she said. 'Only my guard. Bothwell will escort me as far as Callander Castle.'

'Shall I have apartments prepared for the King?'

'No,' she said. 'I – that is – he might not agree to come.'

When she left me she held me for a moment in close embrace. Her cheek against mine was icy.

A week later Bothwell told me that for the King's health a house had been chosen for him at Kirk O' Field, a ten-minute ride from Holyrood. There would be no fierce winds but soft sea breezes, and salt water baths were being arranged. 'He is pleased, for a change, not to parade – embarrassed by his pox marks.' Then he laughed. 'I'm Mistress of the Household here – Her Majesty has asked me to select furniture for their suites since the house is bereft of it. I've done so. It's been carted there.'

I knew him to be a jealous man and I could not imagine his amusement at the Queen lodging with her husband.

'They are reconciled, then?' I asked.

His reply was oblique. 'It would certainly seem so, my lady. She sees to his comforts as any wife would – his favourite wines and foods, clothing . . . and a mix of diamond dust and oils to heal his skin.'

I was puzzled that her hatred of the King had changed to affection. But the explanation was simple: *he* must have changed, and humbly. Her faith had triumphed and I was relieved, for her sake, that the sin of divorce had been denied her.

On 9 February, Carnival Sunday, Her Majesty returned to Holyrood in the early morning and summoned me to arrange her hair. She, and indeed all of us, dressed for the wedding of favourite servants, Christina Hogg and Sebastian Paget, who

233

were married in the chapel at ten. There was a banquet at noon. Shortly after James left for St Andrews, and I heard Her Majesty say in parting, 'I regret that you go, my dear brother.'

Perhaps it was a mere formality, and I hoped so. But perhaps his impeccable behaviour since his pardon had wiled her into renewed trust. There was, after all, the bond of blood. But I was distressed to think that her memory of James's treachery was so short.

In the afternoon I rearranged her hair in a golden snood; she had changed to a willow-green gown and would visit the King, then attend a dinner for the Savoyard ambassador at Lord Balfour's house. Before midnight she was back at Holyrood for the wedding ball, dancing with the bridegroom, with Bothwell and Lethington. But she looked weary. I assumed that reconciliation with the King was no bed of lilies, if indeed they bedded. And if, as I was certain, she loved Bothwell, that would account for her malaise of spirit, though she was gracious to all of the revellers. She retired to her apartments shortly after one o'clock, and I to mine.

The pipers outside gradually silenced and, the curtains drawn about my bed, I sank towards sleep. Then it seemed that the world was rocked with the most tremendous earthquake. Near the casement there was a crash of ornaments on my dressing-chest, falling pictures, and God knows how, trembling as I was, I managed to part the curtains and look out. The fire still burned behind its screen and I could see the ornaments, plants on the sill and a wall cresset broken and bent. Fearing another quake, I sat on the bed, my ears ringing with the reverberation, but it did not come – only the howl of dogs, and now a great stir of men shouting and horses screaming in the courtyard. I went to the fire, made a spill, and lighted candles. Isobel, naked but for a blanket, rushed in and we held one another in panic.

'I must go up to Her Majesty,' I said, or I think I said that; at least that was my intention, for now I realised that the palace must have been attacked by cannon at close range. I snatched a robe and opened the door; Isobel was close behind me. Now we could hear shouting in the corridors and saw guards sweep past us with naked weapons. One turned and called to us, 'Go back, bolt your door,' and we obeyed.

Isobel, mindless of propriety, poured wine for us both and huddled with me by the fire. Gradually we calmed and went to the casement. By torchlight we could see Bothwell ride off with a few of his men, a crowd making way for them. Comforted, I said to Isobel, 'He'd not leave here if Her Majesty were in danger, and if it's an attack he'd not be allowed to escape.'

And then, to our astonishment and relief, someone brought Her Majesty's palfrey and she came out with Captain Erskine and followed, Huntly behind her.

I opened the window, leaned out and called down to the crowd, 'What is it? What has happened?'

I did not see Gaston until he turned and looked up. 'We don't know.'

'Where have they gone?' I asked, but no one heard me.

Isobel was shivering and I ordered her to her bed and sat down by the fire to speculate. I had never heard of earthquakes in Scotland; it seemed to me that we *had* been attacked – and James, supposedly at St Andrews, could have returned and captured the Castle cannon. But that such a small company would have ridden to meet him seemed ridiculous, and Her Majesty had worn neither armour nor helmet.

Surely it was safe to unbolt the door and, though the palace was quiet now, I would find someone awake? Hastily I dressed and, on the way to the chambers Fleming shared with Lethington, made inquiry of a guard. He said he knew no more than I but he thought it a shift of earth from the Salisbury Crags or Arthur's Seat; it had tumbled him to the floor, with the oak chandelier at the staircase.

There was no sound from Lethington's apartments and I did not want to intrude on them, but I did want some explanation and was glad when I saw Lady Huntly's maid emerge from her chamber. Yes, her mistress was awake, and I might go in.

'*What* has happened?' Lady Huntly asked me, coming forward, a tasselled nightcap askew.

I said that I was as mystified as she. Like myself, she believed that James was responsible, that it had been an

235

attack and that Her Majesty had ridden off for a peace parley at the Castle. She was less alarmed than indignant. 'I was bounced from my bed, look at the shambles of my Venice glass . . . and that mirror cracked.'

Then I remembered that Morton's house was not far across the park, behind the palace. If he had set up field guns? But we agreed that the riders had gone in the opposite direction.

Time passed so slowly. Finally, after four o'clock, we heard commotion below, and looked out. Her Majesty, Bothwell and the others had returned. Despite her attire, Lady Huntly and I hurried down the main staircase, others crowding behind us.

Her Majesty looked up. Her face was rigidly composed, her voice steady. She said, 'There was an explosion at Kirk O' Field. The King is dead.'

CHAPTER XIII

At Her Majesty's command the palace was dressed in black. Up from the vaults came woe-weeds to drape over bright tapestries, black carpets, black candles. Before she retired she sent couriers racing to England and throughout Scotland. Others would travel to the Continent.

At noon Her Majesty, after scant sleep, summoned us to hear Mass in the chapel; the funeral would be held the following day to give Lord Lennox time to attend. We Catholics left the abbey and, at her order, joined Protestants in her audience chamber. She sat on her throne under the canopy of state, lifted the mourning veil from her face and addressed us.

'At two this past morning, at our residence at Kirk O' Field, the King, taking his sleep, was apparently hurled from his bed into the garden by the force of gunpowder.'

Who had said, 'Gunpowder is tricky'? Ah yes, James, when Bothwell had set off the frightening blast at Stirling. I glanced at Bothwell, who stood nearest the dais in his silken black. He had never betrayed nerves, nor did he now. Hands calm at his sides, he listened as we did, respectful of her ordeal.

'Strangely, there was not a mark upon him but the scars of his pox, not even ash or powder-burn, nor on the body of Taylor, his valet.' She paused and then said, 'I am so shocked that I'm confused now. I said the force of gunpowder, but it wasn't that which killed them. It appears that they were smothered, the murderers using their victims' nightshirts.' She indicated Bothwell. 'My Lord, as Sheriff of Edinburgh, roused us at the sound of the explosion and we rode there – rode there – and he will tell you.'

He turned; then, facing us, told us that, earlier that evening, Her Majesty had visited Kirk O' Field with himself and Lords Huntly, Argyll and Cassilis who took wine at the

237

King's bedside. At eleven o'clock he had reminded Her Majesty of her promise to attend the wedding ball here, and the King was upset, saying that she had promised him to stay the night. He insisted that she must, but she explained the prior engagement.

'Then', Bothwell said, 'the King extracted another promise, that she be there with her principal nobles at eight of this morning to return him here to Holyrood. To this she agreed and gave her ring in pledge.

'We were dancing here when my page Paris came to me and told me that the King's father had left Glasgow for Linlithgow with a force of men, possibly a battle clan. I warned Her Majesty not to return to the King this morning – I suspected treachery. And' – he turned to Lords Huntly, Argyll and Cassilis – 'these gentlemen are witness to the fact that the King repeatedly demanded that we be at his house *precisely* at eight. Why? I found the house in such pebbles as only gunpowder could achieve, four servants who slept in the cellar blown to fragments, an empty powder barrel . . . in short, whoever devised to kill the King had expected Her Majesty also, and was unaware of the changed plan. Or – more likely – it was the King's plan to kill Her Majesty at two and escape to his father.'

Lethington said, 'Then what went amiss?'

Bothwell said, 'Everything, as any plot would in amateur hands. Until we gather more facts I accuse no living man of the King's murder. But you, my Lords, heard testimony this morning of the woman who lodges near the garden where the King was found. She was awake, tending a sick child, when she heard an explosion, screams, and ran outside with her sister, and heard a man pleading for his life. For some five minutes he repeated, "Pity me, kinsmen, for the love of God." '

Morton and his Douglases were kin to the King. . . .

'Yes,' said Her Majesty swiftly, 'that was the woman's testimony and I take it as honest, she'd have no reason to lie. The King had escaped the blast but must have found the assassins as he fled into the garden. Plot, counterplot . . . a maze we must grope through. Signor Rizzio is aware of warnings we have had from foreign friends.'

238

Joseph Rizzio said, 'They implied that the King was plotting for power. And since Her Majesty did expect to remain overnight, the mining of the house, its explosion at two, does seem designed for her.'

Or, I thought, designed by James for them both. Probably he had instigated this with the help of Morton, then cleverly left town before the deed was accomplished.

'It seems incredible', the Queen said, 'that the house could have been mined without the knowledge of the King or his servants.'

'Aye,' Bothwell said. 'I've ordered all citizens to watch for men whose clothing bears powder-burns, the town watch will halt any who try to leave by the various gates, and I have set a guard on all ports – and at Linlithgow. Lord Lennox's move there is considerably strange, timed as it is.'

The Queen said, 'An hour ago, in reply to the message I sent, Lord Lennox stated "astonished horror" of the act but will not attend the funeral.'

'Afraid to,' Bothwell said, 'since his house was a nest of conspiracy against Your Majesty.'

She nodded. 'So the funeral will proceed without him. It will be held at ten tonight.'

Bothwell took her hand as she came down the steps of the dais and we made way for her as she left, entering her bedchamber, tearless, the black veil flowing behind her. I had no appetite but joined others in the Great Hall where tables had been set up. They were covered in black linen. Rain beat against casements draped in black. Lady Huntly, pausing at the buffet, said, 'What, no black puddings?' and caused a ripple of amusement. In truth, not one of us could mourn the King and so we behaved as naturally as the gloom permitted. I joined Bothwell at the wine table, anxious for more information.

'Do you think that Morton smothered the King?' I asked.

'More likely Archibald Douglas, on Morton's order. Paris found his slipper nearby; I keep it as evidence that he fled the garden and lost it.'

'And who but James ordered Morton?' I asked.

He smiled. 'That would be difficult to prove. The Bastard

always contrives to be miles away in time of tragedy.'

'Shall there be a trial, my Lord?'

'Her Majesty refuses to consider one but I hope to persuade her.'

How very odd, I thought. Then we were interrupted by Arnault who said that the King's body had arrived, that he and Gervais had embalmed it but that there was no casket sufficiently long, only a box of oak measuring six feet. When might Her Majesty be consulted?

'It's hoped she will sleep all day,' Bothwell said. 'Cram the body into the box – who's to know?'

Arnault seemed relieved. 'Of course we do have a fine silken winding-sheet. Another matter, there's a valuable ring on his finger.'

'It belonged to Her Majesty. Keep it for her.'

We attended Solemn Requiem Mass in the chapel. The King was interred in the centuries-old vaults. Afterwards Her Majesty retired, still tearless and outwardly composed. To my relief my brother had arrived and we sat late by my fire. He said that Madame my mother had asked him to invite the Queen to Seton, there to recover from what must have been a hellish experience. I thought it a marvellous idea but we would bide our time before we suggested it.

'It's strange,' I said, 'but Bothwell told me she is reluctant to bring any suspects to trial, yet there is some evidence. . . . Why should she not?'

'Because of Bothwell,' he said. 'Don't you realise he is chief suspect? Who else is known to employ gunpowder? Who but he had motive to kill the King and marry the widow?'

'James—'

'Would be too prudent to ally himself again with Morton. And how do we know that Bothwell – ten minutes' ride from here – did not go to Kirk O' Field, light a slow-burning fuse and return to this palace to be "surprised" by the explosion?'

As I sought words, he said, 'If the King had ordered the explosion, it would have come off at eight o'clock, when Her Majesty and the lords were present.'

'You think that of Bothwell – your friend?'

240

'I think that of Bothwell – *her* friend. I am not sitting in judgement, sister, and this is private between us, but in his love and his recklessness, and because her divorce is impossible, he would be capable of total ruthlessness.'

'Perhaps', I said slowly, thinking it over, 'you're right.' Then I said, 'But you forget Jean. What grounds would he have for divorce?'

'He might have only to ask her. To settle land upon her, and gold. She's never seemed an overly loving wife, content to be away from him.'

I could not quite agree; we had many talks within the next few days but, though he did not try to convince me, his theory made sense. Then one evening Bothwell came to my brother and said that he was away to Crichton – Jean was ill, vomiting and with cramps. He had said to George's inquiry, 'She is not with child.'

Next morning George and I rose early and walked in the gardens, anxious for clean air. At the palace gate we saw guards tearing placards off the wall and George said, 'What do you do?'

'Our duty, my Lord.'

Coming close we saw that the placards were of a redheaded man whose hands dripped blood, and labelled, 'Bothwell, the King's murderer.'

'Who set these?' my brother asked.

The men did not know; they had appeared during the night. They were told that such sketches were nailed throughout Edinburgh – on the Tolbooth door, at the Salt Tron, and some had appeared on church doors. Lord Balfour, too, had been denounced, they said, as confederate. Puzzled, I asked why as George and I returned to the palace and he told me that Balfour had suggested his brother's empty house as a place of convalescence for the King when they had met on the road from Glasgow. But how did townsfolk know that? The King's guards might have talked, surprised at being diverted from Holyrood to the lonely Kirk O' Field.

We asked audience of Her Majesty, and told her. She said she would inform the town watch. I had expected anger, but she spoke listlessly. Her thin body seemed bent under the weight of its dark damask robes; her thin hands moved among the vines of a potato plant, pinching off dry leaves.

George rode into the city and returned to tell me that Bothwell's portrait, labelled the King's murderer, was being sold by street vendors in Her Majesty's name. He threatened them with the death penalty if the goods were not destroyed. The merchants did so in his presence but next morning the placards reappeared on the palace gates.

George came to me shortly after breakfast. 'Her Majesty has agreed to come to Seton – she is packing. Be ready within the hour.'

We rode off, with our guard and hers, through a haar as ghastly, thick and yellow as that which had risen on her arrival in Scotland. And it lingered.

My family were properly attired in mourning, and the house dressed so, but dinner was elegantly served and the food, as usual, superb. Madame my mother asked after the health of the prince and Her Majesty said he was well, the nursery heavily guarded.

'Your Majesty will wish to rest,' my stepfather said as we rose from the table. 'We beg that you consider this a cradle for your comfort.'

She smiled wanly, extended her hand for him to kiss, and retired to her apartments. The sun came out. An hour later Bothwell rode in with Huntly. He did not ask, he demanded to see Her Majesty, and I worried that some new crisis was at hand. But later that afternoon she and Bothwell went off to play golf at the Links, then won an archery match against Huntly and my brother. They returned to dress and George told Madame my mother that he had promised to pay off the wager with a supper party at Tranent.

When they had left, Her Majesty dazzling in satin and jet, my mother said, 'It's not for me to question Her Majesty's – whims, but to frivol so soon after the King's death. . . .'

It had been six days.

One evening in the gardens, at dusk, I turned a corner and saw two cloaked figures embracing, so close together as to seem one. I had a sense of being isolated from such love for the rest of my life; of being denied, of utter sterility. I did not envy their passion but I was wistful for it. For a long time, well into darkness, I lingered in the mews among the calm, caged falcons. One might say that being still only in my mid-twenties there was time for romance; only peasants married early for need of children to till the land or spin the wool. And being wealthy I was all the more marriageable. But I felt as though my heart had been lifted away with Adam's death. There remained only a mind, inimical to the thought of mating for dreary convenience. I was not Jean.

Jean's illness kept Bothwell riding between Seton and Crichton; he said the physicians were mystified. He was visiting her one day when a page came to me and said that Lord James Stuart had arrived but that Her Majesty was asleep. What should he do?

'Send him to me,' I said, for she would want him entertained and my parents were supervising a planting.

He wore black satin with a chain of black pearls. Refusing refreshment, he talked piously of hoping that God would help Her Majesty through these troubled days. An imp of mischief led me to say that Bothwell and her other loyal nobles were her source of greatest comfort. 'Her Majesty has such confidence in Lord Bothwell that she has just given him the command of Edinburgh Castle, governorship of the fortresses of Dunbar and Blackness, control of the port of Leith. . . .'

I knew I had struck and wounded his greedy soul. His mouth turned down, he chewed his lip, his eyes were the green of a frosted pool. Then he said, 'A pity that Lady Bothwell may not live to share his glory – and poison so cruel and lingering a death.'

'What?' I said, leaning forward. 'Who would poison her?'

'One who'd have most to gain,' he said.

For once, I was clever – my hatred of him was so intense that it sparked my wits. 'How terrible,' I said, instead of asking 'How do you know?' I shook my head sorrowfully. 'I hope you won't spare Her Majesty this information. She should know.'

'I'm loath to add another grief,' he said.

'But my Lord, it's your duty, is it not?'

243

He said nothing but I knew he would tell her. I took it upon myself to have Her Majesty awakened, and presently James was sent to her apartments.

A scant twenty minutes later she came to me in cold fury. 'May I burn in hell if I ever receive him again! He came to me with a preposterous story that Jean is being poisoned . . . implying that Bothwell visits her to feed it to her in milk and gruel – oh, and if she *should* die of whatever ails her, he'll speed the story throughout the world, and folk will believe it!'

I calmed her as best I could, pointing out that, after all, even Elizabeth had refused to harbour James in England, that the world knew of his rebellious history. Then she hid her face in her hands and said, words muffled, 'Seton, we must pray for her recovery. I shall send my own physicians. . . .'

Bothwell returned from Crichton that night but neither he nor the Queen appeared for supper. 'She is not ill, I trust?' Madame my mother asked.

'While you were in the fields her brother James arrived. He always upsets her, and she sent him off.'

The French are said to be logical. Madame said, 'She has sent him off so often, as I rip mandrake from the herb garden. He returns like the evil root. The only riddance is burning.'

'Have you burned the mandrake, then?'

Wryly, she said, 'I thought I had. Perhaps I wasn't sufficiently brutal because, do you know, the root screams?'

'You're not serious, Madame—'

'It screams.'

We moved back to Holyrood on advice that Elizabeth's envoy, Sir Henry Killigrew, was expected there on a visit of condolence. This had been achieved by Lethington, who must have counselled Her Majesty that to remain at Seton was to appear to be on frivolous holiday. When we left Her Majesty honoured my family with a most magnificent looking-glass, framed in jewels. I recognised it as the King's.

Before the interview with Killigrew the Queen ordered that I arrange her hair, but when I formed curls she said, 'No, it must be severe, plain.' When one of her tirewomen, Annette, brought paints the Queen refused them, using only kohl on her eyelids. In her mourning coif and veil she looked full thirty years of age, but this was deliberate, as if she were in masque to play an older and tragic role. She wore no jewels, only her marriage ring. In the audience chamber she asked that the woe-weeds be closed against the sunlight.

She commanded me to stay, but before she sent a page for Sir Henry she asked me to wipe off my lip-paint and wash off the musk which perfumed my wrists. This accomplished, and when we were alone, she said, 'Everything – every flick of an eyelash – will be reported to the Queen. And we *are* in deepest mourning, are we not?'

'Truly, Madam,' I said, but, remembering her sport at Seton and that supper party at Tranent, I wondered how she could imagine that *these* matters had gone unreported.

'It is kind of the Queen to send a special envoy,' she said. 'I wouldn't command your presence if I knew him but it's only discreet to have a lady with me.'

Oh Madam, I thought, if only you were always discreet. . . .

'Lord Bothwell's at Crichton,' she said. 'I've asked him to send a messenger if there's any change in her condition, and so admit him even if Sir Henry and I are in deepest discussion.'

I understood all too well; Bothwell had been labelled the King's murderer; if his wife died it would be assumed double murder so that any hope she might have of marriage to him would be doomed. She would demand marriage not only as pledge of love but as purge for her conscience and the requirement of dignity. To remain his mistress would be galling, unthinkable. But if Jean died she would have to remain so until – if ever – rumour died.

Sir Henry Killigrew was admitted; he bowed, kissed her hand, bowed to me when she introduced us. She motioned for me to sit on a window-bench but they remained standing near the fireplace. He was small and thin, legs spiderlike in black hose below puffed black velvet breeches; of middle age, and mellow with charm. For a few minutes he commiserated with Her Majesty over the death of the King. Then from a case he brought out a letter from his sovereign and said, 'This is written in Her Majesty's own hand, of her heart's blood.'

My Queen took it to the taperlight, opened the great seal of England, read it. Tears spilled down and I knew them to be genuine. Then she re-read it aloud: 'My ears have been so astonished and my mind so grieved and my heart so terrified at hearing of the abominable murder of your late husband and my cousin that I have even now no spirit to write about it . . . but I cannot conceal from myself that I am more full of grief on your account than on his. O, Madam! I should not perform the part of a faithful cousin or an affectionate friend if I studied rather to please your ears than to endeavour to preserve your honour; therefore I will not conceal from you what most persons say about the matter, namely, that you will look through your fingers at taking vengeance for this deed and have no intention to touch those who have done you this kindness as if the act would not have been perpetrated unless the murderers had received assurance of their impunity.

'I beg you . . . I exhort you, I advise and beseech you to take this thing so much to heart, as not to fear to bring to judgement the nearest relation you have. . . .'

She put down the letter. 'Her Majesty must refer to my brother James.'

There was a flicker of amusement as he said, 'Perhaps, Madam.'

'Or perhaps she employs a figure of speech. Tell her that Lord James was absent at St Andrews at the time of the murder, so he can't be brought to trial. Lord Lennox wants Lord Bothwell brought to trial – imagine!'

He tut-tutted, but said, 'That might seem unfair to you, Madam, but may I risk saying that Her Majesty would think it wise considering that it would stem gossip that he is – honoured beyond all other gentlemen?'

So Elizabeth had heard that he was her lover. And what about her own? The Earl of Leicester was still prattled about, and his wife's strange death was assuredly murder.

'Lord Bothwell is indeed honoured,' Her Majesty said, 'and rightly. In fact, he himself has suggested that he be tried so that he may clear himself.'

Paris was admitted, and I knew that this must be a message from Bothwell. She paused, read a letter, then – looking at

246

me – said, 'What happy news from Crichton. Dear Jean is very much better. In fact, nearly recovered.'

As if Jean were my best friend, I said, 'I'm delighted.'

Killigrew left us after discussing his return journey and Monday's possible weather. Her Majesty said, looking twenty despite her attempt at age, 'Isn't it marvellous? I did worry about Jean.'

'So did I, Madam.'

'I'll come to you at six,' she said. 'I've a new idea for my hair – a coronet of braids, but with sapphires interlaced. It isn't strict mourning, but then, a few jewels would honour Sir Henry.'

'Yes, Madam.'

'And Bothwell will be here.'

Her Majesty visited the nursery twice a day. She did not cuddle the prince but consulted with the physicians as to how to rosy those sallow cheeks. The March weather was dour, but when there was sun he was taken into the courtyard or gardens. At night, of course, all windows were closed lest he suffer the fevers brewed in darkness. And then, in early April, he was moved to Stirling in the care of Lord and Lady Mar who acted like grandparents.

One reason for the move was that Bothwell's Borderers – more than five thousand – had come to Edinburgh to keep order during his trial at the Tolbooth. They were an inquisitive lot, poking about the city, and one had been caught climbing a wall of Holyrood hoping for a glimpse of the prince. Being merely a burly, simple yokel he was admonished rather than punished.

She was extremely nervous on the eve of the trial, and no wonder. The jury consisted principally of Bothwell's enemies. Caithness, the foreman, was James's closest friend and six were allied in hatred because in years past Bothwell had embarrassed them by loyalty to Mary de Guise while they had plotted with Elizabeth. Several had suffered when he had captured English gold. Then there was Alex of Boyne, a juror who, if he had any lingering fondness for Jean, must have heard tales of her 'poisoning' and been appalled. Four

247

of the jurymen were questionable in their attitude, weather-cocks. Only three were Bothwell's friends.

But, to my astonishment and relief, he was declared innocent of the King's murder after five hours' deliberation. At supper I congratulated him and asked about the proceedings.

'A farce,' he said. 'A dark comedy. No one cared to present evidence against me.'

'Why not, my Lord?'

He smiled. 'Possibly, just possibly, because my Borderers surrounded the Tolbooth. Old Lennox was afraid to come into town and testify on behalf of his son, though all he could have done was to accuse. And Master Buchanan is still accusing, as Scotland's eminent historian. Not an hour ago, I'm told, he said that the jury was bribed to aquit me. Can you imagine Lindsay being bribed? Argyll, Lord Justice? The other assessors? But, Lady Seton, I had my uneasy moments this morning when I learned that James left town.'

'He did?'

'Aye. To visit Paris and Rome. And when the Bastard leaves, he generally leaves a plot to blossom.'

The Queen blossomed as April did, and very gradually shed her mourning. It almost seemed that she had forgotten the murders. But Gaston said to me, when we met in his herb garden, 'A thought recurs, my lady, over and again. The night the Queen escaped and the King stumbled over Signor Rizzio's grave.'

'Yes?'

'She said, "I swear another shall lie as low before a year has passed." And do you realise, it was precisely one year to the night of the King's death?'

Thinking back, I had to agree. 'A very strange coincidence,' I said.

'Coincidence, of course,' he said quickly.

Early one morning Her Majesty came to me to discuss the disposal of the King's effects. She was listing jewels to be sold when she suddenly dashed for the privy. Returning, she sat down on my couch and said, smiling, 'I was ill. Herrings mislike me.'

I offered to mix her a powder Gervais had given me for stomach upsets but she rejected it. Then she said, 'Why should I lie to you, who would guard a secret with her life? I'm with child.'

She said it proudly, serenely, and I ran to her and knelt beside her; she took my hand in hers. Because she was so obviously happy I could only pretend to share it, but it seemed to me another disaster, every obstacle being against the child's legitimacy. First, though Bothwell had been judged innocent of murder, the rumours had not been silenced, partly due to Buchanan's libel of bribery. Secondly, on what grounds could he divorce Jean? Then, even if it were achieved, the Queen could only insult the Catholic world by wedding a Protestant. Lastly, to marry during her period of mourning was unthinkable. She would have to wait another ten months.

'Are you sure, Madam?' I asked.

She nodded. 'I'm two months with child. Arnault, of course, is under oath to say nothing.' Then she laughed. 'Lord Bothwell is not amused but I must say he's enterprising. Last night at Ainslie's Tavern he entertained our Privy Council, twenty nobles and eight bishops, and persuaded them into signing a bond asserting his innocence of murder – and further, swearing them to assist him in coaxing me to marry him.'

'They actually signed a bond to help him? How, Madam, would they agree to it?'

Again her ripple of laughter. 'First they were given quantities of *aqua vitae* – aye, even the bishops were staggering. But my Lord was taking no chances that, when they left, the fresh air would sober them. So all of his Borderers were waiting outside in an armed circle of the tavern.'

'It is marvellous,' I said.

'Today', she said, 'I expect visitors – Argyll, Lindsay, Morton. They will probably tell me that they signed under duress. I shall reject Bothwell's suit as offensive.'

'But Madam – you want to marry him—'

'As I want to enter heaven. But I must appear to be more than reluctant. Dove, I've play-acted often but never for such stakes. Never before for love.'

'But Madam, you can't reject his suit for long.'

'Oh, I shall appear to, furious that a mourning widow should be betrayed by her Lords, even her clergy. But my Lord will *force* me to marriage. He will abduct me to some castle and ravish me.'

Only Bothwell would be capable of such a plan, and his very reputation would create credibility. She said, 'I don't know when, but soon . . . one reason I tell you this is that when you hear of my disappearance you'll know me safe, you won't worry.'

'My principal worry is Jean,' I said. 'She may adhere to love of Alex, but she enjoys the honour of countess, and all of the lands and properties you've given Bothwell. She might not easily agree to divorce.'

Her Majesty said, 'We're cognisant of that; her nature is to gain, not give. But she and all of the Gordons possess loyalty to their sovereign, and if she's told I'm with child she would want that child legitimate. At least, so my Lord says. And he knows her better than I.'

Then she said softly, 'I pray that she isn't in love with him. He insists she's not, but I think him modest.'

Bothwell modest! If the gates of hell opened for him he would swagger through them to challenge the devil and demand cooler quarters.

'Madam,' I said, 'you do me great honour by your confidence.'

She patted my head, and we rose. As she left me she said, 'I am not sure, but I think to journey to Stirling this week and see to the prince's security. If I am abducted on the way back here, you will be as outraged as everyone else.'

She set out for Stirling with Lethington, Huntly, Sir James Melville and a guard of three hundred. During the next two days I busied myself with a further inventory of the King's possessions, which included his horses, saddles and the lions. Her Majesty hated the beasts and planned to send them to young King Charles. I would be relieved at their departure because the spring winds were fierce and they reacted, roaring across the shredded gardens, breaking our sleep.

At dawn of 25 April Fleming received a courier sent by

250

Lethington. She hurried to my chamber and said, 'Her Majesty is taken prisoner by Bothwell – with my husband, Huntly and Melville. At Almond Bridge he overpowered them with a large force of men and took them to Dunbar.'

'But why?' I asked, simulating astonishment.

'My husband says the poor lady is prey to his lust. He heard her scream from a chamber last midnight but there was no way to reach her. . . . He will send another message this afternoon. Isn't it terrible?'

'I can scarcely credit it. I thought Bothwell completely trustworthy.'

'So did I. I thought, in fact, that he loved her, respected her. Now he turns brute. . . .'

Lethington had given no instructions as to rescue and Fleming was afraid to inform anyone without his approval. Dunbar was one of the most formidable fortresses in Scotland and if Bothwell's Borderers were there, she said, it was hopeless.

Just before supper a second message arrived from Lethington. Bothwell was demanding the Queen's hand in marriage. If she refused him he was sure to kill her. Huntly was urging her to sign a promise of marriage which she could later repudiate but she said she would sign no pledge which she would not honour. Lethington was being released to return to Holyrood next day, with Melville and Huntly, to inform the Privy Council that Bothwell's intentions towards the Queen were entirely honourable.

'My husband wants all of this secret,' Fleming said, 'and I shouldn't have told you but I had to talk to *someone*.'

And so, when Lethington returned with the others, I pretended ignorance. They said merely that Her Majesty was at Dunbar and would return in a week or so.

I am not certain who babbled but by now everyone knew of the Queen's detention, and my brother rode in from Seton to say in bewilderment that she had declined help from him as if she were actually enjoying her captivity. 'Bothwell has behaved despicably! He places her in such a position as to enforce her marriage to him. And what of Jean?'

I did not know.

251

Escorted by Bothwell and his men the Queen returned in state, he humbly leading her palfrey. Down the Royal Mile she rode with her own archer guard and halberdiers to Holyrood, signifying to the people that she was not captive. They were, from all reports, as bewildered as my brother who said to me, bitter now against his friend, 'I suppose most rapists don't propose marriage to the victim.'

Had he known about the child he would have been first to sanction their union.

The Queen received me joyfully. 'Jean has agreed to divorce him on grounds of his adultery with Bessie Crawford, a serving wench. The matter should be legal within less than two weeks. Imagine my gratitude, my relief!'

'You love him so much, Madam, that this is all worth it?'

'Yes,' she said, 'all of the heartache, all of the intrigue. There is still intrigue among my nobles – a bond pledged to Bothwell's destruction, obscene playlets put on in Stirling about him. But no one can prevent our marriage.'

Impulsively I blurted, 'James?'

She snapped jewelled fingers. 'In Italy, I believe.'

That night Her Majesty did not appear at supper, and though Bothwell did, he was moody and uncommunicative. Next morning at breakfast they were cool to one another. He must have deeply offended her about something. Joseph Rizzio spent most of that day with her and at the end of it she asked me to join them in the library.

She asked abruptly, 'Would you attend a Protestant wedding ceremony, Seton?'

'Oh no, Madam,' I said. 'No more than you would.'

She turned to Rizzio. 'You see? Lady Seton is young too, but she doesn't share your tolerance. I maintain that every Catholic country will revile me if I marry him in the Protestant faith. I'd lose the support of all my friends, and I shudder to think what the Pope might do.'

I shuddered too. Rizzio said, 'Then, Madam, it's wiser not to marry.'

The poor young man spoke from ignorance of the situation. I said timidly, 'Isn't it possible to persuade Lord Bothwell—'

252

'No! I've tried. Sooner coax a stubborn mule one inch along a puddle.'

'I'd no idea he was so religious,' I said.

'Irreligious,' she corrected me. Then she dismissed Rizzio and said, tears in her eyes, 'I suppose I can only give in; we've argued for hours. Better the shame of my heretic wedding than the shame of bearing a bastard.'

'Better by far, Madam. And you do love him.'

Wearily she said, 'I do. But – ah, well. So be it. It will be punishment for my own sin.'

She was further punished by John Craig, the minister who had supplanted Knox at St Giles. He refused to proclaim the marriage banns without a meeting of the Privy Council at Holyrood. She told me later that he had ranted insultingly, calling heaven and earth to witness that he abhorred the very thought of this marriage as an odious union. On Sunday he preached the same opinion in St Giles, stirring the people against her, insinuating that Bothwell had murdered the King.

Sir James Balfour was present at dinner and told me about it. I said, knowing him to be expert in the law, 'How can this talk prevail when Lord Bothwell was acquitted?'

His teeth were dark, decayed, broken, so that his smile was repulsive. 'Acquitted, aye – but by the force of his own power. Five thousand of his men were not to keep order but to threaten the court.' He took a gulp of wine, wiped his mouth on his sleeve. 'Most folk think that he mined Kirk O' Field, lit a slow-burning fuse and returned here to be "surprised" by the explosion.'

'Indeed,' I said, 'but of course *you* don't think that. You would have guarded your brother's house while the King was in residence, especially as you yourself met Their Majesties on the road from Glasgow and suggested it a fine climate for an invalid.'

He flushed, rumpled his beard. 'High ground is healthy – the mists here are not.'

'And you were – as guardian of the house – unware that it was packed with explosives?'

'Servants tended the cellars,' he said, 'and they were Bothwell's. Or the King's.'

253

I felt that I had ventured too far, and retreated to chatter of food but no subject was safe with this dirty-nailed oaf and so I was happy when Her Majesty left her table and I was free to go to my chambers.

But I was not free of this plague of rumour. And that night, when Captain Erskine spoke of a new command at Edinburgh Castle, I was about to say, 'Didn't you know that the Queen has appointed Lord Bothwell?' When he said, 'Sir James Balfour is in charge.'

I was so certain he was wrong that I went to Bothwell. 'Is it true. . . .'

'It is expedient,' he said, 'for the moment.'

Next day Her Majesty stated, in formal audience of noblemen and ladies, that no one and nothing deterred her marriage. Later, in the Great Hall, she created Bothwell Lord of Shetland and Duke of Orkney and placed a golden coronet on his head. And she signed the marriage contract.

She was besieged by priests and bishops, and I supposed that this was an immense, final plea against heretic marriage. Du Croc and Melville looked grave at supper, deep in talk which I could well imagine: France would be appalled by the marriage; so would England. So, in truth, would the world.

Beaton and Livvy rode in that evening. Fleming and I were as depressed as they.

'If only Her Majesty would wait out her mourning,' Beaton said, 'but who can blame her for the love she feels? True, she loved the little King Francis, but he was a weakling, slow and sickly. The late King – we know what *he* was. Lord Bothwell – I mean, the Duke – is the first real man of her life.'

But a dangerous one. Yet some women, like moths, flirt with fire and the Queen had courage for it.

Beaton said, 'My husband thinks the matter vile, as it affects an innocent – Lady Bothwell. That she granted divorce was admirable, since it was akin to royal command, but what it must have cost her we'll never know.'

I found myself defending Bothwell. 'It must have cost the Duke a great deal in estates. Why else is her mother so calm about the matter? Instead of being vindictive, she is preening in new gowns. As a Catholic, of course, she won't attend

254

the ceremony but see if she doesn't dance afterwards.'

Janet tapped on the door and said, 'Her Majesty commands that you ladies come to her at three this morning.'

'At *three*?' I asked.

'She dresses for her wedding then, my lady.'

The Queen had bathed and was wrapped in white damask, her hair flowing to her waist. She invited us to take wine, and we drank a goblet to her happiness, joined by Lady Huntly and Lady Argyll. Then Her Majesty moved into the tiny dressing-closet with Janet.

We had nothing to say. Perhaps it was the late hour, the darkness, the smell of mould and mice that engulfed Holyrood even when incense burned from its braziers. But trust Lady Huntly to break the silence tactlessly: 'May is ill-luck for brides. I'm surprised she chose it.'

No one replied.

Margaret Carwood came in to replenish the fire, curtsied and left us. The closet door opened and Her Majesty appeared.

She wore a gown of black crêpe bodiced in jet, the flowing sleeves cuffed with jet, a jet coif and a back-flaring ruff of black lace. Still slender, no one could have suspected her with child. Nor would a stranger suspect that she was attired for a wedding. All she lacked for a funeral was a black veil.

But then, she had dressed in black for her marriage to the King to exhibit lack of frivolity; so she had now. At her dressing-chest she adjusted the coif and scented her cheeks and wrists. Then she turned to us. 'I shall expect you at the wedding breakfast.'

We murmured acceptance. The clock struck four. We accompanied her to the door of the Great Hall. When it was opened I saw an altar set up and on it a vase of fading May-flowers, petals spilling. The Bishop of Orkney stood behind the altar; nearest him, Bothwell in dark amber. Livvy gasped as the door closed and in the corridor I said, 'Of course the door was closed on us – we don't *want* to witness a Protestant ceremony.'

'It's not that,' she said. 'I counted thirteen guests.'

'I, too,' said Lady Huntly. 'Ill-omen. . . .'

I, for one, was prepared to dance after breakfast but when

255

we entered the Great Hall – the altar removed, and tables set up – there were no musicians. Her Majesty's table, on its dais, was not decorated, nor her canopy garlanded. Except that the Duke sat beside her sharing a loving-cup it could have been any ordinary breakfast.

Her Majesty rose, lifting the loving-cup, and proposed a toast. 'To my husband, His Grace the Duke of Orkney, King-Consort of Scotland.'

We rose, too, and drank. My brother, who had just arrived, was in time to lift his glass. From the end of the table he waved to me and I thought that his glance was meaningful.

The breakfast was brief. The Queen and the King – for so I must designate him now – retired. George accompanied me to my apartments and said, 'As I came in past the sentries at the gate they were examining a placard. They didn't understand the "foreign words" but though I did, knowing Latin, it seemed wise not to translate. It was a line from Ovid: "The people say that wantons marry in the month of May." '

'How disgusting! We can only hope that the crowd there was ignorant.'

'Crowd?' he said. 'No one was there but the sentries. The whole of Edinburgh knows of this marriage, even to the hour. But no one cared to come and wish her well.'

CHAPTER XIV

W e, her own courtiers, had presented wedding gifts but none
arrived from abroad. Lethington's letters to the Pope had not
moved His Holiness; she was considered heretic. She had lost
the support of all Catholic rulers. Only Elizabeth seemed
pleased by the marriage which, of course, was a setback for
English Catholicism.

Rumour festered at Holyrood, born of bewilderment or
boredom, malice among some, genuine fear in others. Fleming
knew for a fact that Lethington was worried about the situation at Stirling, where the Lords hostile to the King kept the
prince virtually prisoner lest the King kidnap him and kill
him. Her Majesty might visit her child but not remove him
to her husband's care.

There was, Fleming said, Lethington's surmise that James
directed this rebellion from abroad. Indeed, I thought, who
else?

Ambassadors are generally discreet, but Melville was not.
One evening when the King and Queen kept supper waiting
he said, 'I marvel she has any appetite at all.'

I was curious but said, 'Oh? Honeymooners often dine
alone.'

'I cannot share your romanticism, my lady. It is scarcely a
love match.'

This was preposterous. She had given herself to Bothwell –
I *must* title him as King – in love. She had risked, perhaps
lost, the respect of the world and now she faced civil war
because of this devotion.

'Why isn't it a love match?' I asked.

'On the afternoon of their wedding I chanced to pass by

257

their bedchamber and heard them quarrelling; I heard her scream out for a dagger to kill herself.'

This shocked me, yet I felt that he was reporting truth. I said, 'Doubtless she was appalled by that wedding – not a chapel, just an unflowered hall bereft of our saints. Her conscience rose to anger, she must have felt lost in hell. But if she hadn't loved him, she'd never have consented to that hell.'

He was embarrassed. 'Perhaps I've said too much—'

'No.' I felt, almost I knew, that had she not been with child she would have married him anyway. 'But never forget that he is Scotland's only patriot, consistently loyal from the time he was a lad. Not his bitterest enemy can deny that fact – if they care to face it. Master Buchanan may meddle but even he can't distort history because truth does prevail despite gossip, rumour, prejudice.'

He looked slapped. 'Of course what I heard shouldn't be repeated – I never intended you should take it seriously—'

'You did,' I said, merciless. 'And I do take it seriously as an indication of Her Majesty's loyalty to our religion. But that doesn't mean that she is disloyal to the King. I'd be most grateful and you'd be most truthful if you'd let it be known that it is a love match. She has told Lethington to inform her nobles at Stirling that she won't only force them to submission but will demand of Parliament the crown matrimonial for the King.'

'So I'd heard. But I hadn't quite believed it,' he said.

'She said, "I will not lose him. If need be I shall follow him in a white petticoat to the world's end." '

Lethington proved treacherous again, perhaps not in malice but because he considered the Queen's cause hopeless for negotiation. In any case, he and Fleming slipped out of the palace one night with their servants and all of their possessions.

One day at breakfast the King rose and welcomed me with a smile, and when I was seated and served he said, 'Gaston's croissants brighten the dawn.'

'They do, Sire,' I said, nibbling one.

258

' "Sire"? That's a premature title. A mere duke is only "Your Grace." '

'True. But the late King had the title, and it pleased Her Majesty even though she withheld the crown.'

'Call me what you like,' he said. 'What pleases my wife is to assume that the crown will be granted me. If so, I'd best nail it on or some Douglas will steal it.'

'A painful acquisition then.'

'Power is painful,' he said with a chuckle, 'and it creates some ludicrous situations. Our friend Morton is mobilising a rebel army with Kirkcaldy of Grange in command. His couriers ride throughout the country warning the people to rise against "Bloody Bothwell" and deliver the Queen and the prince from the tyranny of this monster, while he holds the prince hostage.'

'And what shall this monster do, Sire?'

He put down the dagger with which he had cut his meat. 'Call all loyal men to arms. It's possible they'll march on Holyrood within the next few days and Balfour urges us to move to the Castle for safety. But we won't fall into that trap.'

'If I may ask, Sire – why did you give Balfour command?'

'To silence him, so that the Queen and I could marry. He was prepared to swear publicly that he saw me light the fuse at Kirk O' Field.'

'How atrocious!'

'Oh,' he said casually, 'I'd gladly have lit the fuse but it proved unnecessary . . . suffice it to say that Balfour was deep in a plot to kill both the King and the Queen. So we shan't remove to the Castle. Today, however, we are storing jewels and state papers in the vaults there to be guarded by my man Dalgleish. And Balfour is netted by our spies.'

He emptied a tankard of ale. 'On the pretext of a Border rising Her Majesty is commanding all loyal men to meet us at Melrose on 15 June with provisions and arms for fifteen days. Tomorrow, 6 June, we ride to Borthwick Castle on the first stage of our journey. We'll gather men there and then move on.'

'Do you know if Her Majesty plans to take me with you?' I asked.

He shook his head. 'Only a tirewoman or two, and a physician. You'll be quite secure here, Lady Seton.'

'I suppose my brother will join you?'

'Aye. Huntly and his Gordons are on watch over Balfour at the Castle. Should you need them, you've only to send a message.'

So we ladies would be alone here except for the male staff, but we were not targets for the rebels and I would not be uneasy, only apprehensive. Then I realised that this was silly; why worry with the King in charge, the wild, passionate loyalty of his Borderers, the Queen's ability to ride into a town, smile, and rally thousands?

As he bowed and left me I thought, whatever he may be he is no weakling. For some odd reason a line from the bible came to me, vanished as dreams do, then came clear. Though the phrase referred to a woman it suited the King when I made a slight change: 'The heart of Scotland may safely trust in him.'

My brother kept me informed of events at Borthwick Castle. Expecting huge forces to arrive there, the King and Queen were disappointed, for less than a hundred Borderers joined them. This was because Morton's agents had visited crofts and keeps stating that the King was holding Her Majesty prisoner after brutally raping her and practising sodomy. They were also made to believe that the King had the prince locked up at Stirling and tortured.

Then Morton arrived with his Douglases and traitor nobles to 'deliver' the Queen from her captivity at Borthwick. The castle resisted siege and, feeling the Queen to be safe, the King disguised himself in womens' clothing, escaped Morton's men and rode to Haddington to rally men from there. It was agreed that on the following night she, too, would escape from the castle and meet the King at a spot designated in the forest. She did so, slipping out disguised as a page. 'But', wrote my brother, 'Lord Borthwick strapped a sword and dagger to her belt when she left us.'

God must have been with her; she avoided Morton's patrols, met the King in the woods and he swept her off to Dunbar, where she summoned all loyal subjects of ages sixteen to sixty

260

to join them. Two days later they left Dunbar for Seton, and in each town their ranks swelled so that by the time they reached our home, a resting place, they numbered about 3,500. The King was loath to march on Edinburgh where the rebels were, and where Balfour had not fired a single Castle cannon in defence of the town. 'He [meaning the King] is renowned as the cleverest forest and hill fighter of our times, and decided to lure the enemy into wild country. So we shall manoeuvre them south to a place near Musselburgh called Carberry Hill.

'Her Majesty, and all of us, are like to perish of the heat as doubtless you do. She asks me to tell you that, in fleeing Borthwick in boy's clothing, she was later forced to borrow a bodice and short kilted skirt from a wench of the garrison and a shady red hat, that her hair is "a tumbled disaster" but she is too occupied with writing despatches to submit to vanity, and that though our mother offered her clothing there is no time to alter it; and this battle-dress, says she, is comfortable and practical. . . . She asks you to pray for her, on this 15 June, and that you will remember that she and the King have been wed exactly one month. . . .'

So Her Majesty was three months with child, and prepared to ride into battle in such heat as I could not recall in the sun of France. It was brutal even here in the stone of Holyrood. I knew the area of Carberry Hill; I had often ridden there. It overlooked the town of Musselburgh and was perhaps a fine defensive point – one could see for miles. But there were few trees, scant shade. One boon was a stream which the rebels would have to ford, and which our forces could use to barrel drinking water.

We ladies dined and supped in near-nakedness in the privacy of our chambers. Lady Huntly, bereft of her corsets, seemed to spread over my couch in layers of fat and cotton tulle. 'My daughter Jean – I *told* you she would marry three times – is being courted by the Earl of Sutherland. Of course he is elderly, but what a catch! And when he dies, there will be another.'

I was amused by her second sight. 'And who will that be?'

'Alex of Boyne.'

261

But Beaton was young, my own age, and healthy.

'You don't believe me,' she said, 'but it will come to pass. Sutherland will give her vast riches but Alex will be, and has always been, the love of her life.'

The heat took such hold that even gossip languished. That night I lay naked on my bed drenched in sweat, the bed-curtains parted for such air as there was. Isobel, though sturdy enough to face blizzards, took ill during this rage of moist, relentless heat and was tended by Gervais, who warned us all not to be tempted to open our casements, for the poisons of night air could cause fatal fevers. But we were tempted, like thirsty seamen who flirt with the thought of sea water. But even if we had admitted air to our chambers it would have been warm, breezeless. At dawn I found slight respite in the arcaded walk that formed the quadrangle of the palace. But then the sun rose in monstrous glare.

George's next message was brief: 'The heat was so intense that many on both sides deserted, seeking the coolness of the stream. But our men, being on the hill, suffered most, and those in armour were roasting alive. The King called it "the most gruelling battle never fought". But we lost. To protect his men the King challenged Morton to private combat to settle the issue honourably but Morton in cowardice refused and delegated the combat to Lindsay who agreed but wished to fight a mile east. They rode there but Lindsay, also a coward, didn't appear.

'In short, the King was forced to leave Her Majesty but by her own command, since she feared he'd be imprisoned and slaughtered. He surrendered his sword to Kirkcaldy and was promised safe conduct for twenty-four hours, later to be declared a hunted outlaw. I am not a soft man, sister, but when I saw the Queen embrace the King, saying farewell before he swung on to his horse – seeing how they could not bear to leave one another – their kisses while the two armies watched – I was close to tears. The rebel lords pledged her their submission since she had dismissed the King. She should soon arrive at Holyrood and my guess is that he is safe at Dunbar and raising another army. Write to me at Seton. . . .'

We waited for the Queen all that morning; Janet had a

bathing-tub ready, the casements open for air, and Lady Huntly and I gathered roses for her apartments.

But she did not come. At night, during supper, we learned that the traitors held her prisoner here in Edinburgh at the Black Turnpike house on the High Street, and that a mob incited by Morton and Lindsay was piling faggots outside for her burning. Even at the gates of Holyrood a crowd shouted, 'Burn her! Burn the whore! Burn the King's murderess!'

I was soul-sick as I had been after Adam's death. I sought Captain Erskine and asked if we could not attempt rescue with the palace guard but he said no guard would live through that howling mob. And then, just as we stood by the draw-bridge, Lethington arrived, dusty from boots to beard, one servant carrying a large case. My first thought was to ask Erskine to pull up the drawbridge but I had no power of command and, chameleon as he was, the Queen had not denied him authority. So I ran to him and said, 'You've heard about the Queen? She—'

'I saw her leaning from a casement and pleading with the mob. I couldn't get through . . . perhaps tomorrow. . . .'

'Have you come to help her?' I asked. 'Tomorrow may be too late.'

He looked and sounded exhausted. 'There is nothing to do at the moment, my lady. A mob is like a child, its anger sub-sides and often pity takes over. If she promises to relinquish her husband she will assuredly return here in state.'

Silently I cursed him. Aloud, 'Is the King safe? Do you know?'

He shook his head. Then, coldly, he passed me and entered the palace. I followed, sought my apartments, sweating and shivering. Prayer is as natural to me as breathing, but I had no breath, no hope, no faith.

Next day Morton arrived at Holyrood and summoned me to the Great Hall where he and Lethington sat in conference. I did not honour him with a curtsey but stood waiting.

'Prepare to ride to the High Street,' he said, as curtly as though I were a serving wench. 'We're escorting Her Majesty here.'

263

In my delight I forgave his crude manner. 'She is no longer imprisoned?'

'She was never imprisoned,' he said, 'only secluded until the temper of the people softened. But her clothing is indecent, her bodice ripped. Carry a cloak to cover her.'

I made haste to gather a bouquet of roses. We set off from White Horse Close, Lord Atholl leading the Queen's favourite palfrey which he had saddled in ivory and caparisoned in green velvet. I rode Fearless and we were followed by three hundred hackbutters and preceded by the archer guard, pipers and a trumpeter.

At the Market Cross there was a dense crowd but, thank God, it was orderly and made way for us when the trumpet sounded. Across the street Her Majesty stood at a casement of the Black Turnpike house and I wanted to weep for her. She tried vainly to cover her breasts with a scrap of scarf, crossing her arms, pulling her long hair forward. Her face was red from sunburn, her lips dry and cracked. She leaned out and stared at us while Morton tethered his horse at the garden gate. Faggots were piled there on all sides.

Morton looked up at her and bowed. 'We've come to escort you to Holyrood, Madam, if you wish.'

She shouted, 'Is this a trick?'

'I swear it's not, Madam. But if you wish to stay here you've only to say so.'

She appealed to the listening mob. 'Many of you have promised to arm yourselves in my defence – the freemen of the trade guilds are doing so now. You've heard Lord Morton vow that I'm not imprisoned but should he break his vow and I do not appear here at the Cross by tomorrow noon you will storm Holyrood.'

I was thrilled, as she must have been, by the approving cheers of the crowd, and their threats to Morton should he trick her were savage. Those who had wanted to burn her now were restrained from burning him when she said, 'Let there be peace – unless I don't return here tomorrow.'

I have heard nothing in all my life comparable to what the usually gentle people of Edinburgh planned for Morton if he broke his vow – nor was Atholl spared. Emasculation was the least of it – to throw his manhood to the dogs and then light the faggots. Not one soul mentioned 'Bloody Bothwell' and one big woman went to the gate and kicked away a placard that reviled him. A mad city had turned sane in regard for Her Majesty but how she achieved this miracle in so short a time I had yet to find out.

When she came out in her cloak, carrying the roses, the crowd blessed her and men fought to help her mount her palfrey. Blessings followed her all the way down the High Street, through the Canongate and into the palace.

As we entered she said, 'Come with me, dove.'

The roses I had placed in her apartments yesterday were wilted but she exclaimed over them just the same, asked Janet to fill the bathing-tub, shed her cloak. While Janet was down for water she said, 'She knows that I'm with child but in this corset it's still not apparent to the others. If I'd not worn this I could have been killed – no rebel would want the King's child alive. Help me remove this cursed thing.'

Cursed it was, of wood and leather, and her waist was lacerated. Further, it had bruised her stomach and so I sent for Arnault to treat the wounds after she bathed. He said that Her Majesty was in remarkably good health despite her ordeal. 'However,' he added when she was clothed in a cotton robe, 'you must obey my command, Madam. Sup here in your apartments, a dish of meat and eggs and milk. Before you retire – and it must be early – I'll return to oil your body.'

So weary she was, yet so bright of eye and hopeful. 'I *must* see my lords at supper – I've so many questions to ask – so much to make clear to them—'

'Very well, Madam. But retire early and eat for the baby's strength.'

He left us. Janet dressed her in thin black silk and I swept up her hair for coolness. There was so much I wished to ask her – principally, where the King was – but perhaps this was secret between them. When I joined her in the Great Hall, I was pleased and surprised to find that Fleming and Livvy had arrived to comfort Her Majesty and celebrate her release.

I supposed that because Morton knew himself guilty of treachery he was unusually subservient, as whipped curs may be. But Her Majesty accepted his attentions as he humbly served as taster for the eggs and milk she ordered, standing by the dias which she shared with Lethington, just the two at table. She talked quietly with Lethington, and I with the two Marys.

But despite the flowers I had ordered placed on all of the tables, and the stream of ivy leaves from plate to plate, there was no semblance of celebration. The wax candles drooped from the tall candelabra and the hall, despite its rock walls, was an oven. One of her tirewomen took a great plume made of paper and feathers and fanned Her Majesty, who seemed about to faint. Arnault rose from his place and went to her, and I think he was urging her to retire at once. I hoped she would because, so clearly, she was suffering.

Morton came out from behind her chair. 'Madam,' he said, 'you must prepare to leave at once.'

Arnault said, 'Madam, please do. You desperately require rest. Ten hours of sleep will restore you.'

As she started to wobble to her feet, supported by Arnault, Morton said, a snarl in his voice, 'Not upstairs. You are taking a journey.'

'*What*?' she asked.

There was silence. Morton looked down at the Master of Horse. 'Are the horses saddled?'

The man bowed, nodded.

Morton said to the Queen, 'Prepare to leave at once. At any moment the people may rise against you.'

What strength she had turned to rage. 'You mean, against you! If I'm not at the Cross at noon tomorrow you know full well what they intend.'

Lethington said calmly, 'So long as your husband is free you and the prince are in grave danger—'

She interrupted him with such a flow of venom that he drew back, cringing. Beside me, Fleming burst into tears. Her Majesty managed to walk a few steps from the table but Morton and Atholl seized her arms. She stood rigidly between them and said, 'Where do you propose to take me?'

'You need seclusion for your protection,' Atholl said. 'Our men will escort you as far as Leith. Lindsay and

266

young Ruthven will accompany you from there on.'

Her Majesty looked at her men servants as though for help; but none was armed; Morton's men commanded her guard by force of numbers. She said, 'Seton, come with me—'

As I jumped up from my chair Morton said, 'None of your ladies accompany you. Only two of your tiring women and Arnault.'

Arnault went to Morton. 'I'm honoured to go with her but I warn you, my Lord, Her Majesty is totally unfit to travel even as far as Leith. Her death would be on your conscience.'

'You are responsible for her health,' Morton said contemptuously. 'As to the journey, if you or the women make any plea of the people on the way, you'll be shot.'

Her Majesty tried to speak but could not. I think she had lost her voice. But I moved towards Morton and said, 'I shall help her pack—'

'Oh no, you won't. You'll bring her a cloak and a night-robe, that is all—'

'I'm not your servant—'

Janet, forgetting her place, ran up and embraced Her Majesty and asked which cloak to bring. Her Majesty whispered something and I said to Morton, 'Doubtless you, too, will take a journey tonight? The climate of Edinburgh is not healthy for you. But should you linger, I shall be only too happy to help the people light those faggots.'

Then I turned on Atholl and Lethington. 'Perhaps you're both in his power, helpless. But if not, you're the lowest curs of the realm.'

Perhaps in fear for me, Her Majesty regained her voice and said, 'May Lady Seton help my maid choose the cloak—?'

'No!' Morton motioned Janet from the room. 'Sit, Madam, and take wine. You've thirty miles to ride.'

Arnault swore as he seated her and, ignoring the decanters, poured *aqua vitae* for them both. Fleming, now beside Lethington, was still weeping and, I am sure, pleading with him. But he said nothing, peeling a pear. The Queen looked down the tables and asked that Jane Kennedy and Maria Courcelles make ready for the journey. I thought it a wise

267

choice; both were young, had been with us in France and were enterprising. Both had courage, neither could be bribed.

Her Majesty, probably desirous of a privy, was escorted out by Arnault, Atholl and Morton following as guard. She stumbled like an old woman and I tried not to think of what a thirty-mile ride might do – if there were hills and peat hags, jolts could cause a miscarriage.

Ten minutes later Her Majesty, in a hooded red cloak, stood ready to leave but Morton, infuriated as a bull by the colour, told Janet to bring a black one. Red, of course, would have been conspicuous and he wanted no rescuers on the road. Finally, they were at the door. The Queen embraced me and the other Marys, then returned to embrace me again. Lips against my ear she said, 'For your safety, don't antagonise them further, appear to relent, talk with Janet,' and then Morton swept me aside and I resumed my place at table – not for need of food, but to join the mourners.

Only Lethington appeared normal, now eating an apple and cheese. Fleming, beside him, still wept. Morton and Atholl came in from the courtyard and demanded dry, chilled champagne. Gaston was summoned and explained that there was no ice. They grumbled and took *aqua vitae*.

I wished someone had removed it to the kitchens for poison. Beaton came to sit beside me and said, 'I can't believe this has happened . . . that Morton has the power—'

'James Stuart has the power over Morton,' I said, 'and the fact that he is absent is further proof of who directs this.' Then I remembered that the Queen had told me to talk with Janet and I caught her glance – she was watching me – and I left the room to await her in my apartments.

'My lady,' she said, sitting at my order, 'the Queen whispered to me that we mustn't despair. The King has not fled Scotland; after the battle she pretended to abandon him so that he might be set free. . . . She was to slip out of here and join him at Dunbar but was captured before she could do so. Could you send him a message?'

I went to my writing desk and wrote swiftly of what had happened tonight. I had no personal courier, and dared not entrust it to the most loyal of servants lest Morton search him at the gates. I wanted no brave man shot. I was wondering what to do when Fleming arrived, and as Janet sprang up to curtsey I said, 'I'm sure you chose the right cloak – neither too thin for the breezes of Leith nor too heavy,' and bade Janet a good night.

Fleming and I were as close as sisters but now that she was married to Lethington I could not trust her; her first duty was to her husband. And so I said nothing of the King's whereabouts – if, indeed, he was still at Dunbar. But to my surprise she said, 'It may be undutiful but I place Her Majesty's safety foremost, beyond any loyalty to William. If only we knew where the King was, to tell him to send rescuers—'

'But we don't know where she's been taken.'

'I know,' she said. 'The isle of Lochleven.'

'Where is that?'

'The mainland village is Kinross, a bit more than thirty miles, I think. A terrible journey for her . . . and at the end of it the loneliest keep in Scotland. It belongs to Sir William and Lady Margaret Douglas.'

'How infamous!' I said, for Lady Margaret was James Stuart's mother. 'I knew James directed this, Morton alone is too stupid.'

She said, 'Morton and Atholl are sufficient for the moment. What I want to do – and my husband mustn't suspect – is to get a message to the King. But where, and how?'

I wanted so to trust her; I almost blurted 'Dunbar.' It was terrible to suspect that Lethington had sent her to me with lies in order to probe what knowledge I might have.

She said, 'Seton, have I ever failed Her Majesty? Didn't she herself sanction my marriage? Think what you will of my husband, but trust me.'

Could I possibly doubt her sincerity, her tear-red eyes? Could I forget twenty years of her kindness? She had never, to my knowledge, lied to me. Often as children she had defended me and lied for me about some prank. Now she extended her hands in a plea for trust and I thought, she could probably command a courier and get the letter safely out.

269

I took a deep breath and made my decision. 'I do trust you. But – I've no idea where the King is.'

She sighed and said, 'I'll not sleep this night.'

Nor would I. For if it were true that the Queen was riding towards Lochleven, to be in the custody of James's mother, no prison could be more effective, no jailor more heartless.

Fleming left me. I took up my letter and tore it to fragments. Then I wrote another: 'Sire, I am told, whether truly or not, that Her Majesty is prisoned on Lochleven Isle, near Kinross, by the Douglas, having been forced to leave this night. . . .'

Far off I heard a clock strike midnight. I changed to riding clothes, cloaked myself, tucked the letter in my belt and slipped out of my chamber. My guard sprang to attention and I said, 'I'm stifled for air,' and smiled and passed him, and at the bottom of the staircase gave the same excuse to the guard there and to those in the courtyard. Then, out of their sight, I ran to White Horse Close. I would saddle Fearless and ride to Dunbar myself.

Pierre, my groom, roused from sleep on the straw of Fearless's stall, blinked in the lanternlight. I whispered, 'Saddle her,' anxious not to wake the other grooms. Pierre was my friend but now he became my protector. He whispered back that wherever I rode he would accompany me.

'Dunbar,' I said, 'to the King.'

'You'd never pass the Netherbow Port, my lady. Any lady would be conspicuous. But I could get past – a thirsty man towards a tavern wouldn't be questioned.'

I thrust the letter into his pouch, with gold. 'May God bless and go with you in the Queen's service . . . but if you're halted destroy this message.'

'I'll not be halted this side of hell,' he said. 'You'll find me here tomorrow night.'

'Ride Fearless,' I told him.

Back in the courtyard I strolled a bit for the benefit of watching guards, lifted my hood from my hair and, yawning, re-entered the palace. Sleep was slow in coming, for I seemed to be riding the night in two directions – with the Queen to

270

Kinross, with Pierre to Dunbar – frightened of bog . . . a swamp . . . a trap.

No mob stormed Holyrood. Morton's forces were too strong and Balfour held the Castle. Taking Her Majesty's advice I was polite to the Lords though I felt degraded in their oafish company.

Since I did not want to rouse suspicion by skulking about, I asked Morton's permission to walk in the palace grounds. He shrugged and said to do as I pleased, that none of us were captive. So at dusk I went to the stables. Pierre was rubbing down Fearless and, since I often visited, the other grooms took no notice of me.

'I saw the King,' he said. 'He will rouse the Hamiltons at Linlithgow, go on to Dunbarton for Lord Fleming's men and says he can depend on Lords Argyll and Boyd. With luck, he can take Lochleven within a few days but is hampered by having to move furtively. There's a price on his head of a thousand crowns.'

'He was in good spirits?' I asked.

Pierre grinned. 'He made a jest of the thousand crowns – he said— I shouldn't repeat it, my lady.'

'Go on.'

'He said that his head was worth less than – than his lower region.'

I laughed; it was so like him. 'But you – wasn't your absence remarked here?'

'It was, of course. When I returned an hour ago I begged my comrades not to question me and I think they suspect but respect that I was on the Queen's duty. There's not one but doesn't hate Lord Morton's men. Already two of the Queen's mares have been taken.' He turned and patted Fearless. 'Might we return her to the old stables?'

'Yes,' I said. 'After you've fed her, lead her out after dark on the road behind the palace and bed her there. I'll send someone to clean your room and light a lantern.'

He thanked me. I think that he loved Fearless as much as I did. But I said, 'Should one of the lords find her, don't protest the theft – let her go. Your life is of more value than—'

271

The Master of Horse came in then and I said, 'Pierre, look to her feeding,' and was starting out of the side door when the Master said, 'My lady, Lord Morton wishes to borrow this mare – only a loan, he says.'

I knew him for a good man, and devoted to our cause. So I said, 'How unfortunate that she is on the way to Seton – I'll inform him myself at supper.'

'Who will ride her, my lady?'

Pierre required rest. 'Sandy. Tell him to be off by eight. And ask him to explain to my parents . . . and give him gold, I'll reimburse you.'

Both men bowed. I left the stables and steeled myself to be clever with Morton.

He himself brought up the subject when I entered the Great Hall, coming towards me from the wine-table with a fawning bow. 'Tomorrow I go to see to Her Majesty's comfort and my horse is lamed. So I wish to borrow yours.'

A lame excuse! He had access to any number of sturdy horses.

'I'm sorry, my Lord – she is nearly to Seton by now.'

'Why?' he asked.

'Because she is ailing of her stomach. She can't retain feed. So I thought to put her to pasture for a while, in the hope that she may recover.'

Thank God, the little pig eyes believed me, and I relaxed. 'Such a beautiful creature to be so afflicted. The late King admired her more than any other.'

'King!' he said, scoffing. 'He was Duke of Albany, Bothwell Duke of Orkney – why refer to them as "kings"?'

'Because it was Her Majesty's pleasure to deem her consorts as kings.'

'Confusing the people, distorting the truth.' I knew he was not as angry about this as he was about the loss of my horse. Then he said, 'I shall require you to help me dispose of the Queen's personal effects before I leave for Lochleven.'

So it was Lochleven, and no longer a secret. I said with deliberate misunderstanding, 'Thank you, my Lord. She will need ornaments, clothing, perhaps furniture?'

272

'No! She has so mismanaged her finances that Balfour says the nation is nearly depleted . . . in debt for her frivolities. We are forced to melt down her silver plate, sell her jewels . . . so that the people may escape starvation. . . .'

Blandly I listened to the lies. He must have thought me stupid indeed to nod and accept them. As he talked my mind raced ahead, wondering how I could conceal the jewellery, the gifts from the Dauphin, Madame Diane, that she treasured. She had with her only the pearl earrings and the pearl combs that bound her hair, her marriage ring and the King's signet ring – the Hepburn motto inscribed: *Keep Trust*.

Keep trust with the King, I thought, as Morton talked on about her extravagance. By now his Borderers must have faced the truth of the Queen's imprisonment, and would rally with the Hamiltons and others. . . .

'After supper,' Morton said, 'you will accompany me to her apartments and we will make a survey.'

If Janet had not sat so far below the salt I could have warned her to hide the Queen's jewel chests – at least a few. But Morton seated himself next to me, Atholl opposite, and there was no escape from them. But, as I had done last night, I signalled Janet by my glance, and held hers. She gave a slight nod.

The difficulty was not only our distance from one another but that I held the key to the jewel chests which I always carried in my bodice, concealed in a little silken pad between my breasts. The Queen, of course, also carried such a key.

Again I glanced at Janet, over the rim of my wine cup, and her eyes sharpened. We understood beyond words, yet were helpless. But bidding Morton to come to me at his pleasure, I went to the door and deliberately tripped on the bearskin carpet.

Janet, of course, reached me first. I said, 'Hide the casket of diamonds,' before Isobel and other ladies surrounded me. The 'gentlemen' were not so solicitous but Lethington helped me to my feet and Morton took my arm. To give Janet time to hide the casket I complained of a sprained ankle and Gurion sat me down and removed my shoe. There being no swelling he said I had strained a muscle, and carried me up the staircase, Morton following with Isobel. At the landing

273

Gurion told me to soak my ankle but Morton interrupted impatiently, dismissing them and ordering me to the Queen's apartments.

Reluctantly I limped into the audience chamber and through into the bedroom. Janet was not there; neither was the diamond chest but I was forced to bring out the others and open them. He pawed through them, then he said, 'I see no diamonds. Where are they?'

I said promptly. 'In the Castle vault. At least she intended they go there so I assume they were sent.'

'Very well.' He went to the bed, took cases from the pillows and emptied the jewels into them. 'This will do for tonight,' he said. 'We'll remove other things in the morning.'

When he had gone I went to Janet's chamber and found her trembling. She had hidden the casket in her fireplace under a pile of charred logs and was terrified he would find it and have her shot. I calmed her, bolted the door and unlocked the chest. The most valuable of all the diamonds was a large, pear-shaped one, the ring Elizabeth had sent her in token of friendship, a pledge which was sacred between them. Whatever happened, this must not be lost so I took it in its velvet case and hid it in my bosom. We wrapped the grimy chest in soiled linens, concealed it under a cloak of Janet's, and I carried it to my bedchamber, hiding it in my fireplace. If it were found my punishment would doubtless be only a verbal lashing.

Usually one goes to bed naked, especially in summer, but I wore a night-dress so that I could conceal the ring in its belt until I could sew in a pocket. At dawn I sat up and placed the ring on my finger to admire it, a dazzle in the semi-darkness. Her Majesty did not wear the ring often; she treated it almost as a holy thing, not because she had reason to love her cousin but because of its promise of assistance in extremity. So I would go to any extreme to preserve it.

I was breakfasting, dressed, when Morton and two of his guards were admitted by Isobel. It seemed to me that the diamond between my breasts fluttered with my heartbeat. He said, 'The casket of diamonds is not in the Castle vaults. Who is said to have taken it there?'

I kept my hands in my lap lest they tremble. 'I don't know, my Lord. I simply heard Her Majesty say that they would be safe there with Balfour during her absence.'

'When was this?'

'Before she and the King marched to raise an army.'

Safe with Balfour – that was an inspiration, I thought. Let the vermin be suspicious of one another. Then I asked, 'If you go to Lochleven today, will you allow me to pack a few clothes for Her Majesty? She can't be "secluded" with none.'

'Lady Douglas will lend what she needs.'

Ha! If Lady Douglas owned sackcloth and ashes, doubtless she would.

'However,' he said, 'I shan't go to Lochleven. There is too much to do here.'

What he meant, and proved that afternoon, was his haste in plundering Holyrood before Balfour or Atholl did or before James arrived. By two o'clock the chapel was desecrated, the golden crucifix and jewelled saints removed; the Queen's private oratory in the audience chamber was stripped of its valuables, its altar kicked to splinters, and every fragment of silver plate removed from the palace, so that night we dined on food held by oaken trenchers and drank from leather mugs because the Venetian glass had been taken. For the welfare of the peasants? Next day our apartments were bereft of Turkish carpets so that rushes had to be spread over rock floors. Treasures of ancient Flemish tapestry disappeared, with vases and pink marble tables. But the portraits remained – and the Queen loved those of her ancestors. Those of herself she thought poor, and none did her justice, even the one by Clouet. No artist saw her truly, and so all painted her differently. The only like features were her remarkably long eyes and, if full length, her graceful slenderness.

Within a few days of the pillage, Lethington and Fleming left for their country castle; Livvy remained, hoping for news of our Queen, but Morton refused to divulge any and, hopelessly, she too left the palace to return to her husband. I longed to go to my family but saw no way of smuggling out the chest, for I felt that Morton was watchful of me. Almost every night he contrived to be near me at supper. There was

275

a sort of quiet lasciviousness in his manner that had always offended me – rather glance than direct action – but I thought I might take advantage of it, for his mind was not subtle and his vanity was such that he had not taken my anger seriously. That he drank heavily was also fortunate, for he was inclined to forget discretion. Several times he stated that Bothwell had abandoned her, and that if only she could be persuaded to divorce him she would be reinstated in honour.

'But she is stubborn,' he said, 'woefully and childishly stubborn. It can only be her Catholic dementia; she must know he never loved her, married her only for power. But, poor lady, she is shackled by her infatuation. We dare not release her for fear the people will tear her to collops – and the prince, too.'

'But he is safe at Stirling—'

'Not if she should escape. Her seclusion is his only protection.'

I think that he actually came to believe in his own lies, that his self-justification was a sort of maniacal sincerity, as John Knox had exhibited, and one cannot reason with that sort even if one dares to try. So, through those weeks, I listened without protest, without argument, learning all that I could. Then, on 20 July, Ambassador Throckmorton arrived from Elizabeth's court and, after a long talk with Morton, walked with me in the gardens. He said that after repeated appeals in the name of his Queen he had been denied permission to visit Lochleven. 'My Queen is outraged that any sovereign should be held captive.'

Naturally; it would establish a precedent.

'And my Queen is further concerned as a woman—'

Yes, I thought bitterly. A jealous bitch but pretending compassion and wondering how she can use this situation to her advantage.

'—because, though she herself is childless, she can sympathise with a mother's heart. That Queen Mary should lose twins—'

'*What?*'

'Didn't you know? She was taken of a flux after stumbling down steps. Arnault and Lady Margaret rowed the – unborn

276

out into the loch and disposed of them in a slide of gold cloth.'

Controlling my sorrow, I asked, 'Could Arnault determine the sex of the children?'

'A boy and a girl. One assumes, the Duke's spawn.'

'No,' I said, careful to keep my rage in check, 'there is no assumption about it. And they were not the Duke's spawn, but the King's children, prince and princess.'

'Oh, of course,' he said. 'One is disinclined in England to refer to a duke as king or to think of an outlaw as such . . . he seems to have disappeared . . . fled, some think, to the Highlands.'

'If he has fled,' I said, 'it's to gather an army.'

At the gates we saw a courier ride in. Morton announced his news at supper. Her Majesty had signed abdication papers. The prince would be crowned king. James would act as regent.

'Until Lord James arrives from Paris,' Morton said, 'my friends and I govern.'

Throckmorton, shocked, said, 'And have you other happy news, my Lord?'

But Morton was impervious to sarcasm. 'Yes. Master Knox has returned to Edinburgh. . . .'

CHAPTER XV

————◆————

It was impossible to believe that the Queen would abdicate of her own free will. I suspected that she had been tortured and much later I learned that I was right. Lindsay had grabbed her shoulder with an iron gauntlet, threatening her with immediate death if she did not sign the papers brought to her bed. Within three days she had lost two children and a kingdom.

The traitor Lords divided their time between Holyrood and the Castle, and I wondered if they had stolen Her Majesty's state papers that she and Bothwell had placed there. For now, to avoid confusion, we no longer referred to Bothwell as king except in our hearts. James VI, thirteen months old, was crowned at Stirling but I refused to attend the celebrations. *She* was rightful ruler and what is signed under duress is said to be worthless and can be repudiated.

I shall never forget the day that James arrived at Holyrood; a day so dark as to recall tales of the moon's eclipse. But he was welcomed to the city by cannon salute from the Castle and rode through Edinburgh down the Royal Mile in drenched dignity, taking brief shelter from the rain in Knox's house on the High Street. At Holyrood he occupied the Queen's apartments and Janet came running to tell me that some of the stolen treasures had been restored there. All within three hours.

James's equerry came to me to ask that I be hostess at supper, since his wife was indisposed. My first impulse was to refuse him but then I thought I might learn something of value if I were tactful, so I agreed. But I dressed in the most obvious mourning.

The Great Hall glittered, all of the candles ablaze, and red roses rioted in the stolen silver bowls and vases. I took my place with him, Morton and Atholl at the Queen's table under the blue and silver starred canopy.

'Lady Seton,' James said, 'you are gracious to be here, considering your mourning. I'd heard your stepfather wasn't well, but not of his death.'

'He is well, my Lord.'

'Then whom do you mourn?' he asked.

I forgot tact. 'Our Queen.'

He smiled. 'But she is no longer queen, my dear lady. She is the Countess of Bothwell until, wisely, she arranges divorce.'

'She is Dowager Queen of France.'

'Oh, that,' he said. 'Of course.'

'But the title dearest to her would, indeed, be Countess of Bothwell, Duchess of Orkney.'

He waited until a servant had poured champagne. Then he said, 'If only she'd relinquish the fellow—'

'You refer to the Duke?' I asked.

There was a sudden bombardment of thunder and we both jumped. Then I laughed and said, 'Do you know, for a moment I thought it was Balfour's cannon? Then I realised he'd *never* direct them on you.'

He ignored that, selecting chicken from a proffered dish. I, too, took a morsel, and peas. Then James said, 'The Duchess refuses to acknowledge the little King. She'd be wiser to display maternal respect.'

'But to her, crowned or not, he is legally the prince,' I said, and then regretted the blunder, for my only purpose in being here was to try to gain information. 'That is, just before Throckmorton left he said that Elizabeth was very much disturbed by the situation and would continue to address Her Majesty as Queen of Scotland.'

'A mere courtesy,' James said.

'When will she be freed, my Lord?' I asked.

'Freed? Oh, you mean released from protection? I'm told she demands trial by the people but the whole matter is relative to her conspiracy with Bothwell in the murder of the late King.'

I had tried to eat; now I knew that another bite would sicken me.

279

'She might possibly establish a modicum of innocence if she will divorce him but thus far she refuses. When I go to Lochleven I pray God to show me a way to persuade her.'

Would God allow the breast screw? The nail rip? Well, had He not permitted Lindsay the iron glove? To doubt God's justice was evil, but James had roused that evil. I raised my glass to the fates: May James Stuart, Regent of Scotland, suffer a death so fierce that hell will seem mild, and may I live to see it.

'I shall take her some clothes,' he said. 'Please be in my audience chamber at nine of the morning.'

'My Lord, you are so kind. . . .'

'One can't have one's sister in rags,' he said.

There were no rags in Her Majesty's dressing-closet; if there had been James would have chosen them. Janet had a great box ready but all he permitted were shoes, two changes of linen and three gowns which were neither furred nor jewelled nor embroidered; those she had worn in the mornings when supervising a planting or a house-cleaning. All of her cloaks were shiningly splendid, even the simplest dark wools lined with marten or ermine or brocade.

'Autumn will be cold on the island,' I said. 'She will need a heavy cloak.'

'My mother will lend one.'

I glanced at Janet; by now we were one in conspiracy. 'My Lord,' she said, 'I have an old woollen cloak the Queen gave me, a bit shabby now but serviceable—'

'Bring it,' he said. After examining it he must have realised that it was not worthy of his wife's adornment or of sale. It went into the box, together with gold and silver thread and her sewing box – that was generous, since the box was of French enamel, but the jewels that rimmed it were merely corals and cairngorms.

To make certain that Janet did not add to the box he ordered her to rope it and had one of his servants remove it. Then he turned to me. 'I should like to see your apartments, my lady.'

'I would gladly send her some of my clothing,' I said as

280

we descended the staircase, 'for we're of one size. . . .'

I was prattling to cover my fear that he would steal from me. And when Isobel admitted us through my bedchamber I remembered the casket in the fireplace and hurried him past it into the anteroom. There he seated himself to my relief and, looking about, said, 'I see the Seton crest on many beautiful things – even carved on the arms of chairs.'

'Yes,' I said. And not only our crest – the initial S was on such small things as gold-cloth cushions and candle holders. S for Seton. S for Stuart?

He had appreciation for art that Morton lacked, admiring some miniatures on the wall, and a Clouet painting of me. 'What a beautiful child you were,' he said, 'and what a beautiful lady you've become.'

The frame was of solid amethyst, laced with gold. 'Thank you, my Lord.'

'You don't mind if I stroll about and admire?' he asked, rising.

'Not at all, my Lord.'

'That lovely painted arch between the chambers,' he said, and went through it. I would have followed him had my legs been sufficiently steady. I did not think he would be so obvious as to pocket my small crystal ornaments – surely not scent bottles or what jewels were out of their caskets or the filigree saints in my oratory? This must be a tour of inspection. Morton had probably told him that I was châteleine of the Queen's treasures and he wanted to ascertain if any were in my keeping.

After ten minutes he returned to me, smiling. 'The fireplace in your bedchamber was particularly interesting – tiles of Delft, I believe? You should instruct your servants to remove that casket before some fool lights the logs and destroys priceless treasure.'

'Oh,' I said hopelessly, 'I always keep my jewels there in summer.'

'But it is not wise, my lady. I strongly advise you to give them to me for safekeeping. And how careless to leave the key in it!'

'But—'

281

'How does it happen that the chest is marked "Marie R"? That the locket holds a lock of the Dauphin's hair? That King Henry's initials form the clasp of a necklace, that the Pope's inscription is on—'

'Take them,' I said.

'You mean, guard them, and of course I shall – as you did.'

Still smiling, he went to the door, bowed, left me.

George rode in from Seton that morning and my depression lifted a little in the safety of his presence and his urgent request that I come home. He said, 'When you sent Fearless I was away but our parents realised what was implied. It's dangerous to stay here.'

'Perhaps it's dangerous to leave,' and I told him that James had taken inventory of my treasures as well as stolen the Queen's diamonds. 'I may return to find nothing.'

'I've brought a wagon. You can take all you like.'

So I set Isobel and a tirewoman to packing my clothing and he sent up two servants to remove the furnishings I wanted. At dinner, within hearing of everyone, he told James that I was leaving for an indefinite time. The Bastard did not protest until I told him that I wanted to take Isobel.

'Impossible,' he said. 'Surely there are adequate servants at Seton?'

'Oh, more than adequate,' George said haughtily. 'It's of small consequence.'

Though I would miss her I did not argue, nor had she asked to accompany us. She would be safe here because she was obedient and would probably serve Lady Huntly. I did not bother to bid that lady farewell; for whatever reason, she was more than gracious to the traitor Lords so I assumed that her son had abandoned Bothwell's cause as so many had.

As soon as we rode out of the palace grounds, I on one of George's Arab stallions, he checked his own horse on the moor. 'I have been at Kinross,' he said, now talking freely. 'The Queen was able to smuggle two letters to me.'

Then he told me of how Lindsay had enforced the abdication. 'But – incredible as it may seem – Her Majesty

282

has charmed her jailors so that she lacks for nothing but proper attire. The men of the household are her slaves. If James knew that his own family provides her with writing materials and other forbidden comforts! That young Lord Ruthven is madly in love and that a young lad, a page named Willie, connives for her escape – well, I've hope for her now.'

'But Bothwell?'

He shook his head. 'Some rumour that he is in the Orkneys seeking help for her there. Within this week I return to Kinross and stay at an inn there as a simple laird interested only in hunting and fishing. When Willie is able to row across the loch he tells me how she fares.

'What is startling is our Queen's new attitude towards Elizabeth. She says that only Throckmorton's efforts saved her from certain death, she completely trusts Elizabeth to depose James as regent once she is free, to invade Scotland and enforce Her Majesty's power with the armed might of England.'

I said, slowly, 'That might be true. Because if one Queen is threatened and deprived of sovereign rights, so may another be.'

Then I told him that Elizabeth's diamond was safely with me. 'My one small triumph,' I said.

'Not small,' he said with a chuckle, and we rode on to Seton.

It was good to be home, and as always I was pampered. On my second evening there, after supper, Madame my mother asked if I would not like some sort of celebration of my return, not merely my relatives but county neighbours.

'As it pleases you,' I said.

'I've been thinking, Mary.' She paused, almost shyly. 'The Queen may not be reinstated for years, if ever. You can't continue to give her what remains of your youth. You'll be twenty-five in December and, if you will reconsider, marriage is such a *blessed* state.'

She did not see me wince.

'Your father is frailer than he seems; I am often plagued of my bones. We should like to see you safe in a husband's care.'

283

I felt so sorry for her – the timidity of this very worldly lady, as though she proposed something offensive rather than protective. The idea was no longer horrendous, for I had buried love of Adam. Conversely, I could not imagine loving anyone else.

'Madame,' I said, 'if you care to introduce me to gentlemen, I shan't object but I can't promise to encourage any. I've met so many—'

'Oafs,' she said. 'Churls, traitors. But here in the country there are loyal men, you know, men of breeding, of integrity. The Earl of— But I do not match-make. I only suggest.'

Because I loved her, I agreed to a supper party for Saturday night, the eve of George's departure for Kinross.

It is surprising I remember that evening, for despite the elegant supper, the lush flowers that created a garden of the Great Hall, the music, the gentlemen were all forgettable. Not an earl, not a lord, not a bonnet laird made the slightest impression upon me. Some were handsome, some were not; all were – I suppose – charming in their various ways. But not one created any fire. They were like so many unlit tapers. Now I fully understood the Queen's devotion to Bothwell; he was a burning flame, rugged, savagely male.

After midnight, when the last guests had left, Madame my mother came to my bedchamber for a sleeping-cup, and to gossip like a girl. Had I fancied so-and-so? Did I mark the admiration of such-and-such when I danced with so-and-so? Had he not pressed a rose into my hand when he kissed it?

'Madame,' I said, 'it was a beautiful evening. I felt like a girl again.'

'And you look like one,' she said. 'So. . . ?'

'But' – I tried to make a jest of the truth – 'I am a spinster at heart now.'

'You were before,' she said with a sigh. 'I suppose we don't change. I shouldn't have expected it.' When she was emotional she spoke French. 'But my dear, these are such troubled times and we do want you settled. George, of course, will protect you always but he risks his life in the Queen's service – his journeys to Kinross terrify us. Lord James's spies are everywhere, most certainly at the inns and around the loch.'

'But we can't dissuade him,' I said. 'And truly, I need no protection.'

She reverted to her usual objectivity. 'Wealth shall be your protection, then. You can travel to safety – France if need be.'

'My darling mother,' I said, 'here I stay with you until the Queen needs me.'

She leaned to press my hand. 'You are so staunch in faith. I doubt she'll ever rule again.' She rose, leaning on her stick, and I hurried to open the door for her. She kissed me and said, 'To be young is to be hopeful, but I. . . .'

Then her taper-bearer appeared and I watched as she was conducted down the long, rock-walled corridor. It smelled of age and of the death of summer.

Early that morning, before George left, I wrote to the Queen telling her all that had happened at Holyrood and that I guarded Elizabeth's diamond. George took the letter to deliver, if possible, to Willie. We held Mass in the chapel before he rode off, taking one servant and fishing gear.

We spent anxious days until his return. Meanwhile, we heard news from Edinburgh. Knox was having senile visions but one pleased me and I hoped it was a prediction that would come true: he saw that the Castle would run like a sand-glass and its commander would be seized and hanged against the western sun. 'Balfour,' I said happily to my stepfather.

'No,' he said, 'James is now in command.'

Extraordinary how superstition can sometimes comfort one! Had I been a man I think I would have found a means to kill James and Morton without a quibble of conscience. Lindsay deserved the torture he had administered to our Queen.

A week, two, three – Madame my mother and I passed the time with needlework, joined by our female relatives too plentiful to name, gentle ladies except when we talked of the traitor lords, when we all became wildcats. I played at golf, I rode Fearless, we were entertained by neighbours, I met new gentlemen but could not even summon sufficient interest to flirt.

285

Finally George returned, to our vast relief. He said that James, Morton and Atholl had been at Lochleven and Willie had not dared to take a boat from the island – hence the delay. But finally they had met on a dark night in the reeds of the shore, exchanged letters and news. Her Majesty had demanded to appear in court and be judged by her people. She had been refused on the excuse that the people would burn her as a conspirator in murder, an adulteress. They claimed to have captured a silver casket of letters from a servant of Bothwell's which conclusively proved that she had pre-knowledge of the crime at Kirk O' Field and had lured the late King to his death there. Another letter proved collusion in the abduction to Dunbar. There were passionate love sonnets indicating that Bothwell had been her lover before the King's death. James had said that any of these if shown in court would doom her and so he 'righteously protected' her. Bothwell had been hunted by Kirkcaldy of Grange; there had been a battle at sea in the Shetlands. Though escaping pursuit, a storm had driven Bothwell to the coast of Norway where he was detained on suspicion of piracy and was confronted by Anna Throndsen, a former mistress who brought him to court on charges of seduction through pledge of marriage. But she was pacified by his gift of a ship. The Norwegian authorities, embarrassed by a king-consort on their hands, put him aboard a ship for Copenhagen. He was assumed to be there now; and the Queen believed that his intention was to beg help for her from King Frederick.

'Through all of this, is she dispirited or hopeful?' I asked.

George said, 'Willie is scarce fifteen years of age and so obviously in love with her that he may exaggerate her courage and coolness. But you can judge for yourself from her letter to you.'

It was not in reply to mine, which she had not received at the time. But certainly it was hopeful and, in a sense, less a complaint for herself than outrage at Bothwell's situation as outlaw. She said she would never divorce him even if she believed that in doing so James would reinstate her. She asked me to pray for her, but the tone of her letter was not melancholy; she even made a little jest, wondering if James

286

had stolen Morton's house. And then, 'I love you, dove . . .' and her name.

There was no excuse for George to return to Kinross. The storms of autumn came and he said that the loch iced over at the first cold; Willie had told him that provisions from the mainland were brought in for the winter as early as October. Thereafter, the island was windswept and boats rarely ventured out.

Nor could we at Seton venture out in the gales that ushered in November. Papa – as I now called my stepfather – fretted about his young trees and then two massive oaks crashed – reputedly planted by Saint Margaret in the eleventh century. So we had more than enough firewood and we kept to our hearths. In December my birthday was celebrated *en famille* – neighbours could no longer visit in time of blizzard. But, aside from news of the outside world, we lacked for nothing. For need of amusement I asked Jacques, one of our chefs, to instruct me in culinary art but, though I was diligent, my efforts were disastrous; what did not burn curdled; what did not toughen cracked or split – like my bread loaves. And so, gravely, respectfully, Jacques said that my mind was clearly on higher matters and recommended that I desert the kitchen.

So I took up weaving with the maids in the wool shed and with some success. But Madame my Mother thought it a bore (as it was) and after Christmas we made a gift that George hoped to smuggle to Her Majesty in the springtime – a cloth of state. Hers at Holyrood was doubtless replaced by James's insignia when he used the throne in the audience chamber. On ivory damask, with infinite care, we reproduced the Queen's. I knew every colour, every stitch of the original and George said that he felt sure she would be allowed it. If James visited, it could be removed lest he punish his family for treason.

Late in March, when the winds had abated, George returned to Kinross. He came back within a week, elated. Two escape plots had failed, but Willie was confident of the next, planned for 2 May. He would be at Benarty Hill that night to meet other loyalists and bring the Queen to Seton.

My mother ordered the preparation of a most beautiful room overlooking the forest; and to joiners, carpenters and artists who were naturally curious about this she said archly, 'For the pleasure of my daughter,' so perhaps they assumed this a future marriage bower. Then to me, with her usual practicality, she said, 'It's no waste. If the Queen cannot come, it is yours.'

By late April it was exquisitely furnished. But we told not even the most trusted servants that we expected a guest. I was careful to say to my maids, 'How I shall enjoy this view . . . I've always fancied a golden bed . . . and this great chair.' The cloth of state, now completed, would be draped above it when she arrived.

George left for Kinross on 1 May, requesting that we tell friends that he had gone to Perth for sport; the same servant always accompanied him as his discretion was absolute. Madame my mother did not order special foods for the morrow, aside from the wild strawberries Her Majesty loved, as we all did. My maid asked if I would occupy my beautiful chamber that night but I said that the robing-closet required new hangings. We could not imagine that there was any suspicion in the household to be discussed in taverns and relayed to James.

I have never known such a wearisome and nervous day as we experienced on 2 May. George had not confided details of the plot for her escape but we knew it to be in amateur hands – Willie Douglas, and George Douglas, Sir William's younger brother. They were not related except in mutual love of the Queen. My mother worried that both were reckless to risk her life and theirs in a third attempt at liberation; if discovered they might all be shot. She sought comfort in her oratory, I in a wild ride on the grouse moor, jumping stiles when I neared our palace and tiring my body; but my mind raced ahead, pushing the day to its close, longing for nightfall.

Midnight passed, but we remained dressed. Hopelessly, at one in the morning, Papa ordered the cressets extinguished but I persuaded him to keep them lit in the courtyard. At a quarter to two we were about to have the fire smoored in the Great Hall when we heard hoofbeats. I ran to the great oak door and ordered the watchman to unbolt it. George was lifting the Queen from a horse, more than a hundred men

288

grouped about – muddy, dusty, laughing. I opened my arms and the Queen came into them, smelling of wind and trees and leather. My parents came forward in welcome and all of the men were invited into the Great Hall after Her Majesty had been seated there at the head of the table. If our servants were pop-eyed with astonishment, they were marvellously efficient in bringing refreshment.

The sixty-mile ride had not tired the Queen. She sparkled, though she wore a rumpled black gown, though her hair hung loose without coif. She called for silence and raised her wine-glass in toast to her rescuers – my brother, Lord Claude Hamilton, John Beaton and all of their gallant men. 'And not least, Master George Douglas of Lochleven and – Willie Douglas, come here.'

A sandy-haired lad, big-nosed, skinny, obeyed her, bowing at her chair. She said, 'I ask you to drink to the extraordinary courage exhibited by this young gentleman.'

We all rose and did so; he turned as red as the Venice goblets. Then she praised Master George, who had left his family for her, the two tirewomen, all of the servants here whom we had roused from sleep on her behalf.

Then she turned to my parents. 'Madame and Seigneur de Bryante, may God bless and protect you always for providing me with shelter and cheer.' And she went to them and conferred the highest honour by a kiss on the lips. I received one too before she retired – but not to her bedchamber. She asked use of the library and, until dawn, wrote despatches which summoned citizens to arms, the meeting place to be Hamilton Palace in Lanarkshire. John Beaton was despatched to Leith to take ship for France and beg ships and soldiers of King Charles. By six of that morning couriers were riding through the mists with messages to Spain and England.

She slept but briefly, awakened to receive, under the canopy of state, loyal Lord Herries and Bothwell's kinsman, Hepburn of Riccarton. Borderers arrived in the courtyard and she said the clang and clash of armed men was sweeter than any music.

During a lull in that busy day she told me that Bothwell had been 'detained' by King Frederick of Denmark, a polite imprisonment until someone offered a good price for him. 'He is a political pawn now,' she said. 'I'm told that Queen Elizabeth is too parsimonious to pay but has asked King Frederick to send my husband to England to be tried for regicide. James wants the Queen to execute him and send the head to Scotland to be raised on a pike at Kirk O' Field.'

But she did not seem frightened. 'If gold isn't offered, I doubt that he will be released from Denmark, and thus far he's treated royally. I've every faith he will escape. But I shall negotiate as best I can.' She smiled. 'I will offer anything asked.'

So calm she was; it was her freedom that made her so despite all the difficulties she foresaw. She told us how Willie Douglas had stolen a gate key the previous night to effect her escape, how she hoped that James would not punish his relatives for carelessness as jailors, that his vengeance be directed on her. Because now that loyalists were massing she felt invulnerable, and though Elizabeth might indeed want Bothwell's trial she was sympathetic to our cause.

When she was dressed – refusing my offer of an elegant gown which was, she said, impractical for a battle journey – I gave her the diamond ring. She wore it, a strange contrast to the black gown. I think she was, for once, superstitious. She had escaped in that gown and so she would triumph in that gown. I begged that she should carry a fardel of my riding attire, and a change of linen, but no, she would travel unencumbered. If need be, clothes could be lent her at Hamilton Palace.

I have never known her so confident; during supper more men arrived in the courtyard, and she left the table to go out and greet each one. She retired well after midnight. We saw her off, with George and all of the men, at sunrise.

That day we held a Mass of petition for her, all of the family and servants gathered in the chapel. That week George sent a courier to inform us that Her Majesty, at Hamilton, had formally repudiated the deeds of abdication in the presence of loyal Lords. She now had six thousand troops well armed; James was said to have only three thousand five hundred. They planned to march on Dumbarton and engage the enemy there, if the enemy were bold enough to appear.

We tried to be optimistic; the weather was fair, her forces were strong, she had even lured over some of James's adherents though not, of course, the principal traitors. When her victory was assured I planned to return to Holyrood and continue in my duty.

Meanwhile we waited for news.

It came by courier on 14 May. The opposing armies had met at a village near Glasgow. History calls it the Battle of Langside. Our troops had been ambushed. After forty minutes of carnage the Queen saw James approaching her and fled for her life.

The courier, one of our halberdiers, said, 'She galloped away with Lords Herries, Livingstone and Fleming, George and Willie Douglas following . . . Lord Seton is taken prisoner.'

My mother, after her initial shock, became practical at once. 'It's of no use to inquire of the Queen's whereabouts, for we couldn't help her if we knew. But George is probably held in Edinburgh Castle and, if so, we can contrive a message to him.'

'How?' Papa asked. 'Political prisoners aren't allowed visitors.'

'Rules are very often relaxed with gold,' she said. 'If he's there we have only to find out the name of his jailor.'

But though we sent trusted men into town to nose about we could gain no information except that George was, indeed, seen to enter the Castle under guard. Even for generous bribes no one was willing to risk James's wrath, nor did we wish to risk the lives of our servants in a hostile climate. All we could do was wait and hope that George could smuggle out a message to us.

One June evening a friar disguised in a red cloak came in on a mule and asked to see Papa. Our palace was often petitioned for funds and we gave alms to help the little chapels – mostly in ruins – which had survived the Reformation. So Father Benedict was admitted. Apparently he worked as a secret agent, and after Papa had talked with him he summoned my mother and me to the charter room where they were taking refreshment.

291

'Please honour my wife and my daughter with your confidence,' Papa said.

George, lodged in the bowels of the Castle, was allowed good food and sometimes exercise on the battlements; he was in no way mistreated. The Queen had fled to the Borders and had been briefly harboured at Dundrennan Abbey by the monks. Then, despite the protests of her Lords and the two Douglas men, she had insisted they take her by boat across the Solway Firth to Cumberland.

'Oh my God!' said my mother. 'But that's *England*.'

'They tried to dissuade her, Madame. They implored, but she was adamant, saying that a ring given her by Queen Elizabeth was her pledge of assistance. And so . . . she is at Carlisle Castle.'

'Is Elizabeth with her?' I asked.

'No, my lady. There seems to be some delay in her progress to northern England.'

That was all he knew. Next day Papa gave him rewards of gold and a fresh mount. That night a ballad peddler told us that a crimson-cloaked priest had been found in a ditch near Edinburgh, his head spilling brains over the side of a mule.

My mother crossed herself, my father cursed. We held Requiem Mass for Father Benedict.

Seeking some task to ease my restlessness, I joined the flower-gardeners in their work about the estate. The sun was not as fierce as the previous July but I was cautious of it. One afternoon, weeding near the lodge gate, I saw James ride in with four attendants. He was splendid in royal purple taffeta and a silver-cloth cape. The Queen's white palfrey was caparisoned in purple, and his servants wore varying shades of that colour. At first I was astonished, then I realised that, as regent, he presumed he was welcome anywhere.

If he noticed me at all my silken sun-mask would have prevented recognition. But he rode on up the aisle of oaks and I followed on to the palace. I went to the Great Hall and found him there with my parents. From his chair near the casement he merely inclined his head towards me.

Smoothly he said, 'I was telling your parents – for your own

292

safety – that it would be best not to plot on behalf of the Duchess.'

'We have not,' Papa said.

'She is receiving letters from Scotland from some source.'

'Why should she not?' my mother asked. 'A guest may receive letters.'

'My dear lady,' he said, 'you are naïve. She is not a guest but a captive.'

'So,' I said, less surprised than angry, 'Elizabeth has broken her royal word.' I did not mention the diamond.

'Queen Elizabeth cannot recognise the Duchess until she's cleared of complicity in murder. Some sort of inquiry will be set up so that she may be judged.'

'By an English court?' Papa asked. 'How can Her Majesty be tried when she is not an English subject?'

This was French logic that James preferred not to probe. 'You can understand a virgin queen's reluctance to accept a proven adulteress—'

'Oh, nonsense,' I said. 'That "virgin" has a remarkable history of lovers—'

'None proven. But we hold papers – letters and sonnets – written to Bothwell.'

Madame my mother never failed to offer refreshment to guests – even wayfarers, the dirtiest gipsies, were fed. I observed suddenly with joy that James had not so much as a cup of ale beside him.

'If such papers exist,' my mother said, 'they could well have been forged.'

'The court will judge whether they are not in the Duchess's own hand. But I didn't come here to quibble. She is at Carlisle Castle, well guarded because some hot-headed fools – Catholics – are dedicated to her escape. Queen Elizabeth is desirous of her comfort and has agreed that two of her ladies may be sent to her: your daughter and Jane Kennedy.'

'Do you mean that I may go to Her Majesty?' I asked, thrilled.

He nodded. My parents exchanged glances and I knew they sensed danger for me, but they also grasped Her Majesty's need of me which, I was certain, would surmount any objec-

293

tion. Papa looked at me and I saw permission in his eyes. I turned to my mother who said gently, 'It is your decision, Mary.'

And it was instant. 'When do I leave, my Lord?'

'As soon as a ship is ready – a cargo ship. Tuesday, perhaps. I will call for you. Kennedy is agreeable to joining you aboard.'

'I'll be ready Tuesday at dawn,' I said.

'Mind that your fardels will be examined,' he said. 'You are not to smuggle gifts to the Duchess or letters. . . .'

Then he left us. Madame my mother embraced me, but not with tears. She said, 'Before you came in I inquired if George might not be released and I think perhaps he will be.'

'So that he may be watched for espionage,' Papa said. 'Never mind, we'll be cautious.'

'I was nearly uncautious,' my mother said. 'There was a terrible struggle between head and heart. My heart insisted that a guest be fed. My head said, "Where else is a low-class person to eat except the barn or kitchens?" So I offered him nothing.'

'As well,' I said. 'He's probably prudent of poison and would have rejected any refreshment here.'

Packing, I selected my simplest attire, and many woollens, for the climate of northern England in winter was similar to our own. I longed to take my portable altar which would comfort the Queen as well; but I was almost certain that it would be rejected when my boxes were examined, and destroyed as 'Popish filth'. But I placed my crosses and the tiny ivory image of Christ in one of my fardels, and my favourite books, playing cards, puzzles, a chess set for Her Majesty's amusement. Probably she was forbidden writing materials but James had not warned me of that so I took a chance and had them packed.

'You will not ride Fearless to Leith,' Papa said. 'James would take her the moment you boarded ship. So, daughter, your mount shall be an old cob.'

I shall not relate the pain of leaving them. I knew that I might never return to Scotland. Suffice to say that when James arrived on the Tuesday we had said our farewells with tears and kisses. James ordered each box and chest unroped. The writing materials and the 'Popish filth' were rejected, but in my belt was a cross the Queen had given me on my sixth birthday. Though the day was warm I was mindful of sea winds and carried my sable-lined cloak – one elegance I could not forgo.

With an escort of twenty we took the road to Leith. On the way I memorised this, my native land – black of crows over gold of grainfields, jagged hill softened with purple of heather, the brass of gorse, the pale yellow of young sheep. And the smells – peat fires of a village as we clattered through a wynd where folk were breakfasting, and the fragrance of barley bannocks. A young man leaned from a casement – rather, a hole in his hut – and shook his fist at James. An old woman at a well spat when she sighted him. No one dared more but I felt the hostility of the people as we passed through Leith. No one cheered us except a small boy, fascinated by our pageant of fine horses. I was content with my cob. Fearless was safe.

Jane Kennedy joined us at the ship. James bade us a cool *bon voyage* and we were rowed out to the little ship – a fleece carrier. When we creaked out with the tide we met on deck and she said, 'My Lady, may I question you?'

'Of course.'

'Were you searched?'

'My luggage, yes.'

'My person', she said, 'was handled by one of Lord James's soldiers. After minutely examining my bosom, he took from my bodice a little crucifix the Queen gave me – my dearest possession. But at Lochleven I learned to control my temper or I'd have scratched out his eyes.'

'I must learn to control mine at Carlisle,' I said. 'Whatever happens there we must work for her. We are both willing tools. . . .'

Her land was disappearing now as the wind ballooned our sails and swept us south. Jane said, 'My Lady, do you think we'll ever return?'

'James – Lord James holds Scotland in an iron gauntlet. Queen Elizabeth will doubtless take advantage of any wind that blows in her favour, as our captain does now. But Her Majesty has a way of winning even in desperate times.'

'Aye.' Jane hooded her dark hair as it slapped her cheeks in the wind of the open sea. We stood in silence, facing the unknown; separate in thought, perhaps, but allied.

CHAPTER XVI

W e had expected to be taken to Carlisle but Her Majesty had been moved to the stronger fortress of Bolton on the Yorkshire moors. Castle it was called, but it had the look of a prison grimly barred, and, gaining entrance, we walked past a hundred English halberdiers before the Queen's jailors – Lord and Lady Scrope – admitted us. They were pleasant, sending Jane to the servants' quarters for refreshment and giving me comfits and wine in theirs. I was glad to see Sir Francis Knollys, another warden, since he was highly in Elizabeth's favour and Her Majesty had seemed to impress him at Holyrood.

When I was allowed up to her small, barred apartments I saw for the first time what prison pallor can mean. Normally pale, she was green-pale for lack of sun. When she embraced me I could feel her ribs through the thin, grey gown that was more a rag than a garment. She wore a dun-colour English shawl and her shoes were broken, the scuffed heels showing as she sat down. But, as always, because of her superb bone structure and the long, deep eyes she was beautiful. And, as always, she was gallant; she had no complaint of the Scropes, who treated her kindly, or of Knollys. She was sometimes allowed to run hares, to bowl in the alley, and she was confident that Elizabeth was not malicious but that Secretary Cecil advised her inordinate suspicion. 'Naturally I can't agree to a trial,' she said, 'since I'm not subject to English law. But Sir Francis says there may be some sort of conference in which I may take part.'

'Madam,' I said, 'your brother says there is evidence of letters you wrote to the King before the late King's death – sonnets too that would incriminate you.'

Almost in a whisper, and with clenched hands, she asked, 'James has these?'

I told her of the captured silver casket. And I thought she would faint and moved to her chair to catch her as she swayed. But she steadied and lifted her head, taking deep breaths. Had I known where water was, or brandy-wine, I would have hurried for it, but she said with great effort, 'I am . . . all right.'

I had known her in stress many times, but never before had she stammered. 'I refuse to – to stand trial or appear in conference. I – I must never consent to – to lower my dignity.'

There was terror in her eyes. 'The – the letter I wrote to my husband from Glasgow was indiscreet – it could be interpreted as approval of – of murder.'

She was shaking, and what I called that red word lay like a millstone between us. But I think I loved her more in those moments than ever before, for now she turned those haunted eyes to me in appeal. They asked mercy, they asked help.

I said as brightly as I could, 'Folk will think those letters were cleverly forged, Madam, if Lord James does present them – and he may not live to do so.'

'Oh,' she said, 'he is ill?'

'No.' But I told her of the hostility of the people. I even exaggerated it a little and gradually she calmed. I asked where brandy-wine might be and she motioned me into the adjoining room. I brought back the decanter and glasses and we both drank. She said with a wisp of a smile, 'Queen Elizabeth doesn't provide the best of brews.'

Nor of furnishings. The painted arras was shabby, the furniture of scarred oak. I said, 'Madam, I longed to bring you the cloth of state—'

'It was more beautiful, dove, than the one at Holyrood.'

' – but dared not. So, with your permission, I'll make you another here if we can get the damask. I have the sewing threads.'

'We will find a way,' she said. 'The Scropes were strict at first, but each day they relent a little and I know they don't enjoy the position thrust upon them. Sir Francis likes me. I

298

have a French and Scots secretary now so I'm allowed to write letters but you may be sure I'm prudent in what I write to my foreign friends, for I'm sure that every letter is opened and examined. I've an apothecary and pages, Willie and George Douglas, and dear John Beaton is Master of my Household.'

Then she asked me to arrange her hair; she had no wigs or face paints but I had brought some and later that day, after she had welcomed Jane, we dressed her for supper in a violet gown of mine. Despite her thinness, she looked like our Queen when we descended to supper. Lady Scrope said to me, 'You know, you were not supposed to have brought the Queen attire.'

So here, at least, she was recognised as Queen. 'It's my own gown,' I said. 'May I not lend them?'

She hesitated. 'Why, I suppose so. I see no harm.'

John Beaton had aged since I had seen him; he had the yellow look of jaundice and he ate sparingly and drank only water. When we had a chance to talk privately after supper in the withdrawing room he said he ailed of his stomach but that our Queen was not to know how severely. As Master of her Household he tried his best to please her educated tastes but the chef was English, which precluded artistry. The finest sauce made under his supervision failed if the moorfowl was tough or the beef overdone. Elizabeth was parsimonious of Spanish and French wines and had insulted Her Majesty by sending her a chest of clothing which contained two old pairs of shoes, two torn linen shifts and two small strips of worn velvet – nothing more. Thus, he said, my clothing was important for her pride. He apologised for my shabby apartments but could do nothing more with such small funds as were allowed him. Our Queen was sure to receive money from France and she had told him, 'We must brighten Lady Seton's life as much as possible.'

Life at Bolton was dull, though we were all compatible. When, rarely, Her Majesty received a smuggled letter from her husband she had to control her excitement – and a mixture of joy and despair. He was still held by King Frederick in Denmark, heavily guarded at Malmö Castle. But she never doubted that he would escape. A man who could escape from Edinburgh Castle could achieve anything.

Her Majesty sent Lord Herries to Elizabeth as envoy to plead her cause but he was refused audience; he remained in London hoping that she would relent – she was famed for indecision, tossed between her own intuitions or whims and the counsel of Cecil.

Autumn came, and the moor winds howled and the wild geese flew south. And in the south Elizabeth ordered a conference to decide my Queen's fate – 'to establish her innocence', Knollys said. On 4 October commissioners met in York, Her Majesty disdaining to be present. Her defenders were her few loyal lords who had accompanied her here, with two of the high clergy. When we learned that James, Morton, Lindsay, Lethington and Lennox would appear as her accusers we both knew the verdict before it was delivered. After much delay, the conference was moved to London and Cecil was ordered to arbitrate. There, in the Painted Chamber at Westminster, James stated that our Queen had plotted and commanded the late King's death, using Bothwell as tool and then marrying him. He produced from the silver casket eight incriminating letters and the passionate sonnets. But Elizabeth's commissioners neither condemned nor vindicated. The verdict, in short, was 'Not proven', which allowed the Virgin Queen to retain the Harlot in custody, but spared her the responsibility of executing her or creating such a precedent. It also spared Elizabeth the bother and expense of invading Scotland to re-establish our Queen on the throne.

Our twenty-sixth birthday was scarcely a cause for celebration. It seemed that she was to be imprisoned interminably, trapped in this illegal farce. She insisted that I was free to leave her service but, though I was fond of my family, she had always been my sun.

In February we moved to Tutbury in Staffordshire, a castle high on a hill overlooking the River Dove, much of it in ruins, marsh-damp, stinking, draughty. There were no drains to the privies so on visits there we held cloths to our noses, and there were cesspools under our casements. The roof leaked so we had to raise woollen tents above our beds. Both Her

300

Majesty and I ached in our bones and became rheumatic; Jane Kennedy, younger than we, limped like an old woman.

Our jailors were the Earl of Shrewsbury and his wife, Bess of Hardwick. She was a hard woman and yet often she could be full of compliments. We decided that she was afraid of Elizabeth but just as fearful of offending us because a number of plots were rumoured that might reinstate Her Majesty as ruler of Scotland. Bess wanted to be on the winning side. Her red-grey curls often adorned with Scots cairngorms, she would wear a shawl of plaid and at the same time she toadied to Elizabeth's fashions and reproved us for wearing a cross. At least she chose to overlook our embroidering damask for a cloth of state with its pieties of gold thread. In a way I felt sorry for her because, inevitably, her husband, the shy, elderly, gouty Shrewsbury, was in love with Her Majesty. Even those men who did not know her smuggled in letters with suggestions for her escape, and many were not even of our faith. A captive queen appealed to the imaginations of young men, both Scots and the northern English. Gradually this led to the plot for a rising on her behalf. While it simmered, I met my second love.

When John Beaton became ill his brother Andrew arrived to assist as Master of the Household. At first I paid him scant notice but Her Majesty teased me that this was sheer snobbery and why not be diverted by a handsome young man who (so she thought) worshipped me. This was flattering, but an heiress, even in exile, is a cynic.

He was very attractive; pale grey eyes, pale blond hair that formed a peak, a tall, slender body, good legs in his puffed breeches. And he was amusing, educated, sharing my passion for the lute and for poetry. We spent hours together and formed a deep friendship. But I would not allow it to develop beyond that; I was afraid that he was merely a diversion and that if and when we were free from this dismal castle we would have nothing.

King Charles of France sent Her Majesty instalments of her dowry from Touraine; we no longer depended on Elizabeth's meagre charity and ate good food and drank fine wines. But ill health prevailed and Elizabeth – out of pity or for some secret reason – had us moved to Wingfield Manor in Derbyshire. Her Majesty had an inflammation of the spleen and her face had swollen, and both of us welcomed the sun on our bones. It also helped Lord Shrewsbury's gout.

News from Scotland trickled in, messages smuggled in a fire log, in Jane Kennedy's shoe. I was allowed into the village, riding for my exercise. The English halberdiers who accompanied me must have been in league with our cause, for they turned away when I was offered a gift of honey or a cloth of herbs. There the messages were hidden.

Some infuriated us: James had plundered all of Her Majesty's lands in Scotland and burned the castles of her friends, excepting ours at Seton. Perhaps he planned to oust my family and live in our palace? In August we learned that he had imprisoned Lethington in Edinburgh Castle because he had reverted to Her Majesty's cause. James's excuse was that Lethington had conspired in the murder of the late King. Bothwell was still held by King Frederick. Paris, his page, had been hanged at St Andrews.

But some messages cheered us. The Northern Rising was imminent; many English Catholics loathed Elizabeth and they would join with our loyal Scots. Her Majesty was jubilant, and so was I.

And so was I, in a different manner, when Christopher Norton joined us as a gentleman of the household; a most striking gentleman, younger son of Sir Richard Norton. After he had kissed our hands and departed for his bedchamber Her Majesty said, 'Dove, it is the first time I've seen you blush at a man's attention.'

'I would hate to be obvious,' I said, 'but, do you know, he reminds me of the King, your husband. '

She nodded. 'The same autumn colour of hair, the full mouth. I hope you will shed your primness so that he will not be discouraged.'

But I knew he was not the sort of man to be discouraged; what he wanted he would take. It was only a matter of days before he spoke to me of marriage but I pretended to hesitate, not wishing to be easily won. Still, we were together almost constantly, and poor Andrew Beaton was miserable but won my admiration by not whining. He remained my friend and

302

told me that in true love one was selfless. If I could be happier with Christopher, then I must marry him.

My Queen did not seek to influence me but I knew that Christopher was her choice for me. He was deep in the plot of the Northern Rising and clever in smuggling messages to and from our adherents. King Philip of Spain had hinted his help with ships and, of course, we had the wild enthusiasm of what I called 'the Queen's young adorers', Scots prepared to join loyalists of Northumberland and Westmorland. Christopher believed that their number exceeded six thousand.

In early autumn Elizabeth commanded us back to Tutbury but despite its stink and its leaks Her Majesty made no protest. Elizabeth had played into our hands; it could easily be captured, vulnerable to even a small army. When we arrived Christopher came to me and said that rescue was imminent.

'Lady Mary,' he said, taking my hands in his, 'at any moment, now or at dawn, this place will be attacked and we'll be freed. Do you come with me or not?'

I clasped his hands tightly. 'I'll come with you.'

He pulled me up from my chair into his arms. His kiss held such desperation, as though it were meant to last a lifetime. But just as we paused and plunged into another his servant tapped at the door with a message: Christopher was summoned to Durham to meet our army; there had been a slight delay of the massing forces. We asked immediate audience of Her Majesty and received her blessing of our engagement, which we would keep secret from the household until I had written to my parents. Then she gave him a talisman to carry into battle – a little silver heart – and we both kissed him. 'You will know how to get past the guards?' she asked.

'Yes, Madam. I leave here unarmed. They will suppose me off to the village tavern for a drink and a wench. . . .'

And so he left us. I was too happy for tears and so was she. For an hour or more we sat by her fire and discussed our escape and my marriage, which would probably be at Seton. Then we prayed, kneeling together under her cloth of state with the candles alight.

'My vow of chastity,' I said as we rose.

'The Cardinal is certain to lift it,' she said. 'He knows

303

it was the vow of a child – so, dove, sleep in peace.'

And so I slept, dreaming of his arms about me.

Two days later armed soldiers – Elizabeth's – burst into Her Majesty's apartments while I was arranging her hair. Wordlessly, with no explanation, they searched her chests, wardrobe, and pawed through her desk. The canopy of state was ripped down on a sword. Then they ordered in Countess Bess and said, 'Search her,' and left us.

The Queen, trembling with rage, submitted to the search, removing all but her shift. Bess whispered, 'Forgive me, Madam,' then went to the door and called through to the soldiers that no letters were concealed on Her Majesty's person. Presently we heard them ride off.

As I helped her to dress, Bess said, 'Queen Elizabeth suspects some plot and has ordered severe restrictions. We're to remove the lock from your door. You may no longer enjoy privacy.'

Her Majesty was always at her best in crises. Coolly she said, 'If there were a plot I'd be the last to know of it – but a plot of what sort?'

'Your escape,' Bess said.

'What a delightfully absurd thought! Seton tells me the village children play a game of Rescue the Queen – is this what started the rumour?' She laughed. Bess asked her to take the matter more seriously. Elizabeth must have some cause for suspicion and she, Bess, could be punished for lack of diligence. Her Majesty graciously said that she understood; nor for the world would she endanger the Shrewsburys. But she wanted her cloth of state restored, and Bess sent a servant to replace it.

Two evenings later Lord Shrewsbury interrupted our supper, hurrying in to say that the north had risen to Her Majesty's cause, that Durham was massed with six thousand men who had burned the Protestant bible in the cathedral and destroyed the pulpit. They were said to be riding towards Ripon and meeting no resistance. 'They are surely on the way here,' he said, 'and so your guard must be strengthened and neither you nor Lady Seton are allowed beyond the privy.'

Thus, for the next ten days, we were humiliated by watching men. No secret message could reach us. On the night of 24 November, as I slept, Bess roused me and said, 'Dress, my lady. We are ordered to Coventry.'

A hard ride through dark miles of wind and rain. Finally we arrived at the Bull Inn where we were confined to two chambers at the top of the house. We spent a week without news of any sort. Then one morning we heard the bells of the town ring out in rejoicing. We looked down and saw our guards celebrating with wine in the courtyard. The Earl of Shrewsbury came to tell us that the Northern Rising had been quelled by Elizabeth's twelve thousand troops. There had been no help from Spain and, in panic, the royalists had scattered and been chased towards Scotland. There had been no battle but hundreds of our men had been taken prisoner, and eight hundred executed.

On our return to Tutbury we saw corpses swinging from gibbets in market towns. There was one in a brown, furred cloak, nearly faceless. A soldier caught me as I fell from my horse in a faint.

Later at night Her Majesty came to my bed and sat there, holding me like a child after I had been given a draught of poppy-drug. I vaguely remember her words of comfort. I would always remember Christopher Norton's wavy hair rippling in the wind.

In the months that followed Andrew Beaton was of supreme comfort. He was brother, father, friend – and had the tact not to speak of marriage. Very gradually it came to me that he, rather than Christopher, was to be my love. Christopher had been a passion but this could be a steady, slow-burning love. The Queen said nothing to influence me but that was her usual behaviour. As for myself, I was content to warm myself at the hearth of Andrew's affection during the long chill of my convalescence from Christopher's death.

January closed in, an icy fist on a ramshackle castle. The Queen fell ill again and took to her bed. But on the night of the twenty-fifth she appeared at supper, escorted by Lord Shrewsbury, wearing a scarlet gown of mine and jewels she had bought herself. When we were all seated she said, 'I never thought to celebrate the death of a relative before, but my lord has received news from Scotland. . . .'

James Stuart had ordered confiscation of an estate near Roslin belonging to a laird, Hamilton of Bothwellhaugh, who was absent at the time. Mistress Hamilton had been driven out, naked, into a blizzard, seeking escape in the Pentland Hills. The next day, when Hamilton returned, he found her wandering in the forest, insane. Hamilton took vengeance for the crime when James rode down the High Street of Linlithgow. Concealed in a shuttered house, he waited until James was opposite him and shot him through the stomach. After eleven hours of screaming agony, James died.

We celebrated despite the Shrewsburys' shock at our behaviour. Later, of course, Her Majesty bade us to her makeshift altar to pray for him but we felt only relief that God had seen fit to remove the devil incarnate. Hamilton was said to have escaped to France and Her Majesty would write to King Charles to see to his safety and have him pensioned.

Now began more intrigue; despite the vigilance of our jailors we smuggled out and received letters and learned that Lennox had become regent of Scotland, that other plots were planned for our escape by the same Catholics who had organised the Northern Rising. Hearing of this, Elizabeth had us moved from Tutbury to the stronger castle of Chatsworth in Derbyshire and we had the boon of sunlight again. We were promised the help of King Philip – an invasion of England – and the assassination of Elizabeth.

More than two years passed of suspense, of boredom, anticipation of rescue, despair, renewed hope. Her Majesty's health declined and Elizabeth moved us to Sheffield, an old Norman castle in Yorkshire where again we were plagued by cold. Had it not been for Andrew and his warmth of spirit life would have been utterly dreary. Our household was reduced from thirty to sixteen. John Beaton died and I had news of my stepfather's death. We learned that Lennox had been shot and stabbed by Kirkcaldy's men and Lord Mar became regent, still guard of King James. But Mar, after dining with Morton, died suddenly of suspected poison and

306

Morton became regent on the same night that John Knox died in bed.

Death was all we seemed to hear of. Elizabeth's ships attacked Leith and bombarded Edinburgh Castle, joined by Morton's men. Lethington was imprisoned by Morton and died – some said of a stroke, others of poison self-administered. Kirkcaldy was hanged.

'Very odd,' Her Majesty said. 'Knox prophesied that the commander of the Castle would hang, facing the western sun, remember? And that the fortress would run like a sandglass. So it did; from its battering came a slide of sand. . . .'

In the summer Bothwell's page Einer arrived from Denmark and was smuggled in to us in a laundry basket. He told Her Majesty that her husband was in the foul, rotting state prison of Dragsholm, kept in an underground cell, chained to a post, shackled on a bed of filth. When Einer was safely out of her apartments she called for me and told me, in tears, 'I can never expect to see him again for he is – is—'

'He was never hopeless,' I said. 'Madam, remember his motto?'

She looked at the signet ring on her finger. 'Keep Trust.' Her hands, twisted with arthritis, went to her eyes. 'But Seton, he has lost his mind. He is green mad.'

The years brought more deaths – that of King Charles, of the Cardinal – and Lady Huntly's prophecy was fulfilled: Jean married the Earl of Sutherland and on his death and Beaton's her long love for Alex of Boyne was consummated by their marriage. I had never before respected visions or the second sight but now I wondered, for when Lord Shrewsbury allowed in a gipsy fortune-teller she told me two strange things: 'The man you most hate will die of his own device. The man you love must never leave this place.'

The man I most hated was Morton, of course, but he was scarcely one to take his own life. Andrew Beaton, as Master of the Household, never left this place except when, rarely, we were permitted to ride a mile or so with Her Majesty. So I dismissed these prophecies. But by now, after so many years

307

of his kindness and comfort, I could not dismiss the idea of marriage to Andrew. I talked it over with the Queen and she was vehement. 'You are thirty-five. You need a man to care for you, for I may not survive another winter and I want you settled. Fortune hunter?' She laughed. 'Not he. Granted he's not of your noble heritage but hasn't he earned your devotion?'

Oh, he had. My snobbery had been childish. And so, with her blessing, we were granted permission from Elizabeth for Andrew to travel to France to obtain release from my chastity vow. After a month of loneliness, of longing, I received a letter from Calais saying that I was released, that he was taking ship and would be with me in mid-May. My Queen immediately began plans for the wedding and together we stitched a white satin gown. But before it was completed there was news of Bothwell's death and so I insisted my wedding be delayed.

And Andrew's sailing must have been delayed. By 26 May we worried about storms, by the thirtieth I was frantic. Early on a June evening Her Majesty came to me, chalk-white as her ruff, and said, handing me a cup of brandy-wine, 'Sit down. There is tragic news. There was a storm . . . Andrew was drowned.'

'The man you love must never leave this place.'

'The man you most hate will die of his own device.'

Morton was tried for complicity in the murder of the King at Kirk O' Field and stated that our Queen had approved it. But he was found guilty of 'art and part' and decapitated at the Market Cross in Edinburgh. This was accomplished by a beheading machine he himself had brought to Scotland from England.

Many plots continued for our rescue and these kept us from total despair because we were ill – she of agonising pains in her side and both of us cramped with rheumatism. But I was ill, too, of a sickness of the spirit, whereas she was bravely optimistic. I felt that my presence dampened this; I could not believe that her intrigues would release us. I desperately wanted to cheer her by play-acting but it would have been false. And, physically, I had scant energy. There were nights when I dragged myself to her apartments to arrange her hair and found my fingers too feeble. More and more often I spent my time in prayer.

One evening, when I was alone with her by her fire, she said, 'Dove, you no longer belong here. Perhaps you never belonged to this sort of world, or to the revels of the court. I can't return you to Scotland but perhaps I could send you to France.'

As I started to protest that I would not leave her she said, 'My aunt, Madame Renée de Guise, orders the convent of St Pierre at Rheims and, as you know, I myself am wistful of such peace as you'd find there. You might take my place.'

'Madam, I'm not worthy of taking holy orders—'

'You needn't. I think nuns are not created at our age. Thirty-nine is late, late for everything but serenity. You'll never find it with me.'

She was right.

'And for the sake of your health, dove – can't you imagine a sunny convent garden, the shade of poplars, the calm, arcaded walks, the silvery sound of bells to sleep and awaken you?'

Yes. 'But I should feel so guilty leaving you.' We had now shared fifteen years of captivity.

'In this case', she said, 'guilt would be only sentimental. I shan't have you slowly losing your life for my sake, another of my victims.'

She was thinking of the thousands of gallant men who had died for her in the various escape plots. 'Seton, it's my command that you go.'

I went to her chair, knelt, kissed the hem of her skirt. She reached down and stroked my hair. 'I'll petition Queen Elizabeth – she shouldn't object to your journey.'

Nor did she; but it was early autumn before arrangements were complete. On the morning of my departure we prayed together at her little altar. We tried to breakfast but neither of us could eat. A wind rose and red leaves fluttered against the barred casement. Then we heard a commotion in the court-yard – my escort preparing for the ride to the coast.

309

She opened her arms and I went into them. Then she drew back and said, as a tear slipped down her cheek, 'I've nothing to give you but my blessing and this.'

She removed a little ivory cross from her belt. As I took it, Lord Shrewsbury came to tell us that it was time to leave.

I memorised her as she stood near the fireplace in a russet gown – tall, greying hair under a heart-shaped cap, her eyes like long jewels set in a pallid face. Leaning on her cane she followed us to the door.

'A safe journey, dove.'

I could not speak.

The convent of St Pierre aux Dames is very beautiful, especially when lilacs lean against the old grey arches, when roses climb the cloisters. Madame Renée became my dear friend, understanding my homesickness, sharing my need to communicate with the Queen, which we did through the French ambassador. But there was scant news from her – Elizabeth suspected everyone, apparently even the Shrewsburys, so we relied on other sources for information.

I cannot say that serenity brought happiness; but, through the years, resignation and sometimes contentment. The nuns were kind to me, often merry when we picked fruit, using it as a pretext for a picnic. My health improved and I could climb up a cherry tree, nearly as lithe as a girl. I learned to preserve the foods of our garden, to brew wines, and so I felt useful. I mourned the death of my mother, and when George died at fifty-five, I felt that the last link was gone. There was a squabble over money among my younger relatives; they granted me very little but I required very little. In winter I wore gowns of simple wool woven of local fleece, and in summer thin damasks and veils to keep my skin from sunburn. This was prudence rather than vanity. There was no vanity at St Pierre unless, perhaps, pride that one or another of us could triumph in the art of composing a peach tart or *salade des légumes*.

It was the custom, during supper, for Madame Renée to read to us; sometimes from the writings of the saints but if she were in lighter mood a poem. On this November evening

310

she chose a sonnet by Ronsard which sent my thoughts like arrows to my Queen:

When you are very old, by candle-glow
You'll sit and spin beside the fire, and sing
The songs I made. And you'll say, wondering:
'Ronsard proclaimed my beauty long ago!'
Some drowsy, shuffling servant bending low
To her dull labour, at my name will spring
To wakefulness, and praise you who did bring
A little surcease to the dead poet's woe.
I'll be a ghost, at ease beyond the tomb,
By the Elysian myrtles' shadowy bloom;
You'll be an old and fireside huddling wife,
Missing my love, rueing your own proud way.
So wait not till tomorrow, live today,
And gather in its hour the rose of life.

She closed the book. 'Ronsard named this "A Sonnet to Hélène". But I have always wondered if it were not intended for another lady.'

She looked at me and I nodded.

'Lady Seton, your opinion?'

I said, 'It was written in 1578 – the Queen of Scots was thirty-six then and, indeed, ageing. But perhaps Ronsard didn't wish to taunt her with the idea of being less than beautiful. He would always remember her as that. Once he called her "The rose of France". So I think, Madame, that the poet used his mistress Hélène as an excuse to address Her Majesty, disguised.'

An older sister said, 'You could be right, my lady. I recall Ronsard at St Germain when he was Her Majesty's verse-master – so in love that he stammered and stuttered like a schoolboy, his arrogance shattered when we accompanied her to her lessons. But why ever did he see her as aged?'

'Poets often see mystically', Madame said, 'if their gifts are from God.'

I had sent gifts to Her Majesty but they were never acknowledged and we believed that she never received them. I often wrote to her, and was careful to say nothing that a jailor might

311

not approve; but there was never a reply. When I had left she was deep in the study of cipher to facilitate secret messages. Her determination to escape was matched by the obsession of her supporters to achieve this. Every day of every year I expected news of her freedom.

In the nineteenth year of her captivity I had not relinquished hope. And prayer is hope. In my retreat I had learned the power of selfless petition based on humility, yet laughed with the nuns when a novitiate said, 'Truly, I'm the humblest of you all.' The laughter was not malicious, but fond. I had become part of a family that I understood as I had my own in Scotland, and they understood my worldliness, my pleasure in their remembering my birthdays. At supper on 8 December young Sister Elizabeth read a verse she had composed:

'. . . so Lady Seton says she is forty-four,
She could be less; she cannot be more.'

In February Sister Mary, who was seventy, became fevered, and I nursed her and in her calm hours read to her as her vision failed.

I was not surprised when, one dawn in early March, I heard death bells from the chapel, then summons to High Requiem Mass. I dressed in black, joined the nuns on the cloistered walk. The sky was a stormy grey but sun shafted through and we walked on cruel blue ice, anxious not to slip, the older nuns assisted by the younger. I remember a flight of crows above the poplars and cypress and how, as we entered the dimness of the chapel, wood doves mourned.

The bishop conferred with Madam Renée. Then, at the altar, he addressed us: 'We have had tragic news. The Queen of Scotland – Dowager Queen of our country – has been put to death.'

Later that morning Madame Renée came to my chamber and found me tearless but shivering by the fire. Tears, I had learned, were for oneself. I was trying to reach across to Her Majesty's joy of heaven but failing. Was she in heaven? I wondered aloud.

'Whatever her errors on earth, she died for our faith,' Madame said, bringing a blanket to place about my shoulders.

312

'She had the choice of being returned to Scotland as prisoner of her son – King James would probably have granted her many favours – or as martyr. She chose the latter.'

'But why did Elizabeth execute her after so many years?' I asked.

Madame said, 'We haven't the full story as yet. But it seems that hot-headed young men plotted assassination of Queen Elizabeth and, at the same time, release of Queen Mary so that she might rule both countries. The plot was discovered, there was a trial and our Queen was found guilty. Still, she had that choice. If she had admitted to guilt she could have been alive today. . . .'

In Edinburgh Castle, politely imprisoned by the young man whom she had never recgonised as King. To her it would have seemed a depth of cowardice, of hypocrisy, a betrayal of Catholicism. I had to ask, 'It was a swift death?'

She shook her head. 'The headsman – sent from London to her prison at Fotheringay – required three strokes of the axe before he managed to. . . .'

The axe! Nobility are executed by the sword.

'. . . but we know of her bravery.'

'Shall there ever be the full story?' I asked, huddling in the blanket.

'There will be legends. But, Lady Seton, since life and death are a circle, unending, how can there be an end to the story?'

As there is no ending to the circle of the seasons. Now, a very old lady, I warm myself on a bench beneath a lace of white lilac and face another springtime. Renewal – the lambs in the meadows; the first flight of fledglings; again, and for ever, the stir of new life in the deep pools of the forest.

No, there is no ending to the story.

313